**Praise for *New York Times* bestselling author
Sharon Sala**

"Drama *literally* invades the life of an A-list Hollywood star, and the race is on to catch a killer."

—*RT Book Reviews* on *Life of Lies*

"A wonderful romance, thriller, and delightful book. [I] recommend this book as highly as I can.... Exciting... and will keep you glued to the pages until you reach the end."

—*USA TODAY.com*'s *Happy Ever After* blog
on *Life of Lies*

"In Sala's latest page-turner, staying alive is the biggest challenge of all. There are appealing characters to root for, and one slimy villain who needs to be stopped."

—*RT Book Reviews* on *Race Against Time*

**Praise for *USA TODAY* bestselling author
Delores Fossen**

"Clear off space on your keeper shelf, Fossen has arrived."

—*New York Times* bestselling author
Lori Wilde

"[*Savior in the Saddle*] takes off at full speed from the first page and doesn't surrender an iota of the chills until the end."

—*RT Book Reviews*

TO PROTECT HIS OWN

NEW YORK TIMES BESTSELLING AUTHOR

SHARON SALA

Previously published as *Gentle Persuasion*
and *A Threat to His Family*

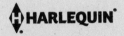

ISBN-13: 978-1-335-40634-7

To Protect His Own
First published as Gentle Persuasion in 2000.
This edition published in 2021.
Copyright © 2000 by Sharon Sala

A Threat to His Family
First published in 2019. This edition published in 2021.
Copyright © 2019 by Delores Fossen

This edition published by arrangement with Harlequin Books S.A.

For questions and comments about the quality of this book,
please contact us at CustomerService@Harlequin.com.

Harlequin Enterprises ULC
22 Adelaide St. West, 40th Floor
Toronto, Ontario M5H 4E3, Canada
www.Harlequin.com

Printed in U.S.A.

CONTENTS

Sharon Sala is a *New York Times* bestselling author. She has 123 books published in romance, young adult, Western and women's fiction and in nonfiction. First published in 1991, she's an eight-time RITA® Award finalist. Industry awards include the following: the Janet Dailey Award; five Career Achievement Awards from *RT Book Reviews*; five National Readers' Choice Awards; five Colorado Romance Writers Awards of Excellence; the Heart of Excellence Award; the Booksellers' Best Award; the Nora Roberts Lifetime Achievement Award presented by RWA; and the Centennial Award from RWA for recognition of her 100th published novel.

Books by Sharon Sala

Secrets and Lies

Dark Hearts
Cold Hearts
Wild Hearts

Forces of Nature

Going Gone
Going Twice
Going Once

The Rebel Ridge novels

'Til Death
Don't Cry for Me
Next of Kin

The Searchers

Blood Trails
Blood Stains
Blood Ties

Visit the Author Profile page at Harlequin.com for more titles.

GENTLE PERSUASION

Sharon Sala

This book is dedicated to a very
special woman who has chosen to share her
gift of being a writer with any willing soul who
has the perseverance to listen and learn.

Not only has she the skill to write wonderful
stories and poetry, but she also has the
patience to share her knowledge.

And what makes her teaching better...what sets
her apart...is the fact that she does it with
love and...*gentle persuasion*.

Ernestine Gravely...this one's for you.

Chapter 1

The doorbell's loud persistent summons pulled Cole Brownfield from the backyard pool. It sent him stomping through the house, leaving a wet trail of drips and footprints in his wake.

"What?" he growled as he yanked open the front door to face a stranger. He knew he was being rude but he'd just gotten home from a three-day stakeout and was bone weary.

He and his partner, Rick Garza, also a member of the Laguna Beach Police Department Narcotics Division, had scrunched themselves in the back seat of a burned-out abandoned vehicle in a less than appealing part of the city. For several hours, they'd watched the constant stream of traffic coming and going from the small, nondescript residence that had tentatively been identified as a crack house. After last night, that had been confirmed.

During their stakeout, he'd been crawled on by bugs and barked at by stray dogs. And sometime during the night, someone had tossed a sack of garbage into the yawning openings of the vehicle that had once been windows. He'd never been so glad to get up and out of a place in his life. The only thing that had kept him sane was the thought of diving into the clear, clean, sparkling waters of his backyard pool. But he'd only made two laps when the doorbell had interrupted his relaxation. The quick dip for which he'd yearned before crawling into bed was fast becoming an impossible dream.

Cole continued to drip as he glared over the man's shoulder to the cab parked on the street.

"Is this the Brownfield residence?" the cab driver asked.

"Yes," Cole answered. "Who wants to know?" Being a policeman made him instantly suspicious of strangers. After the last seventy-two hours, he was in no mood to play twenty questions with a cab driver.

"My fare," the driver answered, and gestured over his shoulder with his thumb. "Here's her bags. But you'll have to help me get her out of the cab. Worst case of motion sickness I ever saw." He walked to his vehicle, leaving Cole to follow along behind him.

Her? Cole didn't like the sound of this. But the driver kept walking. Cole frowned. If he wanted answers, it was obvious that he was going to have to get them for himself.

The warm sunshine had begun to dry the water clinging to his bare chest, but he broke back out in

cold sweat when he recognized the passenger plastered
to the floorboard of the cab.

"Sweet Lord!"

A familiar head of dark curly hair hung limply over
the seat, dangling above the floorboard. "Little Red!
What in hell are you doing here?"

Debbie Randall heard the voice. It was one she'd
traveled halfway across the country to hear. And if the
world would stop swimming backwards, she'd have
time to enjoy the fact that the owner of said voice was
standing before her nearly naked.

He looked fabulous: all hard brown muscles, wide
shoulders, and tapered waist above slim hips. And dripping wet! Her mind boggled at the implications. But as
luck would have it, her stomach changed her mind, and
she made a dive out the opposite side of the cab and
heaved. It was strictly for effect. There wasn't anything
left in her stomach to come up.

Cole was beyond speech. He eyed the look of disappearing patience on the cabby's face, reached into his
pocket to pay the fare, and realized he didn't have pockets. Muttering beneath his breath, he retrieved Debbie's
belongings from the cab, fished a twenty-dollar bill out
of her purse, and paid the man.

The cabby drove away, leaving Cole face to face with
the reason he'd left Oklahoma in a sweat. She might be
a bit green around the gills, but she was still the first
woman who'd sent him running for cover.

In all his years as a cop, Cole Brownfield had seen
a lot of tragedy and dealt with many situations fraught
with danger. But he'd never been as scared as he was
now with nothing between him and one slightly be-
draggled, dark-eyed witch but a Speedo bathing suit.

"Cole," she whispered, blinking slowly as she held out her hand, "please get me off the street and into bed before I shame us both."

Cole staggered. *My God! She hasn't been here five minutes and she's already trying to get me into—* He pulled his wayward thoughts back into gear as he realized that she was referring to the fact that she was sick as a skunked dog. He took her by the arm.

"Come on, girl," he said gruffly. "We'll talk later. Right now you look like you just flew through hell backwards."

"Don't mention flying, please," she muttered, and staggered gratefully into the house.

"Dad! Why am I the last to ever know anything of importance around here?"

Cole's question came as his brother, Buddy, was trying to maneuver their father back into the house from his latest trip to the doctor's office.

Morgan Brownfield sank into his favorite chair and dropped his cane onto the floor. He grunted, lifting his leg as Cole quickly shoved a hassock beneath the heavy cast. He leaned back and stared at his eldest son's angry impatience.

"Yes, the doctor said I'm healing just fine. Thank you for asking," Morgan drawled. Ignoring the look of guilt sweeping across Cole's face, he asked, "Now what are you so worked up about?"

"That...that girl...from Oklahoma is here. You know! Lily's friend... Debbie something or other." He knew good and well what her name was. But he wasn't about to admit to his family that she'd haunted his dreams for months.

"Oh! Debbie's here! Great! Lily called days ago to tell us she was coming. Lily was going to come herself but her doctor discouraged it. She's into her eighth month of pregnancy and too near delivery for air travel. The only way Case and Debbie could talk her out of coming anyway was for Debbie to promise to come in her stead. I was going to have to pay a live-in to help out until I got back to my feet anyway. I'd rather pay someone I know than have a total stranger living in my house."

Cole grimaced. This meant she wasn't here for a day or two. This sounded like weeks, even months.

"Why didn't I know about this?" he asked, and ran his hand through his dark hair in frustration. Bone straight and in need of a haircut, it fell back perfectly into its state of disarray as his fingers raked across his scalp.

Buddy's answer was short and, as usual, to the point. "You didn't know it because you're never here."

"Hell!" Cole said succinctly, and glared at his brother, who calmly stared back, knowing that there was nothing Cole could do to argue the point.

"Where is she?" Morgan asked. "I've been looking forward to her visit."

"She's in bed," Cole drawled. "I don't know who's going to take care of whom. I peeled her out of the floor of a cab and dumped her in Lily's old room. She's suffering from motion sickness. You guys are on your own. I've got to get to the P.D." The Laguna Beach Police Department was Cole's second home.

Cole waved his arms in the air, renouncing the issue as out of his hands, and left. Buddy disappeared into his room, leaving Morgan alone. Silence was a rare occurrence in the Brownfield house, and Morgan relished the opportunity to lean back and close his eyes.

His wife had died years ago, leaving him alone with five children to raise. Lily, his only daughter, was the only one who'd moved out of the house. She and her husband, Case Longren, lived on a ranch outside of Clinton, Oklahoma, and were about to present him with his first grandchild. The way things looked, it might also be his only one.

Cole, a detective with the Laguna Beach Police Department, was a loner. Buddy, his middle son, was a virtual genius and loved only one thing: his computers. The youngest were the twins, J.D. and Dusty, actors who, at the present time, were away on location of the latest film on which they were working.

Morgan opened his eyes, glanced down at his watch, and reached for the remote control of his television. It was almost time for *Wheel of Fortune.* He decided to let Debbie wear off the traces of travel. Tomorrow was soon enough for a welcome.

Debbie rolled over on her back, stared blankly up at an unfamiliar ceiling, then down at herself, and wondered where she was and why she'd just spent the night in her clothes. Suddenly, the memory of yesterday came rushing back along with a sick feeling that the man she'd most wanted to impress had all but poured her into bed. *At least I'm still alive,* she thought. So much for great first impressions.

She rolled out of bed, standing for a moment just to assure herself that the world had finally stopped spinning, and then sighed with relief. Things felt pretty close to normal and that was good enough for her. She pulled her suitcases onto the bed and began to unpack, taking time as she worked to appreciate the very feminine wallpaper and the soft pastel colors on the bed and matching curtains. Framed pictures on the wall indicated she was in Lily's old room. It made this trip just the least bit less uncomfortable, knowing that she was in the room in which her good friend had grown up.

Volunteering to come had been one thing. Giving up her job as a cashier in a grocery store wasn't exactly giving up a life-long career. Now that her brother, Douglas, was finally out of college and more or less on his own, she could think about herself. Knowing that she was going to live in the same house with the first man she'd met in years who had even made her think of lasting relationships had been another altogether.

But the memory of a tall, quiet man's dark eyes and solemn face had been powerful persuasion. The attraction present between them at their first meeting was as fresh as if it had only been yesterday. A neighborhood cookout to introduce Lily's family to Oklahoma had turned into a contest between Debbie and Cole as to who could ignore whom the most effectively.

But it hadn't worked. It was hard to ignore a need to be held. It was impossible to ignore each other. Cole Brownfield had been a man to remember. And she had…for months. Now she was here. It was time for action.

A quick shower and a fresh change of clothing sent her in search of her hosts. She entered the kitchen to find Morgan hobbling from cabinet to table and back again, obviously trying to assemble a breakfast for himself. Debbie's mouth formed a silent *O* as she took a good look at the mess in the kitchen. Chaos reigned.

"Need a little help?" she asked, and returned the smile of welcome that Morgan Brownfield sent her way.

"Debbie! You'll never know how glad I am to see you," Morgan said, "and how much I appreciate you giving up your time to come out and help."

"Oh, I think I can," she answered, as she gave him a quick hug of welcome. "The question is, where do I start first?"

"With breakfast," Morgan commanded. "There may not be order in the house, but there's food. I have Cole to thank for that."

Debbie flushed at the sound of his name. "And I have him to thank for helping ground me yesterday. I've never been so sick...or embarrassed."

"You're young yet," Morgan teased. "There'll be other times and other days."

Laughter was shared along with a quick but filling breakfast as Debbie was brought up to date on Morgan's progress and on the whereabouts of his offspring, as well.

"You won't have to worry about J.D. and Dusty," he said. "They're off on location, playacting again. Bit parts in some low-budget movie," he grinned. "But they're happy and that's what counts."

He pointed toward a closed doorway just off the kitchen. "Buddy's in there. At least I think he is. That's where I saw him last. And, as you probably have guessed, Cole is on duty. His hours are unpredictable, but he's not. He's my responsible son. Sometimes too much so. But my wife's death left all of us with burdens.

Cole took it upon himself to become the father figure to Lily and the boys while I was at work."

Morgan sighed and rubbed his forehead. "I don't know what I would have done without him. For that matter, I still don't."

"I understand," Debbie said. "My folks have been gone for several years now. Dad died of cancer and Mom two years later in an accident. I was nineteen when Mom died. It left me with a seventeen-year-old brother who was nursing a chip on his shoulder. It took me six years to reclaim him and another two to get him out of school. He graduated last year from Oklahoma University with a marketing degree."

"And where did that leave you?" Morgan asked softly. There was a lot of giving in Debbie's story, but not much about what she'd had to give up.

"Free to come take care of you," she answered. "And that's what I'm about to do. Where do you want me to start?"

Morgan shrugged. "Well, I certainly appreciate it, and don't think I don't know what an effort this was on your part. And, as for monetary arrangements, I've opened an account for you at my bank. Your pay will be deposited twice a month. Here are some counter checks until yours come back from the printer."

"I didn't intend for this to be so…businesslike," Debbie said. The mention of money made her blush. "It's not like I had a job I couldn't bear to leave. Grocery checker isn't exactly high on a high school counselor's list of career opportunities. I can have the job back as soon as I return. My boss already said so. I was simply looking at this as a…vacation. I've never been to California."

He smiled crookedly, reminding her of Cole. Just the

thought of him made her lose her concentration. And then Morgan continued.

"As for where to start…look around. It's all a mess, and I don't think this will feel like a vacation. Believe me, you'll earn every penny of it. If you hadn't come, I would have had to hire extra help until I'm well. That wreck on the freeway broke more than my leg. I can't seem to recoup my enthusiasm for anything." He hugged her gently. "I'd a lot rather it be you here than some stranger."

She smiled.

He continued. "And I may have to send you out to buy a whole new set of dishes. I can't seem to find half of them. Glasses are scarce, too."

"Hmm," Debbie mused. "Well, I'll tell you what! Why don't you go out to the fabulous lounge chair by the pool. Take the morning paper with you. I'll be out later with something cool for you to drink. That'll give me time to sort through all this without disturbing your rest."

He readily agreed and disappeared outside, leaving Debbie to set a routine in motion as she began to put the household back to rights. A shadow passing across a doorway nearly an hour later made her look up to see that the Brownfield hermit had finally come up for air.

"Hey, mister!" she called from the living room as she saw Buddy carrying a plate of cookies in one hand and a glass of iced-down soda in the other. "You better say hello to me. Long time no see."

"Uh… Debbie!" Buddy gulped and grinned around a mouthful of cookie. "Yeah! I'd forgotten you were coming. Great to see you again, too."

She gave him a hug and resisted the urge to sit him

down and comb his hair. It looked as if he'd slept standing on his head. Little swirls and spikes of shaggy
brown hair went every which way.

"You, too, Buddy," she replied. "Are you still into
computers?"

"Cole is gone, you know," he answered in Buddy-like
fashion. His mind was always on an entirely different
subject than the one in discussion.

"I know, darling," she said softly, and patted him on
the arm as he disappeared into his room with his snack.
As she watched him walk away, a thought occurred to
her. If she was right, she just may have saved Morgan
the price of a set of crockery.

"Oh, Buddy." She called aloud through the closed
door. "I meant to tell you. You have fifteen minutes to
retrieve every piece of crockery and glassware residing
in your room, or I'm coming in with a bucket of soap
and water and a vacuum."

The door flew back instantly. Buddy stood mouth
agape, half-eaten cookie hanging from his mouth as he
gasped. "No…never…in here. Wait! I'll do…you can't…
I'll only take—"

Debbie waited. He stuffed the cookie into his mouth
and pivoted as neatly as a star running back. She smiled
to herself. Pay dirt! She wisely refrained from making
another remark as Buddy made his first of five trips to
the kitchen. She opened the dishwasher and pointed.
He blinked, chewed, gulped, and swallowed the last
of his cookie.

"Who, me?" he asked, and then stopped at the expression on her face. "Oh! Sure thing."

Debbie left him to his task as she went outside to
check on Morgan. A quick glance told her that he was

still dozing. She quietly scooted the patio table over so that its umbrella would give him some shade and went back into the house just as the phone began to ring.

"Brownfield residence," she answered. The deep masculine voice at the other end made her tilt. She leaned against the wall for support and tried to focus. It was the same feeling she'd had when the plane had taken off yesterday, leaving her stomach somewhere over the red earth of Oklahoma.

"Feeling better?" Cole asked, secretly glad that it had been she who'd answered. This way he didn't have to ask anyone else how she was feeling and reveal the true reason why he'd called.

"Much," she said. "And, Cole..." her voice trailed off into a little silence.

"What?"

"Thanks," she said.

"For what?" he asked gruffly.

"You know what," Debbie said. "For the rescue. For putting me into bed. For taking off my shoes. For bringing my bags—"

"Oh, that," he said, interrupting her recital. "Well, Little Red, that's my job. I'm a cop. Cops to the rescue and all that."

Little Red! It had been months since she'd heard that teasing nickname. It was a play on words. Oklahoma University's football team was affectionately known as Big Red, and she'd been a small but staunch fan; thus the name, "Little Red."

She closed her eyes, swallowed sharply, and pulled herself together.

"Yes, well, I'll have to take your word on that cop business. Yesterday I didn't see a badge on you anywhere. Course I wasn't seeing so good. But from where I was crawling, I saw a whole lot of bare skin. Wet, too. But, no badge. Definitely no—"

"You haven't changed a bit, have you, girl?" he muttered, thankful that she couldn't see the spots of heat that had just flashed across his cheeks. *Damned woman,* he thought. *Men aren't supposed to blush.*

"Guilty as charged, officer," she said. "So what's my fine?"

His swiftly indrawn breath was audible, but Cole refrained from answering. He couldn't tell her what had just come to mind. People got arrested here for less. "Just take care of my family for me," he said. "I'll be home sometime tomorrow and help you work out a schedule. Do you need anything now?"

Cole knew the minute he'd asked that she was toying with the idea of an X-rated answer. He held his breath.

"It can wait," Debbie finally replied.

"See you later," he replied, and disconnected before he came unglued. That woman made him nervous as hell. But it was nothing new. He'd been living with the feeling ever since the day they'd met.

"Dammit, Dad," Cole muttered. "You have to help me. Your leg won't heal right if you don't do these exercises, and you aren't even trying. You're letting me do all the work."

Debbie walked into the living room just in time to hear Cole's remark. She quickly took in the sight of Morgan flat on his back on the floor, the removable cast momentarily off his leg, and Cole kneeling at his feet, trying to coerce him into completing his exercises.

"I don't care what you and those doctors say," Morgan growled. "My leg hurts too much to do this stuff."

"I'm sure it does," Cole answered, trying to maintain his self-control, "but it'll hurt a lot worse and a lot longer if you heal with a limp, and you know it."

Morgan's glare met Cole's frustration. It was time for some gentle persuasion. That's when Debbie stepped in.

"Cole, you're wanted on the phone." She touched him on the arm.

He jumped. He hadn't even heard her approach, let alone the ringing of a phone. "Thanks," he said shortly, refusing to meet her eyes as he lowered his father's leg back onto the floor and went to answer the call.

"I'll bet all this exercise stuff hurts a lot," Debbie remarked as she knelt down at the place he'd just vacated.

Morgan nodded. At last! Someone who understood.

"I'd really hate it if I had to wear this hot old cast day in and day out, too."

Morgan was hooked and didn't even know it. Cole walked back into the room just in time to hear Debbie commiserating with her father. He started to object, thinking that she was about to undo all the good it had taken him days to effect when her next soft remark caught his attention, and he smiled. She was working his father like a pro.

"Here you are stuck in this house during the most gorgeous part of the year and can't even take advantage of that great pool you have outside."

Morgan grimaced, nodding as Debbie's sympathy touched his wounded ego. He didn't even see it coming when she remarked, "You know what? I think I'll just call up that doctor of yours and give him a piece of my mind. Why doesn't he let you do your exercises in the water, Morgan? They would be just as effective, and you'd be much more comfortable."

Cole sighed. All his methods for trying to get his father to do his exercises—all his pleading, all his bullying, all his love—had failed. But Debbie had Morgan all but begging to do them, if he could only get into the pool. Thank God for small favors that came wrapped in enticing packages like Debbie Randall.

"What would you like me to do, Morgan? Want me to call that doctor and persuade him to our way of thinking, or do you want to continue working with Cole?"

"His name and number are on the pad by the phone in the kitchen," Morgan said, waving his arm. "By George, you're right! That pool would be just the thing."

Debbie hid a smile of satisfaction as she patted him on the leg and arose.

"You're dangerous," Cole muttered as Debbie walked past him toward the kitchen.

"Yes," she answered calmly as she passed him by without looking up, "and don't you forget it."

"Kick, Morgan, kick!" Debbie urged, and ignored his grumble. She braced herself against the side of the pool, legs astride, and let all of Morgan's weight rest against her chest. She held him in a floating position as he continued to work his legs back and forth in the water.

"Just a little bit more. Only one more set of scissor kicks and you're through for the day. Then I'll get your float, and you can have thirty minutes of play and relaxation before we put the cast back on. What do you say?"

"I say you're a menace," Morgan wheezed as he worked his injured leg back and forth in the water. "And you're tougher than Cole."

She laughed as his last kick sent water showering into the air, wetting her already damp curls and plastering her face.

"But I'm a lot prettier, don't you think?"

Cole walked onto the patio and stopped in midstride. The sight of his father and that woman...together...in the pool...made him feel slightly jealous and a whole lot stupid.

The droplets hit her face and arms, beading in the bright, afternoon heat like thousands of tiny diamonds. The churning water teased his sight, giving him momentary glimpses of that damned red excuse for a swimsuit. It was two-piece and covered just enough of her body to remind him that there was more to see.

And then he saw weariness on her face. His father's big body continued to buck and jerk in her arms, and he knew that she was probably worn out. It was time for the second shift to take over.

"Hey, you guys." He dropped his towel onto a lounge chair. "Leave some water for me."

Debbie almost dropped her hold on Morgan and succeeded in dunking herself instead as Cole's voice sent her sanity into a tailspin. She thanked the hot sun overhead for its presence. It was a perfect explanation for the red flush that crept up her neck and cheeks.

He had on that same little-bit-of-nothing suit that he'd been wearing the day she'd arrived. Only this time she wasn't sick as a dog. Instead, she was more than cognizant of the fact that he was mildly devastating and overwhelmingly gorgeous.

Cole slipped into the pool, pushing his way through the wake caused by his father's exertions. He walked up behind Debbie and slid his arm up and around her shoulders, allowing her room to duck while he took over her duties.

"Here, Little Red, duck under. I'll spell you for a while. How many does he have left to do?"

Debbie froze. Her hair was soaked and plastered to the sides of her face and neck. Water beads were hanging on the edges of her eyelashes, partially blinding her, but she could still feel. And the feel of Cole's hard body against her back made her shiver in response. "One more set," she mumbled.

"You're shivering," he said as she ducked beneath his arms. "You've been in the water too long. Crawl out and grab a towel."

For once, Debbie was at a loss for words. There were no smart rejoinders on the tip of her tongue. Only the feel of him pressing against her hips, his long, strong arms wrapping around her. She'd never wanted anything as much in her life as to turn and hug him. And that was just for starters.

Instead, she dutifully crawled out of the pool, grabbed the first beach towel she came to, and wrapped it around her. She sat down on the lounge chair and watched as Cole completed the last of his father's exercises, laughing and teasing as Morgan began to rebuke and complain.

"You're just mad cause I'm not Debbie," Cole teased. "I already know I'm not as pretty, Dad. But I didn't think you noticed, too."

Morgan hushed. He realized he'd just sounded petty and complaining. It wasn't like him and he was instantly sorry.

"I'm sorry," he said. "I know I don't appreciate all you do. All both of you have done. But even if I don't say it, I think it constantly, and don't either of you forget it." To lighten the moment before either of them became embarrassed by his compliments, he added. "Don't forget you promised me strawberry shortcake for dessert tonight."

"I won't forget," Debbie laughed. "Just don't either of you forget to save room for dessert. If I'm going to fix it, you two have to do it justice. I'm going to get dressed. You guys are on your own."

She quickly exited the pool area, leaving Cole to spend some quality time with his father. She knew that they were close and suspected that having her as a guest had put a dint in Cole's comfort zone. Especially since she was in the room next to his. She heard everything from the squeak of his bed frame to the water running in his shower. By the same token, she knew that he heard her, too. It kept them just slightly off balance as they met from day to day.

Cole was nearly always gone before their day began, or else didn't come home at all. Debbie tried not to think about the constant danger he was probably in and knew a moment's regret for the fact that she'd fallen in love with a man who was in law enforcement. But her worry came and went as quickly as it had surfaced. Her problem wasn't in Cole's choice of lifestyle. Her problem was getting Cole to realize that she was necessary in his world.

"Did I hear someone mention dessert?" Buddy asked as Debbie walked into the kitchen.

"By all rights, you shouldn't have a good tooth left in your head." She headed toward her room. "I've never seen someone eat so many sweets in my life. I'd be crawling on the ceiling if I ate as much sugar as you do."

"Cole has been here for an hour," Buddy remarked, changing the subject as usual.

Debbie stopped in her tracks. It made her nervous that she was beginning to understand Buddy's odd conversational habits. What he was telling her, in Buddy fashion, was that Cole had been watching them in the pool for some time before coming outside. That also told her that he was interested.

"You get an extra big serving tonight, my friend." She patted him on the cheek. "You're a man worth cultivating."

Buddy smiled, momentarily connecting with her line of thought and then was off in his own never-never land as he closed the door and shut himself away from the world.

"I'll call you when dinner is ready," Debbie said as she walked out of the kitchen. "And tonight is going to be special in more ways than dessert. I can just feel it."

Chapter 2

"Who wants more dessert?" Debbie asked, swirling her finger around in her mouth as she licked the last of the whipped cream off the tip. She amended with a grin, "I mean, who besides Buddy wants more shortcake?"

Cole's bare feet tingled and his toes curled against the red-tiled kitchen floor as he watched her off-center smile and the bit of whipped cream still caught at the corner of her lips. She accidentally found the topping with her tongue. He shuddered as he watched it disappear.

"None for me, thanks," Morgan groaned as he pushed himself away from the table. "Everything was delicious, honey." He hobbled into the living room to catch the late-evening news.

Buddy took his second helping in hand and began a none-too-grateful exit. He stumbled over a chair just as

he was taking a bite of shortcake. A strawberry plopped
out of his bowl and onto the floor.

"Sorry," he mumbled, picked up the berry, looked
at it, shrugged and then licked it clean before stuffing
it into his mouth.

Cole rolled his eyes and laughed as Debbie splut-
tered, "For pity's sake, Buddy, you don't have to eat
off the floor!"

Buddy grinned and disappeared into his room, chewing with relish.

"He's not only lacking in manners," Cole laughed,
"but he's also totally unconcerned with germs. The only
virus that panics my brother is a computer virus. He has
so many safeguards built into his computer programs
that, from time to time, he even locks himself out."

Debbie caught her breath. It was the first time she'd
ever seen Cole laugh so freely. It changed the somber
expression in his dark eyes to one of devilment and joy.
She definitely liked the latter expression more. Then
she smiled as Cole turned to gather the rest of the dirty
dishes from the dining table. Buddy wasn't the only
Brownfield wearing his dessert.

Debbie's hand caught and cupped the side of his face.
His eyes narrowed as he warily allowed her the famil-
iarity. She turned him toward her, teasing as her finger
swiped at the corner of his mouth.

"You saving this for anything special?" she laughed,
waving the bit of whipped cream in his face.

"For you," he said and, without thinking, grabbed her
finger and guided it to her lips. *Oh hell,* Cole thought,
as he watched her lips purse around her own finger
and suck slowly at the stolen sweetness, *why did I just
do that?*

"Thank you very much," Debbie said.

Her slow drawl kicked his hormones into gear, but he wisely ignored them as he answered, "You're welcome."

Chagrin enveloped him at the depth of emotion he felt just being around her.

Debbie stared, lost in the confused passion lurking in his eyes. He wanted her. That much she knew. But he hadn't admitted it to himself. She knew that, too. However, wanting wasn't enough for her. She would have love, or nothing at all.

Cole blinked and took a step backward. He had to. If he hadn't, he would have taken far too many steps forward and Deborah Jean Randall would have been in his arms.

"Dammit, Little Red," he whispered, "you should be declared illegal."

Debbie tilted her face, looked him straight in the eyes, and answered softly, "What I'm wondering is what are you going to do about it, Cole Brownfield?"

Cole sucked in his breath. Muscles he didn't even know he had tied themselves into knots. His fingers clenched. He couldn't decide whether to wrap them around her neck or thread them through her hair. She'd pushed him just about as far as he was going to push. He stepped forward.

The phone rang—loudly, repeatedly. He jerked, spun around, and almost yanked it off the wall.

"Hello?"

"Saved by the bell," Debbie whispered as she began clearing up the remnants of their meal.

Cole's eyes narrowed sharply as his partner began a familiar recital. He listened, cataloging the events that Rick was sharing that related to one of their ongoing investigations. He filed it in his memory along with the way Debbie's hips swayed beneath her shorts as she stepped from table to cabinet and back again and the way her breasts tilted upward as she stretched, replacing the salt and pepper shakers and condiments in the upper cabinet shelves. He could tell by the way she was ignoring him that she knew he wasn't ignoring her.

"Can you come pick me up?" Cole asked.

His question definitely got Debbie's attention. She turned around, eyes wide and nervous, a dish towel dangling limply from her fingers as she stared at the serious expression on his face.

"I'll be ready," he said, and hung up.

He looked long and hard at the near panic lurking in Debbie's eyes. It was the single reason he'd sworn to stay unmarried. This fear was something a cop's wife had to live with. It wasn't something he was ready to share.

"I'll be back late," Cole explained. "And, it's just as well. Whatever you thought was about to happen here, girl, didn't. It's not going to either, so you may as well wipe that look off your face."

"What look?" Debbie asked, tilting her chin mutinously.

"That one," Cole said. His guttural growl sent waves of nervous tension dancing up her backbone as he gripped her shoulders and turned her to face a mirror hanging over the dining table.

They stared at each other, silently assessing the reflections of a tall, dark-haired man and the small, curly haired imp at his shoulder.

"I know what I see, Cole Brownfield," Debbie said quietly. "Or are you blind to that, too?"

She left him standing before the mirror to face the devils within himself that he stubbornly refused to acknowledge.

Cole stared, long and hard. He shuddered. "No!" he said. "No!" He headed for his room.

Three a.m. Debbie gasped and jerked upright, rolled over on her side, and stared at the clock by the bed, trying to decide what had yanked her awake. There! She heard it again, only now she was not lost in sleep.

A floorboard creaked in the hall outside her room and sent her flying to the door. She yanked it open and then blinked, trying to adjust her eyes to the light spilling out of the hallway from Cole's partially open door. It reflected on his bare chest as he came down the hall barefoot wearing a pair of blue jeans with the top two buttons enticingly undone. He looked as if he'd just emerged from the pool. Water was still clinging to his body in interesting patterns, and if Debbie'd had to answer, she'd have had to swear he wasn't wearing anything underneath that denim.

"You're home," she said softly and sighed in relief as she leaned against the doorway.

Yellow silk soft and creamy as warm butter hung from her bare shoulders. Tousled curls, dark and tumbling, framed a sleep-softened, heart-shaped face. Her lips were full and parted, devoid of makeup as was the rest of her face. She looked to be somewhere between sixteen and sexy as hell.

Cole sighed. He was too tired and defenseless to ignore what he was feeling.

"Sorry I woke you, girl," he said quietly, and ran

his finger down the length of her upturned nose. "Go back to sleep."

"I'm glad you're home," Debbie said.

"I'm damned glad to be here, Little Red. More than you'll ever know."

Memories of the horror of the crime scene he'd just left gnawed at his gut. It was hard to go from the hell on the streets to the heaven of walking into a clean, comfortable, quiet home. But the knowledge that it was always here…waiting…was what kept him coming back sane.

"Is everything… I mean…are you…?" Debbie saw the dull, weary look in his eyes and knew that whatever had pulled him away from home earlier had been serious. She couldn't continue. There were no words to express her concern. And there was no need. She simply slid her arms around his waist and laid her head on his damp chest, hugging him in a nonthreatening, comforting gesture.

Cole's arms wrapped around her with a slow, defeated movement. He groaned softly as he felt silk and Debbie sticking to his body, and buried his face in her tousled topknot.

"You feel good. You smell good. And no matter what I say tomorrow, I'm damned glad you're here, Debbie Randall."

His voice was so soft, she almost didn't hear him repeat, "I'm so very glad you're here."

With every ounce of willpower he had and some he had to borrow, he turned her loose and gently pushed her into her room.

"Go to sleep, girl."

Debbie crawled back into her bed, pulled up the covers, and smiled as she buried her face in the pillow. Maybe…just maybe…it was going to be all right, after all.

Cole woke late. Sunrise had already been here and gone as he caught the stripe of yellow high on the wall of his room. It must be nearly noon. Quiet seeped cautiously into his soul. He stretched, sighed, and then stifled a yawn as he realized he had two whole days ahead of him with nothing to do but whatever he wanted.

Quiet! He suddenly realized it was *too* quiet. He rolled out of bed, pulled on a pair of red jogging shorts, gave his face a quick wash, and ran a comb through his hair.

A note hanging behind the Mutant Ninja Turtle magnet on the refrigerator told him why it was so quiet. According to Buddy's sparse shorthand they were: Doctor—Shopping.

Looking around the spotless kitchen he sighed and allowed himself to wallow in something akin to pity. The first time in days that he'd had a chance to have a meal with the family and they were gone. He didn't—wouldn't—admit to himself that the real reason he was feeling sorry for himself was that Debbie was also absent.

A bowl of yellow-and-white daisies sitting on the windowsill told him she'd been here. The coffee maker was on warm, with the pot half full and his favorite mug sitting beside it, inviting him to partake. He poured and complied.

Like the detective he was, he followed the clues of Debbie's presence from the cabinet where plates, bowls, and glasses rested in orderly fashion to the glass-covered cake stand holding a partially eaten coffee cake waiting for someone to finish it off.

And, like the good cop he was, he did his duty. The coffee cake went from plate to microwave to his mouth, and all the way down. Full and replete, he leaned back, closed his eyes, and listened. The house was just like it'd been before his father got hurt, before Debbie Randall came and turned his world upside down. It was clean, quiet, and lonesome as hell.

"Hey, Cole! We're back!"

Tony Hillerman's latest mystery went flying to the concrete as Cole came up and out of the lounger by the pool. He was inside the house in a heartbeat. His brother's bellow told him something he'd been waiting impatiently to hear. Family, noise, and Debbie had all returned.

Buddy handed Cole a loaded grocery sack, cocking his eyebrow as if to say, you know what to do with this, and exited the kitchen. He returned with another sack of equal size and began unloading the purchases, putting them away in shelves and drawers. Cole set the sack down on the counter and stared. He looked past Buddy to his father, who was talking on the phone to one of his golfing buddies, giving him a play-by-play of his latest trip to the doctor. A sack ripped, Cole looked, grimacing as Buddy tore into a package of cookies and sampled them before transferring them to the cookie jar on the cabinet.

One very new, but important, member of their family was notably absent. Debbie was nowhere in sight.

"Where Debbie?" Cole asked.

Morgan waved his arm and mouthed something Cole couldn't understand.

"Buddy, where's Debbie?"

Buddy thrust his arm down to the bottom of the grocery bag and pulled out a six-pack of yogurt.

"Mmm, peach," he muttered, and rummaged in the drawer for a spoon.

Cole took a deep breath and then counted to three. It didn't do any good.

"Dammit to hell, Robert Allen Brownfield. I asked you a question!"

Buddy raised his eyebrows and licked his spoon. "You don't have to yell," he said calmly and then shrugged. "I guess she's still in the car."

Cole was dumbfounded. What in hell was the matter with his family?

"Car? Why wouldn't she come in when the rest of you did? What's wrong with her? She's not sick again is she?"

His voice rose an octave with each question until, finally, even his father realized there was about to be a brotherly confrontation.

"What's wrong with you two?" Morgan hissed, covering the receiver with his hand.

"Why the hell is Debbie still in the car? You act as if she didn't exist."

Cole threw the accusation out into the sudden silence of the kitchen as anger sent him outside to check. Morgan and Buddy stared at each other, recognized the guilt each was wearing, and quickly followed.

"She's asleep," Morgan called, but it was too late. Cole was already gone.

Everything dire that he could imagine came and went as Cole hurried to the family station wagon parked beneath the shady carport. His heart knocked against his rib cage as he yanked open the back door and knelt, expecting the worst.

His hand was shaking as he slid it gently across her face, smoothing the tousled jumble of curls away from her eyes. Her forehead was cool, her breathing slow and even. There was no pale, clammy countenance, only a rosy flush across her cheeks and a soft sigh that escaped from between slightly parted lips as Cole's fingers moved a curl out of her eye.

She was only asleep.

"Come here, Little Red," Cole whispered.

He scooted his hand beneath her shoulder and pulled her toward him, resting her weight against his lap until he could slide his other arm beneath her knees. Then he stood, carefully shifted his load until he had her in a firm grip, and walked back toward the house with her weary head bobbing against his bicep.

The breeze teased at her hair as the sun played across her face. Guilt followed every step. The movement didn't even faze her.

My God! She's got to be exhausted to sleep through all this.

He glared at his father and brother, stalked through the door Buddy was holding open, and left them behind.

Morgan watched the look of protective possession playing across his eldest son's face. A smile came and went. *He's finally coming to his senses,* he thought. Nothing would please him more than to see a relationship develop between those two.

The door to Debbie's room was closed, and rather than take a chance on waking her, Cole chose the only open door down the hall.

His!

He laid her down in the midst of his unmade bed, shifting cover and pillows that he'd abandoned only hours before. The pale-green jumpsuit she was wearing would be wrinkled, but there was nothing he could do about that. The thought of trying to remove it without waking her did cross his mind. But the thought came and went so fast, he knew it was only a notion, not an intent. He unbuckled the straps of her sandals and slipped off her shoes.

The moment Debbie's head touched the pillow, she turned on her side, slid her hand beneath her cheek, and burrowed beneath the loose covers like a little mole.

Cole's smile was as gentle as the touch he left on her cheek. He closed the door and walked away.

"Is she all right?" Morgan asked. "We didn't mean to be thoughtless. She was sleeping so peacefully, it seemed the only kind thing to do." He shrugged, softening his explanation with a smile.

"She's in my bed," Cole said. "She's exhausted. We've been expecting entirely too much of her. Have you looked at her lately?" He fixed Buddy with a pointed stare that sent him scurrying into his computer room without answering. "Hell's fire, she's so damned little, I don't know where she keeps the energy she has, but it's obviously used up. From now on, we give her some space."

"You're right, son," Morgan said. "You're absolutely right!"

Cole nodded, glad that his concern had gotten through to at least one member of this family.

Morgan whacked Cole's back in fatherly fashion. "Tomorrow, she's all yours. You two take the day off.

Go to the beach. Maybe you could do some sightseeing. Whatever Debbie wants. If I need anything, I'll shut the power off in the breaker box. That'll get Buddy out of his room. Anyway, the doctor said I'm healing great. The water therapy was a stroke of genius, and I have Debbie to thank for that, don't I? Whatever it takes, show her a good time, okay?"

Cole took a deep breath. He'd asked for it. He couldn't very well accuse everyone of taking advantage of her good nature and then be the one to refuse to alleviate her duties. He nodded. The smile on his father's face changed. It looked suspiciously like a smirk.

But all day? He hoped he survived. It wouldn't pay to forget she was dangerous to his peace of mind.

Hell! Who am I kidding? I have no peace of mind. All he had was a houseguest from Oklahoma with dark eyes, a slow drawl, and a smile that tied his guts in a knot.

Cole was leaning against the doorway with arms crossed, surveying his bed and its contents. It was the third trip he'd made in as many hours, and he was beginning to worry. By his best calculations, Debbie had been sleeping for the better part of four hours. If she didn't wake soon, he was calling the doctor. Something must be wrong with her.

It took effort, but Debbie maintained her slow, even breathing. She watched Cole with interest. She'd realized some moments before when she'd opened her eyes to find him watching her that he hadn't noticed she was awake. He *was* staring at her, but she could tell he wasn't really *seeing* her. He was lost somewhere in thought, and that was just fine with her. It gave her the opportunity to look back from a very interesting vantage point—his bed.

How she got here was not a question she wanted answered. How she was going to get him to join her would have been much more appropriate to her way of thinking.

He was such an enigma. Debbie was used to men who were more forthright. Men who said what they meant and left you to decide whether you would slap their faces or hug their necks.

The red jogging shorts he was wearing left way too much tan skin showing for her peace of mind. His broad shoulders and flat belly told her that he probably maintained a rigid regimen of physical fitness. And then she remembered his occupation and knew that it was probably not just a choice of lifestyle that kept him in shape. It was also necessity.

"Am I being evicted?"

Her slow drawl made him jump. And then the look in her eyes nearly sent him to join her.

"How long have you been awake?" he growled.

"Long enough," she said softly, and rolled over on her back and stretched.

Cole groaned. Once. Silently. It wouldn't do to let her know that she was getting to him in more ways than lust. His eyes narrowed, his lips firmed as he watched her lithe body coming to life like a cat coming out of a deep sleep. She stretched first her arms and then her legs and then, finally, arched her back and sat up on the side of his bed as if she belonged there. She rubbed her hands across her face, ran her fingers through her hair, and then looked up at him and smiled.

"My word, I'm a mess!" Her clothes weren't just wrinkled, they were a wreck.

"Yes, ma'am, you're that," he said, referring to her presence in his house. She was messing up a whole hell of a lot, and it had nothing to do with laundry.

"Well, thanks for the loan of the bed," Debbie said. "I feel great! I must have needed the nap."

"It wasn't *just* a nap. You've been asleep for nearly four hours. You're worn out, and for the next two days, you're going to take it easy. I've already warned Dad and Buddy, so don't let them coerce you into anything you don't want to do."

Her mouth dropped open, just a little, just once. She quickly regained her composure as she realized he was about to become defensive. He'd obviously revealed more of himself than he'd meant.

"Okay," she agreed, taking the bluff out of the argument he no longer needed.

"Well," he muttered, "just so you know."

"Right, just so I know."

He nodded and started to stuff his hands in his pockets when he realized he didn't have pockets in which to stuff. *Damned shorts. Now what am I going to do with my hands?* He very badly wanted to put them on Debbie.

She leaned over and retrieved her sandals.

Cole couldn't decide whether to walk or run, but either way he had to move. She was coming toward him with a look on her face that he'd seen before. The devils were sparkling in her eyes and tilting the corners of that mouth.

"Look at the wrinkles in my jumpsuit!" And then she grinned and scratched the tip of her fingernail lightly across his bare belly. "You took off my shoes. Why didn't you finish the job?"

"I thought about it," he said quietly.

It wasn't the answer she'd expected him to give. It was one of the few times in her life that Debbie was at a loss for words. A faint blush spread. She looked everywhere and at everything but Cole. But her sense of self-preservation told her she must have the last word.

"Oh! Well, next time, give it more thought."

Cole swallowed.

Debbie hooked her finger on the long zipper at the front of the jumpsuit. She grinned as she walked past him. He followed the sight of her little rear swaying gently as she headed toward her room. He saw her arm move down, heard the rasp of the zipper as it came undone, and walked into his room and slammed the door.

Debbie jumped as the echo reverberated in the hallway and she smiled wider.

"What do you think you're doing?" Cole asked as he walked into the kitchen.

Debbie was pulling a package of frozen chicken breasts from the freezer. "I think I'm going to fix dinner?"

"No, you're not," he said. "Remember what I told you about taking it easy?"

"But—"

"No buts. We'll either eat out or order in. Your choice."

The smile that lit up her face made him forget what the hell he'd been going to say next.

"Really?"

He managed a nod. What in the world had he said to

put that look on her face? When he got his answer, he wanted to laugh at the simplicity of it all.

"I would *love* to order in. Rural Oklahoma offers a world of benefits, but one of them is definitely not take-out food. You either go out to eat or cook it yourself. What can I order?"

Cole grinned. "Just about anything you want," he said.

She nearly clapped her hands. "Let me ask Morgan and Buddy what they'd like to—"

"You choose, honey," he said gently, unaware of what he'd called her. "They'll eat anything."

Her eyes lit up, and she made a half circle of the kitchen floor and then stuffed the frozen chicken back in the freezer.

"Could we have Chinese, with all those cute little boxes of different stuff and lots of eggs rolls and even fortune cookies?"

He laughed long and loud. "Hell, yes, you can have Chinese, cute boxes and all. Fortune cookies added."

"Did someone mention cookies?"

Buddy walked into the kitchen. Cole rolled his eyes.

"Your timing, as always, is impeccable, brother."

"Thank you," Buddy said, uncertain what Cole was referring to, but convinced that, for once, Cole was right.

"We're ordering in," Debbie said. "We're having Chinese."

"Cole's mad at us," Buddy told Debbie.

"Not anymore," she said gently, catching the look of guilty regret lurking behind Buddy's glasses. "It's okay."

"I like sweet and sour chicken," he said, as usual, jumping from one subject to another.

"Egg rolls are my favorite," Debbie answered.

Cole sighed, envious of the instant communication his brother and Debbie seemed to have. "I'll call in the order," he said, and headed for the phone.

"I don't know whose idea this was, but it was sheer genius." Morgan speared another shrimp from the box.

"It was Cole's." Debbie dug through the buffet of boxes on the table. "I think these are my favorites." She poked at the moo goo gai pan, the Hunan beef, and the shrimp fried rice with her chopsticks. "But I sure did like this, too." She was eyeing the sweet and sour pork and the chicken and snow peas.

"It'll keep," Cole teased. "Chinese leftovers microwave pretty good."

The smile on her face was worth a week of stakeouts and sleepless nights.

"Great!"

"Your fortune is in your fingers."

All eyes turned to Buddy, who'd broken into his third fortune cookie and was chewing and reading at the same time. And, who, as usual, had thrown the conversation completely out of sync.

He shrugged, and held up the tiny slip of paper that he'd pulled from the cookie. "My fortune," he explained.

"Wow!" Debbie said, her eyes glowing. "It's true! Your fortune *is* in your fingers, Buddy. Computers... right?"

"Let me try one!" She dug through the box holding the crunchy brown half-moons.

She closed her eyes and picked one as if magic were

hovering at her fingertips. "I choose this one. It feels right."

"Read it," Morgan urged, getting into the joy of seeing something old and familiar through the eyes of someone new.

Debbie broke open the cookie, pulled out the little strip of paper, and began to read. The smile on her face slipped. Her mouth twisted, and then she looked up at the men around the table, who were obviously waiting for her to share her secret. It was impossible. It was too fresh...and too close to home.

"Oh, it's just like Buddy's," she lied, and stuffed it in her pocket.

"Have another," Morgan urged.

"This one's just fine," she said softly, and jumped up from the table. "Anyone need a refill on drinks?"

Buddy followed her to the refrigerator and together the two of them put fresh ice and tea in everyone's glasses.

But Cole was not deceived. He'd seen the look of shock come and go on her face. He knew damn good and well that something on that little slip of paper had rocked her world.

"Let's go out by the pool," Morgan said. "It's a nice night. Bring our drinks. I'll get the tape player. Maybe some jazz or some easy listening would be appropriate."

"I'm going to my room," Buddy said. "My fortune is in my fingers."

Morgan hobbled off to the den and left Cole and Debbie alone in the kitchen.

He walked toward her.

"I'll just put this stuff in the refrigerator before we

go outside," she said quickly, and began closing the tops of the takeout boxes.

Cole slipped up behind her and, before she knew it was happening, had the piece of paper out of her pocket.

"What are you—?"

"Doing my job," he said. "Remember? I'm a detective...and I sense you did not tell the truth about your fortune." His teasing was gentle, but the smile died on his face as he read her fortune.

His heart is in your hands.

"Well, hell," he said shortly.

"Exactly," Debbie answered, took the bit of paper out of his hands, and stuffed it back in her pocket.

"You get the glasses. I'll get the door."

Chapter 3

"Did you pack sun block?"

Debbie dug through her bag and then nodded.

"Do you have sunglasses, something to read, the package of trail mix, the　?"

"I'm ready," Debbie interrupted. "You can't put this off any longer, Cole Brownfield. Take me to the beach, and take me now."

I'd love to take you now, but there are too many witnesses, and I don't think I'm ready for you.

"Get in the car," he ordered. He turned to his father. "Don't expect us until you see us coming. We'll get something to eat before we come home tonight."

Morgan nodded, concealing his glee behind the morning paper. "Have a good time," he said.

"Are you sure you'll be all right?" Debbie asked. "Don't forget, there's plenty of leftovers, and I think there's still some fruit salad if Buddy didn't—"

"Get her out of here," Morgan ordered, smiling as he turned his cheek up for the kiss she was offering.

"We're already gone," Cole said, and ushered her out the door.

The sun was bright and hot and persistent. The windows in Cole's car were down, at Debbie's request. The air tunneled in one and out the other, whipping their hair and clothes in carefree abandon. Her attention was yanked in all directions by the intriguing unfamiliarity of California. She was constantly asking questions. And the palm trees lining the streets seemed to enchant her.

The closer they got to the beach, the more varied and bohemian the sights became. Debbie could hardly wait.

If she'd been given the task of finding the complete opposite of the area in which she'd grown up, she couldn't have picked a better place. Laguna Beach, California, with its sun and surf and tropical atmosphere, was diametrically opposed to the wide, often dry flatlands of western Oklahoma.

Cole needed a chauffeur. Then he could have ridden the way he wanted, with his eyes on his passenger instead of the roadway.

The rambunctious wind kept plastering her clothes against her body, teasing him with reminders that the wind could touch where he dared not. Her breasts were outlined beneath her soft white blouse, revealing the top of her red swimsuit. Her legs, firm and shapely, dangled from the seat in a half-hearted effort to reach the floorboard. He also knew the bottom portion of that red suit was as snug a fit as the top, and ready to be revealed as soon as her brief black shorts were removed.

She was full of anticipation and questions. And she

made him nervous as hell. There was a simmering quality to her personality today that told him he'd better beware.

The Debbie Randall that he'd first met at the Longren Ranch—the one who'd charmed every other member of his family and then ignored his existence, the one who'd lined up five Brownfield men like peas in a pod to assure Lily that her wedding would go off without a hitch, the one that had sent him running in panic from Oklahoma—was back.

He turned off the highway and headed south. Aliso Beach was just ahead. They parked. He grinned as Debbie began grabbing at all the paraphernalia she'd brought along.

"Well, this is it, girl," he said. "We walk from here. Looks like someone besides us decided that this would be a good day to spend at the beach."

Debbie stared. There were cars for miles, gleaming, metallic status symbols as multihued as peacocks, lining the streets and parking area. Just beyond them, she could hear voices and laughter. She grabbed her bag, slid her sunglasses down on her nose, and opened the door, her anticipation mounting as a new adventure was about to begin.

Cole sensed her excitement. It was contagious. He'd gotten a glimpse of her wonderment last night during their impromptu meal. What would today reveal of this charming bit of femininity? And more important, what would be revealed of himself? Each day, it was becoming harder and harder to ignore the fact that Debbie Randall was stuck in his craw. It would take everything he had to insure that she didn't get a toehold on his heart. Cole, male that he was, was blind to the fact that it was already too late. He was long past help.

Vendors lined the boardwalk, hawking their food and souvenirs, their sun block and umbrellas, until Cole thought they'd never make it to the beach. Debbie was entranced by everything and had to see and sample all that was offered. It took them twenty minutes to get from the car to the middle of the vendors' walkway, and during that time, she'd downed a corn dog, a lemonade, and was beginning a frozen yogurt.

"You'll have to wait forever to get in the water," Cole teased.

Debbie shrugged. "It's okay," she said. "We've got all day."

He sighed. That's what worried him.

The people walked in twos and threes and sometimes bunches of eight—families and friends out for a good time and some sun and surf. Long-legged beauties sporting string bikinis and roller blades skated through the crowded throng with skilled precision, announcing their approach by the rumble of wheels on the boardwalk.

Body builders, greasy and brown as a bag full of fries, bulged appropriately whenever anyone was watching, and sometimes just for their own satisfaction.

Skateboards swished and swooped, their lone occupants performing dangerous yet graceful acrobatics, defying the law of gravity, as they came and went through the crowds with unpredictable regularity.

"Clinton, Oklahoma, was never like this," Debbie muttered.

Cole grinned. He knew what she meant. He'd spent

just enough time on Case Longren's ranch to get an appreciation of the peace and quiet the people in rural Oklahoma took for granted. It had been something of a culture shock to him when he'd first seen all that wide, open space and all those cows. But by the time he'd left, the culture shock had been reversed, and it had taken him a week to reacclimatize himself to the sounds of sirens day and night and the growing numbers of people with which he had to contend on a day-to-day basis.

A trio of young males came swooping past, wearing cutoff jeans, frayed and frazzled, with white strings dangling to just above their knees, their bare arms and chests gleaming in a rich array from dark chocolate skin to pink and peeling. Their means of locomotion—the latest fad in skating—roller blades.

Debbie was jostled as they passed. She grabbed at her bag as her sunglasses fell to the pavement. Cole caught her just in time, preventing her from following her glasses' descent.

Something about the trio's frenetic movements alerted Cole. He frowned. They were pushing the limits of what constituted beach etiquette. Granted, it was crowded, but they were still plowing their way through the people with no concerns save their own. A young man staggered as the trio rolled past, and a woman yelled a rude obscenity and flashed a following gesture.

"Are you all right?" he asked sharply.

"I'm fine," Debbie said. "It was just an accident." *Wasn't it?* The last of her statement remained unspoken.

She sensed Cole's uneasiness as she picked up her sunglasses and stuffed them in her bag. She took one quick look at his face. He was watching the trio sweep a path through the crowd.

Suddenly, the boy in the middle did a 360-degree turn around an elderly couple and, before her eyes, snatched the huge beach bag off the lady's shoulder.

"Cole!" Debbie gasped, but it was an unnecessary warning. He'd already seen it coming.

"Wait here," he ordered. He turned to a hot dog vendor and yelled, "Call the police!"

The vendor quickly assessed the situation and grabbed a briefcase from out of a cabinet beneath his stand. A cellular phone appeared in his hands, and he quickly began to dial.

The boy laughed, almost thumbing his nose at the dismay and destruction he left in his wake and gave one last, third-fingered salute to whomever cared to look.

For whatever reason, call it fate, call it bad luck, but the thief's eyes connected with the shocked expression on Debbie's face. For one slow moment in time, everything suspended, movement ceased, motion stopped. There was only Debbie staring into the dark, fathomless eyes of one who'd ceased to care. The connection was unwelcome to both, but it had happened. Debbie shivered, and the moment passed as quickly as it had begun. And then all she could see was Cole running and people screaming as someone called the police.

Cole's first thought as he dashed through the crowd, trying to keep the thief's bare brown backside separated from the other near-nude pedestrians, was that his service revolver was safety locked in the car back in the parking lot. That he was unarmed and chasing a perpetrator gave him second thoughts, but he didn't stop.

The trio was moving fast. Cole knew it was almost beyond hope that he'd ever catch up. He was fast on his feet, but no match for wheels. And the density of the crowd through which he was running hindered him even more. One thing was in his favor; he didn't think they knew they were being followed. He could see them yelling back and forth between themselves, and then he saw the woman's bag drop to the ground.

Hell! he thought. *They've already stripped it!*

Before his eyes, they split and moved in three different directions. Cole muttered a helpless curse as he noticed something else. *They've taken off their skates!* Now they were no longer forced to stay on firm surface to make their getaway. This obviously wasn't their first snatch.

They disappeared into the crowd, leaving Cole to retrieve the only thing he could catch: the woman's bag. He bent down and picked it up, frustrated by the fact that they'd gotten away. The wallet was missing…of course. They were after cash. The rest of the stuff scattered on the street would only have been excess baggage to someone in need of a quick getaway.

He shoved the articles back into the bag and started through the crowd. For the first time since the incident began, he remembered that he'd left Debbie standing in the midst of strangers, witness to a part of his world that he'd learned not to share. He began to trot, anxious and uneasy. She would probably be either mad or frightened or a combination of both. A slow, sick feeling began to grow inside him. *I don't want to lose her.* And then reality surfaced. He couldn't lose something he didn't have.

Cole had been off and running before Debbie registered the fact. She'd had one moment's swift surge of panic, knowing that he was in pursuit of a thief, and then remembered that he did this for a living.

The elderly woman who'd been robbed had fallen to the street, and her husband was kneeling at her side, trying to comfort her.

The crowd of people parted and watched. A few offered help. But Debbie could see that the elderly man was concerned with more than the fact that his wife's bag had just been snatched. Debbie shifted her beach gear to a better position and headed for the couple.

"Are you all right?" she asked as she dropped her bag and beach towels and knelt at the old man's side.

She missed nothing of the woman's pale, clammy complexion. A fluffy white halo of hair framed her features. Heavy slashes of blush traced the high bony structure of her face and enhanced the lack of color beneath. Her thin, knobby knees protruded out from under her culotte skirt. The indigo tracing of aging veins was evident beneath her fragile skin. A tiny trickle of blood was running down her leg. Her matching, tropical floral overblouse that had been knotted loosely at her waist was caught and twisted beneath her arm. Debbie gently rearranged the lady's clothing.

The old man looked up at Debbie, his pale blue eyes wide and watery beneath the fragile, wire-rimmed glasses sliding down his nose.

"Florence has a bad heart."

The statement made Debbie cringe. She stood up, scanning the crowd for the hot dog vendor who'd whipped out a phone earlier.

"Hey!" she yelled. He looked her way. "I think this lady may need an ambulance."

He nodded and grinned. Out came his briefcase.

"Now, Florence," Debbie said, as she knelt back down. "Do you have medicine with you?"

"It was in her bag," the man said as tears began to run silently down his face.

There was nothing to do but wait for help to arrive and keep the couple calm.

"Help will be here soon, Florence," she said, and patted the little woman's leg. "My name is Deborah Randall. I'm from Oklahoma. Have you ever been there?"

The old man's voice lifted. "I'm Maurice Goldblum. Florence and I have a son. His name is Murray. He and his family live in Tulsa, Oklahoma. It's a very small world, isn't it?"

And for the first time since the incident, Florence spoke. "He's a lawyer, with a very prestigious firm."

Debbie smiled. The color was slowly but surely coming back into Florence's cheeks, as was the pride in her voice. She patted Florence and looked up, nervously scanning the crowd around them, hoping for a sign of a policeman or an ambulance or even better—Cole. Someone handed Debbie some wet paper towels. She draped one across Florence's forehead. Maurice took another and wiped gently at the blood running down his wife's leg.

"Let me through!" The authority in his voice, as well as the panic, was evident.

Debbie looked up. Cole! He was back. He was safe. He knelt. Debbie started talking.

"This is Florence and Maurice Goldblum. They have a son named Murray who lives in Tulsa. Imagine that!" Her voice was just the least bit shaky as her eyes spoke what she dared not say. And then she reversed the introduction. "This is Cole Brownfield. He's a policeman."

Cole smiled gently at the look on the elderly couple's

faces. They were hanging on Debbie's every word. Once more, she'd used her gentleness to make a bad situation easier. And then her next quiet statement made him take a second look at the old couple.

"She has a bad heart, Cole. Her medicine was in her bag."

The multistriped carryall was still clutched in his hands. He'd almost forgotten it at the relief of finding Debbie. He quickly opened it and began to shuffle through what was left after the thieves had rummaged. He almost missed it. The tiny, round brown cylinder was caught in the soft corner, stuck deep in the careless folds.

"Would this be it?"

"My medicine!" Florence cried. The towel fell off her forehead into her lap as her fingers closed around the vial, grasping at it in shaky relief.

"Here," Cole urged, "let me help." He removed the cap, and handed it to Maurice.

The old gentleman shook out the correct dosage. Florence opened her mouth like a baby bird waiting to be fed and sighed quietly as the tiny pill went under her tongue.

"Thank you." Maurice Goldblum grasped Cole's forearm with trembling hands. "You saved her life."

The sound of a siren broke the silence of the moment, and Cole quickly began to move away the bystanders. An ambulance pulled into the area. Two EMTs jumps out, grabbed their gear and a gurney, and headed toward the people down the beach who'd wadded themselves into a crowd. A police unit pulled up beside the ambulance. Two officers exited the car. It seemed like hours, but it had only been a few minutes since the drama had unfolded. The crowd began to disperse. Professionals had everything well in hand.

Debbie stepped back as emergency services were being rendered and watched as the elderly couple was taken away. She located Cole, who was still talking to the two officers, and knew that everything was under control. There was nothing for her to do but gather their gear and wait until she was retrieved.

"Hey, lady!" the hot dog vendor yelled. "Have a seat. They'll be a while."

She grinned, dragged their stuff toward the vendor's cart, and, before she knew it, was sitting beneath Wally's umbrella, drinking a lemonade, and listening to him talk about the stock market's latest ups and downs.

Cole had given the officers all the details and learned that this was the twelfth such incident at the beach in less than three weeks. He absently turned around and then faced nothing but milling crowds. Debbie was no-where in sight! Swift panic surfaced. She was such a stranger...and too trusting.

And then he heard her laugh. He followed the sound. And when he finally saw her, feet propped up on Wally's hot dog cart, sipping a lemonade in the shade and sharing conversation with the owner of the cart, relief made him weak. He didn't know whether to shake her or hug her. He settled for a touch on her shoulder instead.

"Hey, Little Red. I lost you," he teased, letting his grip on her shoulder tell her what he could not.

Debbie jumped up and whirled around, threw her arms around his neck, and hugged him. She'd needed to touch him ever since she'd seen him coming back through the crowd with that serious expression on his face. Until she'd seen him, she'd imagined the worst.

Condensation from the icy drink in her hand dripped down the back of his neck. He could have cared less.

"Sorry," he said, grimacing as he unwound her from around his neck. "This isn't such a great start to our day off, is it?"

"I think it was perfect," Debbie said. "You're a hero."

He blushed and tried to ignore Wally's grin.

"No, I'm not. I chased those punks and still let them get away."

"I'm not talking about those creeps. I'm talking about the fact that if you hadn't chased them, you wouldn't have retrieved Florence's bag, and then she wouldn't have had her medicine. I know the ambulance came soon afterwards. But you might just have made the difference, Cole."

"Yeah, buddy," Wally chimed in. "Don't consider this gratuity or nothin', but have a lemonade on me."

Cole grinned as the vendor handed him a tall, ice-cold cup of lemonade. He tipped it in a salute and drank, relishing the tart, refreshing liquid as it ran down his throat and into his stomach.

"Thanks—" he looked down at the side of the cart just to check the name "—Wally." He stuffed the empty cup in the trash, and grabbed up their bags. "Now, come on, girl. It's time to get you wet."

It took a while. They had to make a stop at the rest rooms. And he had to rent an umbrella. But when she came out, Debbie was minus white shirt and shorts. Once again, Cole lost his breath at the small, curvaceous body in the tiny red suit, and tried to ignore the rush of lust that wanted to make itself known. *For God's sake,* Cole told himself, *not now, and not here.*

And then finally, they were on the beach.

The sand was endless and warm and in her shoes. Debbie stepped out of the canvas slip-ons, stuffed them in her bag, and squiggled her toes with relish.

Cole grinned. "Feel good?"

"Feels great," Debbie replied. "Can't do this at home. Too many sandburs."

He laughed. "No stickers here, but watch out for trash. I don't want you to cut your foot on a piece of metal or glass. They police the area pretty well, but sometimes things can get buried in the sand."

She nodded. "Where do we put our stuff?"

Cole had already pinpointed a fairly sparse assortment of sunworshipers and pointed Debbie in their direction. "Just walk that direction and when you see a spot big enough to sit down in, grab it, and don't move until I spread out our towels and plant the umbrella."

"You got it." She grinned and almost danced across the beach in her excitement to begin their day.

None too soon, everything was in place. Debbie was fairly bursting with anticipation.

"Just one more thing," Cole said. "Come here, Little Red. Let's get some sun block on you so that you don't burn."

She grinned. "Only if I get to return the favor," she teased and, cocking her eyebrow at him, raked his long, tanned body with a look that made his blood pressure rise.

He looked down in panic, hoping that it was the only thing rising, and then breathed a quiet sigh of relief, praying that he'd just be able to make it into the water before he embarrassed himself.

The sun block went on, swift and smooth, then Cole all but shoved her toward the water. He had no intention of letting her get her hands on him with that lotion. He was tough, but he'd have to be dead not to react to Debbie Randall.

He followed her path to the water, watching the way her hips swayed beneath that scrap of red fabric, and glared at a couple of young men who whistled and teasingly made a halfhearted grab for her ankles. They yanked their hands back as if Cole had slapped them and then grinned and shrugged as he stalked past. This was going to be more difficult than he'd imagined. If he took her to the beach again, she wasn't wearing that damned red bikini. He'd take her shopping himself and see to it that some more of those tender curves were covered.

He was so busy glaring at every male within a hundred yards, he didn't notice that Debbie had stopped. He bumped into her and sent them both staggering. By the time they'd righted themselves, Debbie had not only stopped, she was backing up. He looked down in surprise at the look of shock on her face and caught her midway in flight.

"Honey! What's wrong?"

The tenderness in his voice was unexpected, but Debbie was so dumbstruck, she didn't even hear it. All she could see was water…going on forever and ever. And the waves coming toward her in ruffled abandon. She swallowed and pointed.

"It's so big!"

Cole wrapped his arms around her shoulders and

pulled her back against his chest. "It's the ocean, Little Red. It's supposed to be big." And then something occurred to him. "Haven't you ever seen the ocean?"

She shook her head, unable to speak for a moment.

"I've seen ponds. I've seen creeks. I've even seen rivers in flood. But every time, I could see land on the other side, too. I've never seen water and not seen it's boundary."

"Well, you have now," he said. "Deborah Jean, welcome to the Pacific." He scooped her up in his arms, and began walking with her toward the waves lapping at the shoreline.

Her arms tightened around his neck. "Cole?"

"I wouldn't scare you on purpose, and you know it. Calm down. We're just going to meet it together."

The look on his face told her more than he'd meant to tell. She saw trust. She saw strength. And she saw something else Cole Brownfield never knew was showing. She saw tenderness…and desire.

At first the water felt cold. But the sun was hot, and the water refreshed them. Cole held her close against his body and let the waters tease her until Debbie felt comfortable with its rhythm.

"You can put me down now," she said. And then when he began to comply, she cautioned nervously, "Just don't go too far."

Cole grimaced. He was already drowning in those wide, dark eyes. He wasn't going anywhere unless Debbie went with him.

It was late. Debbie was asleep beneath the umbrella's shade as Cole kept watch. And he was desperately watching everything and everyone except the woman lying beside him. He didn't care. He'd already tried it and nearly lost his sanity at the thought of stretching out beside her, slipping her against and then beneath him, and losing himself in—

"Hey, Brownfield! As I live and breathe. I never thought I'd see you down here among the pretty boys and beach bunnies."

Cole looked up and grinned, recognizing the smart-ass tone before he saw its owner.

"Hey, yourself, Whaley. I see you're riding herd today." His remark was pointedly aimed at Detective Lee Whaley's two teenage daughters, who were doing their best to attract any or all male eyes their way.

Lee rolled his eyes and grimaced. "I couldn't have had boys. Hell no. I had to have girls—four to be exact. I'll never survive their raising. I'll probably wind up in the stir for murder first."

Cole laughed. "You love it and you know it. And if you hadn't been such a hell raiser when you were a kid, you would trust these boys more."

Lee grinned. He plopped his short, stocky body down beside Cole, patted his head to make sure his well-worn golf hat was still covering his nearly bald head, and picked at a spot on his arm where skin was trying to peel. He kicked a spray of sand on Cole's feet as a retort. It was then that he saw the curvy little female lying beside and behind him.

"What have we here?" he leered, and elbowed Cole in return for the glare he was receiving. "Been holding out on us, have you?"

Cole glared again. "She's a houseguest," he said shortly. "She's my sister Lily's friend from Oklahoma. She came to help out with Dad while his leg heals."

The smirk slid off Lee Whaley's face. "How *is* Morgan, anyway? That was a hell of a wreck. He was lucky he wasn't killed."

Cole nodded. "Thanks to her," he tilted his head toward Debbie, unaware that his expression and voice had softened, "he's doing much better. She's got him doing his exercises, and has him on a regular schedule of healthy diet and rest. She could charm roses into growing without thorns."

Lee grinned again. "Well, she's got her work cut out for her. You're still full of thorns, buddy. In fact, you're prickly as hell."

Cole tried to maintain his disparaging attitude, but it was no use. Lee Whaley was too good a friend, and too close to the mark to deny.

"Say," Lee said. "Why don't you two guys come on over later. We're having a clam bake in the backyard. Remember where we live? Just past the beach, first house on your left. It'll be the one with all the boys lined up at my fence, gawking."

Cole laughed.

Whaley took a lot of teasing about his residence. The ribbing ranged from accusations that he took kickbacks to suggestions he was stealing drug money. But it was all in good fun and Whaley knew it. He'd just had the good fortune to marry his high school sweetheart. She'd had the good fortune to be the only child of a wealthy, retired movie mogul. Ten years ago, her parents had died and left her everything, including a very ostentatious beachfront home. Whaley had taken it in his stride. He was a cop. Just because his wife had money didn't mean he was going to give up his own pension. He had too much pride in himself and his work to do that.

And then Debbie's voice startled them both as she crawled to her knees and entwined herself against Cole's back.

"We'd love to, wouldn't we?" she asked, and slid her elbows on either side of Cole's face, resting them on his shoulders.

The feel of those lush breasts pushing against his spine gave him an instant ache he couldn't afford, especially not in front of Whaley. The little devil. He hadn't even known she was awake. He grabbed her arms and wrapped them around his neck.

Lee smiled, watching them fencing with bodies and words. He vaguely remembered what it was like to be so desperately in love and not be able to do anything about it. Thank goodness he had Charlotte. She'd put up with nearly twenty years of him and police work, plus the fact that he'd refused to give it up. She deserved a medal. But she'd settled for him.

Cole was afraid to let go of Debbie's arms. He never knew what she was going to do, and he didn't want any more surprises in front of Lee. "Are you going to have a crowd?"

Lee nodded. "You know how these things get. Just bring yourselves. We'll eat around sunset."

"We'll be there," Cole said.

Lee nodded his approval, then looked up and saw that his daughters were swiftly disappearing down the beach with several young men in tow.

"Oh hell," he muttered. "I've got to go. I promised Charlotte that I'd sort through the uninvited guests this time. Last time, the girls brought home someone who couldn't speak English, but kept flashing a wad of dough that would choke a horse. Those kind make me nervous. Know what I mean?"

Cole grinned and waved goodbye as Lee made his way down the beach, following in his daughters' wake.

"He's nice," Debbie said.

"So are you," Cole answered as he pulled her around and into his lap.

The look he gave her was one that she'd save forever in her memory.

"Thank you very much, Cole."

Her voice was soft and gentle. He ached to taste the words on her lips.

"You're very welcome," he said, and settled for less.

Chapter 4

"Are you cold?"

Cole's voice wrapped around Debbie's senses, making the breath she'd been taking harder to swallow. She scooted closer to the bonfire and turned her back to the flames, giving equal time to her shivering body.

"Just a little. I think it's the breeze coming off the ocean."

"Hold up your arms," Cole asked.

"Are you going to rob me?" she teased as she threaded her arms through the sleeves of the sweatshirt he was pulling over her head.

"I haven't quite decided what to do with you, girl."

His voice was low and steady, nothing like his heart. It rocked against his chest like a boat in a storm.

She smiled and rubbed her hands against the welcome warmth covering her arms.

"The sweatshirt's either J.D.'s or Dusty's." Cole answered her question before it was asked. "It was in my trunk. I found it when I went to get my sweats. Good thing they're a lot shorter than I am, or you'd be lost in here." He ruffled the top of her curls. "I also found the matching pants. Want to try them? They have elastic at the ankles and a drawstring waist."

"Please." Debbie was trying to keep her teeth from chattering.

She used Cole for a leaning post and quickly thrust her legs into the blue sweats. They bagged around her ankles as she tried to find the drawstring at the waist.

"Here, let me," Cole said, and slid his hands beneath the sweat shirt, fumbling in the semidarkness surrounding the bonfire Lee Whaley had built at the edge of his property.

Debbie held her breath, closed her eyes, and pretended that the touch of his hands at her waist was a prelude to more.

The voices of the other guests at the Whaley residence faded into the background as they ranged from the second-story deck of the home to the water's edge and scattered along the beach. People were more than replete from the evening's meal and trying to walk off their binge.

Cole had wanted to do the same, but for different reasons. He'd hardly eaten a thing, for watching Debbie mingling with his friends. The men had begun to reminisce about a narcotics bust they'd made last year that had made national news. The longer they'd talked, the more graphic their stories became. They were too proud of the fact that they'd taken down one of the larger drug lords in the area to let it be forgotten.

Cole sat and waited for a reaction from Debbie that never came.

She listened. Cole started to think she was going to let it slide. But what she finally said wasn't what he'd expected. It wasn't horror at the tales, and it wasn't a put-down of their occupations. She'd simply caught one of the men in a slight fabrication of the truth.

"I don't see how that happened," Debbie said, trying not to grin at a statement one of the men had just made.

"What don't you see, little lady?" the detective asked. He rolled his eyes at Cole, thinking he was going to get her good.

"Well...just a few minutes ago, you said you fainted at the sight of blood. If that's true, then I don't see how you managed to take the entire bunch into custody alone. You said they were 'all shot up.'"

The men erupted into laughter as the off-duty officer grinned at Debbie's remark.

"Yeah, I do," he'd answered. "But I always manage to slap the cuffs on them before I pass out."

Cole had laughed along with them. Instinctively she'd hit on the right note with these guys. They were serious when it mattered and got through the horror of what they saw by laughing at it.

He wanted to believe she could fit in. He wanted to believe that he could begin a life with her. He wanted to, but the certainty wasn't there. Debbie *might* be strong enough...but he didn't know if he was strong enough to lose her if she wasn't.

He tugged at the drawstrings and then tied them snugly, tucking the dangling ends inside the pants.

"That better?"

Debbie nodded and opened her eyes, willing him to make a move. He did.

"Want to go for a walk?" Cole held his breath, waiting for her to answer.

"I thought you'd never ask."

The tide had swallowed the shoreline as Debbie knew it. It was another something that would take getting used to. In Oklahoma, water stayed put. Except for intermittent floods in certain areas, water pretty much knew its place.

The words of an old Gatlin Brothers' song came to mind. She didn't know about all the gold still being in California, but California *definitely* was a brand new game.

Her foot crunched upon something half-buried in the sand. She bent down, dug until she found it, and lifted it up, using the moonlight to see by. It was a shell. Small convoluted swirls formed the white conical shape into something special and secret.

"Look!" she cried. "My first seashell!"

Cole caught her hand and carried it to his lips. "You've had a lot of firsts today, haven't you, lady?"

There was something about the way he was touching her, something in his voice that gave her hope.

"It was my first time to see the ocean." Her voice was breathless and soft. "It was my first time to eat clams." His hands cupped her face and tilted it. "I found my first—"

His mouth took the rest of her words as his hands stole her heart.

It was better than she'd imagined. His lips were cool and firm, softening and warming as she opened to him.

His hands made tentative forays across her shoulders, then moved back up her neck and threaded the tangled curls around her face.

He shuddered and groaned as her arms wrapped around his waist and pulled him close…too close…not close enough.

Moonlight sliced a thin, silver path across the water, blinding in its intensity, but neither saw it. They were too lost in the feel of being in each other's arms.

And then suddenly Cole couldn't get close enough. He took them to their knees. His hands moved beneath her shirt and around behind her back.

The catch on her red bikini top came undone, and she spilled into his palms with a thrust, yearning to alleviate the pulsing pressure he'd created.

The soft tips went flat against his hands and then, as if they had a life of their own, hardened and pushed against him, reminding him that he'd started something that was aching to be finished.

With no thought of their proximity to the other guests, he laid her beneath him, stretched out above her, and then branded himself with her heat. She was soft. All movement and enticing depths that he wanted to explore. She would let him. Of that, he was certain. Could he let himself? Of that, he was unsure.

The sand made a place for her, generously shifting to allow her room—room for her body and the man above her. Below the surface, it was still warm from the heat of the day. Debbie sighed and lifted her arms, pulling Cole down until there was no room for breath between them. She heard his soft groan and felt his need as his mouth plundered past the neckline of the sweat shirt.

His hands slid up, and then his hands slid down. And Debbie lifted herself to meet them.

"Jesus!" Whether he'd said it as a prayer or an oath, he was uncertain. But nevertheless, Cole rolled off Debbie and sat up, burying his face in his hands as he desperately tried to regain control of what he'd nearly lost. His sanity.

"My God!" he muttered, remembering that he'd left her behind, and scooped her from the sand. He sandwiched her between his knees, fitting her backside to his lap as he tried to get himself in order. "Debbie... I'm sorry. I didn't mean to—"

"For Pete's sake," she mumbled, as his chin nestled in the curls atop her head, "if you ever expect me to speak to you again, at least don't apologize."

He shuddered, wrapped her tightly in his arms, and wondered if he could ever let her go. He rocked them in the darkness.

The moon's silver path on the water beckoned, enticing by its mere presence, promising something intangible if one were courageous enough to chance it.

Both stared, lost in the lure of the night, and knew that if they were only brave enough to walk on water, magic awaited. But neither moved.

The drive home was long; Debbie, strangely silent. It was so unlike her, Cole was uneasy. He couldn't tell whether he'd angered her by initiating the kiss or by stopping just beyond. Either way, she was quiet and he was nervous.

But tonight, he'd realized something. For the first time in his entire life, he was considering the possibility of ending his life as a bachelor. For the first time, he let himself contemplate what it would be like to share his life with another. It would mean that his peace of mind, his sanity, his well-being would not depend entirely upon himself. It would revolve around another person and her happiness and her well-being and peace of mind. It would mean that Cole was not in control. It scared the hell out of him.

"We're home," Debbie said quietly.

It startled him.

She spoke again. "I'll get the bag. You get the rest of the stuff. Just dump the entire mess in the back room, okay? I'll go through it all tomorrow. I'm too tired to deal with it now."

He parked, opened the door, and started around to help her out. But she beat him to it and let herself out of the car. He sighed with frustration, turned, and headed for the back door, key in hand.

She walked past him, into the shadowy depths of the house, homing in on the hall light shining through the kitchen, guiding the way toward their rooms.

"Debbie?"

His voice caught and held her in place. Finally she turned and answered. He was impossible to ignore. "What?"

"Are you all right?"

She shrugged in the darkness, but he still saw...or sensed the motion. "Of course."

"Then...where are you going in such a hurry? I thought you might want something to drink...maybe unwind..."

"I'm going to take a shower," she said quietly. "I need to wash the sand out of my hair."

It left him speechless. Memories of her beneath him

in the sand, and her body soft and inviting, made him instantly hard and aching. She walked away, and he let her.

It was only much later when Debbie lay sleepless, staring out at the moonlight teasing the folds of the curtain at her windows, that she remembered she hadn't told Cole she'd seen the mugger's face.

Morgan sensed something had changed. Ever since their day at the beach, he'd felt the chill between them.

He saw his son's silent anguish. When Debbie came in a room, Cole made an excuse to exit. If she needed something, he was the first to volunteer to get it, but always managed to return and leave it without having to face her. Morgan wanted to shake them both. It would have been obvious to a blind man with earmuffs that they were doing everything but what they wanted...and that was to fall into each other's arms.

Cole had volunteered for a very extended and very dangerous assignment, and Morgan knew it was just an excuse to keep from facing what he was trying to ignore. Debbie. He missed his son, and he worried about him, but except for saying a prayer each night, there was nothing he could do but be there, should they need a sounding board.

Debbie smiled and laughed. She cooked and cleaned. She crawled into the pool and chided and teased Morgan through all his physical therapy. She coerced Buddy into joining them for meals so that she and Morgan wouldn't be alone. There was no way she was going to admit aloud, to anyone, that she and Cole were having problems. She couldn't admit it aloud, because she'd yet to admit it silently, to herself.

He's just stubborn. That was her rationale for everything that made her ache. That was what kept her from packing her bags and taking the next plane back to Oklahoma. That was the only thing that kept her in her own room at night and not across the hall between the covers of his empty bed.

I can be just as stubborn. That was what kept her from falling apart every time she heard a siren. And when she listened to the local evening news, she did not let on, by so much as a gasp, that the latest drug bust had resulted in two deaths.

Learning that the deaths had not been of the officers involved, but of some suspects who'd resisted arrest, did not help. It only served to remind Debbie that during his days on duty, Cole was constantly in the line of fire and in danger of never coming home.

It made her stop. And it made her think. And for the first time, she had a taste of what kept Cole Brownfield out of her arms. She'd heard him say more than once that, on the job, a policeman's first duty was to his partner. It was what got them home safe and sound each day. And that if a man, or woman, as the case might be, couldn't face that fact, they had no business trying to work a family into a policeman's lifestyle. It was what got people killed.

But Debbie knew that she could face sharing Cole. If that was what it took to keep him safe and bring him home, she'd share him with the whole damned department. *I can be stubborn,* she reminded herself. *I will wait until he realizes that, too.*

She sprayed furniture polish on an already gleaming table and rubbed furiously, muttering beneath her breath at the stupidity of supposedly brilliant people.

"Were you talking about me?" Buddy asked as he wandered through the kitchen with an empty plate and glass. He'd long since learned to return his carry-out crockery. It still gave him nightmares thinking about soap and water and vacuums in his inner sanctum.

"What?" Debbie looked up, startled at his appearance and then realized that he'd walked in on the last of her mumblings.

"Brilliant people…were you talking about me?" Buddy grinned.

"You're not nearly as stupid as you let on, are you, Robert Allen?"

"Cole just drove up." He deposited his announcement and his dirty dishes at the same time.

Debbie whirled around, stared through the living room toward the front door and then, before she thought, wrapped her arms around Buddy's neck and planted a big kiss on his cheek.

"Thank you for caring, Buddy dear," she whispered.

Cole walked in. It was the first thing he saw. His brother and Debbie. In the kitchen. Kissing. At least she was kissing, Buddy was grinning down at her like someone had just handed him the keys to the computer brain in Washington, D.C.

Cole didn't think. He just reacted. It had been too long since he'd been home and too long since he'd felt human. He'd never been so pissed off in his life. He pivoted, slamming the door behind him as he made a none-too-graceful exit back outside. This time, he stood on the front stoop, leaned against the door, placed his finger on the bell, and pushed.

Debbie grinned. She'd heard the door open, and then she'd heard it slam. For just a moment, she feared that the impulse she'd given in to with Buddy had been the wrong thing to do. The last thing she meant to cause was trouble between brothers. However, it was obvious from the sarcastic ringing of the doorbell that Cole hadn't mistaken what she'd been doing. He was just mad that it hadn't been him.

"I'm going to my room now," Buddy said. "Thank you for the kiss…and we're out of cookies."

"Okay. You're welcome. And I'll make some tomorrow."

He nodded, secure in the knowledge that he'd done his bit toward family unity.

Morgan hobbled into the room, intent on reaming out whoever was playing at his door, when Debbie made a dash into the living room. He caught a glimpse of Cole's angry face through the sheer curtains, another glimpse of the light shining in her eyes, and did as neat a pivot as his leg would allow.

"I'm going to my room," he announced.

Debbie grinned. "It runs in the family."

He didn't know what she was talking about, but he kept walking just the same. If it was the last thing he saw on this earth, he wanted to see Cole and Debbie together…and happy.

Debbie took a deep breath and opened the door. Cole's glare was as dark as the three-day growth of beard on his face.

"Hi!" she said. "You need a shave."

She turned and walked away, leaving him standing on the doorstep. She hadn't seen or heard from him in more than seventy-two hours. It was the single hardest thing she'd ever done.

Cole stared. *How in hell do you stay mad at some-*

one who won't fight back? He walked in, slamming the door behind him, and followed her into the kitchen on the pretext of getting himself something to eat.

Doors banged, dishes rattled, pots and bowls were shifted, and the remnants of the refrigerator received a thorough inspection. He stared and he glared at everything and everywhere...but at Debbie.

"Looks like you've been busy while I've been gone." The remark was meant to be sarcastic. He was referring to walking in on the kiss.

"Yes. Your dad is now down to a cane instead of crutches. I painted the fence around the pool. The neighbor across the street gave me some apricots today. I froze six quart bagfuls. They're really good. Do you like apricots? I could make a—"

"Dammit to hell, girl. I wasn't talking about apricots."

Her voice was soft, and her touch was gentle. She wrapped her arms around his waist, laid her cheek against his backbone, and hugged.

"Welcome home, Cole Brownfield. You were missed."

As he'd thought before, he wondered, *How the hell do you stay mad with someone who won't fight back?*

His hands caught her wrists, unlocked them, and turned himself in her arms. He pressed her face against his heartbeat, wrapped his hands in her hair, and inhaled. She smelled of soap and flowers...and those goddamned apricots. And he'd never been so glad to be home in his life.

"Is that so?" he asked. "Well, just for the record, I missed being here, too."

"Are you hungry?"

Hell, yes, I'm hungry. I'm starving for you, Deborah Randall.

"A little. I'm more tired than hungry."

She leaned back, using his arms for a brace, and took one long look at the shadows in his eyes. She swiped at the hopelessly straight hair brushing his forehead and gave his cheek a pat.

"Go shower...shave...change. I'll have something ready when you are."

It was the best deal he'd ever been offered. "I'll be right back."

He never made it. Debbie had seen the exhaustion. She suspected what might occur. She'd been right.

She stood outside his closed door, listening. She heard the first shoe hit the floor. Seconds later, after a soft grunt, the other. It was quiet. For long moments, she heard nothing. And then the soft, gentle sound of an exhausted snore.

She pushed open the door. He was flat on his back, one arm slung across his eyes, the other flung across his pillow. His legs dangling from the bed. She went to get Morgan.

"I need help," she said.

Morgan didn't ask. He followed. And when he saw his son and the state he was in, tears threatened.

"He works too damned hard," Morgan said as Debbie motioned for him to pull while she pushed.

Together they managed to get Cole all the way onto the bed.

"He'll sleep better if we could get his jeans off, but I'll settle for unbuttoning the top buttons instead."

Morgan nodded and complied as Debbie went to the linen closet and retrieved a lightweight blanket. It was hot outside, but inside, the air-conditioning kept everything at a comfortable seventy-two degrees. Asleep, that sometimes became too cool for comfort.

She pulled the soft blue blanket over Cole, resisted the urge to lie down beside him, and settled for a pat on his arm instead.

"Come on," she said. "He can always eat later. I don't think he's slept since he left."

The tears were thick in her voice and in her eyes, but Morgan wisely refrained from mentioning the fact. He had to. He was too full of emotion himself to bring it up.

Cole slept the clock around. When he awoke, he could smell coffee and the aroma of freshly baked oatmeal cookies, and he could smell himself. He groaned, rolled over and off his bed, stripping his jeans and shirt as he walked.

The shower came on just as his last item of clothing came off. He walked beneath the jetting spray, reveling in the sting of water yet to warm.

The last thing he remembered was walking in on Debbie kissing his brother. And he vaguely remembered holding her and promising something about "being right back." He grimaced as he reached for the soap and shampoo. It was obvious that he'd never made it.

He stood beneath the shower until the water got hot and then until the water ran cold because he'd emptied the tank. He exited the stall, grabbed a bath towel, and wrapped it around him as he walked back into his room to get some clean underwear.

A steaming cup of hot coffee and a plate with three cookies, still warm from the oven, sat on his bedside table. Startled, he half expected to see Debbie's teasing face peeking out from around some door. But she was nowhere in sight. He sank down on the bed, unmindful of his still-wet body, and inhaled two cookies before he remembered to chew. The last, he savored with the coffee, thinking that a guy could get used to this kind of treatment.

He dried and dressed, gave his hair a half swipe with a comb, and gathered up his empty cup and plate.

"Got a refill?"

Debbie turned at the sink. She dropped the potato she was peeling back into the bowl and stuffed her hands into her apron pockets to keep from throwing them around his neck.

"You look better," she said softly.

"I hope to hell I do," he teased. "I saw myself just before I walked into the shower. It even scared me."

She grinned. Buddy walked into the kitchen.

"Debbie made cookies," he announced.

Cole nodded, holding up his empty plate.

"Chocolate chip is *my* favorite," Buddy said.

Cole privately thought that his brother was nuts. He knew good and well that he'd just eaten oatmeal and raisin. He should. They were his favorite.

"Debbie made oatmeal and raisin," Buddy continued.

Cole's eyebrows shot up toward his hairline. Suddenly, he, too, was beginning to understand Buddy's odd manner of conversation. Especially when he saw Debbie blush at Buddy's last remark. And he knew that Buddy was explaining, in the only way Buddy knew how, that the kiss Debbie had given him had been innocent.

"I know, Robert Allen," Cole said. "You can go to your room now."

Buddy grinned. "I'm going to my room now," he echoed.

They stared at each other and then burst out laughing. It was impossible not to. And for the first time since he and Debbie had parted company after their day at the beach, he felt happy inside himself.

"I'm starving," he said. "What have you got to eat... besides oatmeal-and-raisin cookies?"

"Sit," Debbie ordered. "It won't take a minute. I've got anything you could possibly want." She began rummaging through the refrigerator.

He watched the seductive sway of her body as she moved around the kitchen. His insides twisted themselves into pretzels, but he ignored the twinges. "Yes, Little Red. You certainly have."

Cole and Debbie had come to an unspoken agreement. They'd agreed to disagree on certain issues yet to be resolved. Thankfully, it left the temperature in the Brownfield household somewhere back in the range of normalcy. No more frozen looks or cold shoulders between them, just lots of midnight dips in a chilly pool for Cole and sleepless nights for Debbie. Nothing serious and nothing that couldn't be remedied...when the time was right.

But it took a routine call on a routine day for Cole to realize that time was not always going to be on his side... or waiting. Time had a way of running out when you least expected it. And for Debbie, it almost ran out for good.

"Just drop me off at the mall," Debbie said. "You go on to your appointment, and I'll take a cab home when I'm through."

Morgan hesitated in the mall parking lot. It was broad daylight. Debbie was a grown woman, even if she was tiny. Women shopped alone all over the world… everywhere, every day. He knew he was just being over-protective. But he couldn't help it. This tiny female had come to mean a lot to all of them, especially his eldest son.

"Well…" he began.

"Come on, Morgan. If I go with you and sit and wait, then you're simply going to have to come back with me and sit and wait some more. None of that makes any sense, now does it?"

He sighed and grinned. "You've got me there." And then he pointed his finger in her face. "But when you're ready to come home, call a cab from inside the mall, and then wait at the door until you see it drive up. Don't stand outside. You'll simply be an easy target for some thug."

"Okay, okay," she agreed. "But don't worry. This is no different from any big mall anywhere. I've survived Quail Springs Mall in Oklahoma City. I've survived the Galleria in Dallas. Surely I can survive Laguna Beach's Village Fair."

He nodded. "Do you have enough money?" And then before she could refuse, he thrust several twenties in her hand. "Don't argue with me. It's either this, or you come with me."

She leaned over and kissed his cheek. "See you back at the house."

He waited until she was inside and then drove off, thankful that this little bit of nothing had come into their lives and thankful that he could now maneuver around more or less on his own.

* * *

Two hours and several shops later, Debbie looked at her watch in surprise. It was later than she thought. She'd better hurry. If Morgan got home before she did, he'd send out the troops—or Buddy—to look for her. It would be hard to guess which would cause more commotion, an entire battalion or one absentminded computer genius.

She grinned as she hurried out of the store, her small sack of makeup clutched in her hand. She made a mad dash for the escalator. There was one more shop she wanted to visit. The morning paper had mentioned a sale.

Her foot caught the step as it unfolded and began its ascent toward the next level. She looked up, partly out of habit, partly to see where she was going, and then forgot to breathe.

On the next aisle, coming toward her, coming down, was a young man. His face was familiar...too familiar. And the last time she'd seen it...he'd been flipping off the world and stealing an old woman's purse.

Thomas Holliday was bored. It was why he'd come to the mall. He'd been here most of the day, filching what he could when he could and laughing to himself at not being caught. He was invincible. He was a stud. And tonight, after he picked up Nita Warren, he'd show her what being a stud meant.

And then he saw the woman. At first, he couldn't place her...and then his belly turned and sweat ran. He reacted before he thought.

The escalator was almost empty. Only one woman with two small children behind her...no one behind

him. He could tell she was nervous. That told him she'd
recognized him, too. It made him feel strong.

Debbie looked up, and then she turned and looked
behind her. If the woman and her children hadn't been
there, she'd have backtracked. Now, it was impossible.
There was only one thing left for her to do. She'd ride
up and call Cole. And then everything went black.

Thomas's fist shot out. It connected with her chin as
his hand yanked at the bag on her shoulder. But something went wrong. The purse wouldn't come loose. And
then he noticed that she had it over her head and then
across her shoulder. And he'd just knocked her out!

She went limp and loose as an uncoiled rope as the
stairs carried her out of his reach. He cursed and ran
down the stairs and out of the mall, with the woman
and her children's shrieks ringing in his ears.

"Hey, partner," Rick yelled as Cole came out of the
washroom at the service station. "We just got a call
to go out to Village Fair Mall. Isn't that close to your
house? The call said a lady requires your services."
He smiled and leered, giving his best Groucho Marx
imitation.

"Just shut up and drive," Cole grinned.

He slid into the passenger side of the unmarked unit.
It had been a slow day. They'd simply been following
up on some leads, eliminating the bad, taking note of
the ones that might lead to something more.

They weren't far from their destination. It didn't take
long to get there. It took less time to park. It was not in
their nature to dawdle, even when something was not
earmarked an emergency. But the emergency quickly
presented itself as Cole and Rick walked into the small

security office and Debbie stood up from the chair in which she'd been sitting.

"Cole."

The quiver in her voice was nearly his undoing. But his training stood him in good stead. He saw the new bruise on her face, and the color receding from her face. He caught her just before she fainted.

Chapter 5

"What the—?" Rick Garza took one look at his partner's face and the woman he caught in his arms. The fear in Cole's voice told him the rest.

"It's Debbie," Cole said.

Cole searched her body for further signs of injury beyond what he could already see. The obvious ones were enough to make him sick. He was desperately trying to maintain his rational thinking when all he wanted to do was vent the rage that was threatening to overwhelm him. Someone had hurt his lady.

"*Your* Debbie?" Rick was beginning to understand. Cole had talked of nothing else since her arrival. He was either constantly ticked off because of what she'd done or worried because of something she hadn't.

Cole nodded. *My Debbie!* He shuddered as he lowered her onto a sofa in the outer office of the security department. The mall manager hovered, concerned for the young woman's welfare, panicked that they might be sued.

"What happened?" Cole asked. He was all business. And it was then that he noticed the woman and two children sitting at a table in another room, obviously giving some sort of statement. He caught the look in Rick's eyes and nodded. As usual, they'd read each other's mind.

Rick touched Cole's arm. "I'll see what that's all about," he said, and hurried into the other room.

Cole knelt at Debbie's side. The manager quickly dumped everything he knew about the incident in the officer's lap.

"All we know is that she was riding up an escalator and someone coming down on the opposite side tried to rob her. The woman in the other room saw everything."

Cole's mouth thinned and his eyes narrowed as he carefully felt for Debbie's pulse. Everything about him seemed cool and methodical. He gave a good imitation of calm under fire. What he wanted to do was hit something...or someone.

"Have you called an ambulance? Did the woman say what Debbie was hit with?" His dark eyes raked the purpling bruise on her chin. "Was it some sort of a weapon or...?"

"Miss Randall wouldn't let us call an ambulance. She just wanted us to call you. She said she was fine. Actually, she seemed to be until you walked in." The manager shrugged, as if to say it was out of his hands. "As for the witness, she said the boy just doubled up his fist and swung. Couldn't believe what she was seeing. Then he tried to get her purse but was unsuccessful."

"Hell!" Cole's single expletive said it all.

"I've got a copy of her statement," Rick said as he came back into the room. "She thinks she can identify the man. She's volunteered to go down and look at some mug shots." He looked down at the tiny woman lying so pale and still. "Come on, buddy. Let's get her to a hospital. We'll beat an ambulance if I drive."

Cole looked up, read the concern on his partner's face, and nodded. Debbie was starting to come around.

"Debbie?" Cole's voice was soft and low as he brushed her hair away from her forehead and tried not to look at the bruise on her face and the cut on her lip. "Honey....can you hear me?"

She moaned. Her eyelids fluttered, and her fingers began to twitch as she tightened her grip onto the only anchor she could find... Cole.

"It was him." Her speech was slurred, her eyesight blurry as her makeshift bed tried to go into orbit inside the tiny office.

"Him? Who, honey?" Cole asked.

Her heart thumped as she saw Cole and struggled to sit. *He's here! Thank God!*

"The man from the beach...the one who stole Florence Goldblum's purse...remember?" Her fingers dug into his wrist.

Cole's expression froze. *My God!* "You mean...that day...you saw his face?"

"Yes. I thought you knew," she whispered. "Didn't you?"

"Not really. I was already running, remember?"

Debbie closed her eyes and swallowed. The words came out in a rush. "At the beach...when it happened... he saw me watching him. Today...when we met on the escalator... I don't know who was more surprised, me or him."

"You mean he knows who you are?" The growl was deep, and threatening. Debbie had to look up just to assure herself that Cole's anger wasn't directed at her.

"I guess. At least, he knows my face." And then she moaned as the sofa took another turn around the room.

Cole took a deep breath. He nodded to Rick, again the need for conversation unnecessary. The man had to be found. After what he'd done today, it was obvious that he didn't like witnesses.

"Be still, honey," he cautioned. "We're going to take you to the hospital. I'm going to carry you. I don't want you to move unnecessarily. Just let me do all the work, okay?"

She started to nod and then grabbed her head and moaned. Rick had seen that look before. He reached for the nearest trash can and shoved it beneath her chin just as the nausea caught her unawares.

"Possible concussion," Cole muttered. "Maybe we'd better call an ambulance."

"You get her. I'll get another can. It won't be the first time someone threw up in the car. Remember that time I got a bad burger? I was sick for a week."

Cole tried to smile. But he was too worried to manage more than a grimace. "I owe you."

"I won't let you forget."

"I talked to your dad," Rick said as he walked back into the emergency room.

Cole nodded. He hadn't taken his eyes off Debbie's whereabouts since their arrival. "Thanks," he muttered. The doctor had assured him, after a quick but thorough examination, that she was suffering only a mild concussion, some contusions, and a few scratches. Cole had watched the white knit shirt come over her head, winced at the evidence of more bruising on her shoulder that had probably been a result of her fall, and tried not to curse.

The doctor had then insisted on privacy, at which Cole promptly balked. But the doctor had been firm. And Cole now sat outside the curtained-off area, listening to Debbie's shaky voice explaining the circumstances of her injuries.

"She's going to be just fine," Rick encouraged him.

"Well, I'm not," Cole said harshly. "I just realized that I'm capable of murder. Being an officer sworn to uphold the law, it's not a thing of which I'm pleased to learn about myself. It's just a goddamned fact."

Rick's hand gripped his shoulder in a gesture of understanding. He knew exactly what Cole was feeling. If it had been his Tina, he'd have felt the same.

"I'm going to head on back to the P.D.—let them know what we've been up to today and make your apologies, so to speak. You've got time off coming. Why don't you take a few days?"

"Past getting her home and into bed, I don't know what the hell I'm going to do, but I doubt that I'll sit on my thumbs. I want to make sure the son of a bitch who did this gets caught. Have you heard anything more about the witness?"

Rick shook his head. "But I'll find out and give you a call later this evening. How's that?"

"I'd appreciate it," Cole said. "Did Dad say he'd be here soon?"

"From the sound of his voice when I called, if he

could have flown, he'd already be here. Sounded really worried."

"He likes her a lot." Cole looked toward the curtain. "So does Buddy."

"And so do you, my man. If you can't admit it to me, at least admit it to yourself."

Cole wouldn't look up, but the words came out. "What if she can't handle my job, Rick? I won't give it up. And I've seen too many marriages go to hell because of the crazy work schedules and the constant danger. I wouldn't be able to face losing her."

"If you don't give yourselves a chance, you've already lost her, buddy. Ever think about that?"

Cole buried his face in his hands. Rick slapped him on the back and made a quick exit. He waved at Cole's father as he came hobbling into the hallway and directed him to where Cole was sitting.

"I knew I shouldn't have left her alone," Morgan said as he sank down onto the chair beside his son. "If I hadn't, none of this would have happened. It's all my fault."

Cole frowned. "That's not exactly what you've spent the last thirty-odd years trying to teach me, mister. I thought you always said that whatever was going to happen, would happen, no matter how much hindsight was applied."

Morgan shrugged and then smiled. "You pick the oddest times to remember my sermons." He heard Debbie's voice. "Is she going to be all right?" The worry was back in his voice.

Cole looked at the man who was so like himself, and smiled. "Yeah, Dad. She's going to be just fine. Got a bump on her head and a bruise on her chin, but she's already worrying about who's going to cook dinner tonight. I just heard the doctor tell her to order out. What do you bet we eat Chinese again? All those cute little boxes...remember?"

"My God," Morgan sighed. "The resilience of youth."

"We'll take turns looking in on her," Buddy offered. It was a major concession for him that he would even consider leaving his computer components for a human being.

"I don't usually go to sleep until after the Carson— I mean, the Leno show. I could do it," Morgan offered.

"Thanks. But I'll tend to her," Cole said. "It only makes sense. She's right across the hall. I used to look in on Lily when she was sick, remember?"

Morgan remembered. He also remembered the look he'd seen on Cole's face when he'd first walked into the emergency room. It had been somewhere between desperate and devastated. He was just thankful that Debbie was not seriously hurt. Cole could not have handled anything worse.

"Whatever you think, son," he said. "But if you do need help, you know where we are."

Cole nodded. "The doctor said just to keep an eye on her, make sure she doesn't sleep too soundly or do too much right at first, and—" he shrugged and frowned "—wait for the bruises to fade."

"Where is she now?" Buddy asked. "I could see if she wants something to eat. Maybe some yogurt or—"

"That's great, Buddy," Cole smiled. "She's in her room. Why don't you knock on her door and then ask? I don't think she's doing anything but lying down right now."

Buddy grinned, happy that he'd thought of something useful, and made a dash for the hallway.

"Did you ever think you'd see the day when a woman would get Buddy out of his precious room?" Morgan was grinning.

"No. And it's a good thing that he doesn't see her as a woman. He sees her more as an extension of Lily. I'd hate to have to fight my own brother for her."

Morgan's mouth dropped. He turned and stared, but Cole disappeared into the kitchen, ignoring the bombshell he'd handed his father.

She was sleeping peacefully on her side, rolled up in a tiny ball with the sheets wrapped around and under her like a swaddled baby.

Cole couldn't decide whether to curse or cry. He did neither. Instead, he simply walked over to the side of her bed, lightly felt across her forehead for signs of fever, and sighed with relief as his palm slid over cool, smooth skin.

The urge to unwrap and straighten her covers was strong, but he knew it would be futile. Two hours ago he'd tried and was now staring at the results. If she'd been bagged and labeled by experts, she wouldn't have been packaged any better. He turned and walked away.

Debbie felt his touch, the sigh on her cheek as he leaned over and brushed her forehead with his lips, and then heard his footsteps as he left her alone...again.

She didn't move or indicate by any means that she'd been aware of his presence. Not now, or the other times he'd come into her room when he should have been getting his own rest.

She blinked back tears. When he thought she wasn't

looking, he was so damned gentle it made her heart hurt. Why couldn't he admit that what was between them was more than just casual caring? Why wouldn't he face the fact that they were in love?

The first time she'd seen him standing beneath a shade tree at the Longren Ranch, a plate full of barbecue in one hand and a beer in the other, laughing at something someone had said, she'd been lost.

He was so different from the men with whom she'd grown up. Besides his being from California—and where she came from, that counted as another planet—besides his being a cop, which took her exactly five minutes to discover, besides his being Lily's oldest and best-loved brother—besides all that, he had secrets.

She'd recognized them instantly. They hung just behind the darkest pair of eyes she'd ever seen. And she could tell that the secrets weren't all good. There was a world of sadness behind his laugh. It reeked of too many lonely hours and too many ugly sights. Yes, in the space of five minutes, Deborah Jean Randall had seen all that and fallen in love.

Now here she was, half a country away, after being whomped by a creep who made a habit of preying on helpless women and nearly being eaten alive by a moving, metal staircase, she was next door to the man of her dreams, and he wouldn't let her sleep.

Debbie rolled over, winced as she mashed a sore spot, and stretched, trying to find a comfortable place to settle. Soon, she'd drifted back to sleep to the tune of the floorboard creaking in the room across the hall.

It was halfway to morning. Midnight had come and gone like a bandit, stealing away whatever rest Cole had been trying to find. He cursed the moonlight shining through his window. Cursed fate for what had happened to Debbie. Cursed the creep who was still out there un-apprehended. Cursed everything and everyone except what mattered.

He was not where he belonged. His heart had been telling him that for hours. Finally, in sleepless despera-tion, he rolled off his bed. Moonbeams danced across his bare body, shadowing the hard curves and flat planes of his well-toned torso. He pulled on a pair of red jog-ging shorts and started across the hall. Just for one more look. Just to make sure she was still alive…and breath-ing.

Debbie heard the floorboard creek. She groaned as it woke her and tried to burrow back down into the covers. He was up again. If she could just locate that comfortable spot…but it was gone. And Cole was here.

He leaned over, peering through the shadows, trying to see her face—listening to her breathing—just to as-sure himself that it was gentle and regular.

"For the love of God, Cole Brownfield," Debbie mut-tered. "You won't let either of us rest. If you can't calm down and let me sleep and trust the fact that my next breath won't be my last, then you have my permission to crawl in beside me and listen to me breathe."

She'd startled him. And then he smiled to himself. He should have known it would take more than this to get her down. He looked at the shadowy contours of her sleepy face, saw the invitation, and knew that it hadn't been far from his thoughts since he'd brought her home.

"Do you pull covers?" he asked as he began to un-wrap her.

"You'll soon see," she muttered, and allowed him to straighten the bed.

It took every ounce of willpower he owned, but he crawled in and settled down. For one long moment, neither spoke.

Debbie had issued the invitation out of frustration. He had accepted it out of need. But when his long arm gently snaked beneath her head and pulled her toward him, she sighed. There! She'd found that comfortable spot again, after all. She should have known where it was. It was next to his heart.

Cole gently wrapped her, covers and all, and held her. Long after he'd felt her relax, long after he heard her breathing slow and soften, he watched and he listened. And he fell in love.

"Good morning, honey."

Debbie opened her eyes, stared up into the faces of two extra Brownfields who were grinning down at her, and stretched and smiled. Her arm hit the other pillow and she jerked, suddenly remembering her bed partner. She breathed a quiet sigh of relief. He was gone. It would have been awkward explaining his presence.

"Cole made us get up," Buddy said.

Morgan grinned. "He got an early call. He said to bring your food to you. I'll just set it on the bed here beside you. After you've washed up, you can dig in."

He watched her wince as she tried to smile around the bruise on her chin. A dark anger, similar to the one his son was wearing, began to simmer. He'd give a lot for an hour alone with the man who'd done this. "Can you manage on your own? Maybe you need some help getting out of bed? Are you sore?"

"Yes. No. Yes."

Morgan grinned again. Their old Debbie was back. "I get the picture. Come on, Buddy. We're in the way."

"When it's time, I'll fix lunch," Buddy announced.

Morgan rolled his eyes as they made an exit. "No one wants a diet of pure sugar but you, son. I think we'd better just wait and see if anyone even wants to eat. What do you say?"

He hated to discourage the first normal thing his son had offered to do in nearly five years, but he didn't think any of them was ready for ice cream decorated with dollops of peanut butter and sprinkled with Fruit Loops.

Debbie wanted to laugh. But she wasn't sure her mouth would take the punishment so she settled for a small smile instead. With a little effort and a lot of moaning, she made it into the bathroom and into a pair of shorts and a huge oversized T-shirt that had belonged to her brother, Douglas. The less that touched her body, the better she felt.

She crawled back into bed, dug into the lukewarm toast, the still-hot coffee, and saved the strawberry jelly for Buddy. Bland food was all her stomach could tolerate.

"Yes, darling, I love you, too." Debbie smiled carefully, tucked a stray curl behind her ear, and pivoted on bare feet as she heard someone walk into the kitchen behind her. Her eyebrows raised at the expression on Cole's face, but she continued her conversation, knowing that he'd probably misinterpret it and figuring that it would be good for his blood pressure when he did.

Cole wanted to rip that phone out of her hand, demand to know who the hell she was calling "darling," and then tell them to get one of their own. This one was his.

He caught himself short. *What the hell is wrong with me? I've given her nothing but walls. What makes me think she wants to climb over?*

His eyes narrowed as he watched her body dancing beneath that oversized shirt. He knew she was wearing next to nothing and the thought made him hot... and hard.

"Yes, I promise," she said. "And I'm really having a good time. No. I won't forget. I'm proud of you, and thanks for calling. Yes, I'll look forward to it."

She hung up with a secretive smile and turned. The wall was behind her. She decided to use it for a prop and waited for Cole to ask. He didn't disappoint her.

"Who was that?" His question wasn't friendly.

"Douglas."

He waited. Nothing more was forthcoming. And it was not enough.

"So...you're going to make me ask, aren't you, Little Red?"

She shrugged. "I don't know what you mean." And then her conscience tugged. Last night, after he'd finally let her sleep, had been the best night of her life. She wanted more like it...and often. "Douglas is my brother. He got my number from Lily. He got a promotion and his company is moving him to L.A. Small world, huh?"

"He doesn't know you were hurt, does he?"

Debbie ducked her head and shrugged, then winced at the movement. "No need. I survived."

I don't know if I will. The bruise on her chin made him want to cry. Cole walked over, slipped her oversized T-shirt down, letting the neckline slide off her shoulder. Another bruise was revealed. He'd seen it in the E.R. It wasn't any less faint. Neither was the one on her chin. They were very vivid, very dark swatches of purple and green. The thought of that man—of anyone—hitting her with such savagery...

She looked up. The fury in his eyes made her shake. And she knew it was not directed at her. She pushed herself from the wall, wrapped her arms around his waist, and hugged him.

"I'm okay," she whispered.

"Well, I'm not," he muttered. He didn't know what hurt more: his feelings, for not somehow being able to prevent this when he was supposed to be a cop who took care of people, or his unrelieved libido, for the night he'd spent holding her in his arms.

She loved holding him. Even if it made him nervous. Even if he hadn't instigated the action. His blue jeans were rough against her bare legs, his striped shirt soft against her cheek. He smelled good. All lemony and woodsy. And he felt even better. He was so big and so hard in so many interesting places and—Her hands ceased their movement beneath his jacket. She looked up and forgot what she'd been about to say.

"It's my gun."

She yanked her hands back from around him as if she'd just put them on a snake. It was the leather shoulder holster that she'd felt. And the look on his face told her that she'd done the wrong thing by being shocked.

Cole saw it. He'd been waiting for something like this for weeks. Ever since her arrival, he'd known that someday something was bound to happen that would prove to him that a relationship between them wouldn't work. He'd been certain that his occupation would be abhorred, that his daily lifestyle would be a problem. He'd been waiting…and he was sick to his stomach that he'd been right.

"Well, I know that," Debbie finally said. "I just wasn't expecting it. After all, it's not like I've ever seen you completely dressed that many times anyway."

Her statement hadn't been what he'd expected. As usual, she'd caught him off guard. And her reminder that last night he'd had little to nothing on as they slept the rest of the night away took him aback.

He still wasn't certain that she was revealing her true feelings. There were women he'd known who'd been appalled that he carried a gun. There had been others who'd been turned on by the fact. He wanted someone in between. He'd never found her. He didn't think she existed. At least, he'd believed that wholeheartedly until that damned cabby had dumped a lost tornado from Oklahoma on his doorstep. Now he wasn't so sure. In fact, he hadn't been sure about a thing since.

"I just stopped by to see how you're doing and to tell you that the witness at the mall identified the guy. At least, it's a tentative I.D. I wondered if you'd mind looking at a few pictures…?"

"Are you working on this case?" Debbie was surprised. "I thought you only worked on stuff involving narcotics."

"Not officially."

The tone and intensity of his voice told her more than his terse answer.

"Let's just say I have a…vested interest…in seeing that nothing else happens to you, lady."

Debbie nodded. "Then spread 'em," she mocked.

The look on his face was worth the pain she felt as she laughed. "I mean the pictures, you dork. What did you think, that I was going to frisk you?" She ran her finger down the buttons of his shirt and, when she got to his belt buckle, tapped it sharply with her nail. "That's your job, remember?"

"Hell's fire!"

She cocked her eyebrow, tried not to smile again, and waited for him to show her the pictures. He finally came to his senses, yanked an envelope out of his jacket pocket, and strung several photos on the kitchen table.

"This one," Debbie said quickly. It hadn't taken long to pick out that belligerent face beneath long blond hair.

"Sure?"

"Very. And I can't believe I didn't think to tell you I'd seen him. I guess I just assumed that, because I had, you did, too. If I'd had my wits about me, maybe none of this would've happened."

Cole slid the pictures back in the envelope and headed for the phone. When someone answered, his comment was short and sweet. "It's him. She made a positive I.D." He nodded as he listened, and then quickly disconnected. "They're putting out an APB. Maybe if we catch him, we'll get the rest of that snatch-and-grab gang operating at the beach."

"Good. I'd hate to think about any more nice people like Florence Goldblum getting hurt. The next one might not be as lucky as Florence."

"Lucky?"

Debbie smiled. "Yes, lucky. If you hadn't been there, no one would have retrieved her bag in time to get her medicine." She punched him lightly in the stomach. "And you know it, tough guy."

"Oh, there'll always be a next time. The world's full of creeps like that."

Debbie hugged him, purposely resting her cheek on the bulge of his holster just to prove that it didn't shock her by its presence. "And the world's just as full of nice guys...like you."

His arms tightened, and then he quickly released them, remembering her injuries.

"I've got to get back. I just wanted to make sure—"

"I'm fine. However, I can't promise what condition I'll be in by bedtime."

He frowned. "Why?"

"Buddy wants to cook dinner."

Cole leaned his head back and laughed. He looked down at her face, saw the barely concealed distress, and laughed again.

"I'll try not to be late," he chuckled. "However, if I am, don't feel obligated to hold dinner for me. I'll just grab a bite somewhere else."

"You're lying and you know it." She sighed. "For two cents, I'd go with you. I don't know if my stomach can stand four courses of sweets."

Cole's voice was gentle as he leaned down and swept a quick kiss across her forehead.

"For less than that, I'd take you with me." His dark eyes raked the slender curves beneath her floppy shirt. And then he shrugged. "But duty calls, at least it will, if I don't get myself back in gear. Take care, girl."

Debbie's tone was light, but the shadows in her eyes told him that she dreaded to see him go. "You, too," she said, and absently patted the holster beneath his jacket.

He grabbed her hand, holding it gently but firmly as he made her look at him. He needed to see that the fear wasn't there. He had to assure himself that she wasn't about to fly to pieces over where he was going.

She pulled her hand away and gave the jacket one more pat.

"Just checking," she said. "Wouldn't want you to leave without all your...bulges in place." She made a theatrical leer at the one behind his zipper and then grinned as he blushed.

"I'm already gone," Cole muttered. "Hell, it's safer out on the streets than it is here with you."

"Maybe," Debbie said. "But here, you wouldn't need a gun. I'd go easy."

God almighty! Cole made a beeline for the door. He didn't have time to pursue this interesting line of questioning. And, he had no desire to return to work in any kind of shape that would require explanations. He ignored the ache behind his zipper and focused on the one in his heart. When he got back, Deborah Jean Randall owed him more than answers. He'd been teased and tortured past his limit.

Chapter 6

That laugh! Cole pivoted, nearly dropping his hot dog and cola as he stared at the woman across the street.

It was Debbie!

Pleasure surfaced at the unexpected sighting. He started to yell a hello when a man came out of the men's clothing store behind her and gave her a kiss.

His hands knotted. Lunch was instantly forgotten and so was the fact that he was still holding it. His fingers squeezed into fists and into his meal. His wiener went one direction, his bun the other. He was left holding the chili…and the bag.

What in hell? He'd never seen that man before, and he'd have sworn that Debbie didn't know anyone in Laguna Beach besides his family. If she did, she certainly hadn't mentioned it.

He looked down at the mess in his hands and cursed softly.

"Here, buddy," the vendor said, handing him a handful of napkins. "Looks like you might be needing these."

Cole took them, nodded his thanks, and stared at the back end of that disappearing taxi.

"Want another?" the vendor asked, hoping to make another sale. Cole made a dash for his car. The vendor shrugged.

Cole spun out into traffic and began following the taxi's retreat. Several minutes elapsed before the taxi finally came to another stop.

He frowned. A clothing store? Again? Surely Debbie hasn't been suckered into buying clothes for some gigolo? He couldn't imagine her being suckered into anything. But she was a stranger here, and in Cole's line of work, odder things had happened.

They exited the cab. Cole watched the taxi drive away. Obviously they intended to spend some time inside. He frowned again and tightened his grip on the steering wheel as the broad-shouldered young man wrapped his arm solicitously around Debbie's shoulder and escorted her inside.

He was nearly six feet tall and stocky. Cole took careful note of the fact that he couldn't possibly be older than his early twenties. Dark brown hair. And no tan! He wasn't local. That much was obvious. Someone with that many muscles would also have sported a tan. The two were synonymous in California, especially with body builders.

Cole thought about just getting out of his car, going

across the street, and introducing himself. Then he thought again. How would he explain that he'd known where she was? He didn't want to admit to her—or anyone else—that he'd been following her. It smacked of insecurity. *I'm damn sure not insecure... I don't think.*

He frowned, settled himself into a more comfortable position, and fixed his sight on the front door. Sooner or later, they'd have to come out. When they did, he'd decide what to do next.

Doug Randall kept one eye on his sister and the other on the sales clerk. If that prissy guy brought out any more coordinating pinks and greens, he was leaving. He'd wear white shirts to work every day before he'd button on something sissy.

When Doug wasn't looking, Debbie grinned. It was something to see him well groomed and success-ful. She'd spent too many years worrying if he'd ever amount to anything other than a sometime mechanic and a full-time biker. He'd been Clinton, Oklahoma's, most avid proponent of black leather and Harleys. It had nearly been her undoing.

Somewhere between the age of seventeen and now, Doug had grown up and out of that phase. She'd been constantly thankful ever since.

"You think you're going to like your new job?" Deb-bie watched her brother's glare send the salesman scur-rying back to the racks for another color of shirt.

"The job's not new, Deb. Just the location."

Douglas frowned. She was so pale. And when he'd first seen the bruises on her face, he'd been livid. He'd been all ready to go out and search the streets of Laguna Beach for the creep until she'd calmly informed him that there was already an entire police force on her side. She'd claimed they didn't need his help. It hadn't made him feel much better.

"You could come with me," he persisted. It had been the subject of most of their conversation the entire afternoon. "I've already got a two-bedroom apartment in what I'm told is the 'better' part of L.A." He grinned wryly. "If L.A. has a better part, I've yet to see it."

"You're too country, Douglas. There's much to be said for city living." She ignored his frown. "And for the last time, I'm not moving in with my little brother—" she raised her eyebrows as he flexed his arms in a none-too-subtle reminder of who was really the smaller "—no matter what he says. Besides, think of your love life."

He flushed and grinned. "I don't have one...yet."

"Exactly," she said. "And I'd like to see how fast it progressed with your sister in the next room."

"Still—" he persisted.

"Still nothing," she argued. "Now hush. The clerk's coming back. Oooh, Douglas, I think I like that one." She pointed to the shirt the sales clerk was carrying.

"It still looks sorta pink to me," Douglas frowned.

"Oh no," the clerk said, "this is just a shade darker than mauve and two shades lighter than raspberry. It's in vogue. Trust me."

"Sounds like I should eat it, not wear it," Douglas growled. And then they both laughed at the look on the clerk's face.

"We'll take it," Debbie said.

* * *

Cole was furious. After the clothing stores, they'd gone into a shoe store and then a specialty shop that carried elegant men's accessories. He'd parked close enough to watch them take several expensive ties to the register and then watched as Debbie tried to pay for them.

What was the matter with her? When they came out of this store, he was making his move. He couldn't wait to see the look on her face when he walked up!

"Hey, Sis," Douglas Randall muttered. "I've just noticed that same damned car again. The last three places we've stopped, it's been outside. Once down the street, the last time across the street, and now there it's sitting right outside in plain sight."

"I know," she said, calmly matching ties to the shirts inside the sacks he was carrying.

"It might be that nut who hurt you. I've half a mind to—"

"It's Cole."

"It's who?" Then understanding dawned. "You mean that's the guy who—?"

"That's the one."

"What the hell you suppose he's doing?"

"Following me." She held up a tie. "What do you think? This print's not too fussy and it picks up the mauve pinstripe rather nicely, don't you agree?"

"Whatever." Doug shrugged. "I don't know ties from shoelaces, and you know it. Why do you think I came so far out of my way to get your advice?"

"To check up on me, just like that man out there. You're both just alike."

Her calm, matter-of-fact manner was impossible to argue with. Truth was the truth, no matter where you found it.

"Don't stare," Debbie cautioned. "We don't want to ruin his day by letting him find out he's been—what's the word?—'made.'"

Douglas looked down at his older sister with undisguised admiration. "You're something, Deb. I'm sure going to miss you."

"I love you, too," she said, and gave herself up to his hug. "Easy," she cautioned. "I'm still breakable." And then she sighed at the frown that appeared on her brother's face. She didn't want to get him started again. "Come on. This is enough. Besides, you'll miss your plane if you don't head to the airport soon."

"I've still got time," he argued. "I'll drop you off at the Brownfields' and then head for the airport from there."

"No way," she argued. "You won't have time. Trust me. We'll split up here. I'll take my own cab home. And that's final."

"Well, I'm paying. And that's final."

She grinned. "You sure grew up mean."

"Just be glad I grew up," he said.

"Amen!" Debbie echoed. And they both laughed.

Cole was sick. She'd hugged him! *What did she do that for?* That did it. He wasn't waiting for them to come out. He was going in. *Hell's fire! The guy just handed her a wad of money!* He frowned as his belly turned another flop.

His hand was on the door when the call came in. There was a robbery going down. A silent alarm had just gone off in a jewelry store. Cole listened intently. That address was only a few blocks over. This confrontation with Debbie would have to wait.

He grabbed the mike, gave his location, and slapped his light on the dash. The red light began to revolve as he quickly pulled out into traffic. The run would be silent. No use warning the thief that he was on the way.

Debbie looked up just in time to see Cole leaving. She saw the red light, knew that duty had pulled him away from curiosity, and said a little prayer for his safety.

"Your cab's here," Douglas said. "Take care of yourself, honey. And I'll call you as soon as I get settled. Maybe you could come out for a visit real soon."

"Maybe," she said, but she wasn't committing herself to anything...except possibly Cole.

"I liked your brother," Morgan said, as they sat down to the supper table.

Debbie grinned. "Thanks, I do, too."

"He didn't like me," Buddy said.

She was shocked. "What makes you think that, Buddy?"

"I asked him if he wanted to see my new mouse, and he just stared at me and walked away."

Debbie tried not to laugh, but it was no use. "Oh,

Buddy, you're priceless," she chuckled. "The only mouse Douglas knows about has beady eyes, two little ears, and whiskers. Computers and their attachments are fairly new to him. I'm sure he didn't make the connection. If you'd only clarified yourself…"

Buddy's eyebrows notched perceptibly. "I always clarify myself—" he ducked his head and started in on his food, anxious to get past what he *had* to eat so he could get to what he *wanted* to eat, namely dessert "—given time."

"There's not enough time in my life to understand you, my son," Morgan teased. "Good thing I don't have to understand you to love you."

Buddy grinned and licked his spoon.

Cole turned into the driveway, stared for long, silent moments at the low-slung, ranch-style house and wished he was a thousand miles away. The last thing he wanted to do was go inside and listen to Debbie lie about where she'd been. He slammed the car door and had begun stomping toward the house when a thought struck him. *What if she doesn't even bother to lie? What if he's someone who really matters to her?*

Cole didn't like that thought at all.

He slammed the front door behind him.

"We're in here," Morgan called. "You're just in time for supper."

"Be there in a minute," he yelled, and made a quick run to his room to put up his gun and wash. He looked down at his clothes and decided he'd change while he was at it. There was chili all over his pant leg. Damn stuff would probably never come out.

* * *

Cole came into the kitchen, carrying an armload of clothes.

Debbie looked up. "Put those on the washer," she said. "I'll get to them after we eat."

"Don't bother," he said shortly. "I'll do them myself."

Morgan's eyebrows rose, but he wisely refrained from speaking.

Debbie smiled sweetly. "Whatever you say."

Cole dropped the laundry inside the laundry room and then made a beeline for the table. Regardless of how angry he was, he was also hungry.

"I'm starving," he said. "Something smells good."

"Thank you," Debbie said. "It's Hungarian goulash."

"She made lemon pie."

"Thank you, Buddy. I'll save room." Cole managed to smile at his brother and gave his father the same weak excuse for a greeting. No use including them in his anger. It wasn't their fault the woman at the table was a hussy.

Cole scooped a double serving onto his plate, poured salad dressing onto his salad, and took the first bite. The aroma was good, but the flavor was better. *So the hussy can cook.*

"You really are hungry, aren't you?" Debbie's question was hooked, but Cole never even saw the barb coming until it was too late.

He nodded in agreement and continued to chew, savoring the meal along with intermittent gulps of cold, sweet tea made in honor of Buddy's palate.

"I don't suppose you ever did get a chance to eat."

He looked up and wondered where that remark came

from. How would she know anything about his day? And then suspicion began to grow.

"Well, I did start to eat a—"

"Yes," Debbie said conversationally. "I watched your hot dog committing suicide, although we left before I noticed if you purchased another. However, I don't see as how you had time because you came along so quickly. Did you?"

Cole forgot to chew. "Did I what?"

"Did you buy another?"

He glared.

"Obviously not." Debbie smiled. "Here, honey, have some more."

"I'm not your honey," he snarled. "You save that for the hulk that kept mauling you all afternoon."

"Maul? Me? I think you misread the situation." She lowered her voice to the sexiest possible tone and let her eyelids flutter for effect. "I called that loving. He's real good at it, too."

Cole slammed his fork down and had started to bolt when Debbie stayed him with a motion of her hand.

"Please, don't leave on my account. I'm already through. I think I'll go put your pants to soak."

Cole glared and tried not to blush. It was maddening that his whole afternoon of sleuthing had been discovered and that she'd stood by and let him make a fool of himself.

"Why do you need to soak his pants?" Morgan couldn't resist the question. He'd tried very hard to stay out of the argument, but that statement had been too loaded to miss.

"Chili's very hard to wash out," Debbie said. "I think it's all that grease."

"Sugar washes out much better," Buddy offered. "And it rarely stains."

"Shut up, Robert Allen."

Cole's glare did nothing to deter Buddy. When he was on a roll, he couldn't be stopped. "Douglas ate some of my pudding earlier, and it washed right off his shirt. Remember, Debbie?"

"I remember," she said, and headed for the washer.

"Who the hell is Douglas?" Cole asked, and then answered his own question as he remembered overhearing one of Debbie's phone calls. *Her brother! Oh hell! That was her brother!*

"Douglas is her—"

"Shut up," Cole snapped. And then he relented at the look of surprise on his brother's face. "Shut up, please," he said softly.

"Okay," Buddy said. "And, Cole..."

"What?" he muttered, staring down at his half-finished meal.

"You need to get some extra rest tonight. I think you're about to suffer from burnout. I read somewhere that policemen suffer burnout twice as fast as—"

"Thank you, Buddy. I'll do that," Cole said.

Buddy nodded and made his escape, but not before serving himself with a double helping of lemon pie.

Debbie walked back into the kitchen. "They're soaking, but I'm not going to guarantee anything."

"I will," Cole said quietly.

Debbie turned.

"I guarantee that I will not jump to any more conclusions where you're concerned." His voice was low and defeated.

Morgan grinned and made his getaway.

Debbie walked over to the table and patted Cole's shoulder. She smiled when he leaned his head against her breasts and sighed with regret.

"Yes, you will, Cole. You can't help yourself. It's just a man thing. Now eat your food before it gets cold."

"Yes, ma'am," he said, and picked up his fork.

"Where are you going?" Cole asked. He aimed the television remote and hit the mute button. He took another look at Debbie's attire and turned the TV off completely. She was wearing her swimsuit beneath that oversized T-shirt.

"To swim. The sun's gone down and no one can see me."

"I don't get it. Why would you care if—" He remembered the bruises. "It doesn't matter, honey," he said softly. "They're only bruises, and they'll fade. Want me to come with you?"

She shrugged. "So, you've decided to speak to me?"

Cole flushed. "I never said I wouldn't," he argued. "It should be the other way around. I wouldn't blame you if you never spoke to me again. I don't know what I was thinking. I should have known better."

"Just what *did* you think, anyway?" Debbie asked.

Cole shrugged. "Nothing much, and it doesn't matter now." He waited for her reaction. When there was nothing but a look he didn't want to interpret, he asked, "So, do you want company or not?"

"If it's you, I always want company," she replied softly.

"I'll get my suit."

"Don't on my account," she said, and laughed as his face flushed two shades or red.

"If I had any sense, I'd go to bed," he muttered.

"You're the boss," Debbie teased. "If you don't swim, then bed it is. In fact, that sounds much more interesting than—"

"Get in the damn water, woman," he warned. "Get in and get wet before I change my mind...and yours."

This time, it was Debbie who blushed. She headed for the door.

"Ooh," Debbie sighed. "Now I know how Morgan feels when he does his water therapy. It hurts so good."

Cole's eyes darkened. He'd just put an entirely different connotation on what it took to hurt good. And it had nothing to do with swimming. He stood at the side of the pool and watched the measured control of her movements.

"Are you very stiff?" His question was gruff, but Debbie heard the concern.

"It's not so bad now. The bruises are fading pretty fast."

"Take off the shirt," Cole said.

"But I look so...spotty," she objected, trying to laugh away her embarrassment.

"Spotty is my favorite color," Cole said. "There's no one else around. Be comfortable. You can't enjoy your swim with that long, wet shirt wrapped around your legs."

It didn't take any more urging. Debbie paddled across the pool until she could touch bottom. Then she began fighting the water's pull against the wet, clingy jersey knit. She was fighting a losing battle.

"I need help."

Cole kicked off his deck shoes and slipped into the pool. His long, lithe body cut a silent wake through the clear blue water. Debbie watched, fascinated.

"Don't fight it," Cole said as he reached beneath the surface and grasped the hem of the shirt. "Let me do all the work."

Debbie nodded and tried not to wince as he maneuvered her arm out of the clinging sleeve.

"Sorry, Little Red," Cole whispered. "One more sleeve does it." He pulled at the fabric, stretching it as much as possible before pulling it over her head. "There," he said. "Now you're free."

She wanted to laugh, but tears were too close to the surface. *Free? I'll never be free again as long as I live, Cole.* "Thanks," she managed to say. "That feels much better."

It doesn't look better, Cole thought. The bruises were dark-purple and green swatches on the fragile satin surface of her skin. In spite of his intentions to remain neutral during this swim, he couldn't resist a touch.

His fingertips feathered the darkest spot on her shoulder and then traced a path through the droplets of water clinging to her skin.

Debbie shivered. Cole jerked his hand back.

"Cold?" He had a remedy for that, but he didn't think she was up to it.

"Not really," she said. "Just...oh, I don't know... I guess I've got the willies."

He laughed unexpectedly, lustily. "You have the most unique repertoire of euphemisms I've ever heard."

Debbie grinned. "Have I just been made fun of? Surely you jest. I can't believe that you've never heard of the willies."

Cole splashed her lightly, playfully responding to her attack on his command of the English language.

"You show me the definition in Webster's dictionary, and I'll... I'll cook dinner tomorrow. What exactly are...*willies?*"

Debbie cupped her hands, scooped up a handful of water, and let it trickle sensuously through her fingers onto his broad chest. When it had run its course, she took the palms of her hands and traced the water's path down his belly.

"My God," Cole whispered as he slowly turned to jelly.

Debbie sighed. Her dark eyes shadowed with barely disguised desire as she ran her fingernail lightly against the tan skin of his forearm. And then she pointed.

"Look," she urged.

His eyes followed the path her hands were taking. And when he saw her pointing to his arm, he got the message. He was solid goosebumps, and it had nothing to do with being cold. He was hot from the inside out.

"Those, my brilliant detective, are willies." Her fingertip was squarely atop a patch of goosebumps. "In fact, if I do say so myself, you've got a marvelous case of them."

Cole cleared his throat twice before he could speak. "So, Doc, if I've got them, what's my cure?"

The water's pull kept urging her back into depths

over her head. He watched, fascinated as her slender body kept bobbing lightly up and down while she tried to maintain footing in the pool. Impulse sent his arms around her as he began moving them into deeper waters.

"Oh, Cole," Debbie teased, laughing and spitting water as he pushed her deeper and deeper into the pool until she was only afloat by holding onto his shoulders. "I'm afraid there's no cure."

He frowned. He could have told her that.

"But," she continued, enjoying their little game, "there's a very successful treatment." Her eyes were dancing by this time as she locked her arms around his neck and wrapped her legs around his waist to stay above water. "And you're in luck."

He grinned. "That's all a matter of opinion," he said. *I feel more like I'm in heat than in luck, lady. But I'm not admitting that to you...or anyone else.*

"I just happen to be an expert at administering doses."

"I'm a big man," Cole reminded her. "It'll take a big dose." By now, he knew what was coming. He could hardly wait.

"It would be my pleasure," Debbie whispered against his mouth.

Their lips merged, water slick, cool, and firm. Between them, their flesh warmed as they molded to each other's shape and savored the sensations of the kiss.

Her sigh became a moan and, as his arms tightened, became a groan. Cole dropped his hands instantly, remembering her injuries. But when he turned her loose, she started to sink. It only took a heartbeat to realize what he'd done.

"Lord have mercy," he muttered, dived beneath the

water, and scooped her up before she touched bottom. Surfacing in moments, they both laughed and sputtered as water streamed from their hair into their eyes.

"If you didn't like the treatment, you should have just said so, not tried to drown me." Debbie laughed, as she wiped hair and water from her eyes.

Cole held her tight against his chest as he walked them both into shallow waters. "That's not the trouble, lady. I liked getting the damned condition nearly as much as the cure. I just don't think you're ready for the consequences."

It was one of the few times in her life that she was speechless. It gave her hope. It gave her courage. It was the first time he'd ever openly admitted that there was something between them he wanted to explore.

"That's where you're wrong, mister," she said. Her voice was steady, her confidence sure. "I'll be ready and waiting for the *consequences* long before you see them coming."

He sighed and closed his eyes, for the moment just relishing the feeling of holding her in his arms.

"Are you ready to come inside?" he asked, as he finally set her back on even footing.

"No, I want to stay out awhile longer. But don't let me stop you. If you're tired, go on to bed. I can take care of myself."

He stared long and hard at the small woman with the large bruises and even bigger determination splashed across her face.

"I know you can," he said.

He walked over to the edge of the pool and pulled himself up onto the side. Evening shadows shaded the water. His legs dangled as he watched her swimming back into deeper depths. "But maybe I *want* to help, Deborah Jean."

She didn't hear him. She was too far away.

Chapter 7

Morgan hung up the phone and tried to mask his apprehension before he turned back to take his seat at the dinner table.

"Well, now there's more for me," he said jovially as he reclaimed his seat.

Debbie didn't miss a thing. She'd seen his hesitation. She'd heard the concern in his voice during the conversation. And she'd have to have been blind not to recognize that fake smile.

"What?" she asked.

"Something came up." Morgan shrugged, trying not to dwell on the possibilities occurring to him. Cole had been vague. He always was. But Morgan had heard the tension in his voice. He knew that whatever was "about to go down" was not the last bite of dessert Buddy was eyeing.

"Morgan Brownfield!"

The sharp tone of her voice got his attention.

Even Buddy quit dawdling. His spoon clattered onto the table and bounced onto the floor. He looked down at the spoon. He looked back up at Debbie. When he saw that she wasn't yelling at him, he retrieved his spoon from the floor, stuck it back in his ice cream, scooped, and ate, relieved that for once he was not the one in trouble.

Morgan was getting a first-hand glimpse of the woman who'd tied his son in knots. He started talking. He had no choice.

"I don't know details," he offered. "I never do. But something happened. I don't know whether it was a tip or new information or what. Anyway, as Cole put it, 'Something came up.' He doesn't know when he'll be home." Morgan watched the fear spreading on Debbie's face. "He'll be fine," he assured her. "This has happened lots of times before."

Debbie sat frozen in place. Every word Morgan was uttering was flashing images in her brain she didn't want to contemplate.

"His last orders were for us to take care of you," Morgan added.

Tears flashed. She hadn't even known they were coming. Her mouth twisted. She swallowed a lump of pain that tightened her throat and quietly arose from her chair.

"Well, then that's that," she said. "No need keeping stuff warm." She gathered her empty plate. "Buddy, darling, when you're through, would you carry out the garbage?"

If she'd asked him to strip naked and then paint the garage, he couldn't have been more shocked. And then he caught his father's glare and swallowed the last bit of ice cream stuck on his tongue. It was a little large and a lot cold and made tears come as it hurt all the way down. But he quickly agreed. Something about the way she was standing so small and stiff with her back to the table told him that this was no time to be dense. And when he had to, Robert Allen Brownfield could be very astute. He took out the garbage.

Debbie was exhausted. The last forty-eight hours had been hell. To get past the worry of what might be happening to Cole, she'd cleaned every closet in sight, rearranged cabinets, and polished and repolished silverware and woodwork until Morgan had succumbed to her spree and disappeared to the golf course.

Buddy had locked his door in panic, certain that his precious room would be next in line. When night came on the second day, they'd all fallen into bed, relieved that the worst was over. They'd survived. There was nothing left to clean.

The night was muggy. Debbie lay uncovered, her silky yellow shift bunched around her thighs. She kept trying to find a comfortable position, but her clothes stuck to her body, and her hair wilted against her neck, making sleep impossible.

Knowing that Cole was not across the hall was a constant reminder that she didn't know where he was or what he was doing. She'd tried to ignore the fact that she was more than a little nervous about his safety. So she'd nearly killed herself by staying too busy to dwell on worries. And, it had almost worked. It was only when the house was dark and quiet, when everything was in place and all were asleep, that rest became impossible, though she was tired enough.

Maybe I'm too tired. I just need to relax.

She thought of the pool and the cool, calming water, and made a decision. It would be a quick dip. No need to change into her suit. Everyone else had been asleep hours ago. Her nighttime prowl couldn't possibly disturb them. Their rooms were at the opposite end of the house.

She grabbed a towel from her bathroom and padded down the hallway, a slip of yellow moving through the shadows.

The tall, wooden fence that surrounded the backyard protected property and privacy alike. It was enough. The night was dark and lonesome without the moon's presence. Streetlights from the front of the house stingily shed just enough light with which to maneuver.

The concrete was still warm, a reminder that the day had been hot. Her toes curled with anticipation as the water lapped quietly against the sides of the pool, moving gently in the rhythm of the night's feeble breeze. She stood beside a deck chair, inhaling the scents of a mimosa tree in full bloom and the bird of paradise flowers opening to the night. The darkness was familiar. She relaxed as it wrapped her in its shadows.

The straps of her gown disappeared with her tension. One slipped down and off and the other followed. The yellow gown hung suspended on the thrust of her breasts before she tugged. It fell at her feet, a puddle of sunlight splattered on midnight. She walked to the edge of the pool, lifted her arms above her head, and leaned forward. Her fingertips parted the water, and then it flowed over and around her, caressing her skin like a wanton lover. She surfaced with a quiet laugh and began to swim.

Cole stood in the shadows of the kitchen, moved beyond words at the sight he beheld. He'd walked into the house just as Debbie had walked out. His ears caught the sound of the patio door catching, and instinctively, he went to investigate. He'd expected to catch a thief. And in a manner of speaking, he had. Debbie Randall had stolen his sanity weeks ago. Tonight she'd just stolen his heart.

His breath was tight within his chest. His lungs expanded in shock as he watched her gown come off. She offered herself to the night and the water, and he resented the fact that it hadn't been to him. His feet moved of their own accord as he walked out of the house. Silently, he stood in the shadows and witnessed the water covering her, caressing her. It was more than a man could stand.

He bent down. His shoes came off. He straightened and began to undress. His jacket fell across the patio table, his gun and holster beneath it. Next came his shirt. His fingers paused at the button-fly of his jeans when something—an unbreakable code of honor—made him hesitate. No matter how much a rejection might hurt, he'd have to ask. He couldn't take. Not with her.

"Can anyone join in, or is this a private party?"

His deep, husky voice startled her. She stopped in

midstroke and made a small, splashy U-turn in the pool. Her feet weren't touching, so she paddled until they did, swiped her hair from her face and the drops from her eyes, letting the water's turbulence lap at her breasts.

She stared, missing nothing of the fact that he was nearly undressed. She lifted her arm and motioned, a silent beckoning, then held her breath in wanton fascination as Cole stripped away the last of his clothing, leaving him bronzed and bare in the shadows of the night.

He was already hard and yearning. She tried not to stare at his body, but couldn't resist. He wanted, and it was because of her. It made her own body echo with an ache he could not see.

He stepped into the shallow end of the pool and walked toward her like a man in a trance. The water lapped at his knees and then his thighs. She started toward him, at first moving slowly against the thrust of the water and then faster as she moved toward the shallow end. And then they were face to face.

The water enveloped him. He was hot and hard, throbbing with desire, and knew there was no danger of losing that overwhelming feeling. Not when his lady was coming toward him wearing nothing but diamond droplets of H_2O. They ran in pearlized perfection down her body, illuminated by the faint lights that penetrated the shrubs and trees surrounding the backyard.

The water rested at the boundary just below his navel. Debbie stopped, suddenly a bit wary, a bit afraid of what she'd unleashed with her invitation. This man wore many faces. But the face of a lover was one with which she was not yet familiar. Her breath caught in the back of her throat as his hand reached out and caressed the nearly faded bruise on her shoulder.

"I'm afraid I'll hurt you." His voice was harsh and needy.

Debbie lifted her arms. "Only if you stop."

With a groan, he caught her up, lifting her high, nearly out of the water, and then let her down, sliding her cool, wet body against him, and tried not to shake from the emotions that overwhelmed him.

She was tiny, but so perfect. Her breasts cushioned against his chest as his hands spanned her waist. The curvaceous flare of her hips fit his ache as she wrapped her legs around his middle and let him walk them both into deeper waters.

And then her mouth tilted and caught his next moan, slipping across his lips with wet precision.

"I've never wanted or needed anyone in my life the way I want you, lady."

Cole's voice was harsh and aching. His hands slid around her, tracing the path of her spine as the water enveloped them. Cupping her hips, he let the water rock her against him. He shuddered, wanting to thrust now. Needing to disappear into the woman beneath him. And yet he waited.

Debbie was lost beneath the spell of the night and the man above her. His hands did things of which she'd never dreamed. His mouth wove magic into the act of love. She needed to belong to him wholly, to take the man inside her and feel his heat and his strength. But he resisted the final motion that would complete the thought. Instead, he continued to investigate her body with a mind-bending thoroughness.

"Come here, sweetheart," Cole whispered. He walked them both toward the side of the pool.

Debbie's head touched the edge, and instinctively, her hands went backwards and grasped the sides to keep her from sinking. She knew she was in over her head… in more ways than one. She was helpless at the hands of this man.

Her body arched, parting the water as she anchored herself to the side of the pool. The movement thrust her breasts up and out, enticing and taunting, and Cole could not resist. His mouth swooped and he encircled the tight little bud at the center of one breast, relishing the hard throb of her pulse beneath his tongue. He rolled it gently between his teeth and felt her body buck beneath him as the tiny pain sent shafts of pleasure throughout her system. He laughed once, low and distinct, and then drank from the droplets in the shadowy valley between her breasts as he journeyed across to the other side and took similar license.

His heart pounded. His manhood throbbed. The water was nothing but a silken torture, lapping and teasing with ever-constant movement. His hands slid down below the surface and between her thighs, parting them with gentle persuasion as she opened to receive him.

He might have been able to wait. It just might have been possible to prolong the delicious torture of fluid foreplay, but she moved. And he slid too close to the heat and fell into the pleasure.

For one long moment, neither moved. But their shock at the joining was fleeting as their need grew.

Her grip tightened on the side of the pool as Cole entered her more deeply. Letting her float free, his hands encircled her waist and he began to move.

She moaned once, the size of him more than she'd imagined, yet no more than she could stand. He was hot and hard and silken, a motion of magic inside her body.

Her groan made him panic. "Am I hurting you, baby?" he whispered, uncertain how he'd ever be able to withdraw from the sweetness.

"Not enough...not enough."

Her answer drove him over the edge. Cole caught his breath at the magnitude of feelings that overwhelmed him. For the first time in his life, he was home...and he knew it...and it scared him to death. But he'd needed too much and had stepped over the line.

The water rocked her gently, and then Cole gripped her waist and rocked her again. Slowly at first and then with increasing speed and depth, he took her right to the edge.

Her eyes were closed as she drifted, lost inside herself at the emotions swamping her. Cole gritted his teeth, felt himself losing control, and made one last effort to prolong the ecstasy.

"Lady..."

His agonized whisper brought her back in an instant. She looked up into a black passion and tried to smile. But the feelings were too strong, and she turned loose of the pool and grabbed onto him as he took them down.

She burst from the inside out. Bubbles of pleasure shot out in jet strength to every nerve ending and then drifted lazily throughout her limbs, making her bone-weak and unable to stand.

Cole felt himself die as he emptied inside her. Sinking and sighing, shuddering with a surfeit of passion, he held her tight and took them back to the top with his last ounce of strength.

They burst through the surface, taking in air, holding onto each other, because alone, neither of them would have been strong enough to stand.

They stared long and hard into each other's eyes while their breathing returned to normal and sanity regained its rightful place in their world. But nothing would ever again be the same. They'd crossed over a boundary into uncharted waters. Cole watched the slow smile spreading on her face.

"What?" he asked gently as he bent down and tasted the smile. It was warmer than he'd expected. He smoothed hair and water from her eyes and blessed the corner of her lips with a kiss.

Debbie returned the favor, drinking from the droplets that lingered on his mouth. Letting her tongue rasp over the beard-roughened jaw clenching at her touch. She was tasting and savoring the texture of her man.

"You know what this means, don't you?" she asked.

His arms tightened around her. His body was already reminding him that he'd only gotten a taste of what he still hungered for.

"I know what this means to me," he growled. "I've marked you, woman. You may not see it, and you may not be able to feel it, but you've just been branded as thoroughly as those calves were at the Longren Ranch."

"You're wrong," Debbie whispered as her hands slid down his body and encompassed that which was already changing again. "I can see and feel just fine." She taunted him mercilessly with a gentle upward thrust. "But there's something you haven't realized."

"What?" he moaned as her hands slid up and down the growing length of him. He was desperately trying to concentrate on her words when all he wanted was to concentrate on the mass of feelings she was erecting inside him.

"I won't let you go, Cole Brownfield. Not now. Not ever again. You made the decision for both of us tonight. You belong to me, just as surely as I belong to you."

God help us! Then all prayer was lost as Cole swept her from the water before she drowned them both. Somehow they made it to his room, clothes in hand. He dropped his gun in a drawer and their clothes on the floor. He couldn't think past the woman on his bed and the fever in his brain.

He headed toward the kitchen, following the sound of voices. His shower-damp hair was nearly black against his neck as tiny droplets of water he'd forgotten to dry ran in neat little paths down his clean, dry T-shirt. Long legs wearing denim made giant strides toward her voice. He tried to mask the burst of pleasure that shot through him when he walked into the room. Then gave it up as a lost cause when she turned, spatula in one hand, platter of pancakes in the other, and smiled.

Morgan glanced up from the article he'd been reading in the morning paper.

"Morning, son," he muttered, and started to resume his reading when the look on Cole's face registered. He crumpled the paper in his lap and stared.

Buddy was sopping the last of his pancakes through a pool of syrup. He spoke around the bite.

"Hi, Cole." He chewed.

Cole walked past them, took the plate and spatula out of Debbie's hands, and wrapped her arms around his waist.

"Good morning, lady," he whispered against her ear. "I thought I'd lost you." He was referring to the fact that he'd awakened alone.

"Fat chance." She grinned and turned her face up for the kiss she saw coming.

Morgan gaped. Buddy dropped his fork. Syrup splattered onto his shirt, the table, and the butter dish. He stared openmouthed and then grinned. As if to celebrate what he saw, he swiped his fingers across a droplet of syrup and then licked his finger shiny clean before going on to the next splash.

Morgan rolled his eyes and then tried to glare at the fact that he had a grown son who was licking syrup off the table.

"Mother always said, 'Waste not, want not.' Remember?" Buddy remarked.

"She also said you were a pig," Cole reminded him as he reluctantly turned Debbie loose.

"How many do you want?" she asked, indicating the remaining pancake batter waiting for her to turn it into golden orbs with crisp, lacy edges.

"How many can you spare?" he teased, and bent down and stole one more kiss before she shooed him to the table with her spatula.

"Well!" Morgan finally managed to say. "It's amazing what a good night's sleep will do for a man."

Cole grinned but declined to comment. Debbie blushed lightly, but kept her chin tilted at a proud, nearly defiant angle. There was no shame in her heart. Only joy.

Cole managed to eat without making a total fool of himself. He neatly dodged Buddy's attempt to tease him and ignored his father's prodding comments. *Thank God for years of police work and this poker face,* he thought.

The phone rang. To save himself the indignity of ignoring his father's last question regarding his intentions and Debbie's good name, he jumped up and answered it before its second ring.

"Case! Hi, man!" And then Cole grinned broadly. "Is this call what I think it is?" He whooped. "That's great! They're all right here. Wait a minute. I'll put Dad on."

"Grandpa, it's for you."

Morgan let out an echoing whoop as he hurried to answer the phone. "Hi, Case," he yelled. "Oh, sorry, guess I was a little loud. I'm just excited. A man doesn't become a grandfather every day. What do we have? A boy or a girl?"

He turned and mouthed to the trio behind him. *It's a boy!*

Buddy celebrated by swiping one last droplet of syrup and rushed to take his turn at the phone. He thought he just might like being an uncle, especially since it would be a long-distance relationship that would not require changing diapers and the like.

"Lily had a baby!" Cole grinned as he turned to Debbie.

And then the smile slipped off his face to be replaced

with instant shock. He'd just remembered last night... and the pool.

"My God!" He shook.

"What's wrong?" she asked. His behavior was more than strange. "Nothing's wrong with Lily or the baby? Please, Cole, tell me what's—"

"Last night. I didn't...we should have..."

Relief washed over her. "It's all right," she said, instantly cognizant of his panic. Her voice was barely past a whisper as she caught his face in her hands and pulled him down to her level. "I'm protected. You won't be caught in that trap, mister, not by me." Her tone of voice was almost bitter and full of sarcasm.

He pulled back and threaded his fingers through her hair, holding her in place as his harsh whisper made her blush with shame. "A child—our child—wouldn't be a trap, lady. And I was only thinking of you. Not me."

She shrugged and blinked back tears. "I didn't mean that the way it sounded, Cole. I guess that's an old brand I've carried a bit too long."

He frowned as the tears sparkled behind her gaze. "I don't understand, honey."

"I know you don't," she said. "But while I was growing up, every time my parents had a fight, my existence became a major issue. I was probably about twelve before it dawned on me that I came along before their wedding."

"Well, hell," Cole muttered, and pulled her against him, pressing her face against his heartbeat. It made him hurt to think of Debbie trying to live down someone else's shame. "It's no big deal, you know. I wish they were still alive, girl. I'd like to thank them for putting the cart before the horse, so to speak. I'd hate to think of my world without you in it."

She tried to smile past the tears but never made it. They spilled over and ran silently down her face.

"What's wrong with Debbie?" Morgan asked. He'd relinquished the phone to Buddy and then suddenly became aware of the fact that everyone else wasn't shouting for joy.

Cole answered without looking up. "You know how women are, Dad. She's just happy."

Morgan wrapped them both in his arms. "It's been so long since we've had a woman on the place, I'd forgotten that little trick." He grinned and hugged them tightly. "From the greeting you two gave each other this morning, it looks like I'm about to get a refresher course on it. All I can say is this has been one of the happiest days of my life. I got a grandson and another daughter handed to me."

Cole's eyebrows rose. His smile was lopsided as he stared his father straight in the face and tried not to sound too sarcastic as he said, "Well, Dad, it looks like you have everything all figured out. When you get the details in place, let Debbie and me know what's happening."

Debbie kicked Cole lightly in the shins and then ignored his gasp of pain.

"What did they name the baby?" she asked.

She knew that, with Cole, commitment did not automatically follow the act of love. That he felt deeply for her was an obvious given. He might even love her. But he'd said nothing to her. And when she heard it, it must be from his lips first. She didn't want his father pressuring him into something he wasn't ready to face.

"Oh! Right! A name! Buddy, give me the phone. I forgot to ask."

Morgan made a dive for the phone and relegated Buddy to the sidelines again.

"I'm sorry," Cole said.

"I'm not," she whispered. "Not about one single, solitary thing that's happened between us. Not from the first day I arrived. And not about last night, either. Just because your father assumed something doesn't put you on the spot with me, Cole Brownfield. What happened last night doesn't either. You have to want me as much as I want you, and then we'll talk. Until then, why don't you just go with the flow, darlin'. You California people live life too fast. You need to take it one day at a time." Then she leaned forward and whispered against his lips, "Nice and easy…it's the only way to go."

He grinned and closed his eyes as he tasted her words. They were reminiscent of last night's loving and this morning's breakfast. It was the first time he'd ever realized that making love and maple syrup were alike— both of them slow moving and very, very sweet. And then she walked out of his arms and up to the phone.

"My turn." She smiled as Morgan handed her the phone and a kiss.

Cole watched the expressions coming and going on her face and knew that he was over his head in love with Deborah Randall. What he did about it would be an entirely different matter. For one long, delicious moment he allowed himself to dream—about loving and life and Debbie and babies. And then he saw a familiar brown leather wallet lying on the counter. He walked over and picked it up.

His badge.

He knew instantly when he'd lost it. Last night, when he'd shed every stitch of both clothing and inhibition and crawled into the pool with her.

His fingers traced the outline of his badge, smoothing the cool metal until it warmed beneath his touch. Worry tinged the edges of his conscience, but he shoved it back into a deeper part of his mind. Today was not a day for borrowing troubles. Today was not the day to decide if his life and a wife would coincide. His baby sister was now a mother. It was enough… just for today.

Chapter 8

Thomas Holliday was pissed. He looked at his reflection as he walked past a store window and frowned. He had a deep scratch on his face and two more on his neck.

Damn fool bitch!

Last night Nita Warren had given him some cock-and-bull excuse about not wanting to make it because he wouldn't wear a condom. He'd tried every excuse and plea he could think of and then when she'd persisted, he's slapped her around and done it anyway. He didn't know why she'd cried and argued. Women were all alike. They didn't know what they wanted. But he did. They wanted someone to take control and show them a good time. He was real good at taking control. And he could care less if they had a good time. It was his own pleasure that mattered most.

A police car turned the corner in front of him, and

for one moment, his heart accelerated and jumped into the roof of his mouth. He swallowed it back where it belonged, took a deep breath, and stared at the cruiser's taillights as it went past.

He didn't know why he was so jumpy. But he kept remembering that woman from the beach. It was more than a coincidence that she'd seen him make the snatch, and then saw him again at the mall. It had never happened before. He'd never left witnesses…at least, none that were willing to talk.

He shook off his nervousness. It was only snatch and grab. He didn't know why he was worrying. Cops had bigger fish to fry. He hitched at the bulge behind his zipper and strutted off down the street.

Jackie Warren wiped at his nose with the back of his hand. His sister, Nita, had come home crying last night, claiming that she'd been raped. He'd tried to work up a rage of family loyalty but it had been lost in his need for a fix. Granted he was the man of the family now that his old man was in the joint, but today wasn't a good day for Jackie. At least, it hadn't been until he'd made the rounds. He'd heard on the streets that the cops were looking for Thomas Holliday. It had worked up his weak need for justice and revenge all over again, especially since he knew that he could sell his information and replenish his supply in one fell swoop. Ordinarily, one street-wise tough didn't sell out another. But Jackie Warren held a distinct but little known title. He was what was known as a "source." He sold information to the cops and, in return, kept his nose in business, Jackie Warren headed for the phone. He had an instantaneous need to unburden his soul.

"Don't fix dinner tonight," Cole said, as he started out the door. "We're invited to Rick and Tina's."

"Cole…" His name was a gentle reminder on her lips that he'd told her, not asked. It was also a reminder that he was about to leave without telling her goodbye.

He made it outside before he stopped and turned around, walked back inside the house, and hauled her off her feet and into his arms.

"Lady, you're the only person I've ever known who could draw my name out into more than one syllable."

"You don't like it?"

He nuzzled the side of her neck and traced the inner shell of her ear with his tongue. "It's the sexiest thing I've ever heard," he whispered.

"Good," she answered. "I have nothing against sex." She ignored his laugh. "And now, what was it you were muttering about as you were so rudely leaving?"

"Rick wants us to come over. Tina's been dying to meet you. Are you up to it? Don't feel obligated to come on—"

Debbie's hands slid around his back as her whisper slid across his mouth. "I'm *up* to just about anything that you're *up* to. And I'd love to meet your friends. Tell them we're coming. Morgan and Buddy can eat pizza."

Cole shivered. Her sexy references to being "up" had nothing to do with dinner invitations, and they both knew it. His body ached. It had been too long since he'd shared her bed. Cohabitating in a house with too many people had its drawbacks. Basically, it just couldn't be done without openly admitting it was happening. And, he couldn't bring himself to ignore her feelings. He didn't want her embarrassed in front of his family. But he wanted her. And they both knew it.

"Be ready about six." He kissed her once as he started to leave and then turned. The look he gave her was more than a promise of promptness. It was full of assurances that he would come back. And he would be safe. "I won't be late." And then he was gone.

Debbie wiggled. She wrapped her arms around herself and tried not to smile. But it was no use. Buddy was the first to benefit from her joy. He walked into the living room and stopped, caught in place by the look on her face.

"Uh..." He didn't know whether to run or stand and take it. She didn't give him a choice. She threw herself into his arms and announced, "I love you, Robert Allen Brownfield. In fact, I love all the Brownfields. And just because I do, I'm going to make you a cherry pie."

Morgan walked in on the scene and began to grin. He'd heard Cole leaving. He knew what had put that smile on Debbie's face.

"What about me?" Morgan teased. "I'm a poor old grandfather without sustenance...or sense. If I had any, I'd have dumped these fool sons of mine years ago and found myself someone like you."

"Pooh," Debbie said. "But you'll share the pie, won't you, Buddy?"

His attention wavered. He'd just gotten used to the idea of pie. He wasn't certain about the sharing part at all.

"Can't you, Buddy?" Debbie was persistent.

He caved in. "Lily named her baby, Charles Morgan Longren. I think I'll call him Charlie."

Debbie and Morgan stared at each other, trying to make sense of what Buddy had just said. They knew the baby had been named for both grandfathers. What it had to do with cherry pies was beyond either of them.

"That's a good idea, son," Morgan said as Buddy wandered away. And then he turned and fixed Debbie with a hard, warning look. "If you and Cole have a child like Buddy, I may disown the both of you."

She blushed. First at the thought of having Cole's child, and then at the thought that Morgan knew it might be possible. That meant he knew, or suspected, what had happened between them.

"Don't," Morgan said, instantly sorry for what he'd inadvertently implied. "I'm sorry. I'm just an old man meddling into other people's—"

"You're not old, and you don't meddle." She laughed. "And I've got to go make a pie."

She disappeared into the kitchen. Morgan saw the shadows in her eyes. He knew she masked her apprehension behind teasing and laughter. And he suspected that his son was dragging his feet about commitments. He sighed. *I'm too old for this nonsense,* he thought. *And Cole is a bigger fool than I'd ever imagined if he lets this one get away.*

A smaller version of Rick Garza met them at the door wearing the latest in Batman gear and sporting a Superman cape. Debbie smiled. This kid was hedging his bets. If one superhero failed him, he had another on which to fall back.

"Hi, Uncle Cole. Who's that?" He pointed at Debbie and blew a bubble that popped across his nose and chin.

"That's my girl," Cole answered, and grinned as the small child made a gagging noise and fell to the floor in an exaggerated fit of disgust.

"Yuck," Enrique said, his dark eyes flashing with merriment. He heard his mother coming and rolled to his feet as she came dashing into the room.

"Enrique! Your manners." Rick's wife, Tina, made a flying leap for her child and frowned as he ducked her grab and swooped away down the hall shrieking the theme from Batman.

"I'm sorry," Tina Garza said. "Seven is a difficult age." And then she grinned. "Six wasn't any better and neither was five or..." she shrugged. "You get the picture. Come in. You must be Debbie."

Debbie nodded and walked into a house warm with laughter and love, smothered in jalapeños and cheeses. The aroma of something delicious and Mexican drifted across her path.

She'd already met Rick. Her trip to the emergency room was one she'd like to forget, but not the driver. Rick had been as concerned for her welfare as had Cole. He'd pushed the limits of street safety to get her to the hospital as fast a possible.

The relaxed atmosphere at the Garzas' home was a welcome respite from the busy traffic of Laguna Beach. She took a deep breath and had the most insane urge to kick off her shoes and follow Tina Garza into the kitchen. She felt welcome.

Cole visibly unwound. It was obvious that this was his home away from home.

"Hey, you guys!" Rick yelled from the adjoining room. "You're just in time. The hundred-meter free-style is about to begin. Come on in." He was glued to the set, watching the prerecorded telecasts of the day's Olympic events.

Tina rolled her eyes. "Come with me," she urged, taking Debbie by the hand. "You can help chop tomatoes. Those two aren't worth two pesos when there's a sporting event on television."

Cole disappeared with a shrug and a grin, and Debbie followed Tina into the kitchen, missing nothing of her diminutive height or the slightly rounded belly that gave away the fact that little Batman Garza was about to lose his standing in the family as "an only child."

Tina handed her a bowl of tomatoes and a paring knife.

Debbie began to peel and dice according to her hostess's instructions.

"When are you due?" Debbie's voice was wistful.

Tina rubbed her stomach, and her dark eyes softened perceptibly as her mouth curved upward. "I'm only five months. I have a way to go. But we're hoping for a girl."

"Cole's sister just had a baby boy," Debbie said. "Did you know Lily?"

"Only by name," Tina said. "She'd already moved out of the house when Cole and Rick became partners."

Tina saw the look in Debbie's eyes every time Cole's name was mentioned. All the worries she'd had regarding this woman from Oklahoma who'd captured Cole's heart just disappeared. It was obvious that Debbie was very much in love with the man. She couldn't understand what was holding them back from making an announcement about their relationship.

"So, have you known Cole long?" Tina asked.

"In here—" Debbie touched her heart "—all my life. It just took me a long time to find him."

Tina caught her breath at the lyrical way Debbie described falling in love.

"Then what's he going to do about it?"

The shocked look on Debbie's face had Tina smiling apologetically. "I guess you see where Enrique gets his rudeness. Rick says I have no tact. But I care for Cole and I want him to be happy."

Debbie's hands stilled. Shadows darkened her eyes. "I don't know what he's going to do," she said softly. "I'm just waiting."

"I don't understand," Tina said.

"Sometimes I don't either," Debbie said. "But I think it has something to do with his being a policeman…and not getting married. What do you think?"

Tina threw her hands into the air and let loose with a string of Spanish. Debbie sat on the bar stool, stunned by Tina's volatile outbreak as tomato juice ran down her elbows and onto the floor.

"You're leaking," Rick said, as he swiped a paper towel across Debbie's arms and then down onto the floor. "And we can hear you in the other room, *chiquita*." He leaned down and softened his criticism with a kiss.

Debbie looked down in surprise at the juice on her arms and jumped up, hoping that none of it had gotten on her clothing. She breathed a quick sigh of relief. She'd been spared.

"Now that you've cursed the four corners of the earth, my love, when can we expect our food?"

Tina made a playful swipe in Rick's direction and shoved him away. "Get out of my kitchen. You eat when we're through and not another minute before." Then as he tried to make a graceful exit, she called after him, "Pour yourselves a little tequila. Soften up that fool you call a partner. Maybe my spicy cooking and this pretty woman will make him come to his senses."

Rick's eyebrows arched. His mouth pursed and a knowing expression came on his face. "Now, I know what set you off. You know what I've told you. Match-making doesn't become you. Just let well enough alone, okay?"

Tina ignored him. "We eat in a few minutes. Go back to your Olympic games."

Debbie smiled at the interchange between the pair. It was obvious from the way Rick touched Tina's cheek and then her belly before he left that the love between them was strong. *If only Cole could see, if only he'd let himself realize that marriages can work...and do.*

The meal was finally served. And if Debbie thought the first bite was hot, she was totally convinced by the last one that Tina Garza had no spices left in her kitchen. She'd obviously used them all in her cooking.

"It was too hot?" Tina's dark eyes mirrored concern as Debbie downed another glass of water.

"I'm not sure." Debbie grinned. "But I think it took all the hair off my tongue."

Enrique looked up from his meal and, for the first time since their arrival, took notice of the woman with his Uncle Cole. "You have hair on your tongue?" he asked with interest, and ran his finger across his own, testing the surface.

Laughter erupted. "It's just an expression, son," Rick said. "I think it is probably a special one that only people in Oklahoma use."

"Oh no," Debbie assured him. "My grandmother always said that, and she was from Tennessee." Then she lowered her voice and leaned over until she was eye level with Rick's young son. "And, she also said that eating tomatoes sprinkled with black pepper made hair grow on a man's chest."

Enrique looked with interest at the bowl of pico de gallo that he'd refused all night long. He stared at Debbie and then back at the bowl and nodded sagely as if instantly understanding the logic of such a statement. And when he thought no one was looking, dished himself up a serving of the chopped tomato and onion, sprinkled it liberally with black pepper, and took it like a dose of medicine.

Cole tried not to laugh. But the intensity with which the child was chewing was too much. And when Enrique subversively slid his little hand up beneath the front of his Batman shirt and rubbed his chest, testing to see if anything had sprouted, it was too much to ignore.

"You have just moved up a notch in my book," Tina said. "I've been trying to get him to eat tomatoes for a year."

Debbie looked up and grinned. "It always worked on my younger brother, Douglas. I see that it hasn't lost its magic." Calmly, she mumbled an aside to Cole. "I wonder what would happen if I sprinkled you with pepper?"

Rick whooped at the look of panic on Cole's face. "Man alive, you didn't exaggerate about her, did you, buddy?"

Tina fairly bubbled with glee.

"I guess it all depends where you sprinkle," Cole mumbled, and then joined in the laughter.

"We're home," Cole said, and gently patted Debbie's shoulder.

She'd dozed off less than five minutes after leaving the Garza residence, and Cole had taken the long way home just to give himself the pleasure of watching her sleep.

The word *home* sank into her sleepy consciousness. It sounded so wonderful. If it were only true. She stretched, moaned, and started to crawl out of the car.

Cole met her at the door and slid his arm around her shoulders. Together, they walked into the house and then caught their breath at the quiet...and the note propped against the salt and pepper shakers on the kitchen table.

Thanks for the pie. Buddy and I went to a movie.
We'll be *very* late coming home. Have a good
evening.
Love, Morgan

"We've been set up," Debbie said, handing Cole the note.

"First Tina, now Dad. It looks like I'd get the message, doesn't it?" Cole's smile was forced.

"Oh, you already got the message," Debbie drawled.

"You're just dragging your feet. And, you'd better pick 'em up, cause where I come from, sometimes you come away with more than dirt on them."

She walked off, leaving Cole alone in the middle of the room with a shocked expression plastered across his face.

She was almost to her room when her feet left the floor. Arms snaked around her waist and lifted her up and against a heartbeat out of control.

"Cole! You scared me to death." Her words were sharp, but came out gentle and easy.

"No, lady," he said, pressing her hand against his chest. "This is what scared feels like. But right now, it would feel worse if I let you go. Do you understand?"

She heard what was between the lines of his confession. "I understand, Cole Brownfield. Now, take me to bed, and damn tomorrow. The only thing that matters is what's between us tonight."

There were many things in a man's lifetime that he might regret. But for Cole, loving this woman would never be one of them. He stared at the faint light coming through his curtains and smiled softly to himself as Debbie shifted against his side, nestling herself against him.

If he could only find the nerve to tell her what she meant to him. If he could just trust the fact that she loved him enough to stay and to give him the space to do what he must. Being a cop was all he'd ever wanted. He couldn't—and wouldn't—give it up. Not for anyone. But finding that someone special who was willing and able to share him with his job had seemed impossible. Until now.

An overwhelming need to reclaim her made him shake. It had been less than an hour since they'd made love with a desperation that left them both weak and weary. Now, just the knowledge that she was still here beside him made him hard all over again.

Debbie felt the rhythm of his breathing change. She slid her cheek against his rib cage and felt the rapidity of his heartbeat. Her breasts were lush and soft against him, emphasizing all the more the very special differences between this hard man with a gentle heart and the soft woman with determination made of steel. She'd found her man. She'd do what it took to keep him.

"Lady, I need you...again."

His voice rasped across her senses, making her shiver with anticipation at the delight which he was capable of giving.

"Then take, Cole Brownfield. It's yours. I'm yours."

He rolled over her, coming to a halt just inches above the tilt of breast teasing at his arrival. His body was hard and straining toward home. But this time, there would be no mutual sharing. This time, he needed to give. There would be a time for taking later.

His mouth descended, but skipped her lips and slid down past her chin, taking her breath with him. His hands moved, almost of their own accord, across her body and down the slender shape of her until they came to the parting of her thighs. They stilled, and so did her heart.

"For me, lady. Let this happen for me."

She sighed, dug her hands into his hair, and knew that she'd never be able to deny him.

"I'll do anything for you, Cole."

He groaned—a quiet sigh of desperate need that feathered across her belly. His mouth slid down across the tops of her thighs and sampled the texture, then paused. His breath on her skin was a warning of where he was about to go.

Debbie's eyes flew open in shock and then fell shut, heavy with passion, as Cole moved into unexplored territory with his mouth and hands. She gasped. And then conscious thought disappeared.

Nothing existed outside the man…and his mouth… and what he was doing with his hands. It was all she could do just to focus on breathing. Everything he did seemed to make it stop. Every stroke of his tongue sent shockwaves of sensation rocketing through her, and every caress of his hands turned her body to liquid fire.

Cole felt the impending rush building beneath his touch. Every gasp, every moan she uttered made him crazy with need to be inside her when this happened.

But there was also the need to give without reservation to this woman. She'd already given so much and asked nothing in return. He knew what she wanted, but the only thing he was capable of giving her now, at this moment, was joy. A future was uncertain. He chose to live for the moment.

Sweet heat burst in his hands. He shuddered, feeling her passion as surely as if it were his own. And then it was. Cole moved upward, captured her gasps of pleasure and tasted her cry as release spiraled within her.

"Love you, love you," she whispered against his cheek.

Ah, Deborah Jean, I love you, too. But his thought was never voiced as Cole moved between her legs and settled himself into the heat. A single thrust ended his last sane thought. After that, he could remember nothing save the feel of her legs around him, her hands on his body, and her tears on his face as he took them back into the fire.

"Good morning... California!" the disc jockey cried as Cole's clock radio came on with maddening precision. "It's six a.m. and another day awaits. Here's a slow and easy wake-up call from Miss Bonnie Raitt with her latest hot single. Like the lady says, 'I can't make you love me, if you don't.'"

Deep and husky, the singer's voice wove a plaintive message that made Debbie wish she'd slept through the alarm. *Oh, Cole. Not even my love can make your heart feel something it won't.*

Cole groaned and buried his face in the curve of her neck, unwilling to move or to tear himself loose of his lady. He dozed, unaware that Debbie was already lost in a world of hurt and despair.

Last night had been magic. But it was morning. And Debbie had waited all through the night for a word from this man that would make her world right. She'd been given pleasure. She'd been given joy. But the one thing she'd waited to hear was never spoken. He'd made love to her with deliberate and passionate skill. But he'd never said the words she needed to hear. He wouldn't say, I love you.

The phone rang, jarring the moment, and Cole muttered beneath his breath as he rolled over on his back, taking Debbie with him. He grabbed the receiver before the second ring.

"This better be good," he growled. And then his arms unconsciously tightened their hold on Debbie as he listened. And finally he spoke. "I'll be right there."

Debbie rolled over and out of bed, ignoring her nudity. "It seems I have no clothes," she said, masking her pain with a teasing sarcasm.

"Debbie!" Cole's voice was sharp. But his touch was gentle as she turned back to face him. "Don't shut me out, sweetheart," he begged. "Every time we get close, my job interferes, and then this wall comes up between us."

Debbie smiled through tears. "Is that how it seems?" She shrugged into his shirt, using it for a cover-up, and pulled away from his grasp. "I didn't know." Her voice was shaky, but her meaning was clear. "I didn't know we'd even been close."

She halted his stunned argument with a wave of her hand. "Oh, I know we've been close...bodily." The tears were thick behind her lashes. "But close? As in, heart-to-heart forever-love kind of close—no way, mister. You're the one who refuses to face facts. You're the one who shuts off whenever your job enters the picture. It's not me who's running. It's you."

She walked out of his room. The door shut with a quiet click, and Cole was left to absorb the truth of her accusations. He wanted to shout. He needed to argue... to fling her words back in her face. But he could do nothing in the face of truth.

Debbie slipped into her room and closed the door. She leaned back, letting the tears run. She tried to laugh away her foolishness, but there was nothing behind her lips but a sob. She'd known what she was getting into when she'd promised Lily she'd come. Only a fool would have ignored the warning signs that Cole Brownfield had left behind him when he'd run from Oklahoma.

But, love makes fools of us all, she thought. "Okay, mister. We've played dodge ball of the heart long enough. I give myself two more weeks, and then it's time to pack it in. If you can't see what you'll be throwing away, then I guess *I* was the blind one, after all."

Her muttered vow was harsh. But no one heard. And in the end, it wouldn't have mattered if they had.

Cole was showered and dressed and in the kitchen, downing one quick cup of coffee when she walked into the room.

For one long moment, they stared at each other. He missed nothing of her still-wet lashes clinging together above eyes dark with pain, nor of the way her arms were folded across her chest—body language that told him he'd hurt her, and she was not open for more of the same.

She tugged at the oversized T-shirt skimming the hem of her shorts, and knew that she'd never be able to let him leave with this hurt between them. She sighed. It served her right for falling in love with principles, no matter how misguided.

"I suppose you think you're going to get a goodbye kiss?" she muttered.

The heavy band around his heart loosened just

enough for him to answer. "I'd given it a little thought," he whispered, and then she was in his arms.

"You think too much," she said.

The kiss was bittersweet. The pain was still there. But a promise of something better came in the touching, and Cole left with the taste of her on his lips.

Chapter 9

Thomas Holliday got careless. He was broke, and it *had* been a week since the incident at the mall. It was time to get back on to the streets and do a little hustling. His fingers itched. His adrenaline raced. He swaggered down the steps of a friend's apartment. It was his residence for the week. Next week it would be somewhere else. Where he slept was the least of his worries.

It never occurred to him that he could work for money. That required too much effort and the payoff was, in his estimation, unworthy. It also never occurred to him that he made less as a thief than he would have working for minimum wages in a fast-food restaurant. Thomas Holliday wasn't known for his brains, only his fast hands and quick feet.

"Is that him?" The unmarked police car was parked about half a block away. The driver pointed as his partner grabbed a pair of binoculars and looked. He nodded, the mug shot that lay in the seat between them, a second verification of their prey.

"That's him," he said. "Hell, this is going to be too easy. He's even coming this way."

Thomas Holliday had just decided that he was going to have pancakes and sausage for ninety-nine cents at the drive-in on the corner. But the man getting out of the white car in front of him changed his mind. Holliday had a sneaking suspicion that his food was about to be compliments of the county for some time to come.

"Thomas Holliday, you're under arrest. You have the right to remain silent. If you—"

"I've heard it all before," he snarled.

But it didn't stop the officer as he read him his rights. Holliday cursed long and loud as he was handcuffed, placed in the back seat of the car, and driven away. Several blocks later, they turned a corner, and he saw the drive-in. The breakfast special was off. He should have known. This just wasn't his day. His stomach growled in protest as they continued down the street.

"Cole! Man, I didn't think you'd ever get here," Rick said.

Cole dropped into the chair behind his desk and frowned as the coffee in his cup sloshed over the side and onto some papers.

"Here," Rick said. "I'll blot, you swallow. You're going to need all the control you can muster. Suck that caffeine, buddy."

"What's the big deal?" Cole muttered, as he dabbed at the spilled coffee with a paper towel Rick handed him.

"They pulled him in early this morning."

"Pulled who?" Cole's mind was still on Debbie. But it didn't take him long to get in gear as Rick answered.

"Thomas Holliday. A couple of Laguna Beach's finest picked him up this morning coming out of an apartment. They're talking to him now. It seems the little man has decided that he wants to make a deal. He keeps claiming that his purse snatching is small potatoes to the information he could give us regarding some dealers. He wants to walk for the information."

The coffee cup hit the desk empty. The look on Cole's face was blacker than the liquid he'd just consumed.

"Dammit to hell! No deals! Not with that son of a—"

"I knew you'd feel like that. So, come on, we've got some tall talking to do with the boys down in Theft."

"Detective Brownfield... Garza..."

The lieutenant in charge shook their hands as they walked into his office. He knew both men well. The talk had spread quickly throughout the department that Cole Brownfield had a vested interest in this subject's arrest. It was a matter of courtesy to hear him out. And the information the perp was trying to sell to the cops came under Narcotics' jurisdiction. That *was* Cole's territory. It stood to reason that he and his partner would be called in.

"What has he said? What have you promised?" Cole's anger was obvious and barely contained.

Lieutenant Tanaka frowned. "He's said plenty. We're trying to decide what's valid and what's not. But it seems he's saving the 'big stuff,' as he calls it, for bigger guns, like you boys. He claims to have some inside info on the dealers around the warehouse district."

Cole's heart sank. He knew a petty thief's crimes would fall short of important in the light of something as big as putting a major dealer out of business.

"And we haven't promised him a damn thing." The lieutenant's voice was gruff. "My daughter was raped seven years ago. The bastard never even made it to trial. His lawyer made a deal." Venom poured from the lieutenant's words.

Cole understood. He could still close his eyes and see the shock on Debbie's face when he'd walked into the mall office. And the cuts and bruises on her face and body and the fear in her eyes and the way she'd collapsed in his arms.

"So, can we talk to him?"

"He's all yours. He's waived a lawyer and trial. He just wants to deal and walk."

Cole's mouth thinned. "I'd like to get my hands on him. He'd be lucky if he ever walked again."

Rick's hand closed over his partner's shoulder. "Easy, buddy. We don't need to make matters worse."

Cole nodded. But the anger continued to boil too close to the surface for comfort.

The door opened. Thomas Holliday looked up and then breathed a sigh of relief. He smirked and leaned back in his chair. The big guns had arrived. He could tell these guys were from Narcotics. No uniforms here. Plain clothes, cold eyes, and tight-lipped expressions gave them away.

Cole saw the smirk and resisted the urge to punch it

off the punk's face. Cole shoved his hands in his pockets and stood back, breathing slow and deep to calm his rage as he and Rick made eye contact. Rick nodded.

"So, Holliday, it seems you want to tell us something special?" Rick said.

Rick Garza's soft tone and slight accent were deceptive. It was a valuable quality. He always played the "good cop" during interrogation. He had to. Cole Brownfield would never have fit the part. There was nothing soft or forgiving about the man. Not on the job. He'd seen too much on the street to be lenient with punks like this who'd sell their souls for a dollar. Good-cop, bad-cop routine was a gimmick, but it was surprising how many times it worked.

Holliday nodded. All four legs of his chair hit the floor at once. He leaned forward, resting his arms on the table, and let his confidence show.

"What's in this for me," he asked.

"I might let you live."

The words were not what he'd expected. And they were not coming from the shorter, dark-eyed detective across from him. It was the tall man in the corner who'd spoken. A sudden chill chased across his spine. His eyes narrowed.

"What's the big deal?" he snarled.

"That's just it," Cole whispered, and stuffed his hands in his pockets. "No deals."

Thomas Holliday started to sweat. This wasn't going the way he'd expected. "But I can give you the names and places—"

"That's good, my man," Rick interrupted. It was time he took some control of the situation. He could feel Cole's anger behind him. It was a living, breathing thing and nearly out of control.

"You give us the information, and we'll inform the judge that you helped. But no deals."

"I don't get it! It was only a snatch. It didn't amount to much."

"It was also endangerment and assault and battery," Cole snarled. "The old woman at the beach had a heart problem. You snatched her medicine. If she'd died from the shock, we'd be talking manslaughter, and you assaulted a woman at the mall. There were witnesses."

Thomas's hand slapped the top of the table with frustration. "How was I to know the old lady had a bad ticker? And as for that bitch at the mall, she shouldn't—"

Cole yanked him out of the chair and had him against the wall before Rick could think to move.

"Don't call her a bitch…ever," Cole said softly. His hands tightened just enough around the suspect's neck to get his attention.

"Cole! Man, don't blow it." Rick's nervousness peaked.

"I'm fine," Cole said. "I just want to make a point."

Rick stood back. He trusted his partner. He knew he wouldn't do anything brutal. Thomas Holliday was the one capable of that. Not Cole Brownfield.

"What's the big deal?" Holliday grunted.

"That woman at the mall…?"

Holliday nodded.

"She belongs to me."

"Shit!" The word was short and succinct. It said everything necessary to the situation. Thomas Holliday closed his eyes and cursed again. "Just my luck."

"Your luck consists of the fact that I'm an honorable man," Cole muttered. His breath fanned Holliday's cheeks.

Holliday looked up and saw his mortality flash before his eyes. It was a new thought, and one he didn't like to contemplate. He shrugged and breathed a quick sigh of relief as the officer turned him loose and helped him back to his chair.

"It's no big deal to me if I go up. It only means a place to sleep and three squares. Anyway, winter's coming."

Rick nodded and tried not to show that he'd almost lost faith in Cole's ability to maintain his presence of mind. If it had been his wife, he didn't know if he would have been that controlled.

"So, there's something you wanted to tell us?" Rick's smile was soft, but his eyes were not. He shared his partner's opinions of street scum.

Thomas Holliday shrugged. "Why the hell not? The judge might give me—"

"Don't count on it," Cole said.

Holliday started to talk.

It had been a long, but satisfying day. Cole turned into the driveway, killed the engine, and just for a moment, folded his arms across the steering wheel and rested his forehead against them. Peace enveloped him. He was home, and inside, a woman was waiting who made his world stay in orbit.

A car pulled into the driveway and parked alongside him. He looked up and smiled. His dad was getting his own world back in order. Golf clubs were riding shot-gun beside Morgan Brownfield.

"Here, let me get those," Cole said as he shouldered the strap on the golf bag and accompanied his father into the house.

"What a day!" Morgan grinned. "I finally beat Henry Thomas. The old geezer won't admit it, but I beat him fair and square. He thinks I added my score wrong, but he wouldn't check it for himself." Morgan fairly chor-tled. "He didn't want it to be true, that's why!"

"Looks like we both had a good day," Cole said. "They arrested the man who attacked Debbie at the mall."

"Great!" Morgan cried. "This calls for a celebration. Debbie will be—"

Suddenly they looked at each other. Awareness spread. It was too quiet. Since the day she'd arrived, they'd never walked into the house without being met and greeted.

"Maybe she's asleep," Cole muttered, dropped the golf clubs, and sprinted for her bedroom.

Something told him she wouldn't be there. But he had to check. Her bed was empty. So was the pit in his stomach.

"She's not here," Cole said as he hurried back into the living room.

"Maybe Buddy knows where she is," Morgan of-fered.

"Bu-u-uddy!"

The echoing screech of his name sent Buddy running out of his room in panic. "What's on fire?" He could envision his precious computers going up in smoke.

"Where Debbie?" Cole asked.

The anxiety in his brother's voice told him this was no time to blank out. He vaguely remembered her telling him something… "Uh…um… I think…"

"Robert Allen, I haven't busted your lip since I was six and you were five, but so help me—"

"She went shopping." The reminder of pain was an incentive he could not ignore. "Now I remember. She asked me if I wanted anything from the mall. I told her—"

"She went to the mall…alone?"

Both men were in shock. They looked at each other and turned as one, intent on retrieving their Little Red before anything else happened to her…when she walked into the house. The blurred image of a cab driving away passed between her and the open door just before she slammed it shut.

"Hi, guys," she said as she staggered into the room with her arms full of sacks. "I hope you don't mind, but we're having chicken tonight, compliments of the Colonel."

She dropped two sacks into Morgan's arms and handed one to Buddy, unaware of the panic she'd caused.

"Wait till you see what I bought for the baby!" She handed another sack to Cole.

"Baby?" Cole was the first to speak, and he felt as if he'd just walked into the twilight zone. She'd told him she was protected.

"Yes, baby." She was beginning to realize that something was wrong here. They were behaving as if they'd all had an overdose of bug spray from an orange grove. "You remember him, I'm sure. Your sister, Lily...remember? She had a baby. Your nephew... Morgan's grandson?"

"Oh! That baby," Cole dropped backwards into the nearest chair and held onto the sack she'd handed him as if it were a lifejacket that would keep him from sinking.

Debbie rolled her eyes and stepped back, taking a good look at the trio before her.

"What's going on," she asked.

"You went to the mall." Morgan's voice was slightly accusatory.

"You went to play golf," she retorted.

He blushed and dropped into a seat beside his son.

"Did you get my Pop Tarts?" Buddy asked, and then handed her his sack and bolted for his room when his father and brother glared at his question. He'd suddenly lost his appetite.

"What in the world is the matter with you?" Debbie asked. "Did you expect me to hide in this house for the rest of my stay, just because I got a busted lip? Besides, the man's been arrested. You called and told me that much, remember?"

The rest of her stay? Cole's stomach turned. That meant she'd be leaving.

Morgan decided that an exit at this point was wise and headed to the kitchen with the chicken and fixings.

Cole got up, dumped their sacks onto the floor, and wrapped her in his arms. "I'm sorry I overreacted," he said quietly. "But I came home and you were gone and—"

"You leave every morning," Debbie said. "You tell me you'll be back. I trust you to fulfill your word, Cole."

She doubled up her fist and punched him gently in the chest. "You have to allow me the same."

"But you're so little, I guess that—"

"Bullets are smaller."

Her response shocked and silenced him. She was right.

"I suppose you're going to hold this over my head," he growled as he gave her one last hug before following her into the kitchen.

"Only if you hog all the drumsticks." She grinned, and then she knocked on Buddy's door as they walked by. "Buddy! You can come out now. And I did forget your Pop Tarts, but I brought you one of each of the desserts from KFC, instead."

He beat them both to the kitchen.

It was the witching hour. Cole had tossed and turned until his bed looked as if it had been turned inside out. All through their evening meal, Debbie had studiously ignored him. Oh, she'd laughed and talked and answered when spoken to, but she hadn't made eye contact once.

He wasn't sure what he'd done to warrant this treatment. But gut instinct told him that it was what he hadn't done that was causing her behavior. He'd caught the inference she'd made earlier about "her stay." He'd done nothing to insure that it was permanent. And it was time he did.

The hardwood floor was cool beneath his bare feet as he walked across the hall and paused outside her door. A thin string of light shown beneath, telling him that she was still awake. He knocked once, gently, and called her name. "Debbie, can I come in?"

"It's open," she answered.

He pushed the door inward, and what he saw pulled him into the room in a panic.

Her suitcases were open on the bed, some souvenirs she'd been accumulating were arrayed on table and bed, and some extra clothes were draped across a chair.

"Can't you sleep?" she asked without looking up. She didn't wait for his answer. "Me either. I got to thinking about what I'd accumulated since my arrival and wondered if I'd forgotten a gift for anyone. You know how it is...there's always a few friends back home who expect you to bring them a—"

"No!"

His denial was loud and sharp.

She stopped, turned around, and looked up. There was fear in his eyes.

"What?" she asked, and shrugged, sweeping her arm toward the stuff on her bed. "Don't you ever take back little gifts for—?"

"You can't," he whispered, and pulled her into his arms.

"I can't what?" Debbie asked, struggling away from his grip. "I can't take back gifts, or I can't—"

"You can't go."

She stilled. Her pulse accelerated, and she closed her eyes, willing herself not to hope that he meant what she thought he meant. Then she looked up.

"Basically, the reason I came no longer exists. Your father is nearly well," she said softly. "No one's given me a reason not to leave."

Cole stared at the truth. It was hanging in the shadows of her eyes, accusing him and reminding him that he'd taken from this lady, but he'd given nothing back.

"I *will* stop you. I *am* giving you a reason."

His hands tightened at her shoulders as he leaned forward and swept his mouth across her lips. A faint memory of mint and roses clung to her skin, remnants of her nightly rituals. His mouth coaxed, and her lips opened beneath his touch. Slowly, in spite of herself, Debbie acquiesced. He drank from her sweetness and then couldn't suppress a groan as she tore herself away from his kiss.

"This is not a reason," she gasped. "This is pure, unadulterated need. There's no denying that sparks fly between us. But I choose not to live my life waiting for sparks. I know they can start fires, but you have to remember that fires always, finally, burn out."

"I love you."

The words came quietly, slipping from his lips as naturally and easily as breath is drawn in, and Cole wondered why he'd feared their coming.

She stopped. Motion ceased. For one long moment, time hung suspended, waiting for her reaction.

"Oh, Cole." Her voice shook. Debbie blinked, trying furiously not to cry. But it was hopeless. Her tears bubbled and fell.

"Don't cry," he begged as he scooped her up in his arms. "I didn't mean to make you cry." He feathered tiny kisses of repentance across her face.

"You win." Defeat was in her voice.

"I don't want to *win*, lady. I just don't want to lose."

He swept aside her neatly folded piles of packages

and clothing, and fell into the middle of the bed with her beneath him. Her tears were on his face and her hands around his heart. The feel of her beneath him was more than he could stand. He wanted to come in. He'd been outside alone too long.

"Make love to me, Cole," Debbie whispered as her hands traced the strong outline of his shoulder blades.

"It would be my pleasure," he said. "And I promise, it will also be yours. Just don't ever leave me, lady."

"I promise," Debbie whispered. She looked up into dark eyes full of shadows and passion. "The lights are still on."

"When I'm with you, my lady, there is always light."

Poignantly, passionately, Cole began to touch her. And when she lay unclothed before him, bathed in the soft, muted glow of the lamp, he bowed his head at her beauty and wanted to shout with the joy of knowing she belonged to him.

"I love you so much," Debbie said, and lifted her arms.

"Thank God," he answered, and took what she offered.

Cole couldn't breathe and he was hot as a two-dollar pistol. He opened his eyes and knew the reason why. Sometime during the night, he'd discarded his covers and used Debbie instead. She was wedged lengthwise beneath him, sleeping the sleep of the innocent.

He smiled and yawned, then rolled over to face her and ran his hands through her hair, tousling her curls into even more disorder. The proximity of her backside was too tempting to resist as he cupped her in the palms of his hands and shook her from side to side.

"Hey, sleepyhead. It's late. I need to get up."

"Okay," she muttered. "Be careful. See you this evening." Then she snuggled her chin against his breastbone, intent on getting at least another hour's sleep.

He grinned. "Debbie, open your eyes."

She groaned, mumbling something about paying him back, and then gasped at her first sight of daylight.

"My gosh!" She elevated herself instantly, propping her arms on either side of his torso as she stared blankly around the room. "How did this happen?"

"You don't remember?" He leered and wiggled his eyebrows.

She blushed all over. "I remember plenty," she muttered, and started to move when his hands caught her hips and slipped her back onto a very interesting and sensitive spot that decided to make itself known.

"Oooh."

"My sentiments exactly," he groaned, and thrust upward.

Her eyes closed, her head tilted, and her hands grabbed hold of his shoulders to keep from falling forward. Awareness centered into one spiraling point of heat and pleasure that tightened and tightened until it burst, spilling Debbie forward. She collapsed into his arms.

For long, heart-pounding moments she was held within his strength. When her breathing resumed its normal pace and her sanity returned, Cole rolled her over beneath him, leaned up on one elbow, flicked a curl out of her eyes and whispered, "Good morning, my lady."

She blinked. *His lady!* What she wanted to be was his wife. Last night had been magic. She remembered everything... including the fact that Cole Brownfield had finally said he loved her. For now, it was enough.

"Good morning," she said. " I like the way you wake up."

He leaned his head back and laughed and laughed, his teeth a band of white against his dark, tanned skin. California sun had been good to this man.

"Thank you," he said. "I'm glad I could please."

"Oh, you pleased...very much."

Her husky whisper was giving him ideas that had to be saved for later. He was already going to be late for work. And he didn't give a damn. Rick could tease all he wanted. It had been worth it.

"I've got to go," he said, and gave her a quick but firm and branding kiss. "But I'll be back."

He rolled off the bed, retrieved his shorts, and had started out the door when he realized she'd remained too silent. It reminded him of what he'd walked in on last night before everything had happened. He turned and stared at the suitcase on the floor and the disarray of souvenirs in plain sight.

"I'll be here," she finally answered.

He nodded, satisfied that he'd gotten the answer he needed, and walked away.

It was much later in the day before he realized he'd never finished what he'd started to tell her last night. Yes, he'd told her he loved her. But he'd never asked her to marry him. He'd meant to. But her tears had driven everything out of his mind except regret that he'd made her cry.

He started to pick up the phone and then grinned to himself and dropped it back in its cradle. *What's the matter with you, Brownfield? You can't propose over a phone.* He shrugged and ran his hands through his hair in frustration. He needed to get a grip. There would be plenty of time later.

It was an assumption he shouldn't have made.

Chapter 10

Thomas Holliday was dead. The news had filtered through Narcotics like bad news always does—fast. And the fact that he was supposed to have committed suicide—in Narcotics, they weren't buying it.

Thomas Holliday was a thug and a thief and a coward. Cowards did not usually kill themselves. It was more common for someone to do it for them. That led Cole and Rick to suspect that someone on the outside had gotten wind of the fact that Holliday had talked.

"I wonder if Holliday had any visitors?"

Rick's question echoed a similar one that Cole just hadn't voiced.

"Maybe it's time we checked to see," Cole said.

They headed for the door.

Jackie Warren paced the floor. He didn't know whether to stay put or run. For the fifth time in as many minutes he went to the window and looked out, half expecting to see a police cruiser pulling up.

He'd heard the news this morning. He knew what the reporter had said. But he knew different. Holliday hadn't committed suicide, not technically. What he'd done was react to the message Jackie had been sent to give him. Holliday hadn't wanted to die. He'd just wanted to get away. Confined to a jail cell, he didn't have many options as to how to do that. Holliday had chosen the obvious.

"It's not my fault." Jackie Warren sniffed and shivered. He wasn't cold. He was scared. He was always scared.

The cops wouldn't understand. He knew it. But he'd had to do it. He'd had to deliver the message. His source hadn't given him any choice. And the cops didn't know how bad he'd needed that fix. At the time, he'd have sold his mother for it. As it was, he hadn't needed to. All he did was tell his source where Thomas Holliday was…and then deliver their message to him.

For the life of him, he couldn't understand why Holliday had become so all-fired important. First the cops had been looking for him and then—he shuddered.

"All I did was deliver a message," he told himself. "It's not my fault what happened. It's not my fault. It's not."

If he kept repeating that, maybe someday he'd come to believe it. And then again, maybe not.

The back door to his house opened. He heard the hinge squeaking on the screen. It couldn't be his sister, Nita. She was at work. It could only mean—

His eyes widened. His mouth dropped and he lifted a hand toward the man who walked into the room.

"I did what you asked," he said quickly. "I delivered the message just like you told—"

"I know," the man said. "And I've got something for you."

Jackie smiled with anticipation. He died with a smile on his face.

"This is the address," Rick said as Cole pulled up in front of the bungalow and parked.

The yard was in need of mowing. The shrubbery beneath the windows was overgrown and badly in need of trimming. Kids were playing in the yards across the street, and Cole frowned at their presence. If something went down, he didn't want any innocent people getting hurt.

"What do you think?" Cole asked. "Do we go to the front door together or...?"

"You take the high road, I'll take the low, my friend," Rick said, smiling at his own wit. "From what the boys in vice tell me, Jackie Warren is the type to run. I'll go around back, just in case, okay?"

Cole started to argue. Something about the whole thing was making him nervous. This had blown itself up into a lot more than an arrested purse snatcher committing suicide. Thomas Holliday's street connections obviously went deeper than just snatch and grab.

But Rick was already out of the car. Cole sighed, patted his jacket just to assure himself that his gun was in place, and crawled out of the car.

"Watch yourself," Cole warned. "I'm going to tell these kids to make themselves scarce. Wait for my signal before you come in the back."

Cole's quiet orders sent the children scurrying into

the closest house. The once-noisy neighborhood was suddenly quiet.

Cole waved to Rick and then headed for the front door.

Rick nodded and started around behind the house to get in position.

Then a single gunshot rang out.

Everyone exploded into action. Rick grabbed the hand radio from his belt.

"Shots fired! Shots fired!" he yelled. He quickly gave their location and began to run.

As he ran, he ducked, and using the heavy, untrimmed shrubbery for cover, he made his way toward the front door. He dared one quick glance through the window. The thin curtain gave away only the faintest hint of a man moving through the front room.

Cole crouched, tested the doorknob and, when it turned freely, shoved the door open wide.

"Police!" he yelled. "Come out with your hands up."

A round of bullets sprayed through the open doorway, gouging huge chunks of concrete out of the porch. Cole's heart sank. It figured. The criminals always had the high-powered stuff, while the police were relegated to using regulation weapons that were often outmatched.

Footsteps pounded, running through the small house... running away from Cole's position. He quickly ducked inside the house, his gun held in position, his eyes searching the dim depths of the house for the assailant. He got one quick glimpse of a man lying on the floor. *Jackie Warren?*

The man was heading out the back. And then Cole remembered the bullets. He shouted at Rick as he ran.

Rick heard Cole yell. He positioned his gun and

stance and waited for the door to open. Cole kept shouting something about bullets and cop killers, but he had no time to react to the warning.

The door was kicked open. The man exited on the run, his semiautomatic spraying the entire backyard as he made a dash for the high fence surrounding it.

Rick squeezed off one shot. It hit high on the man's leg. Just for a moment, he staggered, and Rick made his mistake. He stepped out of concealment.

Wild with pain and desperate to escape, the man turned. Rick felt the first bullet catch his side. There was no pain, only surprise. And then nothing at all.

Cole saw it happen. He came through the back door in time to see the man hit and Rick move.

"Look out!" he shouted. But it was too late. The man saw Rick and fired.

Cole shot. The gun bucked in his hands. Rick was down, and still the man kept shooting. Cole shot again, and the man turned. For one long moment, time suspended itself. Cole could see the green flecks in the man's eyes. He could see the pupils dilating with pain, and he saw the man's desperation. It wasn't over.

Bullets sprayed the ground in front of Cole. He emptied his gun, and finally…finally, the man went down. In the distance, Cole heard the sound of sirens. But they were going to be too late. The man was no more.

Then there was silence and the harsh gasps Rick was making as he struggled to breathe past the hole in his lungs and Cole's footsteps pounding across the yard.

Cole groaned softly. *Blood everywhere!* He grabbed for his radio.

"Officer down! I need an ambulance. Fast."

It was a policeman's worst fears. Hearing that call go

out soon had a bevy of cruisers and several unmarked cars converging on the scene. But by that time, the ambulance had arrived and Rick was swiftly being carried away.

Cole was running beside the stretcher as they lifted his partner into the ambulance. He stood in shock, Rick's blood drying on his fingers, as they took Rick away.

"Tough one, Brownfield," one of the officers remarked as he walked up behind Cole. "Say, who got the one inside the house?"

Cole jumped. It was hard drawing himself back to the business at hand. He started to wipe his hand across his face and then took a look at its condition and shuddered.

"The guy out back," Cole muttered. "I don't suppose we'll ever really know why, but I suspect it was to shut him up."

The officer nodded, took a good, long look at Cole and stared at the blood on his clothing. "Maybe you need to get to the hospital and get yourself checked out," he offered.

Cole looked down in blank shock and shuddered. He felt sick to his stomach. "None of it's mine," he muttered, and walked away.

"We interrupt our programming to bring you this bulletin. Today, a detective from the Laguna Beach Narcotics Department was seriously wounded during a shoot-out in a local neighborhood. He was taken to South Coast Medical where the surgeons are now working to save his life. The identification of the officer has been withheld until—"

"No!"

Sheer terror overwhelmed her as Debbie stared at the television. She grabbed onto the nearest chair for support and stood in shock as she listened to the rest of the bulletin. Then regular programming resumed.

"Oh God, oh God." Her legs began to shake. *Morgan! He'll know what to—*"He's at the golf course," Debbie moaned softly to herself. Waiting was impossible. She knew where she had to be. She turned and ran.

"Buddy!"

The shock on his face matched the pain in her voice as the door banged against the wall. He leaped and grabbed her just before she dropped.

"Get me to South Coast Medical Hospital. I don't know where it is and I have to—"

"Are you sick?" Panic etched his face. This was not in his usual list of things to do and venturing away from his list was frightening, especially since Buddy was a man who needed to always be in control of his schedule.

Her chin quivered. Tears blurred her vision, but her grip on his arms was strong, and so was her voice.

"There was a bulletin on television. An officer from Narcotics was hurt during a shoot-out! They wouldn't give a name but it might have been—"

"I'll get the keys," Buddy announced. "You get in the car."

Debbie nodded, calming a bit with the knowledge that they were doing something besides waiting.

Buddy drove as if someone had just announced a sale at his favorite computer store. He turned corners at high speed and ran yellow warning lights, almost daring the Fates to slow him down. Debbie stared in amazement at the look of purposeful intent on his face. It was a complete turnaround from the vague expression he usually wore, and for the first time, she saw the resemblance between him and his brother, Cole. His hand briefly touched her shoulder in a gesture of understanding, and then they roared through the next traffic light just before it turned red.

The hospital stood tall against the skyline, and her heart accelerated as they parked and began to run. When called upon, Robert Allen Brownfield had proved himself worthy.

They emerged from the elevator at a fast walk. A knot of people stood at the end of the hall. Someone was crying. Debbie began to shake all over again. Buddy slipped his hand beneath her elbow for support as they approached the group.

And then they walked into the waiting area and stopped. It was Tina Garza crying. Tears poured down her face as family and friends comforted her. Tina looked up and saw the pair who'd just entered the room. For just one moment, woman to woman, an understanding passed between them.

Buddy's hand on her shoulder refocused her attention. "It's Cole," he said quietly. "Over there."

Debbie took a deep shaky breath. "Thank God! Go tell Morgan he's all right. I'm staying with him. When we need to come home, we'll catch a cab."

Buddy nodded and started to walk away, his own relief making his legs a bit wobbly.

"Buddy." Debbie's voice was quiet, but he heard and turned. She hugged him tightly. "Thank you, darling," she said softly. "When it counts, you're the best."

He grinned and patted her awkwardly and, for one silver second, thought of trading in his computers for someone like her. But reality reared, and he quickly dumped the thought and walked away. The only relationship he wanted was with a floppy disk and a good trade magazine. And when he felt the need, he could always eat a chocolate bar.

Debbie turned. Her attention focused completely on the tall man sitting alone against the wall, staring down at the floor. The dark stains on his clothing made her shudder. She knew what happened had been bad. Tears pricked at the back of her eyes, but she quickly ignored them. He didn't need tears. He needed to be held.

Cole stared blankly at the thread of green marble running through the off-white floor tiles and wondered whose job it was to put in the color. It was an inane thought, but it kept him from thinking about the fact that his friend and partner was in surgery, fighting for his life while his wife sobbed quietly in the opposite corner of the room, waiting to see if today she became a widow.

The ache inside him was blooming. He could feel it spreading in a cold, frosty path throughout his body. If he gave it its head, it would encompass him. He couldn't close his eyes. If he did, he kept seeing an instant replay of Rick going down, then of what had happened afterward. The two scenes flashed back and forth, caught forever in his memory in horrible perfection. He cursed quietly and buried his face in his hands.

"Cole."

It was soft. But it was the most welcome sound he'd ever heard. He stood, afraid to talk. Ashamed, because if he did, he might cry. He'd never cried in front of a woman except his mother in his life.

And then she was in his arms. He pulled her off her

feet and up against him as a swift surge of grief overwhelmed him. "Rick...he's—"

"Sssh," she said. Her hands cupped his face as she rained tiny kisses against his eyes and cheeks. "I know, Cole. I know. And I'm so sorry."

He dropped them both into the chair, adjusted Debbie in his lap, and tried to ignore his overwhelming guilt at the fact that he was still alive.

She wrapped her arms around his neck and leaned against his shoulder as her hands moved across his face and neck, assuring herself that he was still in one piece and breathing.

"It happened so fast." The words came out of him in a swift bulky rage. "One minute Rick thought the situation was under control, and the next minute he was on the ground. The son of a bitch wouldn't stop shooting at Rick. I shot—" Cole shuddered and hushed, instantly.

Debbie's arms tightened around him. Suddenly she understood. Cole was not only dealing with the fact that his partner had been shot. He was trying to deal with the fact that he'd shot and, she suspected, killed the man who'd hurt Rick.

"It's your job, Cole. It's what you do."

He closed his eyes and buried his face in the curve of her neck. He knew that she was right. But he'd never killed a man before. And the man had given him no choice. Inside, the chill kept spreading.

"Mrs. Garza?" The doctor's voice had the same effect on the waiting area as water hosing down a dog fight. Silence reigned. Breathing stopped as all eyes turned to the man in surgery greens.

Tina stood, and then Cole was beside her.

"Your husband is a fighter. He's made it through surgery and is now in recovery. He'll be in ICU for a bit, but barring any complications, which at this early day I still can't rule out, his chances look good."

Tina sagged with relief and Cole's arms came around her. *"Madre de Dios,"* she moaned. "Thank you, God!"

"From the looks of you," the doctor said gently, "I think someone needs to take you home." He was referring to her obvious pregnant state. "Your husband won't know a thing for several hours. You can come back—"

"I'll stay," Tina said firmly. "I'm fine now. Now that I know."

He shrugged and nodded. "At least get off your feet," he ordered gently. "And eat something. You may not be hungry, but I suspect your *niña* will be." His hand was gentle on her shoulder as was his voice.

Cole spoke quietly but firmly. "She'll rest. And she'll eat. Her family will see to that."

The doctor nodded and then walked away. Tina turned and hugged Cole tightly.

"I know what happened, Cole. And I know you. You're blaming yourself for something that couldn't have been prevented. The captain has already been here. He told me everything, including the fact that you probably saved Rick's life, as well as some of the others. He said the man wouldn't stop coming or shooting." She bit her lips. "Sometimes, this job just stinks, *es verdad?*"

"Es verdad," he agreed.

"Is someone looking after Enrique?" Debbie asked.

Tina nodded and welcomed Debbie's hug. "A neighbor took him to my mother's house. He will be fine." Then she smiled gently. "But thank you for asking. You're the first one who thought to ask about the rest of my family. I thank you for that. In times like this, sometimes they get misplaced."

Tina saw the strain on Cole's face. And she saw something else. He'd killed a man today. Despite the fact that the man was a criminal, despite the fact that the crook had shot first and nearly killed an officer, Cole was having a difficult time dealing with the fact that a man had ceased living because of him.

"Cole Brownfield," Tina said. He looked down into her knowing eyes and shuddered. "You did what you had to…and I thank you for my husband's life."

"If we'd been more careful, it might not have happened at all," he said quietly, and walked away.

"Go after him," Tina urged.

"I intend to," Debbie answered. "He's a strong man, but inside, he's very gentle. I suspect it's a hard combination to live with in a job like this."

Tina nodded and then turned back to her family. Her waiting had just begun.

Debbie followed Cole's retreat. "Do you have to go back to the station?" she asked.

Cole sighed and nodded. "I'll have to write a report."

"Can't it wait until tomorrow? It's late."

Cole looked down at his watch. It was nearly eight p.m. He looked outside. It would be dark soon. He shrugged as he looked down at his clothes. Dark stains reminded him of what had happened this day.

"I'll call in from the house," he said suddenly. "I need to take a bath first."

Debbie walked the kitchen floor. She stared out the patio door overlooking the backyard pool and looked up at the sky. It was cloudy and overcast. Rain would come before morning.

Morgan entered the kitchen. "You couldn't sleep, either? Are you waiting for him to come back from headquarters?"

She nodded and wrapped her arms around herself to keep from shaking. But her voice gave her away. "I've never been so scared and then so relieved in such a short span of time. In the space of an hour, my world nearly stopped." Her lips trembled as she walked into Morgan's open arms. "Thanks," she whispered, blinking back tears. "I needed that."

"It's the part of Cole that makes me the proudest and also the most afraid. Honor for what he believes in is as much a part of him as the color of his hair. He's a cop, Debbie. And a good one. Can you live with that?"

"I've already faced it," she said. "I've witnessed the long hours and coped, I think, reasonably well. I've seen him in action, and I've seen him hurting. But he won't let me share his pain."

Morgan nodded and patted her gently. "In time, he will... I think. Don't give up on him, honey. He loves you very much, you know."

Debbie never gave up on something she wanted. She walked away, unable to speak. The pain was too fresh for words.

The key turned quietly in the lock as Cole let himself inside. Raindrops ran off his hair and jacket onto the kitchen floor. He stepped out of his shoes and socks, draped his damp jacket across a stool, and walked barefoot through the house. It had been a long night. The paperwork was finally finished. A review of the shooting would take place, and then everything would go on as before. He had nothing to worry about.

But worry was all he could do. He kept seeing Rick's body buck from the impact of bullets. He shuddered, remembering the sound they made hitting flesh and remembering emptying his own gun into the man before it was over.

All that he'd feared from his job had happened in the space of one incident. His partner had been shot, and he'd killed a man. He took a deep breath and shuddered again.

I got rained on. It's only a chill.

But he knew better. It was getting to him, and he didn't know how to stop it from happening.

He opened the door to his room. The dim glow of a nightlight in his bathroom illuminated the room's interior, and he saw her. She was curled into a small wad, sleeping in the middle of this bed with her arms wrapped around his pillow. Every emotion he'd buried since the incident had happened came hurtling forward. They slammed inside him with rude, unforgivable force. There was no time to undress. He needed to get to her, and he needed it now. If he didn't make it to the bed and her arms, he'd come apart, from the inside out.

Droplets fell on Debbie's bare arms and face and yanked her awake. Cole was unwinding her from his pillow. She could feel his hands. They were shaking.

"You're home," she said sleepily. "I tried to wait up…"

"Just let me hold you," he pleaded softly. Agony was thick in his voice.

"You're wet," Debbie said. Her hands moved across his hair and across his cheeks as her breath caught at the back of her throat. It wasn't rain on his face.

"Come here," she said, and wrapped him in her arms.

In desperation, he clung to her strength and warmth. Words were not possible...or necessary.

Long after he'd finally relaxed in her arms and slept, Debbie was still awake, cradling his head against her breast. Her hands smoothed the nearly dry fabric of his shirt over and over in a gentle caress, a reminder that he wasn't alone. Often, his arms would tighten around her, and he'd begin to mumble. It was then that she'd know that he was starting to dream, to relive the horror of the incident all over again.

"Sssh," she whispered. "It's all right, Cole. I've got you, darling. And I'll never let you go."

His arms relaxed, his breathing evened, and Debbie sighed with relief. She threaded her fingers through his hair, combing gently against his scalp as he quieted.

Hesitant to acknowledge itself, morning finally dawned in a gray and rainy mood.

Exhaustion had finally claimed Debbie. Cole heard the steady rhythm of her heart before he opened his eyes and knew that he'd fallen asleep in her arms.

If I never have to move again, I'll be happy, Cole thought.

And then he looked down at himself and changed his mind. His clothes felt glued to his body. He couldn't remember the last time he'd slept fully dressed.

He shifted slowly, easing himself out of her arms. It only took a few seconds to undress, and then he was back beside her. She sighed softly in her sleep as he nestled her against him. Her arm slipped around his chest as her head fell into the hollow beneath his arm. Her hand was small and warm against his skin. He pulled the covers over them, slid his hand on top of hers, and closed his eyes.

They slept.

Morgan tiptoed down the hall toward Cole's and Debbie's rooms. The night had been long and traumatic for both of them, but in different ways, and he was anxious to check on them.

The door to Cole's room was ajar. He pushed it aside and had started to go in when he saw them. A mist of tears filmed his vision, and for one moment, he remembered his own wife and the precious mornings they'd spent in each other's arms.

They slept so peacefully. And Morgan suspected it had not come easy. He backed out and quietly eased the door shut. Last night was over, but he knew there would be many more nights during which Cole would suffer. What had happened yesterday wasn't something a man could quickly forget. It was something he would have to learn to live with. He prayed that Cole would let Debbie help him.

His hand cupped her breast and then moved slowly across her rib cage, feeling its way across her body like a man lost in a fog locating familiar landmarks to pinpoint his location before moving on to a chosen destination. She moaned and shifted her leg across him, recognizing the feeling that was beginning to build, knowing that it would only take a touch to send sanity flying.

He thrust slowly against her belly, sighing as the pressure intensified and moaning as he felt her mouth against his nipple. He rolled over and inside her before his eyes ever opened. It was with shock that he realized he hadn't been dreaming and that the woman beneath him, the woman he'd just entered, was real and not a figment of his imagination. She moved beneath him. Her body tensed, drawing him deeper, and he shuddered, realizing how quickly he was about to lose control.

Debbie's hands moved of their own accord across his backside. Her legs opened to accommodate him as she felt his muscles tensing beneath her fingers. She arched up in a silent plea for more and then gasped as he thrust. Dreams had never been this vivid. She opened her eyes and then smiled softly as she saw him staring down at her in shock. It wasn't a dream. And it was only beginning.

"I love you," she whispered as he began to move.

"Ah, God, lady... I..." Words became impossible.

Motion became fluid as their bodies merged perfectly into one instrument of pleasure. Nothing existed for them at this moment but the need and the feeling that they each knew was coming.

Heat intensified. Sunlight came through the overhanging clouds and burst through the curtain of his room at the moment he spilled into her. Daylight had never felt so good.

Weak from what she'd taken, strong from the knowledge that it would happen again, he dropped his head

onto her breasts and nuzzled against their pillowed soft-
ness. He finally was able to finish his sentence.

"… I love you, too."

"Oh my God," Cole muttered. "Buddy cooked!"

"How can you tell?" Debbie asked as she walked into
the kitchen several hours later.

"I can smell it," he answered.

Debbie wrinkled her nose and tried not to laugh. She
finally got the message. She smelled a variety of things,
none of which seemed disgusting or burned, but they
all shared one thing in common. The kitchen smelled
like a candy factory. The air was permeated with the
scent of sugar…and chocolate.

"Wonder what it was?" she grinned, trying not to
laugh.

"I can tell you," Morgan groaned as he walked into
the kitchen from the pool. "It was pancakes. Chocolate
chip pancakes. And he ate his with chocolate syrup."
He shuddered. "I've been trying to swim mine off ever
since breakfast. My God, what did your mother and I
do wrong to produce an offspring like him?"

Debbie patted Morgan comfortingly as she went to
prepare an antacid. "Here," she said, handing him the
glass of bubbling effervescence. "And from my point
of view, you did everything right. Yesterday, when it
mattered, Buddy came through. And I don't want any
of you to forget it. Do you hear me?"

Cole heard the strain in her voice and knew that yesterday had been a nightmare for them all. He watched
her closely, searching her features for proof of his worst
fears. He saw nothing but a small frown. And all he

heard was a gentle warning that Buddy was not to be mistreated.

"I love my brother," Cole said gruffly. "But I don't have to love his cooking. Come on, we'll get something to eat on the way."

"Where are we going?" she asked as she headed out of the kitchen to get her purse and shoes.

"To the hospital."

His short answer sent her running to comply.

Chapter 11

Cole walked into the waiting area. His stomach lurched as Tina turned dull, lifeless eyes their way.

"What happened?" He could tell that last night had been rough.

"He took a turn for the worse around four this morning," she said. "They have him stabilized now, but for a while…"

Her lips trembled as she crawled up to a sitting position. She kicked the blanket the nurses had provided for her to the end of the couch and ran her fingers through her hair, smiling weakly as Debbie sat down beside her.

"I shouldn't have left," Cole said. A wave of guilt swept over him as he remembered where he'd spent the night…and how. Why should he have been enjoying life when Rick was fading?

"What would you have done?" Tina asked sharply.

"Bullied the doctors? Cried harder than I did? Killed some one else?"

The color faded from her face. She clasped her fingers to her lips to call back the words, but it was too late. "Oh my God," she moaned, and jumped to her feet. She wrapped her arms around Cole's waist and buried her face against his chest. "I'm sorry. I'm sorry. You know my mouth—it has no brain, only a mechanism that makes it flap."

Debbie was sick. The look on Cole's face—if he'd been slapped, he couldn't have been more shocked. She wanted to shake Tina Garza, but knew that her words had come from exhaustion and fear. There was nothing she could do now but let Tina make her apologies and hope that when this was over, Cole had survived.

"It's okay, honey," Cole said, and patted her shoulder. He felt the slight protrusion of her belly pushing against him. It was only a reminder that Rick Garza had too much to live for to lose it now. "Last night was hell on everyone."

Tina turned away. Shame for what she'd done overwhelmed her. Cole was Rick's best friend, like a brother to her. And she'd done the unforgivable. She'd hurt the man who'd tried to save her husband's life.

"It's just this damn job," she cried. "It's inhuman."

Cole's expression froze. Debbie watched her world falling to bits before her eyes and knew that if she didn't do something now, it would be too late. Tina was simply mouthing Cole's sentiments. It's all she'd heard since she'd arrived from Oklahoma. Cops, marriages, and families don't mix.

She knew there were plenty of policemen and women

who made marriages work...and work well. But the facts were there. There were also plenty that failed.

"Come with me," Debbie said. She slipped her hand beneath Tina's elbow. "Let's go wash up. When we come back, I'll fix your hair. When you put on some makeup, you'll feel like a new woman. Trust me."

Cole watched them walk away. He tried to block out what Tina had just said, but it was impossible. *Cops and marriages don't mix...don't mix...don't mix...*

They came back, but Cole was gone. Two members of Tina's family had just arrived to bring her fresh clothing and news of her son's night at the grandparents' home. For a moment, everything seemed almost normal.

"Did anyone see where Cole went?" Debbie asked.

A man, whom Tina quickly introduced as her uncle, spoke. "He's in Rick's room. The doctor was just here making rounds. He got permission." The last was said for Tina's benefit.

Tina slumped down into a chair and buried her face in her hands. "He doesn't need permission," she said softly. "He's as much a member of this family as any of us. I just hope he can forgive me for what I said."

"Don't," Debbie said softly. "Knowing Cole, he already has."

But Debbie was wrong. Cole hadn't forgotten a thing. And for the next five days, it festered inside of him until he was a fight waiting to happen.

"Dad, I'm going to be gone for a couple of days."

Morgan turned around in shock and dropped the shears he'd been using to trim the shrubbery in the backyard.

"Now? I thought you were taking a few days off since—"

"The man is dead. I couldn't stop it from happening, just like I can't make the world stop spinning, understand?"

"That isn't what I meant," Morgan answered just as sharply.

Cole stuffed his hands in his pockets. The grim expression on his face darkened. "I know it," he said. "And I still jumped all over you anyway. That's why I need to get away. I've got to get back to work, get back on the street..."

He stared into the clear, nearly blue-white waters of the pool. "If I don't do it now, I may never be able to face it again."

Morgan hugged his son. "I didn't realize it was bothering you this much," he said. "I'm sorry."

Cole shrugged. "Nothing anyone can do...except me."

"Does Debbie know?"

Cole turned away. He didn't answer.

"Cole...dammit! Does she?"

"No!"

It was harsh, but it was clear. Cole started into the house.

"Are you going to tell her, or are you leaving that up to me, too?" Morgan was angry. He couldn't face being the one to deliver her hurt.

"I can't," Cole shouted. "God dammit, I can't." The pain was thick in his voice. Tears welled, but refused to flow.

Morgan was sick. He relented instantly, but it was too late. His son was already walking out the door.

Debbie stood in the shadows of the hallway as tears ran blindly down her face. She almost called Cole's name aloud, but she was afraid if she opened her mouth, nothing would come out but a scream. She'd heard everything.

Buddy leaned against the door to his room and stared at the computers winking at him from across the room. He needed to fix this. But he didn't know how to fix broken people, only machines. This was out of his realm of expertise. And then he heard Debbie sobbing. A small streak of Brownfield spirit made him grip the doorknob and open the door with a hard, vicious yank.

Debbie stared, surprised by the unlikely vehemence with which Buddy was moving. He grabbed her by the arm, and began pulling her toward the front door.

"What are you doing?" she said.

He stopped, a stunned expression spreading on his face. He looked down at the firm grip he had on her arm and quickly released it with an awkward apology. "Ummm... I just thought...if you weren't too..." He took a deep breath, yanked his shirttail from his pants and swiped it across her face, drying tears and streaking makeup in one fell swoop. "We're going to get some ice cream," he said.

Debbie's heart skipped a beat. *Oh, Buddy! You dear! Why didn't I fall for someone like you? Someone with no complications?* And then her heart answered her own question. *Because I didn't fall in love with my head, I fell in love with my heart. And my heart belongs to Cole.* She shuddered. *I just don't think he wants it anymore.*

"Thank you, Buddy," she said. "I think I'd like that. Maybe your dad would like to come?"

He smiled, happy that his suggestion was being met

with so much appreciation. "I'll get him," he said, and lurched toward the backyard.

Debbie sighed as she watched him hurry away. At least the rest of the family still loved her. It was small comfort, but it was a comfort nonetheless.

The doorbell was ringing and ringing. Debbie dropped her mixing spoon back into the bowl, ignoring the fluff of flour that poofed over the edge and onto the counter as she ran to answer the persistent summons.

She peered through the peephole and then screamed with delight. The door flew back with a thud and for just a moment the sunlight was blocked by a very tall man wearing a weary smile and juggling a multitude of bags. The woman standing beside him had a bag over one shoulder and a baby on the other.

"Lily! Case! Why didn't you call? Why didn't you tell us you were coming? Someone could have met you at the—"

Case dumped the bags and scooped her up into his arms, laughing as he moved her over to make room for the rest of his family to come in.

"You haven't changed a bit, Deb. You still talk faster than you walk, and that's saying something," he said. "Besides, you know Lily. The moment the doctor said she could travel, we were on the plane. She's been very worried about Morgan."

"Lily! You look great!" Debbie said. "Your dad's next door. He's going to be so excited." And then her expression changed as worry tinged her voice. "I'm in your old room. It'll take me a little while to get my stuff out of—"

"Leave it," Lily said calmly. "I spent my entire life

across the hall from my big brother. I know how cranky he can be in the morning. I don't think he'd appreciate listening to his nephew crying during the night. Are the twins still gone?"

Debbie nodded.

"Good. We'll take their room. It's bigger anyway."

It didn't take long for bag, baggage, and family to be moved into the Brownfield residence. Case wandered back through the house, taking note of the layout and the inviting blue waters of the backyard pool, and found Debbie staring blankly into a bowl of partially mixed dough.

"Did you forget what you were doing?" he teased as he slid a gentle hand across the back of her neck. "You've been a godsend to us, honey. I can't tell you how much we appreciated you coming out when you did. But as you can see, as soon as the doctor gave her the go ahead, Lily was packed. All I could do was follow."

Debbie looked up into those dearly familiar big-sky eyes, so blue they made her heart ache, and promptly burst into tears.

"Well, hell," Case said softly and wrapped her in his arms. He didn't know what had caused this outburst, but during the last few months, he'd learned that it didn't matter what caused them, the proper procedure for healing them was a hug.

"I finally got the baby down," Lily said as she walked into the kitchen and then stopped short. She caught her husband's frown and shrug, and sighed. If Deborah Randall was in tears, she suspected her brother's absence had something to do with it.

Before Lily could offer advice or condolences of any kind, her father's voice sent her spinning.

"Lily Kate! You're home," he said, and engulfed her in a warm, welcoming hug.

Debbie jerked away from Case, mortified that she'd lost control, and quickly swiped at her tear-stained face, unwilling for Morgan to see her in this condition.

"And, Case! It's great to see you, son. I hate to be rude, but where's my grandson?"

Debbie stood back as the proud parents quickly ushered Morgan to the bedroom. He beamed as he looked long and hard at the tiny baby sleeping soundly on the bed.

"He looks like you, doesn't he, Case?" Morgan was overwhelmed by the emotion of seeing such a tiny bit of his own immortality.

"Yes, Dad, he does," Lily answered. "And I can't wait for him to wake up so you can see his eyes. They're so blue…"

"All new babies have blue eyes," Morgan teased.

"Not like these," Lily said. "He has his daddy's eyes."

Case still couldn't get over the joy he felt at hearing those words, *his daddy's eyes.* He couldn't believe that he and Lily were parents. But the proof was there in the middle of the bed.

Debbie started forward when the phone rang in the other room.

"I'll get it before it wakes the baby," she said, and dashed down the hallway to the phone on the table. "Hello!"

Her voice was soft and breathless. Cole groaned and cursed the Fates as he realized he was finally going to have to talk to her, even if it wasn't face to face.

"It's me," he said.

Debbie almost dropped the receiver. It was the first time in thirty-six hours that she'd heard his voice, and even now, he didn't sound a bit better than he had when he'd stormed out of the house.

"So it is," she said shortly, and then waited.

Cole cursed softly. This wasn't going to be easy. "I just thought I'd call and let you know Rick is out of the woods."

"That's wonderful," she said. "Are you still working…or are you just running?"

The sarcasm was not lost on him. It made him defensive…and that was not a wise move. "You don't understand a thing about it," Cole said.

"That's possible." Tension hummed between them. "I can't read your mind. And you certainly haven't talked to me about anything. You slept with me, but you damn sure haven't talked."

"Listen, lady—" he began.

She cut him off short. "No, you listen," she cried. "I know you're going through a bad time, Cole. So is Rick. So is Tina. But they haven't shut each other out. They've been leaning on each other for strength."

"How would you have felt if it had been me instead of Rick? How would you like it if we'd had children and you were left alone to raise them?" Cole argued.

Debbie heard the pain in his voice. But he wasn't listening to her. She had to make him understand. "I know one thing, Cole Brownfield. I would be proud to call you husband. And I'd be strong enough to raise our children alone…if I had to. But we won't have to worry about any of that now, will we? You're too busy trying to fix what never happened. You're too busy assuming that I'd be a quitter." Her breath caught in a sob as she finished. "Well, I'll tell you something, mister. I'm not the quitter. You are."

Case stood quietly at the end of the hall, listening. He wanted to wring his brother-in-law's stupid neck.

He'd never known a family as determined to do everything their own way as the Brownfields. It had taken years off his life, just worrying if Lily would ever get over her hang-up about being scarred long enough to see that he loved her just the way she was. The scars were gone now, but Case hadn't forgotten the pain of wondering. He could tell his friend Debbie was suffering the same way. He headed toward her.

Debbie looked up, saw Case coming down the hall with a determined expression on his face, and thrust the phone into his hands. "Here, you talk to him. I don't have anything else to say." Then she walked away with her head held high and ignored the fact that she was dying inside.

"I don't know what the hell is going on," Case growled into the phone. "And I don't want to. But if you don't do something about it, Cole, I'm going to have to punch your face."

It hadn't taken Case Longren long to get to the point. Cole smiled to himself as he hung up the phone. It was what he'd most admired about the tall Oklahoma cowboy the first time they'd met.

In his heart, he knew that Debbie was right. *He* was the one running from the truth. And the truth was, he loved her to desperation. If he lost her, it would kill him.

Then what the hell am I doing? If I don't get myself together and get home, I've already lost her.

Cole walked back toward his desk. He stared at the mountain of paperwork and wanted to strike a match to it. With Rick gone, he was doing twice the work with half the results. *Damn, but I miss you, buddy. And thank God that you're getting well.*

He made a mental note to swing by the hospital later and check up on the Garzas before going home. *It should be interesting to go home tonight and have everyone watch me make a fool of myself,* he thought, then shrugged. *What did it matter? I've already acted like a fool. One more time isn't going to make that much difference.*

Buddy sat in silent awe, staring at the tiny bit of humanity wiggling around on his brother's bed. The baby's hair was thick and dark and stood up like new-mown grass. His fingers itched to touch, but he feared to make the move. There was no blinking cursor on this tiny little man to tell him where to begin.

The baby began to squeak. That gave him the impetus to introduce himself.

"Hello, Charlie Longren," he said quietly. The baby ceased wiggling instantly as his little blue eyes searched blindly for the location of the unfamiliar voice. "I'm your uncle. My name is Robert Allen Brownfield, but you may call me Uncle Buddy…when you learn to talk."

The baby squiggled and kicked. The soft white blanket covering his legs slipped down and with one more kick, it was in a wad at his feet.

"Yes," Buddy said, conversationally, "I can see that you're very strong. That's good. Obviously like your father, of course. I never was much for feats of physical prowess."

The baby shoved a fist toward his mouth and grimaced when the fist went sailing spastically by.

"You'll get the hang of it eventually," Buddy said, as if he were talking to one of his peers. "Personally, when I was younger, I preferred a thumb. However, you may choose a finger or a combination of several. I understand some do."

Lily blinked back tears. She'd walked into the room, certain that the baby was probably awake and then caught her breath at the sight. Buddy was in love. It was probably going to be his first and only, but that made it all the more special.

"Lily!" Buddy said. "I didn't know you were here."

"I just arrived," she said quickly, not wanting him to know that she'd overheard any of the man-to-man talk that had been going on.

He nodded, satisfied that his secrets were safe. "I think he likes me," he said softly.

The baby began to fuss after hearing Lily's voice.

"He's probably hungry," Lily said. "I brought his bottle. Do you want to feed him?"

Buddy's eyes dilated. His mouth dropped, and his fingers twitched as he considered the possibility. Finally, he answered. "Yes, I believe I would. But you'll have to show me how to pick him up. I wouldn't want to damage him."

Lily grinned. "You won't damage anything, Robert Allen. Just scoop and balance everything wiggling. I'll hand you the bottle."

Buddy stood and walked around the bed, carefully measuring the best angle to make his descent and, when he was satisfied that he'd figured it out, leaned over and deftly lifted the baby from the bed.

It was a perfect lift-off. Lily had expected awkwardness, even nerves. She should have known better. When Buddy did something, he always did it to perfection. The baby was in good hands.

"Sit down," she said, "and cuddle him. Here's his bottle."

"Thank you, Lily. Do I insert it now or...?"

The baby began to fuss at being held in the nursing position.

"Yes, Buddy. Insert it now." She tried not to grin at his terminology.

The bottle went in, and Buddy's face lit up. "Well, now, Charlie. I'll bet that just hits the spot. When you're a little older, I'll treat you to some of my favorite drinks. There's one with two scoops of chocolate and—"

"We call the baby Morgan," Lily corrected. But her brother wasn't listening. As far as Buddy was concerned, the baby was Charlie. She suspected as time passed, he would be Charlie to everyone. Buddy had a way about him.

Cole walked down the hospital corridor, wincing as a nurse hurried past with a capped syringe in her hand and a look of determination on her face. He was heartily glad he wouldn't be on the receiving end of that needle. Soft laughter drifted out into the hall. It was coming from Rick's room.

Cole opened the doorway and paused unobserved. It gave him an opportunity to see for himself how well his partner was healing.

The burden of guilt that he'd been living with, the constant reminder that he'd killed another man, seemed to lessen. In fact, the longer he watched Rick and Tina together, the easier it became to face the fact. Somehow it was finally justified in his mind. If that's what it had taken to keep a good man like Rick Garza alive, then it had been worth it. He stuffed his hands in his pockets and allowed himself a long, slow sigh.

It was then Rick saw him standing in the doorway. "Hey, buddy. Don't be a stranger. Come in and see what Tina has."

Cole grinned. "I heard the laughter all the way down the hall. What's so funny?"

Tina looked up and smiled. "We're laughing at a picture Enrique drew. It is of the little girl next door. We're trying to decide whether to move now or wait until Enrique is a little older before we panic."

Cole looked puzzled. Tina explained.

"We think he's in love. He drew a picture of the girl and put bats all over her clothing. It's a sure sign he likes her, you know. Only the best rate bats."

Cole laughed. He remembered the boy's infatuation with his hero, Batman.

"Better move now, love is hell," he warned.

Tina stopped laughing and stared point blank. "What's going on?" she asked sharply. And then she looked past Cole into the open doorway. "And where's Debbie? I haven't seen her in days. Have you?"

Cole frowned and stuffed his hands in his pockets.

"Tina..." Rick's warning was soft but firm. He grasped her hand. "You're got enough to worry about without interfering with Cole's business."

"It's my business, too," she said. "You don't understand. When you were so sick... I... I lost my temper and said some hurtful things. And I think—" she looked up at Cole with tear-filled eyes " —I think it just may have given Cole the wrong idea."

"Tina! You didn't lose your temper? I'm shocked! What will Cole think?" Rick grimaced as he shifted to a more comfortable position. And then he continued with a sarcastic grin. "Of course you lost your temper. You always do. It's one of the things I love most about you."

Cole listened. Fascinated by their ability to laugh, as if the last few days had never happened.

"But you were so frantic," Cole said to Tina. "You were blaming the job and—"

"And you. Tell the truth," Tina whispered, ashamed of herself but unwilling to ignore what she'd done. And then she shrugged. "I can't help it. It's just my nature. When bad things happen, I always have to blame something…or someone. Then I can get on to the business of fixing it."

"What if this couldn't be fixed?" Cole asked, unwilling to look at his partner's face. But he had to know.

Tina slid her hand beneath her husband's. Her eyes teared as he gave it a gentle pat.

"Then I would have had ten good years to remember and two children to love," she answered. "I knew when I married Rick that he was going to be a cop. I accepted it then. What has happened has changed nothing, except maybe it makes me appreciate him more."

"If you have love, Cole, nothing else matters," Rick said quietly.

Cole stared at the truth on his partner's face. His stomach tilted. He had the strongest urge to go home. Suddenly, seeing Debbie would come none too soon.

"Really glad to see you doing so well, Rick. Everyone sends their best. I've got to be going now. I'll see you later."

He made a hasty exit from the room and missed the knowing looks that passed between the Garzas. Tina leaned her head down on her husband's arm and kissed his hand. She had much to be thankful for.

It hit him like a ton of bricks. The chaos was complete. Cole was speechless at the sight that met him when he walked into the house.

The baby was crying.

Morgan came running from the kitchen with a heated bottle full of baby formula.

Case was competently patting his son's behind, trying to soothe him until the arrival of food.

Buddy had disappeared into his room, convinced that dirty diapers and burping babies left a lot to be desired. He'd decided to admire and cuddle when the opportunity arose, and wait until Charlie could communicate on a higher level than shrieks.

Cole grinned. *Now this is what I call, "coming home."*

"Hi, everyone,' he said. "So, this is my nephew. Hi there, fellow," he crooned, and stroked the baby's crumpled cheek. His little mouth turned automatically toward the touch, and for a moment, his crying hushed. "Aren't things going your way today? Boy, can I ever sympathize. Where's Lily?" he asked, wondering where the new mother was in all this melee.

"Taking a shower," Case said, and resisted the urge to sock his brother-in-law. "If I were you, I'd be a whole lot more concerned about where Debbie was."

Cole's smile disappeared. The sick feeling came back

into his stomach with rude force. "What the hell do you mean?" he asked.

Buddy sauntered into the room. "She's gone."

Morgan thought fast and shoved a chair behind his son's knees just before he hit the floor.

"What do you mean...gone?"

Case already regretted the hasty way he'd announced the fact. They'd all suffered a similar panic only moments before, but his son's distress had taken first place in the sequence of things to be done.

"He means she's packed. She's gone. She's on her way back to Oklahoma. That's what he means," Case said shortly. "I told you things were bad. It took you damn long enough to show up and fix them. Looks like you were an hour late and a dollar short."

"Oh God!" Cole groaned. "When did she leave? Does anyone know when her flight leaves? Maybe I can catch her before—"

"She won't be on the plane."

All eyes turned toward Buddy's bland announcement.

"What do you mean?" Morgan asked. He'd spent too many years seeing that same expression on his son's face at the worst possible moments.

"I mean, she'll miss her flight, that's what I mean," Buddy said, mouthing each word slowly and distinctly, as if his family's elevators didn't go all the way to the top. *It is a trial, living with people who can't understand the simplest facts,* he thought. "Are there any brownies left?" he asked of no one in particular, and started out of the room.

Cole grabbed him by the arm and plastered him

against the wall. The hard stare was unmistakable. Buddy began to get nervous. His brother was mad.

"How do you know she'll miss her plane, Buddy?" Cole's voice was very quiet. "What have you done?"

That he'd done something, there was no doubt. Cole had also known his brother too long to miss the look of feigned innocence.

"Well, it was obvious that you weren't going to do something," he accused, and pushed Cole's hands off his arms. "So it was left up to me, that's all."

"I repeat," Cole said. "What the holy hell did you do?"

"I put my castle and princess computer game in her luggage, that's all," Buddy said.

Cole's mouth dropped. He slapped his forehead with his hand to keep from slapping his brother instead. "You don't mean the—"

Case was lost. He didn't understand these Brownfield men. He was still having a hard time understanding the woman. "I don't get it," he asked Morgan and Cole. "What's the big deal about a game? Everyone has them."

"Not like Buddy's," Cole said. "It's one of a kind, and it looks like a remote control for detonating a bomb. Remember when we came to Oklahoma last year? Well, we spent several hours in LAX trying to explain that our brother is a harmless nut."

Cole spun around and slammed his fist against the wall. "For the love of God, Buddy. You'll get her arrested, and you know it. What were you thinking?"

Buddy looked at them as if they'd suddenly lost their minds. He couldn't understand it. How could he have a family so dense? "I was thinking that you love her but that you're terribly stupid."

"Oh," Cole said. There was nothing else to say. He patted the baby's tiny back. "It was nice meeting you, Charlie," he said quickly. "I'll be back later. I've got a plane to catch."

"She won't be on the plane," Buddy reminded him.

"She will kill us all," Cole said, and made a run for the door.

Chapter 12

If anyone had told her she'd be running away, Debbie would have called him a liar. But the truth was, she'd met her match. It was time to face facts, no matter how much they hurt. Cole might love her, but he didn't trust her. And without trust, there was no love.

Tears sprang into her eyes. Her heart ached. Shaky legs carried her through the thick throng of people coming and going in the busy Los Angeles airport terminal. More than once she was jostled by an impatient traveler hurrying to catch a plane. But she didn't care. The farther she got from Cole, the worse she felt.

Leaving had been her last option. There was a limit as to how long a woman could humiliate herself for love. Everyone in the family knew she loved Cole. And everyone also knew that Cole was doing nothing about it. It was going to kill her, but come hell or high water, she was getting on that plane.

The bag slipped on her shoulder and she gave it another hitch, relocating it to a strong position. All of her other luggage had been checked, but she'd been unable to trust her breakable souvenirs to the baggage handlers.

The closer she got to the checkpoint, the heavier it became. Debbie knew that she was being weighed down by more than souvenirs and hair spray. Guilt was weighing heavily on her heart as well as her mind.

I shouldn't have left him, she thought. *But what else could I do?*

"Place your purse and bag on here, miss," the attendant ordered as Debbie stepped up in the line.

She complied and walked through the metal detector to meet her bags on the other side of the security X-ray. She was standing, staring down at the floor, lost in thought, when alarms began to go off and the attendant shouted and grabbed her arm.

"Get some more security here, on the double. We've got a problem," he ordered.

Debbie gaped. Two uniformed officers appeared and grabbed her, one on either side. With her bags in tow, the trio began a quick walk toward an area designated as off limits to ordinary travelers. People pointed and stared.

"What?" she gasped. "I don't understand. You've made a—"

"Just save it, miss," one of the officers ordered. "You can explain it to the chief."

Debbie rolled her eyes, caught a glimpse of a clock on the wall as she was all but dragged through the hallway, and knew without a doubt that she would not make her plane. She didn't know about high water, but hell had come calling.

Cole made the entire run to the airport with lights flashing, moving unsuspecting citizens out of the way in a desperate attempt to save Debbie the embarrassment of being arrested. The traffic on the freeways was, as usual, a tow-trucker's delight.

The exit leading to the airport finally came into view. He glanced down at his watch and knew that whatever was going to happen already had. Either Buddy's sabotage had failed and Debbie was gone, or she was under arrest. Neither was an option he wanted to consider.

He chose airport parking. If Debbie was under arrest, it would take hours to straighten out this mess. He could still remember his own family's nightmare trip, when they'd had to try to convince the authorities that Buddy's invention was nothing more deadly than a hand-held computer game. And, if by chance Debbie was already gone, he was going to be right behind her. Either way, he wouldn't be needing his car for some time to come.

Stuffing the claim ticket in his pocket, he began to jog. By the time he reached the terminal, he was in an all-out run. Several people stared at the tall, suntanned man dressed in blue jeans and sneakers. And quite a few noticed how well his Forty-niners T-shirt molded to his physique. But it was all they saw. He was merely a blur through the crowd.

Cole was running. One quick look told him her flight had been delayed. *Oh, Lord! That means she's been arrested, and they're probably searching baggage.*

What he had to do now was get to security, and he knew right where it was. He should. He'd spent the better part of three hours there himself.

"You can't go in there," a guard shouted as Cole sprinted down a hallway.

He stopped, breathing hard, and dug in his pocket and flashed his badge. "Detective Brownfield, Laguna Beach Narcotics," he said quickly. "Can you tell me, in the last hour or so, has a young woman been arrested?"

The guard grabbed Cole by the arm and asked, "What do you know about it? And let me see that badge again."

I can see I was right. "Just take me to security," Cole asked. "I can explain everything."

"I seriously doubt it," the guard said.

"Believe me," Cole sighed, as they started down a long hallway. "I can."

Debbie stared at a point just past the officer's shoulder and stifled the urge to scream. She'd been answering the same questions for nearly an hour. It was obvious that they either needed hearing aids or didn't believe her. She opted for the latter.

"So, Miss Randall," Officer Tillet droned, "if you claim you know nothing about how this got in your luggage, maybe you *can* tell me what it does." He pointed to Buddy's computer game, careful not to touch any of the buttons and accidentally activate anything deadly.

She leaned forward, resting her elbows on the table, and drawled, "All I know is that, if you don't turn it on, you can't rescue the princess."

Tillet frowned. *Must be some kind of code. One never knows about radical factions and their crazy plans to save the world.* His pulse soared. This would mean a promotion for sure if he'd accidentally stumbled onto a plot by the IRA to harm the Royal Family.

"Princess, huh? As in Princess Di, maybe? Where were you headed anyway, London?"

"Right," Debbie said shortly, "by way of Oklahoma City, Oklahoma?"

He looked taken aback. "Check that out," Tillet ordered. One of the men scurried from the room.

"If you claim not to know anything about how it got in your luggage, then how do you explain your knowledge of it?" He had her there. He just knew it.

"I didn't say I'd never seen it. I just said, I didn't know Buddy had put it in my bag."

Now we're getting somewhere. She's about to name an accomplice. They always do when they're about to be caught. They never want to go down alone. "So, exactly what's your buddy's real name?" He leaned forward and pinned her with a stare.

"Robert Allen Brownfield," Cole said. "And unfortunately, he's my brother."

Cole was silent, waiting for a response to his announcement. He'd probably get arrested, too. *The Chief would love that,* Cole thought, picturing his boss's face when he tried to explain this mess back at the P.D.

Debbie leaned back in her chair, covered her eyes with her fingers, and pressed tightly. *Thank God!*

Cole saw her actions and felt the floor tilt beneath him. *She's furious. She's never going to forgive me or anyone claiming a remote relationship to a Brownfield.*

Tillet jumped. "Who's he?" he asked.

Cole reached for his pocket. Two officers reached for

their guns. He rolled his eyes. "In my pocket, please," he said.

An officer handed the wallet to Tillet.

A detective...with the Laguna Beach P.D.? What's going on here? They'd better not mess with me. This is my territory. I won't have anyone claiming credit for something I've—

"Brother?" What the detective had said finally registered. "What's going on here?" Tillet asked.

Cole shrugged free of his restraints and claimed his badge. "If I may…" he leaned forward and picked up the offending black box.

Everyone jumped back and several more officers drew their weapons. "Don't shoot," he drawled, "or I'll never get that damned princess out of the tower."

The machine came to life beneath his fingers, and for the first time, he was thankful that this was one of Buddy's games he knew how to work.

Lights came on, a computerized version of trumpets blared, and a tiny, robotic figure appeared on the small screen. It thrust and parried as the game's instructions were given to proceed.

"Prince Robert," Cole grinned, as he introduced the dashing little figure. He looked at Tillet and asked, "Do you want to take the road to Challon or go by water? I'll warn you, if you go by water, there's a hell of a monster just past the first set of cliffs that'll eat your damned boat every time."

The men assembled started to grin. One even stepped forward and held out his hand. "I'll give it a try," he offered. "I'm real good at—"

"Get back to your post," Tillet ordered. He hated days like this. "Miss Randall, I'm sorry you've been detained unnecessarily, but I'm certain you understand our position. We'll give you a personal escort to the plane and see that you get on it. It'll take about a half an hour to reload the baggage, and then you may resume your trip in peace." It was obvious that he'd be happy if he never saw her again.

Cole stepped forward. "That won't be necessary," he said. "If you'd be so kind as to get her bags off the—"

Debbie spoke. "Don't remove a thing. And I'll get myself to the proper gate." She walked out the door.

No!

Cole bolted after her.

Tillet sank down onto the nearest chair and stared at the figure of Prince Robert going down for the third time. A grinning dragon appeared on the screen and then a series of trumpets blared. The dragon had won. The princess was still in the tower, and Tillet was going to be the laughingstock of the week.

"What do you think you're doing?" Cole yelled, ignoring the curious stares sent their way.

Debbie didn't answer. She just kept walking.

"So, you're quitting! It doesn't surprise me," he shouted. "I always knew that my being a cop bothered you."

Debbie frowned. *That's part of his trouble,* she thought. *He doesn't know what I think. He just imagines he does.* She never slowed down.

"If you think I'm going to get down on my hands and knees. If you think I'm going to swear to quit being a cop just for you…"

She didn't respond and Cole picked up his pace. Just as they reached her loading gate, he grabbed her by the arm and hauled her around. "If you think I'm going to let you get on that plane, you're crazy."

He wasn't just warning her. He was desperate and determined. She knew when she'd met her match. But there was no use in spoiling this by admitting it too soon. She shifted gears.

"I suppose you *could* stop me…this time. But there'd always be a next, and a next and a—"

"Why?" The heartbreak in his voice was evident. "I love you, lady. I'm sorry my family caused you so much trouble. I'm sorry I've hurt you." Fear overwhelmed him as he stared at the lack of expression in her eyes. "It doesn't matter to you, does it? If I don't change my occupation, this conversation is null and void."

"I don't remember asking you to quit being a cop." The sharp tone of her voice got his attention…and everyone else's within a ten-yard radius.

Cole rolled his eyes. She was going to make him beg. He was nearly at that point anyway. "Just because you didn't ask doesn't mean I can't read between the lines," he snarled.

"I don't think you can read directions to the nearest bathroom, Cole Brownfield. Don't you dare stand there and tell me you read what I'm feeling."

She huffed herself up with a vengeance. Cole would have sworn he just saw her grow. It was impossible. But she *was* really mad.

"Then what's the big deal? If you love me, and if I love you, then why won't you marry me?"

"Probably because you never asked," Debbie said.

Several people laughed quietly, and one woman sniffed into the stunned silence of the crowd, obviously moved by what she would later claim was better than any soap opera any day.

Cole forgot to breathe. She was right! He'd never said the words. But dear God, he'd thought them, right up until Tina Garza had lambasted police work as being responsible for Rick's condition. He knew that she'd later recanted, but he hadn't been able to get past her fury. All he'd done was transpose her behavior onto Debbie without giving Debbie the benefit of the doubt.

Cole slid his arms around her, clasping her tightly against him, and nestled her against him. He rested his chin on the top of her head. "I meant to," he said quietly.

Debbie shrugged. "But you didn't." She spoke around a shirt button. Her nose was smashed against his collar bone, but she didn't care. She'd never thought Cole would hold her again. This was heaven. But he didn't deserve to be let out of hell. At least, not yet.

"So," Cole stepped back and stared deeply into dark, accusing eyes, "does this mean that I'm too late?"

She shrugged again.

"Does this mean that everything we've shared up to this point was nothing more than a good time? That you can give it up with no more thought than this?"

"I believe that should be my line," Debbie drawled. "I'm the one who gave and gave with no promises, remember?"

He flushed angrily. He hated it when she was right. He also hated the rumbling of the crowd behind him. Unless he redeemed himself fast... He wondered if tarring and feathering was too outdated to worry about.

"I love you, Deborah Randall." Cole got down on one knee and tried to ignore the same woman in the crowd who was now sobbing openly. "Will you marry me?"

"I love you, too," she said, and raked her fingers through his hair, framing his face with her hands.

Relief blossomed until he realized that she'd never answered his question.

"Final boarding call for flight 1207 for Dallas—Ft. Worth and Oklahoma City," the attendant called.

Debbie turned around and started walking toward the gate.

Cole wanted to cry. What else could he say?

"You're leaving me anyway? You're going back to Oklahoma after all we've meant to each other? Why?" he begged. "Just tell me why."

Debbie couldn't prolong his agony any longer. She turned and smiled through her tears. "I'm going to get my mother's wedding dress," she said. "I'm not getting married without it."

Cole started to shake. "I ought to wring your little—"

She was in his arms.

"Last call for flight…"

"I've got to go," she said.

"I'm coming with you," Cole answered.

The small crowd of people who'd witnessed the entire altercation began to cheer and clap.

For the first time since the entire incident began, Debbie was at a loss for words.

"But you can't. You don't have a…they won't let you…."

"I'm a police officer," Cole said quietly. "Sometimes it pays to be special. I think I can talk them into letting me pay at the other end. Trust me?"

"Forever," Debbie said. And she did.

Epilogue

"We're going to be in trouble," Debbie warned as they pulled into the driveway.

Cole grinned. "It won't be the first time."

"They've probably been planning and planning. They're going to kill us."

"So don't tell them," Cole offered.

Debbie stared. "But think of the waste of time and money they'll go to if we don't."

"Think of the fun they'll miss if we do."

Debbie sighed. "We'll see," she said. "Just don't blurt it out too fast. Let's feel them out about the whole thing first."

Cole parked. He couldn't wipe the smile off his face. He'd been trying for the past two days. But it was still there, and he'd be damned if he'd worry about it again.

And, if tonight was anything like last night, it might never come off.

The front door opened and his father and sister ran out.

"It's about time you two go home," Lily cried. "I thought you'd be here yesterday."

"Couldn't get a flight," Cole said calmly.

Debbie's stomach twisted. It wasn't *really* a lie. They couldn't get a flight because they hadn't tried.

Lily sighed and wrapped them both in a hug. "Wait till you see the flowers I've picked out."

Debbie sent Cole a piercing glare.

He shrugged and started loading his arms with bags. They'd packed everything possible and were shipping what hadn't fit.

"Need any help?" Morgan asked. Cole shifted several bags into his arms.

"What about me?" Case asked. Lily smiled at her husband, who sauntered outside as if he were on a weekend stroll. He was way too laid back for California time.

Cole loaded him, too. Finally they were ready to proceed. Debbie sent Cole one last look he couldn't misinterpret. They went into the house.

"So! Tell me everything," Lily said.

Debbie's eyebrows shot up into the fluff of her bangs and her face turned pink.

"Not on your life, Sis," Cole said softly.

Everyone laughed, except Debbie. She was starting to get a guilty conscience. She opened her mouth. Cole saw the look. He braced himself. It never came. Buddy sauntered into the room.

"You've got nerve," Debbie said, as she wrapped her arms around Buddy's neck and gave him a kiss. It was the first time she'd seen or spoken to him since her incident at the airport.

"I rather like to think of it as...initiative," Buddy claimed, and took the kiss as his reward for brilliance.

Cole grinned. "Your *initiative* almost got me shot, little brother."

"You look all right to me," Buddy remarked. And then he stared intently at them both before walking away. "In fact, if I didn't know better, I'd think you looked married."

Debbie nearly fainted. *Is he psychic too?*

For once Cole was speechless.

Everyone stared at them, waiting for them to deny it.

"Buddy!" Lily's shriek woke her baby. She sent Case a look that had him hastening to retrieve their son while she waited for her brother to reappear.

"You woke Charlie," he accused as he stuck his head around the corner.

"Why did you say that?" Lily asked.

Buddy rolled his eyes. Sometimes his family was too dense for words. "I said you woke him because I can hear him crying," he said distinctly. "Before he was quiet. Now he's not. Understand?"

"I think I'm going to kill you," Lily said shortly.

"Won't do any good," Morgan said. "I think he's cloned himself in that damned room. If you hurt your brother, two more like him will come in his place."

Debbie wanted to hide. Cole slid his arm around her shoulders and pulled her gently against him. For better or worse, they were now in all this family mess together.

"I wasn't talking about my son's sleeping habits," Lily said shortly.

Buddy waited.

Lily wanted to strangle him. She'd forgotten how maddening he could be.

"I wanted to know what made you say what you did about Cole and Debbie."

"About what?"

Lily screamed. It was unlike her. She was a lady, always. She never lost her cool. Never. Unless Buddy was around.

"Why did you say Cole and Debbie looked married?"

"Oh, that!" Buddy pointed. "I saw the rings. It's rather obvious, don't you think?"

Everyone gaped. For once, Buddy had them cold. He leaned against the wall and watched his family come to attention. They were a fascinating species.

"It's true." Lily was floored. "She's wearing rings."

"That doesn't necessarily mean—" Cole began.

"Cole, stop it," Debbie said softly. "No more."

He wrapped her in his arms. "You're right," he said. "No more. Not from any of you. Yes, we're married. Not because I wanted to leave any of you out of the ceremony, but because I'd waited long enough for Debbie to be part of this family. I nearly waited too long. I wasn't taking any more chances."

"Makes sense to me," Case drawled as he walked back into the room carrying his son. "Taking chances on women is deadly stuff. I can vouch for that."

Lily smiled gently.

"If you want, we'll have another ceremony," Debbie offered. "I brought my mother's wedding dress, just in case."

"Far as I'm concerned, save it for your daughter's wedding," Case said. "Getting married once is enough for any man. Twice is above and beyond. Besides, if I remember my own, you two should be about ready for the honeymoon. Where are you going?"

"We'll be gone until Wednesday," Cole said.

His brother-in-law grinned at the neat way he'd side-stepped the question. It was understandable.

"Where will you live when you come back?"

Lily's question took them all by surprise.

Morgan's face fell. He could hardly face the thought of Cole leaving. And Debbie had become another daughter. But it was only fair that they had their time alone.

Buddy lost his calm demeanor. He'd come to depend on Debbie greatly. He liked having someone fuss over him, and he definitely liked the way she cooked. What would he—?

"Who'll make me chocolate chip cookies?" Buddy asked aloud.

"I will, darling," Debbie said. She felt Cole's arms tighten around her. She could feel his approval. "And while we're gone, I expect you to keep your room clean."

Buddy nodded vigorously.

Cole laughed. *My God, but marriage to her is going to be one wild ride through life! I can't wait!*

"And, I don't want to come back and find out that there are no plates and glasses in the cupboards. Remember?"

"I remember," Buddy promised.

"Morgan—"

He jumped to attention. Obviously he wasn't going to escape the orders either. "If the twins come back while we're gone, explain the situation. And, I don't want to find out that you've quit your therapy."

Her warning was enough. He hugged her and smiled. "I promise, too, girl."

"How about me?" Cole whispered.

"Are you still here?" Debbie asked with practiced surprise. "Why aren't you packed? We've got a honeymoon to start."

"I don't need to pack," Cole drawled. "I sleep in the buff, remember?"

She blushed. It was just like him to tease her in front of the whole clan. "Yes, I remember it very well," she chided. "But what's that got to do with the trip?"

"Well, if we never get out of bed, what will I need with clothes?"

As usual, Debbie got the last word in...and the last laugh.

"After I'm through with you," she drawled, "they'll have to bury you in something. Pack your good suit. You'll want to look nice for the funeral."

Cole looked stunned. And then he laughed.

"It won't take long," he said. "I've only got one suit."

* * * * *

Delores Fossen, a *USA TODAY* bestselling author, has written over one hundred novels, with millions of copies of her books in print worldwide. She's received a Booksellers' Best Award and an RT Reviewers' Choice Best Book Award. She was also a finalist for a prestigious RITA® Award. You can contact the author through her website at deloresfossen.com.

Books by Delores Fossen

Harlequin Intrigue

The Lawmen of McCall Canyon

Cowboy Above the Law
Finger on the Trigger
Lawman with a Cause
Under the Cowboy's Protection

HQN Books

Lone Star Ridge

Tangled Up in Texas
That Night in Texas (ebook novella)
Chasing Trouble in Texas

A Coldwater Texas Novel

Lone Star Christmas
Hot Texas Sunrise
Sweet Summer Sunset
A Coldwater Christmas

Visit the Author Profile page at Harlequin.com for more titles.

A THREAT TO HIS FAMILY

Delores Fossen

Chapter 1

Deputy Owen Slater knew something was wrong the moment he stopped his truck in front of his house.

There were no lights on, not even the ones on the porch or in the upstairs window of the nursery. It was just a little past eight and that meant it was his daughter Addie's bedtime, but she always slept with the lamp on.

If the electricity had gone off, the nanny, Francine Landry, would have almost certainly texted Owen to let him know. Besides, Owen had already spotted a light in the barn. That wasn't unusual since the light was often left on there, but it meant the power definitely wasn't out.

Because he was both a father and a cop, the bad thoughts came and his pulse kicked up hard and fast. Something had maybe gone wrong. Over the years, he'd made plenty of arrests, and it could be that someone wanted to get back at him. A surefire way to do that was to come here to his home, to a place where he thought he and his child were safe.

The panic came, shooting through him when he thought of his daughter being in danger. Addie was only eighteen months old, just a baby. He'd already lost her mother in childbirth and he couldn't lose Addie, too.

That got Owen drawing his gun as he started running. He fired glances all around him in case this was an ambush, but no one came at him as he barreled up the porch steps.

Hell.

The front door was slightly ajar. That was another indication that something wasn't right. Francine always kept things locked up tight now that Addie was walking and had developed some escape skills.

Owen didn't call out to Francine, something he desperately wanted to do with the hope he'd hear her say that everything was okay. But if he called out, it could alert someone other than the nanny. Still, he prayed that she would come rushing in to give him some account for what was happening. But no good explanation came to mind.

Owen tried to rein in his heartbeat and breathing. Hard to do, though, when the stakes were this high, but he forced himself to remember his training and experience. That meant requesting backup before he started a search of the area. He quickly texted his brother Kellan to get there ASAP so he'd have some help if needed.

The tight knot in Owen's gut told him it would be needed.

And Kellan was the best backup Owen could ask for. Not only was he the sheriff of their hometown of Longview Ridge, he lived just two miles away. Kellan could be there in no time.

Using his elbow, Owen nudged the door open all the way and glanced around. His house had an open floor plan, so with a single sweeping glance, he could take in the living room, kitchen and dining area. Or at least he could have done that had it not been so blasted dark. There were way too many shadows. Too many places for someone to hide.

Owen flipped the light switch. Nothing. That snowballed the wildfire concerns because it meant someone could have cut off the power to the house. He doubted this was some kind of electric malfunction because if it had been, Francine would have gotten out the candles and flashlights since she was well aware of Addie's fear of the dark.

Even though his brother would be here in minutes, Owen didn't want to wait for him. The thought of his baby hurt and scared got him moving. With a two-handed grip on his gun, he checked behind the sofa, making sure he continued to keep watch. No one was there, so he moved to the dining room. Still no one.

But he heard something.

There were footsteps upstairs. Not Addie's toddling feet, either. These were heavy and slow, probably the way his own steps would sound if he were up there looking around. Owen turned to head in that direction in case it was Francine, but that was when he noticed the back door was open, too. And there were sounds coming from the yard.

"Shh," someone whispered. "We need to play the quiet game."

Because the voice was so ragged, it took Owen a moment to realize it was Laney Martin, his ranch manager. That sent him hurrying straight to the door, and he saw Laney running toward the barn. She had Addie clutched to her chest, her hand cupping the back of the baby's head.

Owen didn't call out to them, but he did catch a glimpse of Laney's face as they ducked into the barn. She was terrified. He hadn't needed anything to up his own level of fear, but that did it. He ran across the yard and went straight into the barn. He heard another sound. Laney's sharp gasp.

"It's me," Owen whispered just in case she thought it was someone else who'd followed them in there.

Laney had already moved to the far corner of the barn next to a stack of hay bales. When she shifted her position, Owen could see his baby's face. Addie was smiling as if this were indeed a fun game. It was good that she was too young to realize the danger they were in.

"Where's Francine?" he asked. "Is she in the house?"

Laney shook her head. "The nursing home called about her mom a half hour ago." While her voice was level enough for him to understand her, each word had come through her panting breaths. "Francine asked me to watch Addie while she went over there to check on her."

Francine's mom had dementia so it wasn't unusual for the nanny to get calls about her. However, this was the first time she'd left Addie with Laney. Maybe, though, Francine had done that because she'd known Owen would soon be home.

An intruder who'd been watching the place would have known that, too.

"Who's in the house?" he asked.

Another head shake from Laney. "A man."

Not that he needed it, but Owen had more confirmation of the danger. He saw that Laney had a gun, a small snub-nosed .38. It didn't belong to him, nor was it one that he'd ever seen in the guesthouse where Laney was staying. Later, he'd ask her about it, about why she hadn't mentioned that she had a weapon, but for now they obviously had a much bigger problem.

Owen texted this brother again, to warn him about the intruder so that Kellan didn't walk into a situation that could turn deadly. He also asked Kellan to call in more backup. If the person upstairs started shooting, Owen wanted all the help he could get.

"What happened?" Owen whispered to Laney.

She opened her mouth, paused and then closed it as if she'd changed her mind about what to say. "About ten minutes ago, I was in the kitchen with Addie when the power went off. A few seconds later, a man came in through the front door and I hid in the pantry with her until he went upstairs."

Smart thinking on Laney's part to hide instead of panicking or confronting the guy. But it gave Owen an uneasy feeling that Laney could think that fast under such pressure. And then there was the gun again. Where had she gotten it? The guesthouse was on the other side of the backyard, much farther away than the barn. If she'd gone to the guesthouse to get the gun, why hadn't she just stayed there with Addie? It would have been safer than running across the yard with the baby.

"Did you get a good look at the man?" Owen prompted.

Laney again shook her head. "But I heard him. When he stepped into the house, I knew it wasn't you, so I guessed it must be trouble."

Again, quick thinking on her part. He wasn't sure why, though, that gave him a very uneasy feeling.

"I didn't hear or see a vehicle," Laney added.

Owen hadn't seen one, either, which meant the guy must have come on foot. Not impossible, but Owen's ranch was a good half mile from the main road. If this was a thief, he wasn't going to get away with much. Plus, it would be damn brazen of some idiot to break into a cop's home just to commit a robbery.

So what was really going on?

Owen glanced around the barn, also keeping watch on the yard in case the intruder followed them out here. Part of him wanted that to happen so he could make the piece of dirt pay for putting Addie and Laney through this.

There were no ranch hands around that he could see. Not a surprise. He ran a small operation and only had three full-time hands and Laney, who managed the place. Other than Laney, none of the others lived on the grounds. Not even Francine, since she had her own house only a couple of miles away.

He glanced at the light switch and considered turning it off, but that might only make things worse. If the intruder saw it, he would know they were in the barn, and he might come out there with guns blazing.

Owen's phone dinged with a text message from Kellan.

I'm here, parked just up the road from your truck. Where is he?

Owen texted back.

Still in the house, I think.

But the moment he fired off the message, Owen saw something in the back doorway of the house. The moonlight glinted off metal and he caught a glimpse of the gun. That confirmed his worst fears, though he couldn't actually see the person holding the weapon. That was because he was likely dressed in all black and staying in the shadows.

Owen ducked back to avoid the barn light. That light probably helped Addie since she wasn't fretting as she usually did in the dark, but it might seem like a beacon to some thug looking to start trouble.

"Stay down," Owen instructed Laney. "I'll see if I can draw this guy out into the open—"

"You could be shot," she said before he even finished, her voice shaking.

Yeah, he could be, but if anyone was going to become a target, Owen wanted it to be him. He didn't want any shots fired into the barn or anywhere near Addie.

He texted Kellan to let him know that he was about to head out the back of the barn. He could then use the corral fence and nearby shrubs for cover to circle around the house.

Keep watch of the front, Owen added to the text.

He didn't intend to let this joker get away. He wanted to know who he was and why he'd broken in.

Owen eased the barn door shut and moved a saddle in front of it to block it. It wouldn't stop anyone for long, which was why he had to hurry. He ran to the back of the barn and climbed out through the opening sometimes used to push hay into the corral. When his feet hit the ground, he took a quick look around him.

No one.

No sounds, either. If the intruder was coming their way, he was being quiet about it. Owen tried to do the same as he made his way to the front side of the barn to take a look at the back porch.

Owen cursed.

The guy with the gun was no longer in sight, but the door was still open. Maybe he'd stepped back into the shadows to look for them. But that didn't make sense, either. By now, the intruder must have spotted Owen's truck, which was rigged with a police siren, and would have known that he had called for backup. That meant he possibly could have already fled the scene.

His phone dinged again with a text message. Owen was about to look down at the screen when he heard a sound he didn't want to hear.

A gunshot cracked through the air.

It didn't go into the part of the barn where Laney and Addie were, thank God, but it did slam into the wood right next to where Owen was standing. That forced him to move back. And to wait. He didn't have to wait long. However, this time it wasn't another shot. It was a man's voice.

"Elaine?" a man yelled. "I know you're out there."

Owen had no idea who this Elaine was, so maybe this was a case of the thug showing up at the wrong place.

Except, wasn't Laney a nickname for Elaine?

Was this man someone from Laney's past? Maybe an old boyfriend who'd come to settle a score?

If so, she'd never mentioned it and nothing had shown up about relationship issues in the background check he'd run on her, and he'd been pretty darn thorough since Laney would be living so close to Addie and him. While he continued to volley glances all around him, Owen checked his phone screen and saw the text from Kellan.

I'm moving to the right side of your house.

Good. There was a door there, just off the playroom. Maybe Kellan would be able to slip into the house and get a look at this guy. Or, better yet, arrest him.

"I'm Deputy Owen Slater," Owen called out. "Put down your weapon and come out with your hands up."

It was something that, as a cop, Owen needed to say. He had to identify himself in the hope it would cause the idiot to surrender. Of course, it was just as likely to cause him to fire more shots. If he did, Owen would be justified in using deadly force.

But no other shots. Just another shout.

"Elaine?" the man yelled again.

Owen used the sound of the man's voice to try to pinpoint his location. He was definitely no longer by the back door. Nowhere near it. This guy was in the guesthouse, where Laney lived. How he'd gotten there, Owen didn't know, but it was possible that he'd climbed through a window.

Since the intruder was now on the same side of the

yard as Owen, it made him an easy target, and that was why he hurried back into the barn. He glanced at Laney. Or rather, where he'd last seen Addie and her, but Laney had moved a few feet. She had positioned herself behind the hay bales and was using one as support for her shooting hand.

"Where's the baby?" Owen immediately asked.

Just in case wasn't looking very good right now. But at least they were all still safe. He heard Addie then, and she wasn't fussing. It was more of a cooing babble, so the necklace must have been holding her attention.

"Elaine?" the man called out. He had moved since his last shout, but Owen wasn't sure to where. He also wasn't sure of Laney's reaction.

The color had blanched from her face and he didn't think it was because of the danger. Owen didn't have to be a cop to figure out what that meant.

"You know this guy," he said.

She didn't deny it, causing Owen to curse under his breath.

"What does he want with you?" Owen demanded.

She didn't get a chance to answer him because the man shouted again. "Elaine, let's do this the easy way. Come out now and leave with me, and no one will get hurt."

Hell. There was a good bit of anger now mixed with fear for his daughter. Anger that this thug would try to bargain like this. No way was Owen going to let Laney leave with a man who'd just fired a shot at him.

"Watch out!" someone yelled. Not the thug this time. It was Kellan. "He's coming right at you."

That wasn't the only thing that came, either. There

was a gunshot, quickly followed by another one. From the sound of it, the second shot had come from a different weapon.

Maybe Kellan's.

Owen hoped it had anyway. Because he didn't like the odds if this intruder had brought his own version of backup with him.

He debated opening the barn door so he could help his brother, but since this guy was likely coming for them, Owen's top priority was to make sure that Addie was protected. He hurried to Laney and Addie, standing guard in front of them and waiting for whatever was about to happen.

Owen didn't have to wait long. Someone kicked the barn door hard, and bits of wood went flying. The saddle shifted, too, and Owen steeled himself to fire. He was about to do that when he got a glimpse of the person who'd just broken down the door. The man, dressed in black, took aim at them. However, before Owen could pull the trigger, shots blasted through the barn.

Laney had fired.

And she hadn't missed.

The bullets, first one and then the other, slammed into the man's chest and he dropped to the ground like a stone. If he wasn't dead, he soon would be, because he was already bleeding out.

Addie started to cry so Owen hurried to her. The relief came flooding through him because his baby was okay. She hadn't been hurt.

He didn't scoop her up into his arms, something he desperately wanted to do. First, he had to wait for the all clear from Kellan, and that might take a couple of minutes. In the meantime, Owen would need to hold his position. However, that didn't stop him from asking one critical question.

Owen's eyes narrowed when he looked at Laney. "Start talking. Who the heck are you?"

Chapter 2

From the moment this nightmare had started, Laney had known that question—and many more—would come from Owen.

Who the heck are you?

No way would Owen Slater just let something like this go. Of course, he probably thought her answer would help him understand this mess. It wouldn't. In fact, it was going to make things even worse.

At least he and Addie hadn't been hurt. And the toddler was so young that she hopefully wouldn't remember anything about this attack. However, the assault would stay with Owen for the rest of his life, and Laney was never going to be able to forgive herself for allowing things to come to this.

Sweet heaven. She could have gotten them killed.

With his scalpel-sharp glare, Owen reminded her

that he was well aware of that, too. In fact, the only reason he likely didn't take Addie from Laney when she picked up the baby was that he needed to keep his shooting hand free in case someone else fired at them.

She glanced at the man she'd just shot. Who the heck was he? How had he known who she was? And why had he done this? He hadn't given her any choice, but it still twisted away at her. A man was dying or already dead because of her. And worse, this wasn't over. If she'd managed to somehow keep him alive, he might have been coerced into telling her who'd put him up to this, but she'd had no choice but to take that shot.

"Who are you?" Owen repeated.

Judging from the tone and his intense glare, he no longer trusted her. Good. Because Laney didn't trust herself.

It crushed her to have it all come to this. She'd thought she was safe, that Addie and Owen would be safe, too. Obviously she'd brought her fight right to their doorstep.

"I was Elaine Pearce," she said, speaking around the lump in her throat, "but I changed my name to Laney Martin."

Of course, that explanation was just the tip of the iceberg. Owen would demand to know about not only the name change, but also how it connected to the dead man. And how it connected to this attack.

Owen sent a text to someone. Probably to one of his fellow deputies to do a quick background check on Elaine Pearce. It was what Laney would have done had their positions been reversed.

"I want you to put your gun on the hay bale," he instructed. He sounded like a cop now, and he looked at her as if she were a criminal.

Laney did exactly as he said, knowing the gun would be taken as part as of the evidence in what was now a crime scene. An investigation would quickly follow, which meant she'd be questioned and requestioned. Soon, everyone in town would know who she was, and she'd be in more danger than she already was. That was why she had to figure a way out of here—fast.

"Elaine Pearce," he repeated. "And you didn't think that was something I should know?" Owen grumbled. "You didn't bother to mention that you weren't who you were claiming to be?"

"No." Laney took another deep breath. "I thought I'd find the info that I needed and be out of here before anything could happen."

"You were obviously wrong about that." He gave a disapproving grunt and went to the man, kicking his gun farther away from where it had fallen from the shooter's hand. Owen then touched his fingers to the guy's neck.

"Dead," Owen relayed as he did a quick search of the guy's pockets. Nothing. Of course, he hadn't expected a hired gun to bring an actual ID with him.

"You recognize him?" Owen asked.

Laney somehow managed to stand upright, though every part of her was trembling. She also moved closer to Owen and then made another quick check on Addie. The little girl's cries were already starting to taper off, but she'd obviously been frightened by the noise of the gunshots.

A muscle tightened in Owen's jaw and, though Laney hadn't thought it possible, his steel-gray eyes narrowed even more when he glared at her. He made a circling motion with his index finger for her to continue, but before Laney even had the chance to do that, his phone rang. She saw his brother's name on the screen. In the months that she'd been working for Owen, she'd met Kellan several times and knew he lived close by. She had figured Owen had called him or their other brothers for backup.

"This conversation isn't over," Owen assured her as he hit the answer button on his phone. He didn't put the call on speaker, but Laney was close enough to hear Kellan's voice.

"There's a second intruder," Kellan blurted out, causing a chill to ripple through her.

Laney hurried back to Addie and pulled the little girl into her arms. Because of her position, she could no longer hear what Kellan was saying. But judging from the way Owen's gaze fired around, he, too, was bracing himself for another attack. He didn't stay on the phone long and, once he was finished with his conversation, maneuvered himself in front of them.

"The second guy was in the guesthouse," Owen told her. "He ran into the woods across the road. Kellan and Gunnar are searching for him now and they've called Dispatch for more backup."

Gunnar was Deputy Gunnar Pullam, someone else that Laney had seen around town. Like Owen, he was an experienced lawman. Something they needed right now. Maybe they'd find the second man and stop him from circling back to try to kill them again. The thought didn't help with her heartbeat, which was already thudding out of control. Addie must have picked up on that, too, because she started to whimper again. Laney began to rock her.

"Kellan said the second man had something with him when he ran out of the guesthouse," Owen went on. "A bag, maybe." His back was to her now, but she didn't need to see his face to know he was still glaring. "Any idea what he took?"

Laney's thoughts were all over the place as she tried to fight off the panic, but it didn't take her long to come up with an answer. "Maybe my toothbrush or something else with my DNA on it. Something to prove who I am."

Other than changing her hair and wearing colored contacts, she hadn't altered her appearance that much. If they'd looked closely enough, whoever was after her could have recognized her from old photos she was certain were still out there on the web. But a hired gun would have wanted some kind of proof to give to his boss and DNA would have done it.

That didn't feel right, though.

She fought through the whirlwind of thoughts and spiked adrenaline, and remembered that one of the intruders had called her by her real name. Elaine. And the one she'd killed had come into the barn to either take her with him or gun her down. So maybe they hadn't been looking for someone to prove who she was. Maybe they'd been after something else in the guesthouse and the man she'd shot had been just a distraction for his partner.

"My laptop," she added on a rise of breath. Though everything on it was password protected or stored on a cloud with several layers of security, a good hacker would be able to find what she had there.

"Keep talking," Owen ordered her while he continued volleying glances between the front door and the window at the back. "Why'd you lie to me about who you were?"

Again, this would only lead to more questions, but she doubted that she could stall Owen, especially since the sense of danger was still so thick around them.

"I lied because I didn't want anyone, including you, to know my real identity." Laney paused when her breath suddenly became very thin. "I'm working on an investigation, and the clues led me here to Longview Ridge."

Owen pulled back his shoulders. "Are you a cop?"

"A private investigator."

Owen growled out some profanity under his breath and looked as if he wanted to do more than growl it. He'd kept it quiet, no doubt because his daughter was right there, but thankfully Addie was falling asleep, her head now resting on Laney's shoulder.

"So, you're a PI and a liar," Owen rumbled. Obviously he didn't think much of either. "I obviously missed way too much about you when I did your background check. And now you've put my little girl, me and now Gunner and my brother in danger."

Yes. She'd done all of those things and more. "I'm investigating Emerson Keaton."

She saw the brief moment of surprise, followed by a new round of silent profanity that went through his eyes. "My brother-in-law. Addie's uncle."

Laney could add another mental *yes* to that. Emerson was indeed both of those things, along with being the town's district attorney. She was also convinced that he had a fourth label.

Killer.

Of course, there was no way Owen would believe that, and she wasn't going to be able to convince him of it now. Laney couldn't blame him for his doubts. Nearly everything she'd told him had been a lie, including the résumé and references she'd manufactured to get this job.

Owen's intense stare demanded that she continue even though they obviously still had to keep watch.

"Seven months ago, my half sister was murdered. Hadley Odom." Laney had said Hadley's name around the thick lump in her throat. "We were close."

Not a lie. They had been, despite the different ways they'd chosen to live their lives.

"What the heck does your half sister's murder have to do with Emerson?" Owen snapped.

"Everything," Laney managed to say, and she repeated it to give herself some extra time to gather her words and her breath. "Hadley and Emerson had an affair."

"Emerson?" Owen challenged when she paused. There was a bucket of skepticism in his tone. With good reason. Emerson was the golden boy of Longview Ridge. He had a beautiful wife, two young kids and a spotless reputation. "I've known Emerson my whole life, and there's never been a hint of him having an affair."

"He and Hadley kept it secret. Not just for Emerson's sake but for Hadley's. Hadley and I had the same mother, but her father, my stepfather, wouldn't have approved." Actually, Laney hadn't approved, either, but it was impossible to sway Hadley once she'd had her mind set on something.

Owen stayed quiet for a moment, his expression hard, ice-cold. "You have proof of this?"

"I heard Hadley talking to him on the phone, and I saw them together once when they were at a restaurant."

Of course, that wasn't proof she thought Owen was just going to accept. And she was right. Owen's scowl only worsened.

"Hadley told me they were having an affair." She spelled it out for him. "She also told me that she got very upset when he broke things off with her. In anger, Hadley threatened to tell his wife and, less than twelve hours later, she was dead."

"And you think Emerson killed her." It wasn't a question.

Owen wasn't believing any of this. Neither had anyone else she'd told, but Laney had plenty of proof that she was pushing the wrong buttons with her investigation.

She tipped her head to the dead man. "He came here after me. Why else would he do that if I weren't getting close to proving what Emerson did?"

Owen didn't roll his eyes, but it was close. Then he huffed, "If you're really a PI as you say you are, then I suspect you've riled some people. You've certainly done that to me."

"Yes, but you don't want me dead. Emerson does."

However, she had to mentally shake her head. Someone wanted to kill her and the most obvious suspect was the one she was investigating. But there was someone else and her expression must have let Owen know that.

"Remembering something else?" Owen snapped.

No way did she want to lie to him again, but before Laney could even begin to answer him, she heard foot-.

steps outside the barn. That gave her another shot of adrenaline and she crouched again with Addie.

"It's me," someone said.

Kellan.

Not the threat her body had been geared up to face. However, like Owen, Kellan was scowling when he came into the barn. He glanced at his brother and niece. Then at the dead man. Then at Laney. She didn't think it was her imagination that she got the brunt of the scowl he was doling out.

"We got the second intruder," Kellan explained. "He's alive."

Laney released the breath she hadn't even known she'd been holding. "Who is he?" she blurted. "Has he said anything?"

"Oh, he's talking a lot," Kellan grumbled. "He's demanding to see you. He says he's a friend of yours, that you're the one who hired him."

"No." Laney couldn't deny that fast enough. "He's lying."

Judging from the flat look Kellan gave her, he wasn't buying it. Apparently, neither was Owen because he walked closer and took Addie from her. He immediately moved next to his brother.

"There's more," Kellan added a moment later. "The intruder says that you hired him to kill Owen."

Chapter 3

Owen hadn't wanted to spend half the night in the sheriff's office, where he spent most of his days, but he hadn't had a choice. This was not just a simple B and E, and with the shooting death of one of the intruders, it was a tangled mess.

One not likely to be resolved before morning.

That was because Laney had denied hiring the intruder, and the intruder was insisting he was telling the truth. That put them at a temporary stalemate. Or at least it would have if Owen had any faith in the intruder. Hard to trust someone who'd come to his home and broken in while his baby daughter had been there. Of course, the reason the intruder had come was Laney.

That meant this was another stalemate.

One that he hoped to break soon.

There was an entire CSI team going through his

place, which meant he wouldn't be going home tonight. The only silver lining was that Francine had taken Addie to her place. Not alone, either. Owen had sent Gunnar with them just case this "mess" got another layer to it with a second attack.

In the meantime, Owen had been in the mind-set of collecting as much information as he could through phone conversations and emails. He hadn't done all of that under Laney's watchful eyes and alert ears, either. He'd left her in his office for some of those calls and was now trying to process everything he'd learned.

Laney hadn't been idle, either. She'd made a call, too. With a cheap, disposable cell phone, he'd noticed. And Owen had made sure he kept his ears alert during her conversation. She'd spoken to someone she called Joe and told him to be careful.

That was it.

The chat had lasted less than five seconds and then Laney had immediately surrendered the phone to Owen. Not that it had been of any use to him since Joe hadn't answered when Owen had tried to call him. Laney had briefly—*very briefly*—explained that Joe Henshaw was her assistant, and that she didn't know where he was. Neither did Owen or the San Antonio cops helping him look for the guy.

"I didn't hire that man to kill you," Laney repeated when Owen finished his latest call, this one to the medical examiner.

Declaring and redeclaring her innocence was something Laney had been going on about during the entire five hours they'd been there. He suspected she would continue to go on about it until the intruder either recanted or Kellan and he were indeed able to prove that he was lying.

Owen figured proving it wouldn't be that hard.

However, they couldn't even start doing that because the guy had lawyered up and they now had to wait for the attorney to arrive from San Antonio. Until then, they were holding not only the intruder but also Laney. Owen had not yet decided if she was a suspect, but he was pretty sure Laney—or rather Elaine—was going to be the key to them figuring out what the hell was going on.

"The guy you shot and killed was Harvey Dayton," Owen told her. He'd just gotten the ID during his call with the ME. "Ring any bells?"

"No," she answered without hesitation. "And I'm sure I've never seen him before, either. His prints were in the system," Laney added in a mutter. "That's how you got the ID this fast?"

He nodded. "Dayton had a record," Owen settled for saying.

What he didn't spell out for her was that the rap sheet was a mile long, and yeah, it included a couple of assault charges with a pattern of escalating violence. Along with a history of drug use, which made him a prime candidate for becoming a hired gun for people who wanted cheap help.

"Did Dayton say what he took from the guesthouse?" Laney asked.

Good question because, other than a gun, Dayton hadn't had anything on him when Kellan and Gunnar had found him. The CSIs would search the area, but Dayton had been captured by the road, a good quarter mile from Owen's ranch. There was no telling where he'd put whatever it was he'd taken.

"Your laptop is missing," Owen added, and he instantly saw the frustration and anger in her eyes.

"I keep copies of my files in online storage," she said with a heavy sigh. "But everything was also on my hard drive. It means whoever took it won't have trouble accessing everything."

Later, he'd want to know more about exactly what was on it. For now, Owen went with giving her more info that would then lead to more questions. Hopefully, more answers, too. "Your toothbrush was there, so that axes your DNA theory. Your purse was open, and your wallet and cell phone were gone. No jewelry around, either, so if you had any—"

"The only jewelry I have is this." Laney touched her fingers to the gold dragonfly necklace that she'd gotten back from Addie. There was also a small key on the chain. "It was a gift from my sister." She paused. "You really think the motive for this was robbery?"

"No." Owen didn't have to think about that.

The gunman had called her by name and come to the barn. Plus, nothing was missing from his house. If this had been a robbery, they would have taken his wallet and anything else of value. They also would have had a vehicle stashed nearby, and so far, one hadn't turned up.

"And the second man, the one who's lying about me, any ID on him yet?" she queried.

"Rohan Gilley." Owen watched for any signs of recognition.

She repeated the name several times, the way a person would when they were trying to jog their memory. But then Laney shook her head. "He had a record, too?"

Owen settled for a nod. Gilley's rap sheet was almost

identical to Dayton's, just slightly shorter. They'd even served time together.

"Gilley's lying to save his hide," Laney grumbled. "Or because someone put him up to it." She added some muttered profanity to go along with that.

The last five hours hadn't improved her mood much. She was just as wired as she had been during the attack. At least, though, she wasn't trembling now. For reasons he didn't want to explore, the trembling got to Owen, and right now the only thing he wanted to feel for this woman was the cool indifference he felt toward anyone who'd been involved in any way with a crime.

But indifference was impossible.

If she was telling the truth about not hiring Gilley— and he believed that she was—then that meant she was a victim, one who'd saved his daughter by getting her out of harm's way. Hard for something that big not to be on the proverbial table.

Laney's tough exterior, or rather the front she'd tried to put on for him, cracked a little. She didn't go back to trembling, but it was close, and before she could gather her composure, he caught another glimpse of nerves.

Big ones.

She was a PI—he'd confirmed that—but this could have been the first time she'd actually been in the middle of an attack. Maybe the first time she had been a target, too.

Along with having a good aim, she had an athletic build and was on the petite side, only about five-three.

And attractive.

Something he hated that he noticed, but it was impossible to miss. Being a widower hadn't made him blind. However, he still had plenty of common sense that reminded him that Laney had way too many secrets behind those cool blue eyes.

"The CSIs found a jammer," Owen went on a moment later. "That's how Dayton and or Gilley cut off the electricity."

She stayed quiet for a moment. "That proves I'm innocent. I wouldn't have needed to jam the power since I was already in the house." Her eyes widened. "Did you check to make sure Francine really had an emergency? Those men wanted me there, and they could have tricked Francine into leaving."

At least Laney wasn't accusing the nanny of any wrongdoing, but it was a clever observation. An accurate one, too. "The call from the nursing home was bogus." Of course, Francine hadn't learned that until she'd gotten there to check on her mom. By then, the attack at the ranch had already been in progress.

"More proof," Laney said under her breath. She looked up, her eyes meeting his. "If I wanted you dead, I wouldn't have kept Addie there. I would have told Francine I couldn't watch the girl so that Francine would have had to take Addie with her."

That was the way Owen had it figured, too, which was why he was leaning toward the conclusion that Laney was innocent. Of the attack anyway. But there was a boatload of other troubling concerns here. Not just the lies that she'd told him about her identity and work résumé, but there was also the problem with the accusation about Emerson.

"Go back over what you told me in the barn," Owen insisted. "Tell me about your half sister's murder."

This would be a third round of Laney doing that, but thanks to an emailed report he'd gotten from the San

Antonio PD in the past hour, Owen knew that Hadley's death had indeed been ruled a murder. She'd died from blunt-force trauma to the head. No eyewitnesses, no suspects. Well, no official suspects for SAPD. Laney clearly felt differently about that.

"Hadley and Emerson had an affair." Laney stared at him. "I'm not going to change my story, no matter how many times you have me repeat it."

That was what he figured, but this was another square filler, like calling out his identity to the intruder. It was especially necessary because she'd lied to him about who she was.

Something that still riled him to the core.

Hell, here he was a cop, and he hadn't known one of his employees was living under an alias. Of course, there was no way he would have hired her had he known who she was and what she was after. That got Owen thinking—exactly what was she after anyway?

"Did you think I was covering up about my brother-in-law?" he asked.

"Yes." Her answer came quickly, causing him to huff. If she truly believed Emerson had murdered her sister, then she'd just accused Owen of assorted felonies by not reporting the crime and obstructing justice. An accusation she must have realized because her gaze darted away. "I know you're close to him."

Yeah, he was. Emerson had helped him get through Naomi's death. Those days had been so dark, Owen would have slid right down into the deepest, darkest hole if it hadn't been for Addie and Emerson.

Of course, Emerson had been grieving, too, since he'd lost his only sister that day. Naomi and Emerson had been close, and while Owen didn't have the deep connection with Emerson that Naomi had, Owen respected the man, especially after Naomi's death when Emerson and he had been drawn together in grief. Maybe "misery loves company" had worked for both of them. Though there were times when Owen wondered if anything had actually worked. The grief could still slice through him.

"Tell me why you think Emerson killed Hadley," Owen demanded. "And stick to only what you can prove. Gut feelings don't count here."

Her mouth tightened a little. "Hadley told me it got ugly when her relationship with Emerson was over. Like I said, she threatened to tell his wife, and then Emerson threatened her. He said he'd hurt her if she didn't keep her mouth shut."

Emerson could have a hot head. Owen had even been on the receiving end of one of his punches in high school when they'd disagreed over the score in a pick-up basketball game. But it was a big stretch to go from a punch to hurting a woman, much less killing her.

"That isn't proof," Owen quickly pointed out. "It's hearsay."

Laney didn't dodge his gaze this time. "I have pictures."

That got his attention. There'd been nothing about that in the police report. "Pictures?" he challenged.

She nodded. "Of Emerson and Hadley together." Another pause, then she mumbled something he didn't catch. "Hadley told me about them and said she kept them in a safe-deposit box."

Owen wasn't sure what to react to first. That there could be pictures or that this was the first he was hearing about it. "And you didn't bother to tell the cops that?" he snarled.

"I did tell them, but I didn't know where they were. Hadley hadn't given me the name of the bank where she had the box." Her forehead bunched up. "I didn't ask, either, because I didn't know how important those pictures were going to become."

"They still might not be important. If the photos exist, they could possibly be proof of an affair and nothing more." Though it twisted at his insides to think Emerson could have cheated on his wife.

Laney made a sound of disagreement. "They're important. Because they're the first step in proving that Emerson carried through on his threat to hurt her."

Owen glanced at the key on the chain around her neck and groaned. "That's for the safe-deposit box?"

Her response wasn't so quick this time. "Yes, I believe it is. And I'll give it to the cops when I find out which bank has the photos. By cops, I mean the San Antonio Police, not anyone who has a personal connection to Emerson."

Of course. Laney wouldn't trust him with the key because she believed he would tip off Emerson. Or destroy the pictures.

He wouldn't.

If Owen did find something like that, he would do his job. But he doubted he could convince Laney of that. Doubted, too, that he could convince her of anything else right now.

"If there are photos and a safe-deposit box, they could be anywhere," he pointed out. "You need help finding them… Joe Henshaw's helping you with that."

She nodded. "He's a PI, too, and we became friends

in a grief support group. He lost both his parents when they were murdered. Sorry," Laney added.

The apology was no doubt because his father had been murdered, too, about a year ago, not long after Owen had lost his wife. His father had been gunned down by an unknown perp who was still out there. Owen had hope, though, that the case would be solved since they had an eyewitness. Too bad the witness had received a head injury and couldn't remember squat about what had happened. But maybe one day she would remember.

One day.

Even though it had nearly killed Owen to lose Naomi, it was a deeper cut to lose his father. Naomi's death had been a medical problem. A blood clot that had formed during delivery. But his dad's life had been purposely taken. Murdered. And all of Owen's skills learned in training as a cop hadn't been able to stop it. Or bring the killer to justice.

Owen pushed that all aside, as he usually did when it came to his father, and went to the next item he needed to discuss with Laney.

"Tell me about Terrance McCoy."

She raked her finger over her eyebrow and shifted her posture a little. "SAPD told you about the restraining order." That was all she said for several moments. But yes, they had. "Then you also know that Terrance was a former client who wasn't happy with the outcome of an investigation I did for him."

That was a lukewarm explanation of a situation that had gotten pretty intense. Apparently, Terrance had hired Laney to do a thorough background check on a woman he'd met on an online dating site. When Laney hadn't turned up any red flags, Terrance had continued to see the woman, who ultimately swindled him out of a sizable chunk of his trust fund. He blamed Laney for that and had even accused her of being in cahoots with the swindler. No proof of that, though.

"Terrance assaulted you," Owen reminded her, letting her know what info he'd been given about the restraining order. "And he's been out of jail for weeks now. He could have hired those men who came after you tonight."

She looked him in the eyes again when she agreed with him. "Yes, and Joe is looking for Terrance now."

Apparently that had come up in the short conversation she'd had with Joe. Or maybe Joe agreed that Terrance was definitely a person of interest here.

"The San Antonio cops are looking for Terrance, too," Owen added.

After what had just happened, Terrance was at the top of their list of suspects. Ditto for anyone else Laney might have rubbed the wrong way. There were maybe other former clients out there. Dangerous ones. And because of the danger to Laney, Owen wasn't going to forget that Addie had been put in danger, too.

"I hate to ask, because I know it's just going to rile you even more than you already are," Laney said, "but could this be about your father?"

Yes, he'd considered it. Briefly. And then he'd dismissed it, and Owen was pretty sure the dismissal had been objective. Hard to be completely objective when it came to that kind of raw grief, but he thought he'd managed it.

"I'll be investigating all angles," Owen assured her.

But he'd be looking especially hard at any of those directly connected to Laney.

Laney and Owen both glanced up when there was movement in the doorway of his office. She practically jumped to her feet when she saw their visitor.

Emerson.

The man was wearing a rumpled suit, sporting some dark stubble and equally dark circles beneath his eyes. Emerson looked about as happy to be there as Owen was.

It probably wasn't a surprise to Laney that Owen had called his brother-in-law. Nor was it a surprise that Emerson had come. It'd taken him a couple of hours to get there because he'd had to drive in from Austin where he'd been away on a business trip.

Emerson frowned at Laney after sparing her only a glance, and then he looked at Owen. "Please tell me you have her accusations cleared up by now so I can go home and get some sleep."

"He hasn't cleared it up." Laney jumped in to answer before Owen could respond.

Emerson gave a weary sigh and rubbed his hand over his face. "Has she given you any proof whatsoever?" he asked.

Owen went still. It was a simple enough question, but it didn't feel like the right thing to say. He would have preferred to hear Emerson belt out a denial, tacking on some outrage that anyone was accusing him of cheating on his wife. There was something else that bothered him, too.

"You know Laney?" Owen asked him. "Elaine," he corrected. He waited because he had already seen the recognition in Emerson's eyes.

"I know her," Emerson stormed. "She's the PI who pestered me with calls about her sister. I told her to back off or I'd get a restraining order."

Arching his eyebrow, Owen shifted his attention to Laney and she acknowledged that with a nod. So, before tonight, Emerson had known about Laney's accusations, but he hadn't said a word about it to Owen. Something he should have done. Then again, maybe Emerson hadn't considered Laney enough of a credible threat.

"Emerson?" a woman called out, causing the man to groan.

Owen wasn't pleased, either, or especially surprised when Emerson's wife, Nettie, came hurrying through the front door, heading straight for them. "When you didn't answer your cell, I called the house, looking for you," Owen explained to Emerson. "Nettie answered, but I didn't tell her about Laney or the attack."

Emerson nodded and gave a resigned sigh. "Something like this won't stay quiet for long."

No. It wouldn't. And Nettie's expression was sporting a lot of concern. Ditto for the rest of her. Nettie was usually dressed to the nines, but tonight she was in yoga pants and a T-shirt. Her blond hair hadn't been combed and her eyes were red, as if she'd been crying.

"God, you're all right." Nettie threw herself into Emerson's arms. "I was so worried."

Owen glanced at Laney, and as expected, she was studying the couple. There was a different kind of worry and concern on her face. She was looking at them the way a cop would. No doubt to see if there were any signs that this was a marriage on the rocks because of a cheating husband. No signs, though. Emerson brushed a loving kiss on Nettie's forehead before he eased her away from him.

"Could you give Owen and me a minute alone?" Emerson asked his wife. "I won't be long. It's business."

Nettie studied him a moment and nodded before her attention went to Owen. Then Laney. There was no recognition in Nettie's icy gray eyes.

"I'll wait by the reception desk," Nettie said. She whispered something to Emerson, kissed him and then walked out of the office.

Emerson didn't do or say anything until his wife was out of earshot and then he tipped his head to Laney. "Anything she tells you about me is a lie, and I've wasted enough of my time dealing with her. Are you okay?" Emerson added to Owen. "Is Addie okay?"

Again, that bothered Owen. As Addie's uncle, it should have been the first thing for Emerson to ask. Of course, Owen had verified the okay status when he'd had a quick chat with Emerson earlier, so maybe Emerson thought that was enough.

But it wasn't. At least it didn't feel like it was.

Owen silently cursed. He hated that Laney had given him any doubts about Emerson. Especially since there was no proof.

"Addie's fine," Owen answered. "Francine said she would text me if Addie has any nightmares or such." Owen cursed that, too, but this time it wasn't silent. Because there could indeed be nightmares.

"I'll check on her first thing in the morning," Emerson volunteered. "Anything else you need or want me to do?"

Owen muttered his thanks and then nodded. "You'll have to make a statement about Laney's accusations."

Emerson gave another of those weary sighs. "I'll come by in the morning to do that, too."

Owen was about to ask him to go ahead and do it now. That way, Laney couldn't say that he'd given Emerson preferential treatment. Of course, she'd likely say that anyway. However, he didn't even get a chance to bring it up because Kellan appeared in the doorway. One look at his brother's face and Owen knew that something else was wrong.

"I just got off the phone with San Antonio PD," Kellan said, looking not at Emerson or Owen but at Laney. "They found your assistant, Joe Henshaw." Kellan paused. "He's dead."

Chapter 4

The shock felt to Laney like arctic ice covering her body. She blinked repeatedly—hoping she had misunderstood Kellan, that this was some kind of cop trick to unnerve her. But she knew from the look in his eyes that it was the truth.

"Oh, God." That was all she managed to say. There wasn't enough breath for her to add more, but the questions came immediately and started fighting their way through the veil of grief.

"How?" she mouthed.

Kellan's forehead bunched up, but he spoke the words fast. "He was murdered. Two gunshot wounds to the chest. That's all we know at this point because the ME has just started his examination."

Murdered. Joe had been murdered. The grief came, washing over her and going bone-deep.

"Joe's apartment had been ransacked," Kellan added a moment later. "Someone was obviously looking for something."

"Terrance," Laney rasped, though first, she had to swallow hard. "Joe was looking for him, and Terrance could have done this."

Since neither Owen or Kellan seemed surprised by that, she guessed they'd already come to the same conclusion. Good. If that snake was responsible, she wanted him to pay. But then if Terrance had killed Joe, he'd done it to get back at her.

She was responsible.

This time she wasn't able to choke back the sob and Laney clamped onto her bottom lip to make sure there wasn't another one. Sobs and tears wouldn't help now. Not when she needed answers. Later, when Owen and Kellan weren't around, she could fall apart.

"The San Antonio cops found him in his apartment," Kellan went on. "It appears someone broke in and killed him when he stepped from the shower. No defensive wounds, so it happened fast."

That last part was probably meant to comfort her. To let her know that Joe hadn't suffered. But in that instant, he would have seen his attacker and known he was about to die.

And all because of her.

Joe had not only been looking for Terrance, he'd also been looking for the safe-deposit box with those pictures. Someone had killed him because he'd been following her orders.

Laney groped around behind her to locate the chair because she was afraid her legs were about to give way. Owen helped with that by taking hold of her arm to help her sit. He was studying her, maybe to gauge her reaction. That was when she glanced at Emerson, who was doing the same thing.

"I suppose you'll say I had something to do with this, too?" Emerson snapped, his words ripe with anger.

Laney didn't have a comeback. Couldn't even manage a glare for taking a swipe at her when she'd been dealt such a hard blow. But then the swipe only confirmed for her exactly what kind of person Emerson was. Not the sterling, upstanding DA of Longview Ridge. A man who was capable of striking out like that could be capable of doing other things, too. Like cheating on his wife. Of course, it was a huge leap to go from that to murder, but Laney wasn't taking him off her very short suspect list.

"Emerson," Owen said, no anger in his voice, though there seemed to be a low warning, "come back tomorrow and I'll take your statement."

Owen got a slight jab, too, when Emerson flicked him an annoyed glance. However, the man finally turned and walked out. Kellan looked at Emerson. Then at Owen. Finally at her.

She had no idea what Kellan was thinking, but something passed between him and Owen. One of those unspoken conversations that siblings could have. Or rather, she supposed that was what it was. She'd never quite managed to have a relationship like that with Hadley.

"SAPD will want to talk to Laney tomorrow," Kellan said to Owen. He checked his watch. "But it's late. Why don't you go ahead and take Laney to the ranch so you two can try to get some rest?"

Laney practically jumped to her feet. "No. I can't go there. It could put Addie in danger."

"We're taking precautions," Kellan assured her. "And I didn't say to take you to Owen's but rather the ranch. You can't go back to Owen's place because the CSIs are there processing the scene, but our grandparents' house is in the center of the property. No one lives there on a regular basis, so it's been kept up for company, seasonal ranch hands and such. Plus, it has a good security system. Addie, Francine, Gunnar and Jack are headed there now."

Jack was Kellan and Owen's brother. And he was also a marshal. Another lawman. But that didn't mean Laney could trust him.

"What about your fiancée?" she asked Kellan. Laney knew her name was Gemma, and she'd met her several times. "She shouldn't be alone at your place."

"She won't be. She'll be going to my grandparents' house, too. Eli's taking her there."

Eli was yet another brother and a Texas Ranger. So, she would be surrounded by Slater lawmen. Not exactly a comforting thought, but it could be worse. As Addie's uncles, they'd do whatever it took to protect the baby.

"I'll have two reserve deputies drive Owen and you, and once Eli and Jack are in place at the ranch, I can have them come back here to help with the investigation," Kellan told them. "With Owen at our grandparents' house, Addie won't have to be away from her dad."

Until he'd added that last part, Laney had been ready to outright refuse. She hadn't wanted to do anything to put the child in more danger, or to separate father from child. Still, this was dangerous.

"There's a gunman at large," she reminded him. "If he comes after me again, I shouldn't be anywhere near Addie, Gemma or Francine."

Owen stared at her a moment. "Whoever sent that gunman could try to use Addie to get to you. They would have seen the way you reacted, the way you tried to protect her. They would know she's your weak spot."

Addie was indeed that. It had crushed Laney to think of the baby being hurt.

Owen dragged in a weary breath before he continued, "It'll be easier to protect you both at the same time, and it'll tie up fewer resources for Kellan. He needs all the help he can get here in the office to work the investigation and try to get a confession out of Rohan Gilley."

She mentally went through what he was saying and hated that it made sense. Hated even more that she didn't have a reasonable counterargument. She was exhausted, and it felt as if someone had clamped a fist around her heart. Still, Laney didn't want to do anything else to hurt Owen's precious little girl.

"I'm a PI," Laney reminded Owen. Reminded herself, too. "I can arrange for my own security. I'll be okay."

She saw the anger flash in Owen's eyes, which were the color of a fierce storm cloud. "I don't need to remind you that your assistant is dead. Or that you're in danger. So I'd rather you not add to this miserable night by lying to yourself. Or to me—*again*. When it comes to me, you've already met your quota of lies."

This was more than a swipe like the one Emerson had given her. Much more. Not just because it was true but especially because it was coming from Owen. It drained what little fight she had left in her and that was why Laney didn't argue any more when Owen gathered up his things and led her out the front door to a waiting cruiser.

Obviously, Kellan and Owen had been certain they could talk her into this. Which they had.

"This is Manuel Garcia and Amos Turner, the reserve deputies," Owen said when he hurried Laney into the back seat with him. The deputies were in the front.

Laney recognized both of them. That was because whenever she was in town or dealing with the other ranchers, she'd kept her eyes and ears open. For all the good it'd done. Owen's ranch had been attacked, Joe was dead and she was no closer to the truth than she had been when she'd lied her way into getting a job with Owen.

It would have been so easy to slip right into the grief, fear and regret. The trifecta of raw emotions was like a perfect storm closing in on her. But giving in to it would only lead to tears and a pity party, neither of which would help.

"I'm sorry," she said to Owen. That might not help, either, but she had to start somewhere. "Believe me when I say I didn't mean for any of this to happen."

The interior of the cruiser was dimly lit, yet she could clearly see Owen's eyes when he looked at her. Still storm gray. It was a different kind of intensity than what was usually there. When he'd looked at her before—before he'd known who she was and the lies she'd told him—there'd been...well, heat. Though he might not admit it, she'd certainly seen it.

And felt it.

Laney had dismissed it. Or rather she had just accepted it. After all, Owen was from the superior Slater gene pool, and the DNA had given him a face that hadn't skimped on the good looks. The thick black hair, those piercing eyes, that mouth that looked capable of doing many pleasurable things.

She dismissed those looks again now and silently cursed herself for allowing them to even play into this. She had no right to see him as anything but a former boss who had zero trust in her. Maybe if she mentally repeated that enough, her body would start to accept it.

"Believe me when I say I'm sorry," she repeated in a whisper, forcing her attention away from him and to the window.

Some long moments crawled by before he said anything. "You were close to your assistant, Joe Henshaw?"

The question threw her. Of course, she hadn't forgotten about Joe, but she'd figured that learning more about the man hadn't been on the top of Owen's to-do list. Plus, he hadn't even mentioned whether or not he would start to accept her apology.

"We were close enough, I suppose," she answered. "He worked for me about a year, and I trusted him to do the jobs I assigned him to do."

"Did he ever come to my ranch?" Owen fired back as soon as she'd answered.

Oh, she got it then. Laney knew the reason he'd brought up the subject. He wanted to measure the depth of her lies. "No. I only had phone contact with Joe when I worked for you. I didn't bring anyone to the ranch," she added.

From his reflection in the mirror, she could see that he was staring at her as if waiting for her to say more. Exactly what, she didn't know. When she turned back to him, Laney still didn't have a clue.

"I just want to know who and what I'm dealing with," Owen clarified. "Joe was your lover?"

"No." She couldn't say that fast enough and shook her head, not able to connect the dots on this one. "He worked for me, *period.*"

Now it was Owen who looked away. "Just wanted to make sure I wasn't dealing with something more personal here."

"You mean like a lover's spat gone wrong," she muttered. The fact he had even considered that twisted away at her almost as much as the regret over lying to him.

"No. Like Terrance McCoy killing your assistant as a way of getting back at you."

Everything inside Laney stilled. Only for a moment, though. Before the chill came again. Mercy. She hadn't even considered that. But she should have. She was so tied up in knots over Emerson having killed Hadley that she hadn't looked at this through a cop's eyes. Something she'd always prided herself on being able to do. She'd never quite managed it with Hadley, though.

"Hadley's my blind spot." Laney groaned softly and pushed her hair away from her face.

She steeled herself to have Owen jump down her throat about that, to give her a lecture about loss of objectivity and such. But he didn't say anything. Laney waited, staring at him. Or rather, staring at the back of his head because his attention was on the window.

"Addie's my blind spot," he said several long moments later. "I didn't want her in the middle of whatever this hell this is, but she's there."

Laney had to speak around the lump in her throat. "Because of me."

"No. Because of whoever hired those men to come to my house and go after you." He paused, turning so they were facing each other. Their gazes met. Held. "Don't ever lie to me again."

Not trusting her voice, Laney nodded and felt something settle between them. A truce. Not a complete one, but it was a start. If she was going to get to the bottom of what was going on, she needed Owen's help and, until a few seconds ago, she hadn't been sure she would get it.

The deputy took the turn off the main road to the Slater Ranch, which sprawled through a good chunk of the county. Kellan ran the main operation, just as six generations of his family had done, but Owen and his brothers Jack and Eli helped as well, along with running their own smaller ranches.

Separate but still family, all the way to the core.

It occurred to her that she might have to go up against all those Slater lawmen if it did indeed come down to pinning this on Emerson. But Laney was too exhausted to think about that particular battle right now.

"For the record," she said, "I told you the truth about most things. I grew up with horses, so I know how to train them. And every minute I spent with Addie—that was genuine. I enjoyed being with her. Francine, too," she added because the part about Addie sounded...personal.

A muscle flickered in Owen's jaw. "What about the day in the barn?" He immediately cursed and waved that off.

When he turned back to the window, she knew the subject was off-limits, but it wasn't out of mind. Not out of her mind anyway. And she did not need him to clarify which barn, which day. It'd been about a month earlier after he'd just finished riding his favorite gelding, Alamo. Owen had been tired and sweaty, and he'd peeled off his shirt to wash off with the hose. She'd walked in on him just as the water had been sluicing down his bare chest.

Laney had frozen. Then her mouth had gone dry.

Owen had looked at her and it had seemed as if time had stopped. It had been the only thing that had stopped, though. Laney had always known her boss was a hot cowboy, but she'd gotten a full dose of it that day. A kicked-up pulse. That slide of heat through her body.

The physical need she felt for him.

She hadn't done a good job of hiding it, either. Laney had seen it on his face and, for just a second—before he'd been able to rein it in—she had seen the same thing in Owen's eyes.

Neither had said anything. Laney had calmly dropped off the saddle she'd been carrying and walked out. But she'd known that if she hadn't been lying to him, that if they'd been sitting here now, with no secrets between them, she would have gone to him. She would have welcomed the body-to-body contact when he pulled her into his arms. And she would have let Owen have her.

Owen knew that, too.

Just as they had done that day in the barn, their gazes connected now. They didn't speak, and his attention shifted away from her just as his phone dinged with a text message.

"Jack's got Francine and Addie all settled in," Owen relayed. He showed her the picture that his brother had included with the text. It was of Addie, who was sound asleep.

Laney smiled. Addie looked so peaceful and, while

it didn't lessen her guilt over the attack, at least the little girl didn't seem to be showing any signs of stress.

Laney was still smiling when she looked up at Owen and realized he had noticed her reaction. And perhaps didn't approve.

Despite that shared "barn memory" moment, he probably didn't want her feeling close to his daughter. Laney certainly couldn't blame him. She was about to bring up the subject again about her making other arrangements for a place to stay, but Owen's phone rang.

It was Kellan and, while Owen didn't put the call on speaker, it was easy for Laney to hear the sheriff's voice in an otherwise quiet cruiser.

"Just got a call from the CSI out at your place," Kellan said. "They found something."

Chapter 5

A listening device.

That was what the CSIs had found in the bedroom of the guesthouse where Laney had been living. Owen figured the thug who'd broken in had planted it there, but that didn't tell him why. What had those men been after? What had been so important for them to hear that they'd been willing to risk not only a break-in but also a shoot-out with a cop?

It was those questions and more that had raced through his mind half the night.

The other half he'd spent worrying if he'd done the right thing by bringing Laney here to his grandparents' old house. He needed to talk to Kellan about other options, but he figured his brother was getting some much-needed sleep right now. Owen hoped he was anyway, since Kellan had opted to stay the night at the sheriff's office.

Owen got out of the bed he'd positioned right next to Addie's crib—one they had borrowed from Francine's friend. Addie was still sacked out, thank goodness, and since it was only 5:00 a.m., she should stay that way for a while. Just in case she woke up, though, he took the baby monitor with him into the adjoining bathroom. Francine had a monitor, too, and she was right across the hall, bunking with Laney in the master bedroom. Gemma was in the only other bedroom upstairs.

Owen grabbed a quick shower, dressed and headed downstairs to make coffee, but someone had already beat him to it. Someone had obviously beat him to getting up, too, because Eli and Jack were at the kitchen table, drinking coffee. They looked as if they'd been at it for a while.

"Get your beauty sleep?" Eli asked. His voice was like a grumbling drawl, and Owen figured the comment was just his way of showing brotherly "affection." Eli showed it a lot.

Owen had never been able to tell if Eli was truly just a badass or if he'd just been in a sour mood for the past decade. Either way, he appreciated him being here. The nice thing was, he didn't even have to say it. This was the sort of thing that family did for each other.

"The question should be—did our little brother get his beauty sleep *alone*?" Jack smiled as he gulped down more coffee.

Owen shot him a scowl, not completely made up of brotherly affection because he didn't like even joking about this. "I'm not having sex with Laney."

Both Eli and Jack raised eyebrows, causing Owen to curse and repeat the denial.

"Maybe you didn't last night…" Jack took his life into his own hands by continuing to smile.

"Never," Owen insisted, pouring himself some coffee as if he'd gone to battle with it. "Laney works for me—*worked* for me," he corrected. "And I shouldn't have to remind you that she lied to me about who she was."

"Yeah, but you didn't know about the lie until last night." Jack again. "There were plenty of nights before that when sex could have happened. Laney's a looker."

She was, and before he could rein it in, Owen got a flash of that look she'd had on her face when she'd seen him in the barn. There'd been a whole lot of lust in the air in that moment.

"Hard to believe you wouldn't go after her," Jack commented.

Owen's scowl got a whole lot worse. "Are you looking to get your butt busted before the sun even comes up?"

Of course, Jack smiled.

Eli shrugged and kept his attention on his coffee. "Well, then, if you're not interested in Laney, then maybe I'll ask her out."

Owen hadn't thought his scowl could get worse, but he'd been wrong. "Laney lied to me," Owen emphasized in case they'd both gone stupid and had forgotten. "And because she lied, I didn't know there was a possibility that thugs could come to my house."

Eli lifted his shoulder again. "Bet she didn't know it, either. Plus, she lied because she wants justice for her sister. A good cause even if she didn't go about it the right way." He paused. "She's taken some hard hits, and she's still standing. Sounds like my kind of woman." He gave a satisfied nod. "Yeah, I'll ask her out."

Owen felt the snap of anger as he caught Eli's arm, ready to drag him out of the chair. The fact that Jack kept smiling and Eli didn't punch him for the grab clued Owen into the fact that this had been some kind of test. A bad one.

"Told you Owen was attracted to her," Jack said with a smirk.

Yeah, a test, all right.

Eli shook off Owen's grip the same easy way he shrugged, took out his wallet and handed Jack a twenty. So, not just a test but also a bet. One involving his sex life.

Owen was about to return verbal fire, but the sound of footsteps stopped him, and a moment later Laney appeared in the doorway. She immediately froze, her gaze sliding over his brothers before it settled on him.

"Did something else happen? Is something wrong?" The words rushed out and alarm went through her eyes.

"No," Owen assured her. Nothing wrong other than him wanting to throttle his brothers.

Laney released the breath she'd obviously been holding and put the laptop she'd tucked beneath her arm on the table. "Good. That's good." She fluttered her fingers to the stairs. "Addie's still asleep, but Francine and Gemma are in there. Gemma wants to hold her when she wakes up."

Owen had suspected as much. His little girl would get lots of attention today. Too bad it was because of the attack. Addie had been in danger, and it was going to be a very long time before he or anyone else in his family got past that.

Laney looked at his brothers again, probably thinking she'd interrupted a sensitive conversation about the investigation. She hadn't, and there was no way in hell he'd tell her about the bet. But it was time for him to get his focus back where it belonged. Better to deal with the investigation than to notice the fit of the jeans Laney had borrowed from Gemma.

"The Ranger lab has the eavesdropping device," Owen said, turning to get her a mug from the cupboard. "They might be able to find where the info was being sent."

That eased some the alarm on her face, and she poured herself some coffee. "The audio was being sent to a receiver or computer?"

"It looks that way." And since he'd started this briefing, Owen added, "Terrance is coming in this morning."

"Terrance," she repeated, her voice strained. "I want to be there when you question him."

Owen shook his head. "I can't allow you in the interview room—"

"I can watch from the observation room." She paused, met his gaze. "I just want to hear what he has to say."

He didn't have to think too hard on this. Owen had to take Laney in to make a statement, so she'd already be in the building when Terrance arrived. Since there was no harm in her observing, he nodded and then tipped his head to the laptop. It, too, was a loaner from Gemma.

"Have you been able to access copies of the info you had stored on your computer?" he asked.

"Not yet. But I will. I've been going through Joe's files on our storage cloud."

Owen immediately saw the shimmer in her eyes. Not alarm this time. She was fighting back tears.

"I need to find Joe's killer." Her voice was just above a whisper. "I need to put an end to this so your life can get back to normal."

He nearly laughed. It'd been so long since he'd had normal, Owen wasn't sure that he'd recognize it. First, losing Naomi and becoming a single dad, and then losing his father. Yes, it had been a while.

"I emailed both Kellan and you the link and password to the files," Laney said a moment later. "Joe was more tech savvy than I am, so I'm hoping he has hidden files. It's a long shot, but something might turn up."

"Gemma could maybe help you with that," Jack said. "Or I know someone else who might be willing to take a look. She's in WITSEC, but she's got good computer skills."

"Caroline Moser," Laney provided.

Owen hadn't been sure that Laney would know who Jack was talking about, but Longview Ridge was a small town with lots of gossip. Plenty of people knew that Caroline and Jack had been lovers. In love, Owen mentally corrected. But Caroline had been injured in an attack and couldn't remember any of that. Ditto for not remembering the crime she'd witnessed.

His father's murder.

When Caroline got her memory back, they'd know the truth. Well, maybe. It was possible that she hadn't even seen the killer. Obviously she had recalled how to work a computer, so that was a good sign. What they needed, though, were a lot of good signs, not just for his dad's killer but also for the attack at his place.

"Don't involve Caroline in this just yet," Owen advised Jack. He wanted Caroline to concentrate on recovering so they could get those answers about his father even sooner.

Jack nodded in a suit-yourself gesture. "What about the gunman you have in custody? Rohan Gilley. He couldn't have killed Laney's assistant because he was in jail at the time, but maybe we can use the murder to twist him up a little? Maybe let him believe his boss is tying up loose ends and he could be next?"

It was a good angle, and Owen would definitely try it and others. It riled him that he might have to offer Gilley some kind of plea deal, but that might be the fastest way to put an end to whatever this was.

And that brought Owen to the next part of this conversation. A part that neither of his brothers was going to like. Neither did he, but it was something they needed to know.

"About a week ago, I asked a PI out of Austin to take a look at the file on Dad's murder," Owen started. "I just wanted someone with a fresh eye."

That definitely got Eli and Jack's attention. Laney's, too. "I'm guessing the PI didn't find anything or you would have told us," Jack remarked.

"You're right. But I have to consider that Dad's killer might have found out and decided a *fresh look* wasn't a good idea, that it would lead us to him or her."

Since his brothers didn't seem the least bit surprised by that, Owen knew they had already considered it.

"I do new runs on the info all the time," Eli commented. "Calls, going out to the crime scene, and I'm not quiet about it. It seems to me that if the killer was keeping tabs on us, he would have come after me. I'd be the easiest one to get to."

He would be. Unlike Jack, Kellan and him, Eli didn't have any full-time help on his place, only a couple of part-time hands who checked on his horses when he was working.

"I do runs, too," Jack interjected, "and if the killer came after one of us, I figure it'd be me. Because I'm the smartest," he added, no doubt to lighten the mood.

It didn't work, but then nothing could when it came to the hell they'd been through for the past year.

Owen finished off his coffee and put the cup in the dishwasher. "I'll go up and check on Addie." He looked at Laney. "Then I'll call the reserve deputies to escort us to the sheriff's office so I can get ready for Terrance's interview. You can give your statement while we're waiting for him."

Owen headed for the stairs, but he only made it a few steps before his phone rang, and he saw Kellan's name on the screen. The call got his brothers and Laney's attention, because they all looked at him. Waiting.

Since this could be an update on the investigation, he went ahead and put it on speaker.

"Eli, Jack and Laney are here," Owen said in greeting to let Kellan know their conversation wouldn't be private.

Kellan didn't hesitate. "The lab just called and they found where the info from the eavesdropping device was being sent." Kellan paused and cursed softly. "You should come on in so we can discuss how to handle this."

Owen silently groaned. If Terrance was behind this,

then Kellan would have quickly volunteered that information. "Did Emerson set the bug?" Owen came out and asked.

"No." Kellan paused again. "But according to the crime lab, his wife did."

Nettie Keaton.

The woman's name just kept going through Laney's head while she drove with Owen and the reserve deputies to the sheriff's office. And there were questions that kept repeating, too.

Why had Nettie done something like this? Had the woman also been responsible for the attack?

Not only was Nettie the DA's wife, she was also Owen's sister-in-law. Family. From all accounts, Nettie had been there for Owen after he'd lost his wife and had even taken care of Addie until Owen had been able to find a nanny. It was an understatement that their tight relationship wouldn't make the interview with her pleasant. But Laney hoped that it would be objective, that Owen would dig hard to get to the truth.

"The CSIs didn't find dust on the listening device," Owen said, reading from the report that Kellan had messaged him just as they were leaving the house. "But since it'd been planted beneath the center drawer of your desk, it's possible dust wouldn't have had time to accumulate on it."

In other words, there was no way to pinpoint how long it had been there. It turned Laney's stomach to think that maybe it had possibly been there for weeks. Or maybe even the entire time she'd worked for Owen. Of course, that only led to another question—had Nettic known who she was when she'd come to Longview Ridge?

Laney had already searched back through her memory to try to figure out if her sister had ever mentioned meeting Nettie. She didn't think so, but Hadley hadn't told her everything.

"The audio feed from the listening device was going to a computer registered to Nettie," Owen noted.

Yes, she'd already come to that conclusion from what Kellan had said earlier. "I'm assuming Kellan will get a search warrant for it?" she asked.

Owen looked up from the report and his eyes narrowed for just a moment. Then he glanced away as if frustrated. "Kellan and I aren't wearing blinders when it comes to Nettie. If she's done something wrong, we'll get to the bottom of it."

After just seeing his reaction, Laney didn't doubt that part, but there was another layer there. Some more fallout. Because this could add another family scar on top of plenty of other wounds.

"Emerson knew who you were," Owen said a moment later. "If Nettie did, too, then this could have been her way of keeping tabs on you. It doesn't make it right," he quickly added. "But if she was worried about you coming after Emerson, that could be her justification for doing it."

True, and Nettie wouldn't have had trouble getting into the guesthouse. Heck, she probably had a key. There'd been plenty of times when Laney had been in the pasture working with a horse and wouldn't have been near the guesthouse. Nettie could have easily gotten in without anyone noticing.

Owen's gaze came back to her. "Of course, you know

I don't believe Nettie would put me or Addie in danger by sending those thugs to the ranch. And I just can't see her hiring a hitman to go after your assistant."

Laney gave that some thought and considered something else that Owen wasn't going to like. "Maybe she didn't think things would go that far. You were still at work, and she might have thought Francine would take Addie with her to the nursing home. She might have *justified* what she did by believing her niece wouldn't be in harm's way."

A muscle flickered in his jaw, but his eyes didn't narrow again. Nor did he dismiss what she was saying. That meant he'd likely already considered it. *Was considering it*, she amended. It wouldn't be easy for him, but he would do what was right. So would she. And maybe what they found wouldn't hurt him even more than he already had been.

The reserve deputy pulled to a stop in front of the sheriff's office. When they went inside, Laney steeled herself to face Nettie and Emerson, who would almost certainly be there with his wife. But they weren't in the waiting area.

However, Terrance was.

When he looked at her and smiled, Laney forced herself not to take a step back and kept her shoulders squared. That was hard to do. Even though she hated feeling it, Laney remembered the way he'd attacked her, that look in his eyes clearly letting her know he'd wanted to kill her.

Terrance was masking that look today. Maybe because he no longer hated her, or perhaps he'd just managed to rein it in. If so, Laney needed to do some restraining of her own. It was best not to show any signs of fear or weakness around a man like Terrance.

It was the first time she'd seen Terrance since she'd testified against him at his trial for assaulting her. That'd been six months ago and his short stint in jail hadn't changed him much. With his acne-scarred face and beaked nose, he was still a very unattractive man in an expensive suit.

Next to Terrance was another suit and someone else she recognized. The bald guy reading something on his phone was Terrance's lawyer. He, too, had been at the trial and had tried every dirty trick in the book to have his client declared not guilty. It hadn't worked, which was probably why the man gave her an unmistakable sneer.

"Laney," Terrance greeted her, getting to his feet. "Did I scare you?" That oily smile still bent his mouth a little.

"No." Laney made sure she looked him straight in the eyes. "Why should I be afraid of you? We both know if you touch me again, you'll spend a lot longer than six months in a cage."

Terrance's washed-out blue eyes dismissed her with a glance before he turned to Owen. "I'm guessing you must be Deputy Slater, the local yokel who ordered me here for an interview?"

"Deputy Slater," Owen confirmed, ignoring the insult as Terrance had ignored Laney's comment. Instead he looked at Kellan, who was stepping into the doorway of his office. "I was about to send our guests to an interview room where they can wait until you're ready to talk to them."

"We've already waited long enough," Terrance snapped.

"And you'll wait some more. Interview room." Owen pointed up the hall, his voice and body language an order for them to go there. "Since you're on probation, it probably wouldn't be a good idea for you not to co-operate with the cops. Even when they're local yokels," he added a heartbeat later.

Apparently, Owen hadn't ignored the insult after all, and it caused Laney to smile. Not for long, though. She spotted Nettie sitting in Kellan's office. Terrance, who looked in at the woman, too, as his lawyer and he walked past Kellan, cast a glance at Laney over his shoulder. She wasn't quite sure what to make of that look, but she dismissed it when Nettie jumped to her feet.

"You planted that bug so that I'd get blamed for it," Nettie immediately blurted. "Well, you won't get away with it. I won't have you telling lies about me."

Laney had already considered that Nettie might try to blame her for this, but it was odd that the woman was the one making the denial. Laney had thought it would come from Emerson first.

As she'd done with Terrance, Laney faced Nettie head-on. "I didn't plant a bug, didn't tell lies about you and I certainly didn't have men fire shots at Addie, Owen and me."

There was a bright fire of anger in Nettie's eyes as she glared at Laney before snapping at Owen. "Please tell me you don't believe her."

Owen dragged in a breath and put his hands on his hips. "I believe her. Laney could have been killed in that attack, so she's not the one who set this up."

Nettie opened her mouth, closed it and then made a sound of frustration that might or might not have been genuine.

"I have no motive to plant a bug and link it to you," Laney reminded the woman.

"But you're wrong about that. You do have a motive. This could be your way of getting back at Emerson."

That got Laney's attention and she stared at Nettie.

Nettie practically froze, but Laney could see the woman quickly gathering her composure. "I don't know exactly what grudge you have against my husband," Nettie amended, "but I believe that's why you're here. Why you came to Longview Ridge. Whatever it is you think about him, you're wrong. Emerson's a good man."

"Is he?" Laney challenged.

Nettie made a sound of outrage and turned to Kellan this time. "Can't you see that I'm being set up?" She flung a perfectly manicured finger at Laney. "And that she's the one who's trying to make me look guilty of something I didn't do."

Kellan dragged in his own long breath. "The eavesdropping device was linked to a computer registered to you. Before Owen and Laney came in, I told you that I needed to have the CSIs do a search of your house to find that computer—"

"No." Nettie practically shouted that and then, on a groan, sank down into the chair next to Kellan's desk. "If you do that, then Emerson will know about these ridiculous allegations."

Owen and Laney exchanged glances. "Emerson doesn't know?" Owen asked, looking first at Nettie and then Kellan.

Kellan shook his head. "Nettie asked me to hold off telling him until she had a chance to clear this up."

"I don't want Emerson bothered by this nonsense," Nettie piped in.

"There's no way around that," Kellan assured her. "I have probable cause to get a search warrant, and I'll get it. The lab will go through all the computers in your home and, from the preliminary info gathered, there'll be a program to link to the eavesdropping device found in the guesthouse where Laney lives."

Laney braced herself for another onslaught of Nettie's temper, but the woman stayed quiet for a moment. "Someone must have broken into my house and added the program," Nettie finally said and then her gaze slashed back to Laney. "You did it. You broke in when I wasn't there so you could set me up."

Laney sighed and was about to repeat that she had no motive, but Owen spoke first. "Just let the CSIs look at the computers and we'll go from there. The techs will be able to tell when the program was installed, and if someone did that while you weren't there, then you might have an alibi."

Nettie didn't jump to agree to that and nibbled on her bottom lip for a few seconds. "Would Emerson have to know?"

Kellan groaned, scrubbed his hand over his face. "Yes. He's the DA, and even if he wasn't, this sort of thing would still get around."

Yes, it would get around, and then Emerson would likely hit the roof when he found out that CSIs were in his house looking for evidence against his wife. Laney was betting he'd accuse her just as Nettie had done.

"You're right," Nettie said several long moments

later. Instead of nibbling on her bottom lip, it trembled. "Someone will tell him, but he'll know I don't have any reason to plant a bug. Emerson will be on my side. He won't believe I could do anything like this because I just wouldn't."

Laney didn't know Nettie that well, but it seemed as if the woman was trying to convince herself of Emerson's blind support. She decided to press that to see if it led to anything.

"Emerson's never mentioned me to you?" Laney asked.

Nettie's head whipped up. "What do you mean?" The anger had returned and had multiplied.

Laney decided to just stare at the woman and wait for her to answer. Kellan and Owen obviously decided to do the same, and their reaction brought Nettie back to her feet. However, the fiery eyes stayed firmly planted on Laney.

"I know you've told lies about my husband," Nettie said, her tone sharp, edgy. "I don't know the details, but I've heard talk. It's lies. All lies."

So, Emerson hadn't told his wife about his affair with Hadley. Of course, that probably wasn't something he'd wanted to discuss with her, especially since Emerson was claiming he was innocent.

Nettie hiked up her chin. "I suppose you want some kind of statement from me about that bug?" she asked Kellan.

He nodded. "And permission to search your house for the computers. If I don't get permission, then I'll have no choice but to get the warrant. Then plenty of people will know about this."

She squeezed her eyes shut, her mouth tightening

as she took out her phone. "Let me call Emerson first." Nettie didn't wait for permission to do that. She walked out of the office, through the squad room and to the reception desk before she made her call.

Laney turned to Owen to get his take, but before she could say anything, she spotted Terrance again. He was outside the door of the interview room—where he could have heard the conversation they'd just had with Nettie.

"I don't owe you any favors," Terrance said to Laney, "but I'm going to do one for you anyway."

"What favor?" Laney didn't bother to tone down her very skeptical attitude.

Terrance gave her another of those slick smiles. "A couple of months before my trial, my legal team started gathering information that they thought would help with my defense. They hired PIs to follow you and people connected to you."

Laney's heart sped up. Hadley had been murdered just a month before Terrance's trial. Terrance had an airtight alibi for the murder—he'd been at a party and there were dozens of witnesses. But his PIs could have seen something.

"Did you know you were being followed?" Owen asked her.

Laney shook her head, her attention still fixed on Terrance. "You know who killed my sister?" She heard the quiver in her voice, felt the shudder slide through her body.

"No. But my lawyers were having Hadley followed. Not full-time but on and off to see if there was something they could use to prove my innocence."

"Cut to the chase," Owen demanded. "What the hell do you know about Laney's sister?"

Terrance smiled again when he tipped his head to Nettie. "Why don't you ask her?" He continued before any of them could attempt to answer, "The DA's wife was with Hadley the night she was murdered."

Chapter 6

Owen stared at Terrance, trying to figure out the angle as to why the man had just tossed them that lie. But there was nothing in Terrance's expression or body language to indicate that he was telling them anything but the truth.

Hell.

Was it actually true? Had Nettie not only known Hadley but also met with her?

Owen shifted his attention to Laney and noted that hers was a different kind of body language. A highly skeptical one. She huffed, folded her arms over her chest and stared at Terrance.

"Why would you volunteer that information to me?" Laney demanded.

It was a good starting point as questions went, but Owen had plenty of others for the man. And then he would need to confront Nettie if he felt there was any shred of truth to what Terrance had just said.

Terrance flashed the same smile he'd been doling out since Laney and Owen had first laid eyes on the man in the sheriff's office. He was a slick snake, the type of man who assaulted a woman, and Owen had to rein in his temper because he wanted to punch that self-righteous smile off Terrance's smug face. That wasn't going to solve anything, though, and would make things a whole lot worse.

"I volunteered the info because I'm doing my civic duty," Terrance answered, and there was nothing sincere in his tone. "As Deputy Slater pointed out, I'm on probation. Withholding potential evidence could be interpreted as obstruction of justice. I wouldn't want that, because it could violate the terms of my parole."

Owen stepped closer and met Terrance eye to eye. "Yet if this so-called evidence is true, you withheld it for months."

Terrance lifted his hands palms up. "I've been in jail and I've been focusing my time and energy on… rehabilitation."

"My client didn't know the information was important," the lawyer added. When he took a step closer, as if he might come into Kellan's office, both Kellan and Owen gave him a warning glance that worked because he stayed put.

"It's true," Terrance agreed. "Until I overheard the conversation just a few minutes ago, I didn't make the connection between the DA's wife and Laney's dead sister." He turned to Laney then. "Here all this time, you thought your sister's killer was Emerson, and now

I've put a cog in your wheel by handing you another suspect."

Laney continued to stare at him. "Two other suspects," she corrected. "You're high on my list of people who could have murdered Hadley."

She'd sounded strong when she said that, but Owen knew that, beneath the surface, this was eating away at her. After all, she was facing down the man who'd assaulted her and put her in the hospital.

"Do you have any proof whatsoever of what you're saying?" Owen demanded.

Terrance lifted his shoulder. "Reports from my PIs. It's possible they took photos, but if so, I don't remember seeing them."

Reports could be doctored. Photos could be, too. Still, Owen would need to treat this as any other potential evidence that fell into his lap. Because if Nettie was indeed connected to Hadley's murder, then she could have had something to do with the attack at his ranch.

That put a hard knot in his gut.

"I'll want everything from your PIs ASAP," Owen insisted.

Terrance nodded. "I'll get right on that. Wouldn't want it said that I didn't cooperate with the law." He glanced at Nettie, whose back was to them. She was pacing across the reception area while still on her phone. "And what about her? You think she'll cooperate?"

"She's not your concern," Kellan assured him, sounding very much like a sheriff who'd just given an order. "Come with me." He led Terrance and the lawyer into the interview room and shut the door before he came back to them.

"I didn't know Terrance was having me followed," Laney immediately volunteered. "I'm a PI, and I should have noticed something like that."

No way was Owen going to let her take the blame for this. "If Terrance didn't lie about the timing of this alleged meeting, you would have been in the hospital and then recovering from the injuries he gave you. A broken arm, three broken ribs and a concussion. That's a lot to distract you."

Laney quickly dodged his gaze while the muscles in her jaw tensed. Maybe she hadn't wanted him to dig into her medical records, but Owen considered it connected to the investigation of last night's attack. At least, that was what he'd told himself. After reading the police report of Terrance's assault, Owen now had to admit that it had become personal for him.

And that was definitely something he didn't want.

"I have no idea if Terrance is telling the truth about Hadley and Nettie," Laney went on a moment later. "Hadley never mentioned meeting Emerson's wife."

Owen had to consider that was because Hadley had never gotten a chance to tell Laney. After all, Terrance had claimed his PIs saw the two women the same night Hadley had been murdered. That still didn't mean Nettie had killed her. Didn't mean that anything Terrance had told them was the truth.

Before Owen could talk to Kellan about how they should handle this, Nettie finished her call and came back toward them. "Emerson just left for a business meeting in Austin and will be gone most of the day," she said and then paused. "I didn't tell him about the eavesdropping device."

Owen only lifted an eyebrow, causing Nettie to huff, "You should have told him."

Nettie shook her head. "I know it's all some misunderstanding, that I had nothing to do with the eavesdropping device, so there's no reason to worry him." She turned to Kellan. "Go ahead and get someone in the house to take whatever you need. Just try to be finished with the search before Emerson comes home. Test the computers and have them in place so that he doesn't know."

No raised eyebrow for Kellan. Instead he gave Nettie a flat look. "I can't guarantee that. In fact, I'm pretty sure it'll take a couple of days to go through the computers once I get everything to the lab. You'll need to tell Emerson," he quickly added. "He'll hear it sooner or later, and I'll give you the chance to have him learn about it from you."

Nettie volleyed some glances between Kellan and him as if she expected them to budge on their insistence that she tell her husband what was going on. They wouldn't. And Owen made certain that his expression let her know it. It didn't matter if this was all some kind of "misunderstanding." It still had to be investigated.

As did Terrance's accusations.

"If you want to interview Terrance, I can get a statement from Nettie," Owen offered his brother.

Nettie blinked, pulled back her shoulders. "A statement?" Her voice was sharp and stinging. "I've already told you I had nothing to do with that stupid bug."

"Why don't we take this to the second interview room?" Owen suggested, hoping this wouldn't escalate.

But it did.

Nettie didn't budge when Owen put his hand on her

arm to get her moving. "A statement?" she repeated. Not a shout but close. She slung off Owen's grip and snapped at Laney. "You're responsible for this. You've somehow convinced them that I'm a criminal. I'm not. You're a liar, and now you're dragging me into those lies."

"Nettie," Kellan said, "you need to calm down and listen."

The woman ignored him and charged toward Laney. Nettie had already raised her hand as if to slap Laney, but both Laney and Owen snagged the woman by the wrist. The rage was all over Nettie's face now and she bucked against the restraint.

"I don't only need a statement about the bug," Owen snapped. "But also about your meeting with Hadley Odom."

Nettie's rage vanished. In its place came the shock. Only for a second, though. "I have no idea what you're talking about."

Because Owen was watching her so carefully, he saw something he didn't want to see. Nettie touched her hand to her mouth, then trailed it down to her throat. She did that while staring at him, her eyes hardly blinking. All signs that she was lying.

"You've never met Hadley Odom?" he pressed.

Her hand fluttered to the side of her face and she shook her head. "No. Why would I have met her? I don't even know who she is."

Kellan and Owen exchanged glances as Kellan stepped in front of Nettie. "What if I told you there could be proof that you not only knew this woman but that you met with her?"

Nettie huffed, "Then I'd say someone lied. Or that you're mistaken. I have to go," she added, tucking her purse beneath her arm. "Make those arrangements for the computers to be picked up. I need to go to Austin and talk to my husband."

Owen didn't stop Nettie when she walked out. She wasn't exactly a flight risk and, once they had more info on the computers—or from Terrance—they could bring her back in for questioning. It'd be necessary because Owen was certain that Nettie knew a lot more about this than she was saying.

Nettie paused when she reached the door and glanced at them from over her shoulder. "Emerson's going to ruin both of you when he finds out how you've treated me," she declared just seconds before she made her exit.

Owen kept his eyes on Nettie until she was out of sight, then turned to get Kellan's take on what had just happened. But he noticed Laney first. She was pale and looking a little shaky.

"Nettie could have killed my sister," Laney said, sinking down into the nearest chair.

Owen wanted to curse. He'd been all cop when he'd been listening to Nettie and hadn't remembered that this was more than a murder investigation to Laney. She'd lost a member of her family, and he knew what that was like. Knew that it could cut to the core. It would continue to cut until Laney learned the truth and found justice for her.

He knew plenty about that, as well.

"I'll take the interview with Terrance," Kellan advised.

Still looking shaky, Laney got up. "I want to listen to what he has to say."

Judging from the way Kellan's forehead bunched up, he was likely debating if that was a good idea. But he finally nodded. "Take her to the observation room," he told Owen.

Owen did, but that was only because he knew he wouldn't be able to talk Laney out of it. Besides, she knew Terrance, and she might have some insight into whatever he said. Owen was betting, though, that Terrance wouldn't reveal anything incriminating. No way would he risk going back to jail, unless he was stupid.

And he definitely didn't strike Owen as stupid.

Just the opposite. Terrance could have told them about Nettie and Hadley's meeting as a way of covering himself. By casting doubt on Nettie, Terrance might believe it would take the spotlight off him when it came to Hadley's murder. It didn't. He had motive and means. As for opportunity... Yes, he had an alibi, but he could have hired someone to do the job.

Laney's top suspect in her sister's murder was Emerson. Or at least it had been before Terrance had just thrown Nettie into the mix. But Owen was going to take a hard look at Terrance himself.

"Are you all right?" Owen asked Laney when they stepped into the observation room. It was a small space, not much bigger than a closet, and it put them elbow to elbow.

"I will be," she answered after a long pause. That meant she wasn't all right at the moment. Of course, he hadn't expected her to absorb it all and look at this through a PI's eyes. Not when there was this much emotion at stake.

She kept her attention on the two-way glass window where Kellan, Terrance and his lawyer were filing into interview room. "I'll be better if I can figure out a way to put him back in a cage."

Owen made a sound of agreement and because he could feel the tight muscles in her arms, he put his hand on her back and gave her a gentle pat. That took her gaze off Terrance. She looked at him. Then she groaned.

"You're feeling sorry for me." She said it like an accusation. There was some anger in her eyes and her voice. "You're thinking about the way Terrance beat me up and how that's weighing on me—"

Owen didn't let her finish. He snapped Laney to him and kissed her. What she'd said was true, but for some reason, her anger riled him. It had obviously made him stupid, too, because his go-to response had been a hard kiss. That didn't stay hard. The moment his mouth landed on hers, everything changed.

Everything.

The anger melted away from him, along with the rest of his common sense, and in its place came the heat. Of course, the heat had been stirring for a while now between them, but the temperature inside him soared to scalding temps when he tasted her.

Oh, man.

He was toast. That taste and the feel of her in his arms worked against him when she moved right into the kiss. Apparently she'd gotten rid of her anger, too, because she certainly wasn't fighting him. In fact, he was reasonably sure Laney was also feeling plenty of the heat.

The memories of that look in the barn slammed into him, mixing with this fresh fire and making this so much more than just a mere kiss. That, of course, only made him even more stupid. He shouldn't be lusting after her. Not with the chaos that was in their lives. And he darn sure shouldn't be wondering if he could take this kiss and let it lead them straight to bed.

She slid her arms around him, first one and then the other. Not some tight grip that would anchor him in place, which made it all the more dangerous. Because he suddenly wanted the anchor. He *ached* for it. Owen wanted to feel every inch of her against him. He silently cursed himself. And he cursed her, too.

When Owen heard Kellan's voice, he automatically tore himself away from Laney. It took him a moment to realize his brother wasn't in the observation room with them but that his voice was coming from the intercom. Kellan wasn't speaking to Laney and him, either. He was reading Terrance his rights.

Great. He'd gotten so tied up in that kiss and in the thoughts of bedding Laney, he'd forgotten there was something very important going on just one room over. They were there to hear what Terrance had to say, to try to look for any flaws or inconsistencies in his statement. Not for a make-out session. Even if that session had been damn good.

"Don't you dare apologize to me for that," Laney warned him. She ran her tongue over her bottom lip, causing his body to clench and then beg him to go back for more.

Owen stayed firmly planted where he was, though it was still plenty close to Laney. "I'm sorry that I lost focus," he settled for saying. "Not as sorry as I should be about the kiss."

It was the truth, but it was also true that it would happen again. That was why Owen groaned and cursed. He didn't need this kind of distraction, not with so much at stake, but his body didn't seem to be giving him a choice.

"We should have done something about this in the barn that day," he grumbled. "Then we would have burned it out of our systems by now."

At best, that was wishful thinking, but Laney didn't dismiss it. That told him she believed this was just lust, nothing more. But maybe that, too, was wishful thinking.

She smiled, but then quickly tightened her mouth to stop it. "I still have dreams about that day in the barn," she said.

Great. Now that was in his head. Dreaming about him having sex with her. Or rather, him wanting to have sex with her. The urge to do just that had been plenty strong that day. Still was. And Owen figured he'd be having his own dreams about not only that but the scalding kiss they'd just shared.

Thankfully, Kellan got their minds back on track when he sat across from Terrance at the table and opened with his first question.

"Where were you last night?"

The lawyer immediately took a piece of paper from his briefcase and handed it to Kellan. "We anticipated that you'd want to know that, so there's my client's alibi. As you can see, he was having dinner with several friends. I've included their names and contact information should you want to verify."

Slick move, Owen thought, and he had no doubts that the alibi would check out. That didn't mean Terrance hadn't been involved, though. Nope. He could have hired those men to break in. Heck, he could have hired them to plant the bug and set up Nettie.

Kellan looked over the paper the lawyer had given him. "Did you have a PI tail on Joe Henshaw, too?" he asked Terrance.

"Not recently, but yes, before my trial I did," Terrance admitted. "I've already told you that I had Laney and anyone connected to her under watchful eyes in case something turned up that I could use in my defense."

"You do know that Joe was murdered last night?" Kellan threw it out there.

Terrance nodded. "But I didn't see him, if that's what you're about to ask next." He tipped his head to the paper. "And that proves I was elsewhere when he died."

Kellan didn't even pause. "You'd be willing to turn over your finances so I can verify that you didn't hire someone to kill him and hire others to attack Laney and kill Joe?"

Terrance smiled, definitely not from humor, though. It was more of amusement, and then he waved off whatever his lawyer had been about to say. "I'll turn them over to you if and when you get a warrant. I'm guessing, though, you don't have enough probable cause to do that, or you would have already gotten it."

"You're right. I don't have probable cause, not yet, but it's still early," Kellan answered. "A lot of hours left in the day, and I don't think it'd take much to convince a judge that I need a look at your financials. Not with your criminal record. Judges are a lot more apt to help when a convicted felon's name comes up in a murder investigation."

The anger flared in Terrance's eyes. Heck, his nostrils did, too, and that caused Owen to smile. It was nice to see Terrance get a little comeuppance, but it wasn't enough. They needed to get into his bank account, and despite what Kellan had just threatened, it might not happen. Terrance's lawyer would almost certainly stonewall any attempts at a warrant.

"How much did the woman he met online steal from Terrance?" Owen asked Laney.

"According to Terrance and the lawsuit he filed against me, it was about three million."

Owen's mouth fell open for a moment. "Damn."

Laney made a sound of agreement and glanced up at him. "A judge threw out his lawsuit, but from what I could gather, that three million was about two-thirds of Terrance's entire inheritance. His family wasn't happy about that."

No one other than the swindler would be happy about that. And with Terrance blaming Laney, it gave him three million motives to get back at her. Maybe even enough to kill or hire killers.

However, if Terrance had indeed paid someone to do his dirty work, his old-money background might have given him the skills to hide transactions like that. There could be offshore accounts. Heck, the funds could have come from a safe with lots of cash. Still, Owen would press to get that warrant. Right now, it was one of the few strings they had to tug on Terrance. If they tugged hard enough, things were bound to unravel and get them the proof they needed for an arrest.

"I've heard you have one of the so-called gunmen in custody," Terrance went on a moment later. "I gather he hasn't said anything about me hiring him, or you would have used that to arrest me."

There was enough snark in Terrance's tone to let them know it was a challenge of sorts. No, the gunman hadn't pointed the finger at Terrance. Maybe he never would. But the longer they held the gunman, the higher the chance he might start to get desperate. The guy could ask for a plea deal in exchange for giving up his boss. Owen figured it would make plenty of people happy if it turned out to be Terrance.

Kellan stared at Terrance for several snail-crawling moments. "A lot of hours left in the day," he repeated. "Who knows what kind of dirt we'll be able to turn up on you."

This time Terrance flashed one of those cocky smiles, and Owen thought he saw some honest-to-goodness frustration slide into the man's eyes.

Terrance leaned forward, resting his forearms on the metal table. "Let me make your job easy for you, Sheriff Slater, because I want you to get off my back. I didn't hire any gunmen. I also didn't kill anyone, but I might have some more information that can put you on the right track."

Owen didn't miss the *more* and he found himself moving even closer to the glass. However, he also reminded himself that anything that came out of Terrance's mouth could be a lie or something meant to throw them off his track.

"I'm listening," Kellan said to the man.

Terrance opened a bottle of water first and had a long drink. "I've already told you that I hired PIs to follow people connected to my trial. That's how one of the PIs saw Nettie with Hadley." He paused. "But that wasn't the only time they saw Hadley."

That grabbed Owen's attention. Laney's, too, because she moved in closer, as well.

"I'll give you the reports from the PIs, of course,"

Terrance went on, "but I can tell you that about two days before Hadley was murdered, one of my men followed her to Austin."

Austin was a city only about an hour from Longview Ridge. Owen glanced at Laney to see if that rang any bells as to why her sister would go there, but she just shook her head.

"Hadley had a package with her," Terrance continued a moment later. "She went into the First National Bank on St. Mary's Street, stayed inside about a half hour, and when she came out, she didn't have the package with her. I know I'm not a cop, but I figure what she left there is worth you checking out."

"The photos of Emerson and Hadley," Laney said, snapping her eyes toward him. "Owen, we have to go get them now."

Chapter 7

Now didn't happen. Despite Laney's insistence, she and Owen still did not have the photos even after Terrance had given them the name and street address of the bank where his PIs had seen Hadley.

Laney tried not to be frustrated and impatient about that, but it was impossible not to feel those things. And more. The urgency clawed away at her. She was so close to the evidence she needed to nail down Hadley's killer. She knew that in her gut. But she was going to have to tamp down that urgency because of one simple fact.

There was no safe-deposit box in Hadley's name at the First National Bank in Austin.

That meant either Terrance had lied about it or Hadley had used an alias. Laney was betting it was the latter. Hadley had wanted to make sure Emerson couldn't get to those pictures because she'd seen them as some kind of insurance policy. Proof of an affair with a married man.

Hadley had likely believed that as a DA, Emerson could have used his contacts to do searches of banks. And maybe he had indeed managed to do just that. But Laney wasn't giving up hope yet.

She would *never* give up hope, even if her patience was wearing thin.

Laney was pacing across the living room floor of Owen's grandparents' house—something she'd been doing a lot since they're returned an hour earlier from the sheriff's office. She stopped when Owen came in. One look at his face and she knew he didn't have good news for her.

"We're having trouble getting the search warrant for the bank." He sounded as frustrated as she felt. "The judge wants more verification that Hadley actually had a box there, and we just don't have it."

She touched her hand to the chain around her neck. It now only had the dragonfly pendant. "The bank manager has the key."

"A key that may or may not belong to one of the boxes," Owen reminded her. It wasn't his first reminder, either.

She wanted to argue with him. But she couldn't. She'd found the key in Hadley's apartment shortly after she'd been murdered. Laney had no proof that it was the one for the safe-deposit box Hadley had told her about. But Laney believed that it was. She believed it with all her heart. Too bad the judge wouldn't take her gut feeling as more verification for the search warrant.

"Even if it is the right key," Owen went on, "the manager says the bank employees can't just test that key on the boxes to find the right one."

"So, we need either the name Hadley used to get the box or the box number," she said, talking more to herself than to Owen. Laney forced herself to think, to try to figure out where Hadley might have left information like that.

Owen nodded, but it wasn't a nod of total agreement. "If the bank gets the right box and opens it, the manager says he can't release the contents without proper authorization."

Laney knew that, of course. Kellan had already told her that when she'd given him the key. The key that he'd then passed along to the bank manager. It still didn't make it easier to swallow. Plus, there was the hope that if and when the box was opened, there might be enough inside to spur the manager to help them get that warrant. After all, the photos could confirm motive for Hadley's murder.

Could.

Again, it would take some convincing with a judge, but at least they'd have tangible evidence. Emerson might fall apart and confess everything when confronted with pictures of him and his lover. At a minimum, it might cause Owen to start doubting him so that he and Kellan would take a much harder look.

"What about the PI report from Terrance?" Laney asked, but then she immediately waved that off.

That wasn't *proof.* Far from it. Terrance was a convicted felon and probably still held a grudge against her. He could have given them this info to send them on some wild-goose chase. One that would take the spotlight off him. One that would put her in an extra frazzled frame of mind. If so, it was working because that was where she was right now.

"Kellan's bringing in the PI who claims he saw Hadley go into the bank," Owen told her. "If the PI will sign a sworn statement as to what he saw, we can go back to the judge."

It was a long shot, but Laney refused to believe it wouldn't work. They had to find that box and get into it.

Owen walked closer to her, but still kept some distance between them. Something he'd been doing since that kiss in the observation room. Despite Laney telling him not to apologize for it, she could tell he was sorry. And that he regretted it.

"The bank manager did agree to go through all the names to see if there were any red flags," Owen said several moments later. "Is there any alias you can think of that Hadley might have used?"

It was something Kellan had already asked her, and Laney had come up with zilch. However, she had given Kellan the full names of Hadley and her parents, their pets and even childhood friends in case her sister had used any one of those.

"What about the PI report of the meeting between Nettie and Hadley?" she asked. "Has Terrance sent that to Kellan yet?"

"He emailed it, and Kellan sent me a copy."

Laney huffed. She wasn't frustrated that Terrance had sent it but because she'd wanted to see it as soon as it arrived.

"You read the report," Owen said, obviously picking up on her frustration. "It's on my computer."

Upstairs and in his bedroom. Or, at least, that was where his laptop had been the last time she'd seen it.

Upstairs was also where his brother Eli and Gemma were. Addie and Francine, too. And while Laney liked all of them, she'd wanted to give Owen some space to be with his daughter and the rest of his family.

Owen motioned for her to follow him as he headed for the stairs. She did. "The reason I wasn't jumping through hoops to tell you about the report Terrance sent is that there's nothing in it other than what he told us at the sheriff's office."

That wasn't a surprise, but it was an annoying disappointment that only added to her frustration. Still, there was no way Terrance would give them anything they could use against him, and the PI likely wouldn't have realized the importance of a meeting between the two women. Still, Laney wanted to read it, study it, because it could possibly have something they could use.

"There are probably other reports," she said as they walked up the stairs. "Ones that maybe Terrance is holding on to. He can maybe use them as bargaining chips if it comes down to that."

His quick nod let her know that Owen had already considered it. "Kellan will try to get a search warrant on Terrance, too."

It would be easier to get that than it would be to get one for the bank, but Laney was betting Terrance had covered his tracks and there'd be nothing to find. There would definitely be nothing on his personal computer since he wouldn't risk going back to jail.

When they made it to Owen's bedroom, she was surprised that it was empty, but she could hear the chatter next door in the master bedroom. Chatter that she was betting wouldn't stop Eli from keeping watch. He was just doing it from the upstairs window now instead of the downstairs one. Laney had thankfully seen no lapse in security, which would need to continue until they found the person responsible for the attack.

Too bad they weren't any closer to doing that.

Owen's laptop was on a small folding table in the corner and he pulled out the chair for her to sit. The report was already on the screen. She noted the date and time.

"Lee Kissner," Laney said, reading the PI's name aloud. "I don't know him personally, but he has a good reputation."

"A good rep, but he was working for Terrance," Owen pointed out.

She nodded. Shrugged. "I sometimes took on slime-ball clients who were trying to clear their names." Laney could see this from that side of things, but it didn't make her feel better that Terrance had had her sister and her followed.

Laney read through the report, noting the description of the clothes Hadley was wearing. Red dress with silver trim and silver heels. Her sister did indeed have an outfit like that. In fact, the details matched all the way to the purse.

"According to the notes, Hadley didn't talk to anyone before going into the bank," Laney pointed out. "But someone—an employee—inside would have spoken with her. I'm assuming they've all been questioned?"

Owen nodded again. "One of the clerks thinks she might have remembered her when Kellan showed Hadley's photo. That's not enough to get a warrant," he quickly added. "The clerk isn't positive and doesn't remember why Hadley was there."

Laney groaned softly. She'd never been to that particular bank, but she'd checked the facts about it online, and it was huge. In addition, this visit would have happened months ago. That wasn't going to help, not with the steady stream of customers who would have gone in and out of there during that time.

As she continued reading, Laney could feel her frown deepening with each sentence. Her sister had spent a half hour inside the bank. That was plenty of time to not only open an account for a safe-deposit box but also enough time to lock the pictures inside and then come out.

Hadley hadn't spoken to anyone as she'd walked back to her car. She had simply driven away. The PI hadn't followed her since he was waiting on further instructions from Terrance. According to Lee Kissner, those instructions had been to suspend, at least temporarily, following Hadley. Too bad he hadn't stuck with her because it might have given them more clues about her killer.

Laney finished reading the report, stood and started to pace again, hoping that she could come up with an angle they could use to sway a judge. But nothing came to mind. Given the way Owen's forehead was furrowed, he was drawing a blank, too.

"I shouldn't have kissed you," he said. So, no blank after all. His mind hadn't been on the report, though she was certain he'd already given it plenty of thought.

"Yes," she agreed. "Loss of focus, blurred lines, bad timing." She'd hoped her light tone and dry smile would ease the tension on his face, but it didn't.

"Heat," he added to the list. But Owen didn't just say it. There was also some heat in his voice, along with a hefty dose of something Laney had been feeling all morning. Irritation and annoyance.

Owen looked at her the same moment she looked at him, and their gazes collided. Oh, mercy. Yes, there it was. So much fire. Way too much need. Way too much *everything.*

With all the memories going through her head, she wanted to smack herself as the image of Owen in the barn jumped right to the front of her mind. Followed by the more recent image of their kiss. Her body reacted and she felt that heat trickle through her.

"It's too dangerous for me not to be able to see all of this clearly," Owen added.

Until he'd said that, Laney had been about to go to him and kiss him. Nothing hard and deep like the one in the observation room. Just a peck to assure him that the heat could wait. It would have maybe sated her body a little, as well.

No assuring and sating now, though. They were just standing there, much too close, their gazes connected, the weight of the attraction and their situation bearing down on them.

It stunned her when Owen leaned in and brushed his mouth over hers. Stunned her even more that just a peck from him could dole out that kind of wallop. It was a reminder that any kind of contact between them was only going to complicate things.

"Sorry to interrupt," someone said from the doorway. Jack.

The man moved like a cat. And, despite the fact that he'd no doubt just witnessed that lip-lock, he didn't give his brother a ribbing smile.

"Just got a call from one of the hands," Jack told

them. "Emerson's at your house, and he's demanding to see you."

Emerson had likely heard about Kellan taking the computers from his home. Or maybe Nettie had finally filled her husband in on everything.

"Emerson's already spoken to Kellan," Jack went on. "Guess he didn't get the answers he wanted, so he drove out to the ranch. I'm thinking it's not a good idea to have Emerson brought here."

"No, it's not," Owen agreed. He paused, his forehead bunching up even more. "Tell the hand to keep Emerson at my place. I'll drive over there to see him."

"Not without me—" Jack immediately said just as Laney piped in, "I want to see him, too—"

She knew Owen wasn't going to argue with his brother about going, but considered he would nix her request. He surprised her when he didn't. He gave her a nod.

"Just let me check on Addie first," Owen muttered.

Jack stepped to the side so that Owen could head there.

"No one in the room will bite," Jack added under his breath to her. "And if anyone can lighten the mood around here, it's Addie."

Jack was right. The little girl had a way of making everything better. Laney thanked him for the reminder and followed Owen, intending to stay in the hall and just get a glimpse of Addie. She didn't want to interfere with Owen's time with her. But Gemma remedied that as she took hold of Laney's arm and led her into the room.

Eli was in the exact spot that Laney thought he would be. Keeping watch at the window. Francine, seated near him, was sipping coffee. Laney smiled when she saw

Addie on the bed, playing with a stash of stuffed animals, blocks and books. Addie smiled when she spotted her dad and put aside a toy horse to scoot toward him. Owen picked her up and kissed her cheek.

"Da-da," she said and dropped her head in the crook of his neck. The loving moment didn't last, though, when Addie's attention landed on Laney. "Aney," she attempted to say.

Laney didn't know who was more surprised when the little girl reached for her, but she felt a lot of relief. She'd been so afraid that Addie would associate her with the loud blasts from the gunfire and the terrifying run to the barn, but apparently she hadn't remembered that as well as she had Laney's name.

Owen passed Addie over to her, and when Laney had her in her arms, she had another surprise when Addie kissed her. The little girl babbled something that Laney didn't understand, but she caught the word *horsey*, so maybe she was talking about her toy stash.

Jack stepped up to Eli, probably to tell him about Emerson's arrival. When Jack went back into the hall, clearly waiting, that was Owen's cue to get moving.

Owen took Addie from Laney, giving his daughter another kiss before putting her back on the bed.

"My advice?" Eli said. "Put on a flak jacket because Emerson won't be a happy camper."

No, he wouldn't be, Laney thought. And it was possible that Nettie hadn't even told him the whole truth. The woman certainly would have put her own slant on things, and that, in turn, could cause Emerson to aim even more venom at Owen and her.

With Eli following them, Jack, Owen and Laney went back downstairs, and she heard Eli reset the security system as soon as they were out the door. They hurried into the cruiser so they wouldn't be out in the open too long. Of course, even a minute was probably too long as far as Owen as concerned.

Laney waited for Owen to remind her that it was an unnecessary risk for her to insist on going to this meeting. But he didn't. Maybe because he knew it wouldn't do any good. Besides, just seeing her might trigger Emerson into a fit of temper that could get him to spill the secret he'd been keeping about Hadley.

When Owen's house came into view, she immediately saw the crime scene tape fluttering in the breeze. Laney also noticed the sleek black car parked in front just a split second before she spotted Emerson. He was talking on his phone while he paced the front porch. And yes, he was riled. Every muscle in his body and face showed that. She had even more proof of the man's anger when they got out of the cruiser.

"What the hell do you think you're doing?" Emerson barked. The question wasn't aimed at Owen but rather at her.

"I'm trying to find out who nearly killed me and Owen," Laney answered. She didn't dodge Emerson's fiery gaze and definitely didn't back down. That was one of the few advantages of being just as riled as he was.

Despite the thick tension in the air, Owen somehow managed to stay calm as he unlocked the door. "There's a hired killer still at large, so we'll take this inside."

Emerson looked ready to argue, but he probably would have argued about anything at this point. He was spoiling for a fight.

Owen ushered her in first and Laney immediately

saw that some of the items had been moved. Likely the CSIs' doing. She was betting the entire place had been checked for prints and trace evidence. An attack on a police officer's home would have caused everyone involved to be on the top of their game.

"You convinced Kellan to have a CSI go into my home," Emerson ranted at Laney as he came inside. He was still aiming his rage at her, too. "You upset my wife."

Owen didn't say anything until he had the door shut, and then he eased around to face his brother-in-law. "Nettie gave us permission to get the computers and have them analyzed. Did she tell you why?"

"Yes," Emerson snapped while Jack went to the living room window to keep watch. "It's because someone set her up so that it looks as if she planted a bug in your guesthouse." His narrowed eyes cut to Laney. "*You* set her up."

"I have no reason to do that." Laney tried to restrain her temper enough to keep her voice calm as well, but she wasn't quite as successful as Owen.

"Yes, you do, because you have some kind of vendetta against me." Emerson opened his mouth as if to say more, but then he closed it.

"What else did Nettie tell you?" Owen asked.

Silence. For a very long time. Emerson finally cursed under his breath and leaned against the wall. "Nettie said she met with her—" he tipped his head toward Laney to indicate the *her* "—sister." While there was still some anger in his voice, she thought she heard disgust, too.

"Hadley," Laney provided, though she was certain he knew her sister's name. "Hadley Odom," she said, spelling it out because she wanted to try to gauge his reaction.

Emerson dismissed her with a glance before his attention went back to Owen. "Nettie heard rumors that I was having an affair with *Hadley.*" He said the name as if it were venom. "I'm guessing your sister started those rumors. So, Nettie confronted her. Apparently some private investigator witnessed the meeting and told Kellan about it."

"Did Nettie also confront *you* about the affair?" Owen asked.

Another long pause. "No. I didn't know that Nettie had heard those rumors until about two hours ago when she told me what's been going on."

"Rumors?" Owen questioned.

Since it sounded like the accusation that it was, Emerson cursed again. Then he groaned when Owen continued to stare at him. "I knew Hadley."

For only three words, they packed a huge punch. Finally, Laney had heard the man admit the truth. Truth about knowing her sister anyway. But she figured Owen was experiencing a gut punch of a different kind. As a cop, he wouldn't have wanted to hear his brother-in-law just confess to a relationship that was now a motive for murder.

Owen dragged his hand over his face and did some cursing of his own. "I need to read you your rights."

"I know my damn rights." Emerson pushed away from the wall. "I'm the damn DA!"

Owen went closer until they were toe-to-toe. "Then act like it and tell me what happened between Hadley and you. *Everything that happened,*" Owen emphasized.

Emerson's glare went on for so long that Laney

thought he was going to clam up or demand that she leave. Maybe even ask for a lawyer. He didn't. He stepped back, shook his head. When his gaze returned to Owen, some of the anger was gone.

"I didn't kill her..." Emerson started. "I swear, I didn't kill her." He looked at Laney when he repeated that. "And I don't care what she told you. There was no affair. I barely knew her."

She studied his eyes, looking for any signs that was a lie, and Laney thought she detected one. However, she didn't know Emerson well enough to use his body language to try to convince Owen that the man wasn't being honest with them.

"How'd you meet Hadley?" Owen persisted when Emerson didn't continue.

"At a party that I attended in San Antonio. She came onto me, and I brushed her off. Told her I was a married man, that I didn't play around on my wife." Emerson glared at Laney as if challenging her to prove him otherwise.

She couldn't.

She'd never personally seen the two of them together, but she'd believed her sister when Hadley had told her about the affair. And, just as important, she didn't believe Emerson. Yes, she could see Hadley coming onto him, but Hadley was a very attractive woman. She could have likely had her pick of the men at that party and wouldn't have come onto Emerson had he not been sending off the right signals. Or in this case, the wrong ones, since he was a married man.

"I never saw Hadley again after that night," Emerson went on. "But she called me and claimed I'd given her some kind of date rape drug at the party. I denied it, but she didn't believe me. She cried and carried on and told me that I'd be sorry."

Owen jumped right on that. "She threatened you?"

Emerson shook his head. "Not then, not with actual words anyway, but I knew she was very upset and believed I'd actually drugged her. So upset that when I first heard she was dead, I wondered if she'd killed herself to set me up, to make it look as if I'd murdered her. The woman was crazy," he added in a mumble.

"Hadley didn't commit suicide," Laney insisted. But she would give him a pass on the crazy part. Hadley could be overly emotional. Still, Laney didn't believe she'd lied about having an affair with Emerson.

That meant Emerson was lying now.

"I agree about her not killing herself," Emerson said when Laney just kept glaring at him. "I realized that when I read the police report about her murder. The angle of the blunt-force trauma wound was all wrong for her to have done that to herself."

For just a moment Laney saw something more than anger. Maybe regret? Or it could be that Emerson had once had feelings for Hadley. That didn't mean, though, that he hadn't murdered her.

"There's more," Emerson continued, his gaze firing to Laney again. "And if you're responsible, so help me God, I'll make sure you're put behind bars."

Laney raised her hands. "What the heck are you talking about?"

"Blackmail." Emerson let that hang in the air.

Owen didn't even glance at her to see if she knew what Emerson meant, and that helped ease a little of the tension in her chest. Twenty-four hours earlier, if Emerson had accused her of something, Owen would have considered it a strong possibility. Or even the truth. But he now knew she wouldn't do anything like that.

"A couple of days ago, I got a phone call," Emerson explained. "The person used one of those voice scramblers, so I didn't know who it was. Still don't. But the person claimed to know about the so-called affair I had with Hadley and threatened to tell Nettie if I didn't pay up. He said he had some kind of proof, but that's impossible. There's no proof because there was no affair."

Owen kept his attention nailed to Emerson. "You paid the blackmailer?" he snapped.

"No. Of course not. I'm not going to pay for something I didn't do. I put the person off, said that I needed time to get some money together. I've been using that time to try to figure out who's behind this."

Owen huffed and Laney knew why. Emerson's first response should have been to go to the cops. To his brother-in-law, Owen. Of course, that was the last thing a guilty man would have wanted to do.

"And did you find out who's behind this?" Owen challenged, the annoyance dripping off his tone.

Emerson shook his head, took out his phone. "I got another call yesterday. I recorded it and had a private lab analyze it. They were unable to get a voice match because of the scrambling device the person used, but the tech thought the caller was male. You can listen to the recording if you want."

Owen nodded.

Both Laney and Owen moved closer to Emerson's phone before the man hit the play button on his phone.

"I made it clear that I want thirty grand to keep your dirty little secret," the caller said. "Since I don't have it yet, it's gonna cost you a whole lot more." The person rattled off a bank account number. "Fifty grand should do it. If I don't have the money in forty-eight hours, the amount doubles and then I go to your wife. I'll go to the press, too. Think of all the damage to your reputation when this comes out. You'll never be able to get the mud off your name."

Emerson clicked off the recording. "Don't bother tracing the bank," he said. "It's an offshore account."

That would indeed make it almost impossible to trace. But a conversation with the blackmailer might have given them plenty of clues. Laney so badly wanted to say that Emerson should have gone to Kellan and Owen with this, but she figured the man had already realized that.

"I won't send money," Emerson insisted. *"Can't,"* he amended. "Even if I had done something wrong, you know I don't have those kinds of funds. You know how little a DA makes in a small town. And I won't go to my wife's trust fund to pay a blackmailer to keep a secret that I don't even have."

Laney had known about Nettie's trust fund and that she was from a prominent family. It had come up when she'd run a background check on the woman. But Laney had assumed that Emerson had money of his own. Apparently not.

Emerson closed his eyes for a moment before he continued, "I don't want Nettie to know anything about this supposed affair. It'll upset her, and there's no reason for it."

Owen dragged in a breath. "Upsetting Nettie is only one part of this, and right now it's a small part. You withheld potential evidence in a murder investigation.

That's obstruction of justice and you, of all people, should know that."

Laney figured that would bring on another wave of Emerson's rage, but it didn't come. The man merely nodded, as if surrendering. "I intend to talk to Kellan about that. In the meantime, I'll send you a copy of the recording from the blackmailer and will cooperate in any way the sheriff's office needs."

"Even financials?" Owen quickly asked.

Emerson didn't nod that time. He stared at Owen, and Laney wished she could see what was going on in his head. Obviously there was hesitation, but there seemed to be something more.

"Nettie and I don't have shared accounts," Emerson finally said. "That's the way it's written in her trust fund, that it can't become a joint account. I can give you access to mine but not hers."

"That'll do for now," Owen assured him.

Laney figured either Kellan or Owen would soon press Nettie to do the same.

Emerson made a sound to indicate that he would. "Just keep Nettie out of this, and I'll cooperate in any way that I can." He started for the door but then stopped when he reached Laney. "I didn't have an affair with your sister," he repeated.

She stood there and watched Emerson walk out. He drove away as soon as he got in his car, leaving Laney to try to sort through everything he'd just told them. That sorting, however, was getting some interference from her own emotions.

Emerson had stayed insistent about not having the affair, but he'd admitted to the obstruction of justice. Admitting to the first might cost him his marriage, but the second could put him behind bars. Why admit to one and not the other?

"You believe him?" Owen asked.

"If I do, it means my sister lied." She groaned softly, pushed her hair from her face. "Hadley could be irresponsible about some things, but lying about this wouldn't be like her." And Laney hated the words that were about to come out of her mouth. "Still, it's possible she did."

Owen nodded, not giving her his take on what he thought about all of it. But he was probably leaning in Emerson's direction. Specifically, leaning toward believing Emerson hadn't killed Hadley. After all, Owen didn't know Hadley, and it would make his personal life much easier if he didn't have to haul in his brother-in-law for murder.

He shut the door, took out his phone, and she saw him press Kellan's number. "I want to get that recording analyzed by the crime lab," he said. "And Kellan will need access to Emerson's phone records. We might be able to find out who made the two calls."

Maybe, but she figured a blackmailer would use a burner cell, one that couldn't be traced. Especially if Terrance had been the one to make the calls. He was too smart to get caught doing something that stupid.

"Terrance knew about the meeting between Nettie and Hadley," she said while they waited for Kellan to answer. "The blackmail could be a way of his recouping some money he lost from his trust fund. It'll barely put a dent in what he lost, but he could be planning on going back to Emerson for more."

Owen made eye contact with her to let her know he

was considering that, but he didn't get a chance to say anything because Kellan came on the line.

"I was just about to call you," Kellan volunteered. "We got a lucky break. The banker in Austin found the box. It's under an alias, Sandy Martell."

"How did they find out it belongs to Hadley?" Owen wanted to know.

"Because Hadley put Laney's name on it. There's a condition, though. Laney can only get into the box if she has the key. How convinced is Laney that the key she gave me is the one to the box?"

Good question, one that Owen had already asked Laney.

"I believe it is," Laney said. "I'm not positive, though."

Kellan stayed quiet for a moment. "All right. Then I'll meet you at the bank so I can give you back the key. Owen needs to get you there ASAP because the manager's going to let you have access."

Chapter 8

A lot of thoughts went through Owen's mind, and not all of them were of relief.

Having Laney's name on the safe-deposit box meant it would eliminate hours and maybe days of red tape to not only locate the box but to gain them access to it. It also meant they might finally have those photos Hadley had claimed would prove her affair with Emerson.

However, for them to get the photos—or whatever was in the box—meant taking Laney off the ranch and all the way to Austin. That wasn't his first choice of things to do when someone had already attacked her. She'd be out in the open where hired guns could come at her.

"Talk to the bank manager again," Owen told Kellan. Laney moved closer to him, no doubt so she could listen to the phone conversation Owen was having with his brother. He considered putting the call on speaker, but the truth was, he didn't mind her being this close to him. It eased his suddenly frayed nerves more than it should. "See if there's a way for us to get access to the box without Laney actually being there."

From the other end of the line Owen heard his brother sigh. "I already asked. Or rather, I demanded, and he said Laney had to come in person with a picture ID. Either that, or we have to go the search-warrant route."

Owen had expected that to be the manager's response, but he still cursed. "Try again." He dragged in a long breath. "Emerson just left here, and I don't like the way things are starting to play out. He claims someone's trying to blackmail him."

"Blackmail? Did Emerson admit to the affair with Hadley?" Kellan quickly asked.

"No. He denied it. He's got a recording of the blackmailer's demand. This might not have anything to do with Laney, but I don't like the timing."

"Neither do I," Kellan agreed. "I'll call the bank manager one more time and see what I can do." His brother paused. "How deep do you think Emerson is involved in this?"

Judging from Laney's expression, she wanted to say "very," but Owen still wasn't sure. "Emerson gave us permission to look into his financials," Owen settled for saying. "I'd like to get that started."

"You think Emerson could have paid for those hired guns?" Kellan pressed.

"I just want to be able to rule it out, and this is a start." Maybe not a good start, though, because someone as smart as Emerson could have a hidden account. No way would he have paid for hired killers out of his checking account and then offered to let Owen take a look at it.

"Yeah," Kellan said a moment later, both agreement and concern in his tone. "I'll let you know what the bank manager says."

When Owen ended the call, he turned back to Laney and saw exactly what he figured would be there. Hope with a hefty layering of fear. "I'll have to go to the bank," she insisted before he could say anything. "I need to see what's in that safe-deposit box, and me being there is the fastest way to do this."

She did need to see the contents of the box. So did he, but Owen was still hoping the bank manager would come through and Laney could then view the box through a video feed. *Safely* view it. Owen stared at her, trying to come up with some argument that would convince her of that, but he drew a blank on anything he could say to change her mind.

A blank about the argument anyway.

Unfortunately his mind came up with all sorts of other possibilities. None good. But plenty of them were pretty bad. Because they involved kissing her again. Heck, they involved taking her to bed.

Silently cursing himself, Owen slipped his arm around her waist and pulled her to him. Since Jack was only a few yards away and still at the window, his brother would no doubt see the embrace and give him grief about it later. But this was like the close contact he'd gotten from Laney when she'd been listening to Kellan's call. Owen needed this, too.

Apparently, Laney needed it as well, because she sighed and moved in closer.

Owen didn't dare pull back and look at her since that

would have absolutely led to a kiss, but he pressed her against him and let the now-familiar feel of her settle him. Ironic that Laney would be able to do that.

The settling didn't last, though. That was because the other thoughts came. The guilt. The feeling that he was somehow cheating on his wife. Again, ironic. Naomi wouldn't have wanted him to go even this long without seeking out someone else. He'd been the one not willing to jump back into those waters.

Until now.

Owen might have considered that progress if it hadn't been stupid to get involved with someone in his protective custody.

His phone rang, thankfully putting a stop to any other thoughts about kissing Laney. He frowned when he saw the caller. Not Kellan. But rather Terrance. Laney frowned, too, and that expression only deepened when Owen answered.

"Ask Laney what the hell she thinks she's doing," Terrance snarled the moment he was on the line.

"Anything specific, or is this just a general rant?" Owen countered.

"Yes, it's specific. Someone's following me, and I figure she's responsible. The Longview Ridge Sheriff's Office doesn't have probable cause to put a tail on me."

"You're wrong about that. You're on probation, and you're a person of interest in an attack. We have a right to tail you."

But that was just a reminder, not something that'd actually happened. Kellan hadn't put a deputy on Terrance. He glanced at Laney just to make sure she hadn't hired someone to do that, and she shook her head. Not that Owen had thought for one second that she would without talking to him.

"Who's following you?" Owen asked Terrance.

"How the hell should I know? Someone who's driving a dark blue sedan. I figure it's either your man or Laney's. Maybe one of her PI friends."

"Well, it's not. I would say it's your imagination, but since you've got a lot of experience putting tails on people, you should know the real thing when you see it. Where are you?" Owen asked, not waiting for Terrance to gripe about the comment he'd just made.

"My lawyer and I are on the interstate, and the car's been following us for about ten miles now. You're sure it's not someone you know?"

"No," Laney and Owen answered in unison.

He would have pushed Terrance for more info than just the vague response "on the interstate," but Terrance hung up.

"It could be a ruse," Laney immediately said. "Terrance might think he'll be less of a person of interest if he makes us believe someone's after him."

Owen couldn't agree more, but he had to look at this from both sides. They had two other persons of interest: Emerson and Nettie. If one of them was guilty, then Terrance would make a fine patsy, and they could pin all of this on him.

He was about to put his phone away, but it rang again. This time it was Kellan so he answered immediately. Owen put the call on speaker so that Jack would be able to hear.

"It's a no-go from the bank manager," Kellan told them right away. "He needs Laney there with her ID. If not, then we have to wait for the warrant."

Owen didn't even bother to groan since it was the answer he'd expected. "How close are we to getting the warrant?"

"It could come through later today now that we've got the box narrowed down. Still, the bank manager is saying if the key doesn't match, then he'll fight the warrant. Apparently, Hadley emphasized that condition in writing when she set up the safe-deposit box."

Hadley had likely done that as a precaution, to make sure no one got into it by posing as Laney or her.

"There should be two keys," Kellan noted. "The second one wasn't found on Hadley's body or in her apartment or vehicle. Any idea who she would have given the other key to?"

Since that question was obviously aimed at Laney, Owen just looked at her.

"No," Laney admitted. "She didn't actually give one to me. I found this one when I was going through her things." She paused. "But it's possible she had the key with her when she died, and if so, the killer could have taken it."

Kellan didn't disagree. Neither did Owen.

"But her killer might not have known the location of the bank," Laney added. "He or she might have been looking for it all this time."

Again, that was true, and Owen only hoped the killer had managed to get to it before they did.

"Jack and I will drive Laney to the bank," Owen explained to Kellan. "You're still planning on meeting us there?"

"Yeah. I'll have one of the deputies with me," Kellan assured him, and he ended the call.

Four lawmen. Maybe that would be enough.

Jack went to the front door, opened it and glanced around. He still had his gun drawn. Owen did the same, waiting until Jack gave the nod before he took hold of Laney's arm to hurry her to the cruiser. It wasn't far, only about fifteen feet away, but it still meant being out in the open.

Jack went ahead of them but stayed close, and Owen positioned Laney in between them. The bad feeling in the pit of his stomach hit him hard just as they reached the bottom step. It wasn't enough of a warning, though, for him to do anything about it.

Because the shot blasted through the air.

The sound of the shot barely had time to register in Laney's mind when Owen hooked his arm around her and dragged her to the ground.

Her pulse jumped, racing like the adrenaline that surged through her. Sweet heaven. Someone was trying to kill them again.

Just ahead of them, Jack dropped, too, and both Owen and he fired glances around, no doubt looking for the shooter. Laney forced herself to do the same, though it was hard for her to see much of anything because Owen had positioned his body over hers.

Another shot came, slamming into the ground between Jack and them. Laney couldn't be sure, but she thought the gunshots had come from her left, where there was a pasture.

And trees.

Some of the oaks were wide enough to conceal a gunman. If so, he was in a bad position. Well, bad for them. Because he would have a clear shot if they tried to get to the cruiser. He'd have just as clear a shot if they tried to scramble back onto the porch. They were trapped and with very little cover.

"There," Jack said, tipping his head toward one of the oaks.

Owen nodded and turned his attention in that direction. Not Jack, though. He kept watch around them. Something that caused Laney's heart to jump to her throat. It meant Jack was watching to make sure there wasn't a second gunman.

Or even a third.

The hired guns could be closing in on them and there was nowhere for them to go. But even with the terrifying realization, Laney had to wonder who was behind this. Who wanted her dead?

A sickening thought twisted at her. Terrance's call could have been meant to pinpoint their location. For that matter, so could Emerson's visit. Word about the safe-deposit box could have leaked, and now someone was going to try to kill her rather than give her a chance to reach Austin and get her hands on those pictures or whatever else was in the box. Unfortunately, Jack or Owen could be collateral damage.

Another bullet rang out, then another. These two shots blasted into the side of the porch, which confirmed to her that the shooter was definitely behind the tree. Maybe now that they knew his location, either Jack or Owen could stop him when he leaned out to fire again.

"Can you keep him busy while I get Laney to the cruiser?" Owen asked his brother.

Her gaze zoomed across the yard to the cruiser. It was closer than the porch but not by much. And the cruiser doors were closed. Jack would be able to open it with the remote on his keys, but to get the door open, he would have to leave what little cover he had.

"Yeah," Jack verified. "Move fast in case we get company."

That certainly did nothing to slow down her thudding heart. Laney shook her head. "It's too dangerous."

"So is staying put," Owen pointed out just as quickly. "Stay as low as possible, hurry and get underneath the cruiser. I'll be right behind you."

At least they weren't going to try to open the doors, and the cruiser itself would indeed give them some protection. Still, getting there wasn't going to be easy.

While there was another round of gunfire, Owen sent a text. Probably to Kellan to let him know they needed backup. The hands from Kellan's place would be able to get there faster than he would. Maybe in only a couple of minutes. And that gave her some hope that they might actually survive this.

Owen glanced back at her again. "Go as fast as you can," he told her.

That was the only warning she got before he moved. Not forward. He pulled her to his side so that he'd be between the gunman and her, and then he gave Jack a nod. Jack immediately levered up just enough to send some bullets in the direction of the tree.

And Jack started firing.

Owen started moving, and Laney scurried along beside him, digging her elbows and knees into the ground to get some traction. Each inch seemed to take an eternity, and there were more shots. Wild ones that she suspected the gunman was just blindly firing off with the hope of hitting them.

Along with a fresh hit of adrenaline, the raw fear

came roaring through her. Fear not just for her safety but for Jack and Owen. Once again, she'd put him and a member of his family in danger. Once again, she was the reason he might die, that by helping her, Owen might never see his little girl again.

Owen, though, had obviously figured out a way to get past the fear and focus on getting to the cruiser. The moment they reached it, he practically shoved her beneath it. Laney moved over far enough for him to get under there with her.

He didn't.

"Move," Owen called out to his brother. With his body only partially beneath the cruiser, he started firing, sending a series of shots in the direction of the gunman.

Jack turned and, staying low, crawled toward them. When he got closer, Laney took hold of him to pull him in next to her. Owen sent another round toward the shooter and then joined them.

The gunman was still firing so there was no way Laney could relax, but because they were no longer in the direct line of the shots, she did feel some relief.

It didn't last.

When the gunshots abruptly stopped, Laney heard another sound. Someone revving up a car engine. She hoped it wasn't one of the hands who would come charging in. If so, he or she could be shot, too.

"Hell," Jack swore.

Since she was between the two men again, Laney couldn't see what had caused him to curse. But she heard the car engine again. Closer this time.

"Hold on," Jack warned them.

Owen threw himself over her, gathering her beneath

him just seconds before the crash. There was the deafening sound of metal colliding with metal, and from the corner of her eye, she saw the tires of the other vehicle. It had rammed into the cruiser, bashing in the side enough so that the tires were nearly right on Jack. He scrambled back, bumping into Owen and her.

The engine revved up for a third time and she could see the vehicle reverse, readying to bash into them.

Owen moved fast, rolling her until they were out from beneath the cruiser and into the yard. Jack was right behind them. And not a second too soon. The cruiser was no doubt reinforced, but there was the horrific sound of metal being crunched.

"Keep an eye on Laney," Owen told his brother, rising as he passed her off to Jack.

She wanted to yell for Owen to get back down, but Laney realized what he was doing. With the cruiser between him and the vehicle that'd been ramming them, Owen started firing, almost certainly aiming his shots at the driver.

Laney sucked in her breath, so hard that she felt the pain in her chest. Mercy. Owen right there, putting his life on the line. He could be killed.

There was another squeal of brakes and Laney braced herself for another jolt. It didn't come. Instead of coming toward them, she heard the vehicle speed away.

Owen took off running after it.

Chapter 9

Owen stood in the observation room of the sheriff's office and watched Laney as she gave Kellan her statement about the attack. Owen had already done his report, but each word he'd written had only fueled his rage. It didn't soothe his temper one bit hearing and seeing Laney replay the ordeal.

He wanted to curse himself, but he didn't even know where to start. He'd screwed up way too many things today—things that could have gotten people killed.

Here, he'd ignored his gut instinct and allowed Laney to be put in yet another dangerous situation. One that had not only involved his brother but also his daughter. All those shots had been fired way too close to the house and Addie.

Owen had known it hadn't been a good idea to take Laney to the bank, had known her being out in the open was just asking for trouble. And trouble was exactly what they'd gotten.

However, that was only the start of things that he'd botched. The driver of the SUV that had nearly killed them had also gotten away. Now the ranch was yet another crime scene, and he had nothing to show for it. No shooter and no safe way to get Laney to Austin. Whoever was after her would just use that trip to make another attempt on her life.

When he saw Laney push back from the table and stand, Owen went back into the hall so he could see her. She wasn't crying, wasn't shaking. That was something at least, and she looked less on edge than he felt.

"Still beating yourself up?" she asked, sliding a hand down his arm.

Kellan came out of the room, his glance at Owen connecting long enough for them to have one of those silent brotherly conversations. At the end of it, Kellan only lifted an eyebrow.

"Laney held up just fine," his brother told him before he headed back to his office.

Owen was glad about the "holding up" part, but it didn't let him off the hook. "I deserve some beating up," he told her.

Laney made eye contact, too, but it was more than a long glance with those baby blues. "You saved my life" was all she said before she leaned in and brushed a kiss on his mouth.

He didn't know what stunned him more, the kiss or the fact that she seemed sincerely grateful even though he'd nearly gotten her and others killed by not listening to that bad feeling he'd had in his gut.

"I can see you don't want my thanks," she whispered.

"You want to beat yourself up for something that was out of your control. Should I beat myself up, too? After all, I'm the reason for the danger."

Owen cursed. "I knew it was a mistake to try to take you to the bank."

"I pushed you into it," Laney insisted and then paused. "Maybe we can beat ourselves up together?"

Laney added what might have been a smile to that, but he didn't want any attempt at being lighthearted right now. He was angry...and scared. Because no matter what he did, he might not be able to keep Addie, Laney and the others safe.

She stayed close, right against him, while she looked up at him. She seemed to be holding her breath as if waiting for something.

Behind them, he could hear the chatter in the squad room. Could also hear Kellan talking to someone on the phone. There was so much to do with this new investigation, but he didn't budge. Owen just stood there. Until he gave up on the notion of common sense.

And he kissed her.

He instantly felt the relief, the tension, draining from his body. Of course, he got a tension of a different kind. The heat from the attraction. But he didn't care. Right now, he just needed this, and he was pretty sure Laney needed it, too.

She moved against him, slipping right into his arms. Moving into the kiss, too. He took in her taste, her scent, and likely would've have taken a lot more than he should have if he hadn't heard the footsteps.

Owen pulled away from her and turned to see Gunnar coming toward them. If his fellow deputy had seen the kiss, then he wisely didn't say anything about it.

"I just had another go at questioning Gilley," Gunnar explained.

Owen certainly hadn't forgotten about the hired gun they had in a holding cell, but he'd moved the man to the back burner. He was glad, though, that Gunnar hadn't because right now Gilley was the one person who might be able to give them answers.

"Please tell me that Gilley's talking," Owen said.

Gunnar shook his head, but then he shrugged. "He's not talking about the attack, but when I mentioned that someone had tried to kill Laney and you again, he didn't exactly seem pleased about that. He got nervous and then demanded to speak to Emerson."

"Emerson?" Laney and Owen repeated at the same time.

"Did Gilley say why he wanted to see him?" Owen asked.

"No, but I figure Gilley's still wanting a plea deal, and he wants to go straight to the source."

Maybe. But with everything that had gone on, Owen had to wonder if Gilley wanted to talk to his boss, the man who'd hired him. And that man could be Emerson.

"I called Emerson to let him know about the *request*," Gunnar went on, "but he didn't answer, so I left him a voice mail." Gunnar stared at him. "You don't think it's a good idea for Emerson to see Gilley?"

Kellan had almost certainly filled Gunnar in on the investigation. All aspects of it. But it was possible that Gunnar didn't know that Owen now considered the DA a suspect in Hadley's murder.

"No, it could be a very good idea." Owen thought about it for a second. "But if Emerson shows for that talk, I'd like to be here to listen."

Gunnar nodded, started to walk away and then turned back. "Jack checked out the car that Terrance said was following him, but when he didn't get any hits, he went ahead to the ranch. He said he figured you'd want him to be there with Addie and the others."

Good. He did indeed want his brother at the ranch to make sure Addie stayed safe. Maybe the same at-large gunman was the one who'd attacked them, but it was just as possible there were several of the hired thugs. Either that or the shooter had manager to get away from the tree and into that SUV darn fast.

"I need to get some paperwork done," Owen told Laney after Gunnar had left. "You should try to get some rest in the break room."

She shook her head. "I can work, too, if I can borrow a computer. I need to touch base with the San Antonio cops to see if they're making progress on Joe's murder. I also want to contact some people who knew him and try to come up with a lead." She paused, met his gaze. "It's very likely that his killer and our attackers are one and the same."

Owen couldn't dispute that. He hated that her mind would be on murder when she was clearly exhausted, but if their positions had been reversed, he'd be doing the same thing. Any thread they could latch onto right now could lead them to an arrest and put an end to the danger.

"You can use my desk," he offered as they headed for the squad room. "I'll work in Kellan's office with him. Just stay away from the windows."

And Owen hated that he had to add a reminder like that. Not while the memories of the most recent nightmare were so fresh. Still, they had to take precautions even in the sheriff's office since one of their suspects was the district attorney who could easily gain access to the building.

"You do the same." Laney stopped as if she might say something else. Or kiss him again. But then she managed a thin smile before she went to his desk.

Kellan was on the phone when Owen walked into his office. Owen didn't know who he was talking to but, judging from his brother's tight jaw, it wasn't a pleasant conversation. Kellan wrote something down on a notepad, finished the call and stared at the phone for a few seconds before he put it away and looked at Owen.

"The link for the eavesdropping device was on one of the computers we took from Nettie and Emerson's house," Kellan finally said. "Specifically, it was on Nettie's laptop."

Owen understood his brother's tight jaw. Oh, man. This wasn't going to be pretty.

"The techs got not only a date but the exact time of installation." Kellan passed him the notepad and Owen saw that the software had been put on the computer less than a week earlier at four thirty in the afternoon. "Obviously, I'll need to get both Emerson and Nettie in here to see if they have alibis."

"They do," Owen immediately said. "That's when they had a big birthday barbecue for Nettie. I even dropped by with Addie." Owen cursed. "And that means Emerson and Nettie will claim one of the guests or someone from the catering company could have slipped inside and done this."

"Yeah," Kellan grumbled profanely. "I don't have to ask if you saw anyone suspicious."

Owen dragged a hand through his hair and tried to

pull up the memories of the party. "No, but there were a lot of people that I didn't know. Some of Nettie's old college friends and some of Emerson's business associates. Addie was fussy—teething," he added, "so I didn't stay long. Only about half an hour."

Still, Owen would go back through what he could remember of the day to see if there was anything to recall. One thing was for sure, he hadn't remembered anyone who'd looked like a hired thug. That would have certainly snagged his attention.

Kellan put his hands on his hips. "Let's go with the theory that Nettie knew about her husband's affair. An affair that her husband claims never happened. But maybe she wants to know for sure, and the best way for her to do that is to listen in on what Laney is saying."

"And have a look at her computer files," Owen piped in, agreeing with his brother's theory.

Kellan nodded. "Nettie could have hired someone to put the program on her computer, and the party would have been a good cover. Her hired man could just pose as part of the catering crew or a guest. Or Nettie could have even slipped away and installed the software herself."

Both were possible. Ditto for Emerson being able to do it, as well. No one would have thought anything about the host disappearing for the handful of minutes it would have taken to plant the device.

So they were right back to square one. Not a good place to be with the possibility of another attack looming over them.

"The next question is how Joe Henshaw fits into this," Owen noted, still going with Kellan's train of thought.

Maybe Laney had heard him say her assistant's name because she hurried to the doorway and volleyed glances at both of them. "What happened?"

Owen and Kellan looked at each other and Kellan gave him the go-ahead nod to answer her question.

"The eavesdropping software was on Nettie's computer," Owen explained. Then he filled her in on the time of the installation and the party that either Nettie or Emerson could have used as an alibi.

When he finished, Laney's only reaction was a long exhale of breath. Obviously the news wasn't a surprise to her, so the frustration he was seeing on her face was for him. Because she knew it wasn't easy for a member of his family to be a murder suspect.

"I don't know if Joe found something to link Nettie or Emerson to Hadley's murder," she said after she'd taken a moment to absorb everything. "I've been going through his files, and I haven't found anything like that. Maybe Nettie or Emerson didn't want to risk him, or me, learning something."

Owen tried to wrap his mind around Nettie and Emerson committing cold-blooded murder. He couldn't, but they likely hadn't been the ones to put the bullets in Joe. Maybe hadn't even been the ones who'd personally murdered Hadley. However, they could have hired someone to do their dirty work.

"Emerson gave us permission to review his financials," Owen reminded Kellan.

Kellan nodded again. "I got them just a couple of minutes ago. Nothing pops, but I haven't had time to take a close look."

"I can do that for you," Owen offered. But Emerson's bank accounts were only half of the picture. "Is the eavesdropping software enough for us to get into Nettie's accounts?"

The sound Kellan made let Owen know even with that kind of connection, it wasn't going to be easy, but he took out his phone anyway. It rang before Kellan could make a call.

"It's Austin PD," Kellan relayed to them. He didn't put it on speaker, but whatever the caller said to him had Kellan blowing out what sounded to be a breath of relief. Relief that didn't last long, though. "No. That's not a good idea. There's been another attack, and it's not safe." He paused, obviously listening, and ended the call with "Good. I'll get right on that."

"What happened?" Owen immediately asked.

Kellan typed something on his laptop keyboard. "The search warrant on the bank came through, *finally*, and since it's not safe for Laney to go there, I convinced the Austin cops to do a video feed for us when they open the box."

Owen didn't exactly cheer, but that was what he felt like doing. He'd wanted to know what was in that box without putting Laney in harm's way, and this was the best way to do it.

"I'm setting up the feed now," Kellan explained. He continued to work on the laptop while he turned the screen so that all three of them could see it.

Laney automatically moved in closer and, while she didn't say anything, Owen knew this had to feel like a victory for her. She'd been looking for this safe-deposit box for months because she believed it held the photos that would confirm her theory that Emerson had killed Hadley.

And maybe it would.

Owen certainly wasn't feeling victorious about that. Yes, if Emerson had indeed murdered Laney's sister, he wanted the man brought to justice. But that wasn't going to be easy when the photos might only prove an affair and nothing else. Of course, it was possible Hadley had something else in there.

As they waited, Laney took hold of his hand just as the images and sounds popped up on the computer screen. The audio feed crackled with static, but Owen had no trouble seeing the two uniformed cops go into the vault area. Owen didn't know who was operating the camera, but it didn't pan around much. The focus stayed on the box that a guy in a suit—probably the bank manager—pulled from one of the slots in the wall.

The suit set the box on a plain table that reminded Owen of the ones they used in the interview rooms, and he took out a key.

"Is that the key we got from Laney Martin?" Kellan asked the cop.

The uniform nodded and, several moments later, they had confirmation that it was when the manager used it to open it the box.

The person holding the camera immediately moved closer, zooming in on the interior.

Owen immediately cursed when he saw what was inside.

Chapter 10

*E*mpty.

That definitely hadn't been what Laney had expected when the bank manager opened the box. Nothing. Not even a scrap of paper.

Her thoughts immediately started to run wild.

"Maybe it's not the right box." Laney threw the possibility out there.

Owen made a sound of agreement. Kellan wasn't paying attention because he was already on the phone with the bank manager.

The cops cut the video feed, leaving her to stare at the blank screen. Mercy. Why couldn't there just have been pictures inside? Or something that would have confirmed what Hadley had told her about the affair with Emerson? Now they had nothing, no reason to go after Emerson so they could stop another attack.

If Emerson was to blame, that was.

"My name was on the box," she added, talking more to herself than Owen. Still, he answered her, along with sliding a soothing hand down her back.

"It was the right key," he pointed out, "but Hadley could have moved the contents."

That was possible, but it didn't answer why her sister would have done that, especially without telling Laney. After all, Hadley had volunteered the info about the pictures, but maybe she'd been murdered before she could let Laney know they'd been moved.

Kellan was cursing when he finished his call. "The bank manager said someone—a woman—accessed the box yesterday."

That got her attention and Laney's gaze shifted from the laptop to him. *Yesterday.* So, Hadley hadn't been the one to empty the box. But that left them with a huge question of who exactly had done that.

"Any reason the bank manager didn't tell us this sooner?" Laney demanded.

"He claims that he couldn't release any info about it until he had the search warrant." Kellan glanced down at the notes he'd taken during the call. "The person had a picture ID with Hadley's name, and she must have also had a key."

"The missing second key," Laney said under her breath. She wanted to blurt out some of that same profanity Kellan was using. "And she must have used a fake ID or one that she stole from Hadley when the key was taken."

Kellan stared at her. "Could Hadley have given the second key to someone else?"

Her mind was whirling so it was hard to think, but

Laney forced herself to focus. "She could have perhaps given it to Joe." But almost immediately she had to wave that off. "He would have told me if she'd done that—especially after she was murdered. He would have known it could be critical to finding her killer."

So, not Joe, but maybe a friend. Still, a friend should have come forward by now, which led Laney to consider that Hadley's killer might have taken the key. The only problem with that was why the killer had waited all this time to access the box.

"Hadley might have left it at Joe's place without him knowing," Owen suggested several moments later. Obviously they were all trying to work this out.

That was possible, but another thought flashed into her mind. Not a good thought, either. "Joe had…feelings for Hadley. Actually, I think he was in love with her. So, if she gave him the key and asked him to keep it a secret, he might have, especially since he knew I had found a key in her apartment."

Still, she was going with the theory that Joe hadn't known. And that the person who'd murdered him had searched his place, maybe found the key and then used it. That would explain why the killer had taken so long to get into the box. Maybe a female killer.

Maybe Nettie.

Of course, it was just as likely that Terrance or Emerson had hired a woman to pose as Hadley.

"The timing works," Owen said as if reading her thoughts. "Whoever broke into Joe's could have gotten the key and used it to go to the bank."

She shook her head. "But how would the person have known which bank?" Laney stopped, her eyes widening. "Terrance. He had the PI report, so he knew the location."

Owen was taking out his phone to call Terrance before she'd even finished. Because she was right next to him, she heard the unanswered rings and, a few seconds later, the voice mail message. Owen left a message for Terrance to call him back ASAP. Whether the man would actually do that was anyone's guess. If he was guilty, Terrance might even go on the run rather than answer any questions that could lead to his arrest.

"I'll get the footage on the security cameras from the bank, and that way we can see who went in there. I also want Terrance's financials," Kellan grumbled. "And on any other PI reports he might not have shared with us." He looked at Laney. "Do you still have any PI contacts?"

"I do. You want me to make some calls to see if Terrance hired anyone else that he hasn't told us about?"

Kellan nodded. "I'm especially interested if he had a female investigator who could have passed for your sister. Of course, he wouldn't need a PI for that because he could have hired anyone, but we might get lucky."

It was a long shot, but at this point, it was all they had. Laney went back to Owen's desk where she'd left the loaner laptop and got to work, finding contact numbers for every PI she could think of. Too bad her cell phone had been taken in the break-in because she'd had plenty of the numbers in it.

Laney had just finished a list when the front door flew open. Owen came rushing out of Kellan's office and he automatically stepped in front of her and drew his weapon. But it wasn't a hired gun who'd come there to attack them.

It was Emerson.

Along with being out of breath, the DA looked disheveled. His suit was wrinkled, his hair messed up, and there was a fine layer of sweat on his forehead. He opened his mouth and then glanced around at the two other deputies and the dispatcher before he motioned toward Kellan's office.

"We need to talk," Emerson said, his voice a little shaky.

Owen studied him for a couple of seconds before he got moving, staying between Emerson and Laney as they entered Kellan's office. Emerson immediately shut the door.

"The blackmailer called me again." Emerson took out his phone, put it on Kellan's desk in front of him and hit the play button.

"Time's run out, DA," the caller said. It was the same mechanical voice they'd heard before. "You've got an hour to get me that fifty thousand or I tell your sweet wife what's going on. No routing number this time. I want cash, and I'll be in touch as to where you can leave the money."

Kellan listened to it again and checked the time on the call. "It's already been nearly an hour."

Emerson nodded. "I figure he'll call me back any minute now. I don't have the money," he quickly added.

"You shouldn't be paying him anyway," Owen insisted. He moved so that Emerson and he were eye to eye. "You need to tell Nettie. That won't give this snake anything to hold over you. It'd be a lot better for her to hear it from you than him."

Obviously that wasn't the solution Emerson wanted because he huffed. Then he groaned and squeezed his eyes shut for a moment. "Nettie could believe the lie about the affair. She could leave me because of it."

"Maybe," Owen said. "But she's going to find out one way or another." He paused. "Besides, Nettie might have her own secrets."

"What do you mean?" Emerson snapped, his attention slicing to Owen.

Owen dragged in a long breath. "Go home, Emerson, and talk to your wife."

Emerson's stare turned into a glare. He held it for so long that Owen figured the man was about to have a burst of temper. But Emerson finally just shook his head. "I want to clear up this mess with the blackmailer first." His gaze shifted to Kellan and now there was some temper in his eyes. "If you can't or won't help me, then I'll have to handle it myself."

"I wouldn't advise that," Kellan told him.

Emerson's glare intensified as he snatched up his phone, obviously ready to storm out.

But Owen stopped him. "Rohan Gilley wants to talk to you."

Laney studied Emerson's expression, and she figured Owen and Kellan were doing the same. Something went through his eyes, something she couldn't quite peg. Frustration maybe? Or maybe something more. Fear? Of course, she could just be projecting that.

"I don't have time for Gilley right now," Emerson snapped. "Tell him that. Tell him I'll get back here when I have some things settled."

Emerson walked out, leaving Laney to wonder if that had been some kind of assurance or even a veiled threat for the gunman.

Kellan sighed. "I need to get both Nettie and him in

here, *together*, for a face-to-face interview. An official one where I ask some hard questions. I think a good air clearing might help all the way around since both of them have motives for the attacks."

Owen shook his head when Gunnar stepped in the office doorway. "Emerson won't be talking to Gilley for a while," he told his fellow deputy.

"I'll let him know, but that's not why I'm here." Gunnar paused. "It's bad news. We have a dead body."

Owen stared at the photo the Austin PD had just sent them and felt the punch of dread when he saw the dead woman's face. A face he'd seen on the surveillance footage that the bank had sent over earlier. He had no doubts that she'd been the same person who'd gotten into the safe-deposit box with Hadley's fake ID.

And now she wouldn't be able to tell them what she'd taken or where it was.

Laney touched her fingers to her mouth as she studied the photo, and Owen saw her blink hard. No doubt fighting tears. "She doesn't look like my sister. Not really."

No. The hair color was the same, but that was about all. It was something the woman could have easily dyed to come closer to a physical match for the person she'd been impersonating.

"What happened to her?" Laney asked, glancing at Gunnar before her gaze went back to the photo.

"Two gunshot wounds to the chest," Gunnar explained. "Point-blank range. She had two IDs on her. One in your sister's name and the other was her own driver's license. Her prints were in the system, so they were able to confirm her identity as Nancy Flanery."

Laney's forehead creased, and she repeated the name as if trying to recall where she'd heard it before. "It sounds familiar, but I don't recognize her."

"Austin PD's running a background check now. I'm doing the same," Gunnar added a moment later. "She's from San Antonio and is a criminal informant."

That got Owen's attention. "A CI?" he said under his breath. "For Austin PD?"

"San Antonio," Gunnar clarified. "She has a record for drug possession, but her latest arrest was three years ago. She seems to have stayed clean since then. Or maybe she just hadn't gotten caught."

Either was possible. Obviously she had crossed paths with someone who'd either paid her to impersonate Hadley or had forced or coerced her into doing it.

"Someone must have hired her to go to that bank," Laney said.

That was Owen's top theory, too. Hired her, used her to get their hands on the photos and then murdered her so that she wouldn't be able to tell the cops who'd paid her to get into that safe-deposit box.

"Oh, and I thought this was interesting…" Gunnar continued, reading from his notes. "According to the preliminary report, Nancy Flanery had gunshot residue on her hands, but there was no weapon found on her."

Owen thought about that for a second. "Maybe because her killer took it. But she could have gotten off a shot first."

With luck, perhaps she could have even wounded her attacker. If so, Austin PD might find blood other than the victim's at the crime scene.

Laney went into the squad room and brought back the laptop she'd been working on. "Let me do a search of my files to see if anything pops up. Like I said, her name sounds familiar, so it's possible she was connected to one of my investigations."

She put the laptop on Kellan's desk and, leaning over, typed in "Nancy Flanery." She frowned when nothing came up. "Let me switch to Joe's files." Laney repeated the process.

Then she froze.

"She's here." Laney turned the screen so that Kellan, Gunnar and Owen would better be able to see it. "A week ago Joe talked to her after he'd gotten a tip that she knew something about Hadley's killer. Nancy claimed she didn't, but Joe apparently didn't believe her." She tapped the screen to show the triple question marks Joe had added at the end of the short report.

"Did you ever meet this woman?" Kellan asked.

"No. I'm almost positive I didn't. According to these notes, this was the first time Joe had met with her. Since it was only a week ago, I was already at Owen's. I didn't do any interviews after I moved there."

She looked at Owen and once again he saw the apology in her eyes. He definitely didn't like that she'd lied to him, but with the attacks, he knew why she had been so cautious.

"Do you think she's the one who killed Joe?" Laney asked. "If she's working for the person who attacked us, then she could have gone after Joe." But she waved that off. "I know it's a long shot."

It was, but it could still be a connection. Joe might not have had his guard up if someone he'd known had approached him, and it was possible Nancy had murdered Joe and then gone to the bank in Austin. The timing would work. If she had indeed committed murder and then fraud, the woman would have been a bad loose end.

And it had likely gotten her killed.

"I'll try to put a rush on that background check," Gunnar offered. He headed back into the squad room just as Kellan's phone rang.

Kellan scrubbed his hand over his face and showed them the name on the screen. Nettie. After blowing out a huff of frustration, he answered the call and put it on speaker.

"Emerson's missing," Nettie blurted out before Kellan could even issue a greeting. Her voice was practically a shout. "You've got to find him now."

"Nettie, he's not missing," Kellan assured her. "He was just here in my office."

She made a hoarse sob. "He's there? I need to talk to him."

"He left already." Kellan huffed again. "I was hoping he'd go home to you."

"He hasn't been here. What did he say?" Nettie demanded, her words running together.

Owen could tell from his brother's expression that Kellan was trying to figure out how to answer that. He took several moments and the woman continued to cry. "What's this about, Nettie?"

Nettie took a couple of moments, as well. "His assistant said Emerson was very upset, that he grabbed some things from his desk and practically ran out. She'd never seen him like that, and was worried about him, so she let me know about it. But when I tried to call him, he didn't answer. Something's wrong, and you need to find him now."

That didn't help ease the frustration on Kellan's face.

"I'll see what I can do. If I find out anything, I'll let you know."

"Emerson could be meeting with the blackmailer," Laney said the moment Kellan ended the call with Nettie.

Kellan made a sound of agreement and stepped out into the squad room. "Raylene," he said, speaking to one of the deputies, Raylene McNeal. "I need you to find Emerson. Make some calls, ask around, see what you can come up with."

Since Raylene had witnessed Emerson storming out earlier, she didn't seem especially surprised by the request. She just nodded and took out her phone.

Owen was about to volunteer to help, but he saw their visitor walking toward the front door. Terrance. The moment he was inside, he flicked Laney a glance before his attention zoomed to Owen.

"I couldn't take your call, but your voice mail sounded...urgent," Terrance said. "What can I do to help?" As usual, there was a chilly layer of indifference in his tone and expression.

"It is urgent," Owen assured him. "A woman was murdered, and I want to know if one of your PI tails happened to see her."

Terrance shrugged his shoulders. "I can ask them, but why would they have done that? Does this dead woman have a connection to Laney?"

Owen held off on answering. Instead he turned the computer screen toward Terrance so he could see the photo Austin PD had sent them. "Her name is Nancy Flanery."

The indifference vanished and Terrance whirled toward Laney. This time, there was fiery anger in his eyes. "What kind of sick game are you playing?" he demanded.

That rage was in his voice, too. So much rage that Owen actually stepped between Laney and him. Laney didn't let that last long, though. She moved to Owen's side and faced Terrance head-on.

"I'm not playing a game," Laney insisted. "Do you know that woman?"

Terrance had to get his jaw unclenched before he spoke. "Are you trying to set me up?"

Owen figured Laney looked as surprised as he did. "Why would you think that?" Owen demanded.

Terrance jabbed his index finger at the picture on the screen. "Because Nancy works for me."

Chapter 11

Laney wasn't sure what she'd expected Terrance to say, but that wasn't it. She shook her head. "Nancy was a criminal informant."

Terrance groaned and, with his gaze back on Nancy's picture, sank into the chair next to Kellan's desk. Laney couldn't tell if he was genuinely upset or if this was all some kind of act.

"Nancy sold info to the cops every now and then," Terrance admitted. "But I'd also hired her to keep an ear out for any information about Hadley's murder." He looked at Laney again and some of his anger rekindled. "I figured eventually you'd try to pin your sister's death on me. Just to get back at me. If you ended up doing that, I wanted some ammunition I could use to defend myself."

Laney didn't take her gaze from his. "I want to find her actual killer, not simply *pin* it on someone."

"Right," he said as if he didn't believe her. He tipped his head to the photo. "Who did that to her? Who killed her?"

Owen stepped closer, standing directly in front of Terrance. "That's what we're trying to find out. Start talking. When's the last time you saw her?"

It was a simple enough question, but it only seemed to bring Terrance's rage. "I didn't kill her, and I refuse to stay here and be accused of it." He sprang to his feet, obviously ready to bolt, but Owen took hold of his arm to stop him.

"You can either answer that here, or I'll arrest you for obstruction of justice and withholding evidence," Owen warned him. "Then you'll wait in a holding cell until Austin PD can come and pick you up."

Terrance slung off his grip with far more force than was necessary before he got right in Owen's face. "Are you doing Laney's bidding now? Her witch hunt?" Terrance practically spit the words out.

"I'm asking a question." Owen definitely didn't back down. "One that it sounds like you're evading. When's the last time you saw Nancy?"

They continued to glare at each other for several long seconds before Terrance ground out some raw profanity and dropped back a step. "Three days ago. She called to say she needed some cash and wondered if I had any jobs for her. I told her I didn't, but that if I found something, I'd get back to her." He paused. "Did she do something stupid to get the money she needed?"

"It looks that way," Owen conceded. "Posing as Hadley, she went into the very bank where your PI had followed Hadley shortly before she was killed."

Terrance cursed again, but this time when he spoke,

his voice was much softer. "Someone obviously hired Nancy to do that and then killed her after she'd finished the job. And no, it wasn't me," he quickly added. He shook his head. "I wouldn't have had a PI on her or the bank so I can't tell you who did this."

Laney considered not just what he'd said but also his body language. Terrance looked and sounded sincere, but this could definitely be an act. If so, then why had he used one of his own employees to get into the bank? Maybe it was some sort of reverse psychology. By putting himself in the center of this, he perhaps thought it would make him appear innocent.

Laney had no intentions, though, of taking him off her suspect list.

"I'll speak with my PIs," Terrance said, glancing over at Kellan before staring at Owen. "Do you plan to arrest me?"

Owen took his time answering. "Not yet, but we'll need an official statement."

"I'll take it," Kellan volunteered.

Terrance's mouth tightened again. "I'll want my lawyer here."

"Then call him and tell him to get over here ASAP. Until he arrives, you can stay in the interview room." Kellan led him in that direction.

Laney waited until they were out of earshot before she turned to Owen. "I just don't know if what he said was true," he commented before she could ask. "But even if it was, I still don't trust him."

So they were on the same page and, while it was comforting to have him on her side, they were in a very frustrating position. Someone else was dead and they still didn't have the photos or whatever else her sister had left in the safe-deposit box. Worse, they couldn't arrest anyone to make sure no one else got killed. Or that there were no more attacks on Laney and him.

Owen stared at her a moment, slipped his arm around her and eased her to him. "I'd like to be able to get you out of here, to take you back to my grandparents' house."

She filled in the blanks. Yes, he wanted to do that, but it wasn't safe. "We can stay here as long as necessary." Laney paused. "Maybe we should put out the word that we're here. It could put off someone sending hired guns to the ranch."

He pulled back, met her gaze. "And make ourselves targets. Especially you." Owen cursed softly. "You're thinking of Addie. Thank you for that."

"You don't have to thank me. Of course, I'm thinking about her. I'd rather thugs come after me here than there. In fact, maybe it's time to use me as bait."

This time his profanity wasn't so soft and he jerked away. "No," he snapped. "No." When he repeated it, his voice was a little softer, but filled with just as much emotion. "And that doesn't have a damn thing to do with that kiss. Or this one."

She didn't even see it coming, but his mouth was suddenly on hers. Taking. And his right hand went to the back of her neck, holding her in place. There was no gentleness here, only the raw emotion of the moment. It was rough, punishing, but even then she could feel the heat in it. Could feel the need that it stirred in her.

"No," he repeated for a third time. His hand was still on her neck, his fingers thrust into her hair, and he stayed that way for several moments before he finally backed away from her.

"I just want Addie safe," she managed to say when she gathered enough breath to speak. "I want *you* safe."

The corner of his mouth lifted, but the amusement vanished as quickly as it had come. "Now, that's the kiss talking."

No, it wasn't. It was what she felt for him, but rather than say that, Laney kept things light. "Well, it was a good kiss. Memorable," she added, trying out one of those partial smiles. Like his, hers was short-lived. Because it hadn't been just memorable.

The kiss had been unforgettable.

Owen was unforgettable.

And when this was over and they'd caught the person trying to kill them, she was going to have to deal with not only the aftermath of the violence but also something else. Having her heart broken into a million little pieces.

The thought of having sex with him flashed into her head, and she nearly blurted out that they should go for it at least once so they could burn off some of this fire that was flowing through them. Thankfully, she didn't get the chance to spill all—something she would have no doubt regretted—because someone came in through the front door of the squad room.

Nettie.

Great. Laney didn't have the mental energy to deal with the woman, and she figured Owen didn't, either. But Nettie stopped the moment her attention landed on them. Laney was no longer in Owen's arms, but she realized that he hadn't taken his hand from her hair. He eased his grip away as he turned toward Nettie.

"I'm glad you have time for that sort of thing," Nettie said, irony and bitterness in her voice.

Laney was a little surprised when Owen didn't move away from her. He stayed shoulder to shoulder with her, still touching her as they faced the woman.

"You're supposed to be looking for Emerson," Nettie added. She marched toward them. "But I find you here with your hands on the very person who's responsible for the mess we're in."

"Excuse me?" Laney said at the same moment Owen snarled, "What the hell does that mean?"

"We didn't have trouble until she came here. She lied to you, turned you against Emerson and me, and now Emerson is missing." Each of Nettie's words snapped like a bullwhip, but the fit of temper must have drained her because on a hoarse sob, she sagged against the door frame. "I need to find my husband. Please." She looked at Laney when she added the *please*.

Laney wasn't immune to the woman's pain. That seemed like the real deal. But she didn't trust Nettie any more than she did Terrance or Emerson.

"I take it that Emerson didn't return your call?" Owen asked as he helped Nettie to a chair. He also turned the computer where the photo of the dead woman was still on the screen.

"No. I called him six times. Maybe more. And he hasn't answered." A fresh round of tears came, but Nettie quickly brushed them away. She looked up at him. "Tell me what happened to him. I have to know what's going on." Nettie added another whispered *please*.

Owen stared at her a moment then dragged in a long breath. "Just know that Emerson isn't going to thank me for telling you this." He paused several long moments. "Someone's been trying to blackmail Emerson."

Nettie looked up at him, blinked. Judging from her

stunned reaction, she hadn't been expecting that. "Wh-what?"

"A blackmailer who's called him several times to try to extort money from him."

Nettie shook her head and volleyed wide-eyed glances at Laney and him as if looking for any signs this was a joke. "Blackmail him for what?"

Owen just stared at her.

The woman did another round of glancing before she shook her head. "No. My husband didn't have an affair with her sister." She flung an accusing finger at Laney.

Laney figured she was the one who looked surprised now. "What do you know about my sister?" she prompted. Of course, Terrance had said there'd been a meeting between Hadley and Nettie, but Laney hadn't known if he was telling the truth or not.

"I know my husband didn't have an affair with her." Nettie seemed adamant about that, too, and when she got to her feet, she seemed a lot stronger than she had just seconds earlier. "Yes, I've heard talk, but I know it's not true. Emerson wouldn't cheat on me."

Laney didn't argue with her, but she would mention something else. "Why else would someone try to blackmail your husband?"

Nettie's chin came up. "There are plenty of reasons. Emerson's an important man, and he's prosecuted a lot of bad people. One of them could be trying to get some revenge."

"This doesn't seem to be about revenge," Owen quickly pointed out. "Blackmailers usually want money to keep a secret. Of course, they usually end up wanting more and more money."

Nettie stared at him again and Laney thought she

was maybe trying to find a reasonable comeback. But Nettie only huffed, "I don't know why someone would demand money. But it's not because he cheated." She started to pace across Kellan's office. "It probably has something to do with that mix-up about the eavesdropping program being on my computer."

It wasn't a mix-up. The program had been there, but obviously Nettie wasn't going to accept responsibility for that.

"Was Emerson upset about that?" Owen asked, sounding very much like a cop who was fishing for information from a potential suspect.

"Of course, he was. But he knows I was set up, that there's no way I would do something like that." Nettie stopped the pacing so she could glare at Laney. "Why would I care about eavesdropping on you anyway?"

Laney didn't even have to think about the answer to that. "Because you're worried that your husband did indeed have an affair with my sister and you wanted to know if I'd found any proof of it."

"No!" Nettie's glare got worse. "I didn't do that because there's no proof to find. I know you want to find your sister's killer, but you'd better keep my husband and me out of your lies."

Owen took Nettie by the shoulders. "What if she's not lying?" he asked. "What if Laney's telling the truth?"

Laney steeled herself for another lash from Nettie's temper, but the woman stilled and shook her head. There was nothing adamant about that head shake, though, and the tears shimmered in Nettie's eyes again.

Owen turned at the sound of footsteps. When Kellan stepped into the doorway, he looked at the three of them, obviously piecing together what had been going on. He motioned for Owen to join him in the squad room and extended the gesture to Laney. They stepped out, but Kellan didn't say anything until he was back in the hall and out of Nettie's earshot.

"Terrance called his PIs," Kellan told them. "All of them claim they hadn't seen Nancy in days and that they don't know who hired her to go into the safe-deposit box."

"You believe them?" Owen asked.

Kellan lifted his shoulder. "Terrance put the calls on speaker so I could hear, and the PIs seemed to be telling the truth. Of course, Terrance could have coached them to say that. After all, we would have found the connection between Nancy and him, and he would have known that would eventually lead to us talking to his PIs."

Yes, it would have, and coaching was something Terrance would have done. He would cover any and all bases rather than go back to jail.

Laney glanced in the direction of his office just to make sure Nettie hadn't come out. She hadn't. "As far as we know, Terrance is the only one of our suspects who knew Nancy."

Kellan nodded. "So, I ask myself, why would he use her? But maybe he did that because he might not be the only one of our suspects with links to Nancy. I want to take a look at Nancy's phone logs and financials that Austin PD will be getting. There might be something there to help us with our investigation."

Laney agreed, and her gaze drifted back to Nettie. "And her financials?"

"I'm working on it," Kellan said with a sigh. He opened his mouth to say more but a loud shout stopped him. It had come from the squad room, and it had both Owen and Kellan drawing their weapons.

"Get out here now!" someone yelled.

Emerson.

Kellan and Owen both moved in front of Laney and rushed into the squad room. From over their shoulders, she immediately saw Emerson. And he wasn't alone. He had a man with him.

Emerson was also armed.

He had a gun pointed at a man he was dragging in by his collar. When Emerson slung the man onto the floor, Laney could see that his hands were tied behind his back.

"I had him meet me," Emerson huffed, his breath gusting. His clothes were torn, too, and there was a bruise forming on his right cheek. "And then I bashed him on the head so I could bring him here."

"Who is he?" Kellan asked.

"The blackmailer." Emerson spit the word out like a profanity. "Arrest him now."

Owen had already had too many surprises today, but obviously they weren't finished when it came to that.

"Give me the gun," Owen ordered Emerson.

Owen intended to get to the bottom of…well, whatever the heck this was, but he didn't want to start until he got that weapon out of Emerson's hand. That wild look in his brother-in-law's eyes let Owen know this was still a very volatile situation.

"Arrest him now," Emerson repeated.

"I'll start doing that when you give me your weapon," Owen countered. He made a quick check to see if Kellan was still in front of Laney. He was. Kellan also had his arm hooked around Nettie, no doubt to prevent the woman from rushing to her husband.

The fire in Emerson's eyes heated up even more, and it didn't look as if he had any intentions of surrendering the weapon. Not until Nettie spoke.

"Emerson, you're hurt," she said, her voice cracking. "He needs an ambulance," she snarled to Kellan.

Emerson glanced at his wife, at the man on the floor, and seemed to realize what he'd just done. He passed the gun to Owen, and Owen handed it off to Gunnar.

"What happened?" Owen asked Emerson.

But he didn't get a chance to answer. Nettie broke away from Kellan and ran to her husband. She landed right in his arms. Owen considered pulling them apart so he could pat down Emerson for other weapons, but Kellan came forward to do that. Judging from both his and Nettie's glares, neither cared much for that.

"He needs an ambulance," Nettie repeated. She was crying now, but they all ignored her. Even Emerson. Though she did gently touch her fingers to that bruise on his face.

"I did what I needed to do," Emerson snapped. "What you wouldn't do." He glanced at both Owen and Kellan when he added that. "He was blackmailing me, and I put a stop to it."

"I wasn't blackmailing him," the man insisted. There was a bruise on his cheek as well, and the anger radiated over every inch of his face. "I told this nutjob he has it all wrong."

"He met me to take the money that he'd demanded," Emerson insisted. "I didn't have the cash, but I'd stuffed some newspapers in a big envelope to make him think I had it. That's how I got him close enough to hit him."

"I didn't know it was blackmail," the man snapped. "I was just doing somebody a favor."

A bagman. Or else he was claiming to be one.

"Who are you?" Owen demanded. He hauled the man to his feet so he could pat him down. No weapons, and his hands had been secured with a pair of plastic cuffs.

"Norman Perry." The sour tone matched his expression.

"Running him now," Gunnar volunteered.

While Owen waited for Gunnar to do that, Nettie looked up at her husband. "What happened? Why would this man be trying to blackmail you?"

It wasn't a question Owen had intended to ask—because he already knew the answer—so he paused to give Emerson a chance to tell his wife. Emerson certainly didn't jump to do that. He took his time while he looked at everyone in the room but Nettie.

"Someone lied and said I did something I didn't do," Emerson finally said. He tipped his head to Perry. "He had a gun, but I took it from him. It's in my car, and it's unlocked out front."

"I'll get it." Gunnar volunteered. He had his phone pressed to his ear as he went out.

With a firm hold on Perry's arm, Owen led him to the chair next to Gunnar's desk and had him sit. He hadn't done that for Perry's comfort but rather so he could get Laney away from the front windows. When she followed him, Owen motioned for her to go back toward the doorway to Kellan's office. She'd still be able to see and hear everything, but it might keep her out of harm's way.

"What you did was stupid," Kellan said, and he

wasn't talking to Perry but rather to Emerson. "You confronted an armed man who could have killed you."

"I wasn't gonna kill anybody," Perry snapped.

Emerson came closer, practically toe-to-toe with Kellan. "You wouldn't stop him, so I did."

Nettie shook her head. "What's going on here? Why wouldn't you stop someone who was trying to blackmail my husband?"

"I didn't get a chance to stop him," Kellan assured her. "I only recently found out about the blackmail, and Emerson stormed out of here before giving me a chance to do anything about it."

They all looked at Gunnar when he came back in. He'd bagged a gun and was off his phone. "His name is Norman Perry. Age forty-three. He lives in San Antonio. No police record."

Now, that was another surprise. Owen would have thought the guy had a rap sheet. "Is the gun legal?" Owen asked Gunnar.

"I'll run it, but he's got a permit to carry concealed."

Another surprise, though Owen figured that people with permits could and did commit serious crimes. And this was indeed serious. Well, it was if Emerson had told the truth about the man.

"I took the classes for carrying concealed," Perry grumbled. "You've got no cause to hold me."

"He does," Emerson practically yelled. "He tried to blackmail me."

"No, I didn't." Not quite a shout from Perry, but it was close to one. "My girlfriend works for a company, Reliable Courier. She's sick, and her boss was swamped, so I said I'd make the delivery and do the pickup. That's all. Call Rick at Reliable Courier if you don't believe me."

This time, it was Kellan who made the call. While he did that, Owen continued with Perry, "Who hired Reliable Courier to meet with Emerson?"

"Wouldn't have a clue," Perry answered. "You'd have to ask Rick."

Owen was certain Kellan would do just that. "What were you supposed to pick up and deliver?"

Perry huffed, "Don't know that, either, but you can see for yourself on the delivery. The card is in a small envelope in my wallet. I put it there because it was little and I didn't want to lose it. My wallet's in the back pocket of my jeans."

Owen put on a pair of plastic gloves that Gunnar handed him. Without cutting off the restraints, Owen retrieved the wallet and pulled out a small envelope, the size that would be on a gift bouquet of flowers. There was a card inside, and someone had written what appeared to be the URL for a website. Beneath it was more writing labeled as a password.

"What is this?" Owen asked Perry.

"Hell if I know. Like I said, I'm just the deliveryman."

"He is," Kellan verified a moment later. He was still on his phone. "I'll check it all out, of course, but according to the owner, Perry was indeed just doing him a favor. He's getting me the client info now on the person who wanted this pickup and delivery."

Good. That might clear things up. Owen bagged the card and envelope, and Gunnar took it, first putting the official info on the bag and then taking it to the computer.

"Can I go now?" Perry complained.

"Not yet." Owen went to the computer to watch as Gunnar typed in the website, and Laney joined him. Nettie was still fussing over Emerson's injuries, but Emerson's attention was nailed to the monitor.

Gunnar entered the password, waited, and the images loaded on the screen. Photos.

"That's a photo of the safe-deposit box at the bank," Laney said, studying the image.

It was. Whoever had taken the picture had made sure the number was clearly visible.

Gunnar went to the next shot. A photo of the box open to show the manila envelope inside. Owen couldn't be sure, but it could have been the one from the photograph Terrance's PI had taken of Hadley the day she'd visited the bank.

"This is a hoax," Emerson said, and he hurried to Gunnar. Owen stepped in front of Emerson to stop him from doing whatever he'd been about to do. "Obviously this is just part of the blackmail scheme," Emerson insisted. "It'll be lies. All lies."

Owen wasn't sure about the lies part, but yeah, it was likely part of the blackmail. He held off Emerson while Gunnar loaded the next picture. It was a shot of photographs that appeared to have been removed from the manila envelope.

Photos of Emerson and Hadley.

"What is that?" Nettie asked. She moved closer, too, her gaze slashing from one image to the next.

"They're fake," Emerson growled, but the color had drained from his face, making that god-awful bruise stand out even more.

Owen didn't think so. There were two rows of photographs. The ones on the top row were semiselfies with Hadley awake and in bed, next to a sleeping Emerson. Since Emerson was on his back, it wasn't hard to miss that he was naked, and he certainly wasn't being restrained. His arms were stretched out like a sated man getting some rest.

The shots on the bottom row were ones that looked as if Hadley had taken them on the sly. Emerson in a glass shower and then while dressing. Owen couldn't tell if Emerson had been aware of the shots beings taken.

"They're fake," Emerson repeated, his voice wavering now.

Nettie didn't seem to hear him. She continued to study the photos.

"Rick at Reliable Courier got the name of the person who arranged for pickup and delivery," Kellan said. "He claimed his name was James Smith. The guy paid in cash, so I'm betting it's an alias."

Yeah. Owen figured that would prove to be true. He was also betting this James Smith was yet another hired gun. But why had the person who'd hired him left the blackmail to a courier company? That was something Owen needed to dig into.

Nettie shook her head. When she finally looked up at Emerson, there were tears in her eyes. She didn't have the distraught expression she'd had when she'd entered the sheriff's office. Now there was only hurt.

"You had sex with her," Nettie muttered. "Admit it. I want to hear you say it." Emerson reached for her, but she batted his hands away. "Say it!" This time her voice was a lot louder.

Emerson stared at her. And stared. "I had sex with

her," he finally admitted. His gaze immediately flashed to Kellan. "But I didn't kill her."

The silence came, and it felt as if the entire room was holding its breath, waiting for whatever was about to happen.

Nettie finally broke that silence. "You lied," she said and, without even looking at Emerson, she headed for the door.

The first word that came to Owen's mind was *broken*. Nettie was broken.

"Wait!" Emerson called out as he rushed after her.

Nettie didn't stop. She just kept on walking, Emerson trailing along behind her.

"I'll go check on them," Gunnar said. "Should I bring them back inside?" he added to Kellan.

Kellan shook his head. "Not yet. Just make sure they aren't going to attack each other or anything. Then, once they've cooled off, I want Emerson back in here for questioning."

About a possible murder.

Hell. Owen groaned. Emerson had been denying this affair, but those pictures proved otherwise, which meant the man had been lying through his teeth.

But what else had he lied about?

Had Emerson actually been the one to kill Hadley?

Owen glanced at Laney, expecting to see some "I told you so" on her face, but there was none. There was only grief. No doubt because all of this had brought back the nightmarish memories of her sister's murder. She'd been right about Emerson lying about the affair, but sometimes being right didn't fix things.

"Emerson's not a flight risk," Kellan noted, "but I'll

feel a lot better after Gunnar's brought him back in and I have him in the interview room."

Owen felt the same way.

"Can I go now?" Perry snapped.

Dragging in a frustrated breath, Kellan went to him and cut the restraints. "I'll need a statement first and then you can go." He tipped his head toward his office. "In there."

Only then did Owen remember they still had Terrance in the interview room, which was why Kellan hadn't sent Perry there.

"Let me get this website to the lab guys, and I'll talk to Terrance," Owen offered.

Owen started to do just that when his phone rang and he saw Eli's name on the screen. Since his brother was still at their grandparents' house with Addie and the others, Owen answered it right away.

"We got a problem," Eli immediately said. "One of the hands just spotted a gunman on the ranch."

Chapter 12

Everything inside Laney was racing. Her heart, her breath and the adrenaline. Just seconds before Eli's call, so many thoughts had been going through her head, but now there was only one.

Keep Addie safe.

Sweet heaven. The little girl had to be okay.

"Drive faster," Owen ordered his fellow deputy Raylene McNeal.

The deputy was behind the wheel of the cruiser with Owen and Laney in back. It had taken a stern, direct order from Kellan to stop Owen from driving, and Laney had been thankful for it. She figured his thoughts had to be racing even more than hers were.

Raylene mumbled something about already going too fast, but she sped up anyway. With the siren howling and the blue lights flashing, she raced down the road that led out of town and toward the ranch. At this speed, it wouldn't take long to get there, but every mile and every minute would feel like an eternity.

Owen had his gun drawn and had his phone gripped in his left hand. He no doubt wanted to be ready if Eli called him back with an update. And Eli would. But he obviously wouldn't be able to call if the ranch was under attack.

"You shouldn't have come," Owen said to her.

He'd already told her variations of that since they'd rushed out of the sheriff's office. Kellan hadn't issued her one of those stern orders but instead had given her a gun. It made sense. After all, she was a PI, knew how to shoot and Owen might need more backup than Kellan could provide. Still, Owen would see this as her being in danger again.

And he could be right.

But there was no chance she was going to stay back. Kellan had had no choice about that since someone needed to man the office, but Laney had had a choice. One she'd made despite Owen's objections.

Owen's phone dinged with a text, the sound piercing through the silence. "Gunnar's on his way to the ranch," he relayed when he read the message. "Kellan called him and pulled him off Emerson and Nettie."

Good. They might need all the help they could get. Plus, Emerson and Nettie might welcome the time to figure out how they were going to handle the bombshell of the affair. And then maybe Kellan could just go ahead and arrest him. Of course, Kellan would need some kind of evidence.

The photos were proof of an affair but not of murder. Laney kept watch around them, knowing full well that the gunman at the ranch could be a ruse to get them on the road for another attack. But Laney didn't see anything, not even another vehicle.

The silence gave her mind a chance to stop racing, and maybe it was that temporary calm that allowed a fresh thought to creep into her head.

"Why would Hadley have taken those pictures?" Laney hadn't meant to say that aloud, but she had, and Owen had clearly heard it. Since he had, she continued, "She said he threatened her when he broke things off, but those photos were obviously taken when they were still together."

He glanced at her before he returned to keeping watch. "You think she was going to try to blackmail him?"

She shook her head. "Not for money. But maybe for emotional blackmail." Laney paused, forced herself to give that more thought. "Maybe Hadley thought she could use the pictures to force Emerson to stay with her."

Before Owen could respond, he got another text from Eli.

Gunman spotted just off the road leading to the ranch. Approach with caution. I'm in pursuit. Jack and one of the hands are in the house with Addie.

The road leading to the ranch was less than a mile away so Laney moved to the edge of her seat to try to spot him if and when he came into view.

"This had better not be a trap to lure Eli away from the house," Owen said under his breath.

And that sent her pulse into a full gallop. A gallop

that was almost impossible for Laney to tamp down. "We're almost there," she reminded Owen, and in doing so, she reminded herself, so she could try to stay calm. "We need to keep an eye out for both the gunman and Eli."

Taking her own advice, Laney did just that while she kept a firm grip on her gun. Unfortunately, this stretch of the road was lined with fences, ditches and trees. Too many places for someone to hide. There was also another possibility: that the gunman had already driven off. It was possible he'd left a vehicle on the road, sneaked onto the ranch and, when he'd been spotted, could have run back to whatever transportation he'd used to get there.

"Kill the sirens," Owen told Raylene, and the deputy shut them off. No doubt so they'd be able to hear whatever was going on outside. Going in hot might drown out sounds that could lead them to the gunman's exact location.

Raylene slowed as she approached the turn for the ranch, and again Laney tried to pick through all the possible hiding places to spot or hear him. Nothing. No sign of Eli, either, though she was certain he had to be somewhere in the area.

"There," Owen said, pointing toward the fence.

Laney immediately shifted her gaze in that direction, but she still didn't see anyone. Not at first anyway. And then she saw the blur of movement as someone darted between two trees.

"That's not Eli," Owen added.

No, it wasn't. Eli was tall and lanky, and this guy had bulky shoulders and a squat build. From the quick glimpse she'd gotten of him, Laney had thought he was armed with a rifle. That made sense because he could use it to fire from a distance. Heck, he could fire from this spot, depending on how good a scope he had. He likely wouldn't be able to fire into the grandparents' house, but the idiot could shoot at Eli.

Or at them.

And that was exactly what happened. Laney had no sooner had the thought when the bullet slammed into the window right where she was sitting. The safety glass shattered, but it held in place.

Cursing, Owen dragged her down onto the seat. Not a second too soon because three other shots blasted straight toward them, all hitting the glass. This time, it didn't hold, and the shards fell down onto them.

The sounds of the shots were still ringing in her ears, but Laney heard something else. Other rounds of gunfire, and these didn't seem to be coming from the shooter.

"Eli," Owen said. He kept her pushed down on the seat, but he levered up. Now that the glass had been knocked out, he took aim through the gaping hole.

He fired, too.

It was just a single shot, but it seemed to be enough because almost immediately she felt him relax just a little.

"The gunman's down," Raylene relayed.

Good. Laney didn't want the snake in any position to hurt Addie or anyone else. Maybe, though, he was still alive so he could give them answers.

"Pull up closer to Eli," Owen instructed Raylene. When the deputy did that, Owen moved off Laney. "Raylene, wait here with Laney," he said just seconds before he threw open the door.

Laney didn't get out with him, but she levered herself up so she could look out the window. She saw Owen running toward the man on the ground. Eli was also approaching him from the direction of the ranch. Owen reached the guy first and, after he kicked away the rifle, he reached down and touched his fingers to his neck. She didn't need to hear what the brothers said to each other to know that the shooter was indeed dead.

She heard the sounds of sirens. Gunnar. The cruiser was speeding up behind them, but as Raylene had done, Gunnar turned off the sirens as he came to a stop. The deputy barreled out of the car and ran toward Owen and Eli. Again, she couldn't hear what they said, but it didn't take long before Owen started quickly making his way back to Raylene and her.

When Owen got into the cruiser, he looked at Laney. Not just a glance, but more of an examination to make sure she hadn't been injured. She did the same to him. Thank goodness they hadn't been hurt. Not physically anyway. But this had put more shadows in his already dark eyes.

"Take us to my grandparents' house," Owen told Raylene.

Owen took hold of Laney, sliding her against him. Away from the glass and into his arms. For such a simple gesture, it did wonders. It steadied her heart enough that it no longer felt as if it might beat out of her chest. He didn't say anything but instead brushed his mouth on the top of her head. Another gesture that was anything but simple. It soothed her, aroused her and made her realize something.

She was falling in love with him.

Great. Just what she didn't need—and what Owen wouldn't want.

When Raylene pulled to a stop in front of his grandparents' house, she spotted two ranch hands, one on each side of the house. Jack opened the front door and, with his gun ready, stepped out onto the porch. No doubt to give them cover in case there were any snipers still around.

Owen didn't remind her that they'd have to move quickly. They did. Raylene, Owen and she all rushed out of the cruiser and into the house. The moment they were inside, Jack shut the door and rearmed the security system.

"I would ask if you're all okay," Jack said, "but I figure the answer to that is no. How about Eli?"

"He's with the dead gunman," Owen answered.

Jack gave an approving nod and tipped his head to the stairs. "Addie, Francine and Gemma are in the master bathroom. I told them to get into the bathtub and stay down."

Now it was Owen who gave a nod as he started up the stairs. Laney headed in that direction, too, but she stopped next to Jack. "I'm sorry."

He cocked an eyebrow. "I only want one apology and it's from the SOB who put all of this together. It took plenty of bucks to hire this many thugs to do these attacks and kill at least two people."

Yes, it did. "Both Terrance and Nettie have money like that."

"And Emerson," Jack quickly added. "No trust fund, but you can bet he could figure out a way to tap into his wife's money. Heck, Nettie's so much in love with him that she might have given him the cash with no questions asked."

All of that was true, and it was yet another reason for them to take a look at their financials.

Jack gave her a friendly, almost brotherly nudge on the arm before she tucked her loaner gun into the back waistband of her jeans and went up the stairs. She followed the sounds of the voices and found them still in the bath. Addie was in the giant tub, playing with a stash of toys, and Gemma, Francine and Owen were all sitting on the floor next to her.

The moment Laney stepped in, Addie looked at her and smiled. Like the way Owen had held her in the cruiser, that smile worked some magic.

"Horsey," Addie said, holding up one of her toys. It seemed to be an invitation for Laney to come closer. So she did, kneeling down beside the tub. Thankfully, the little girl didn't seem to be aware that she was in this room because there had been another attack.

"You think it's okay for me to go to the kitchen?" Francine asked Owen.

He nodded. "Just stay away from the windows."

Francine thanked him as she got to her feet. "I think I need a cup of tea."

"I need a drink," Gemma added, getting up, as well. "A strong one with lots of booze, and then I'm going to call Kellan."

Laney nearly told the women there was no reason to leave on her account, but she realized she wanted this time with Owen and Addie. Even if it was for only a few seconds.

Gemma gave her arm a gentle squeeze, a show of support, which Laney greatly appreciated.

After the women were gone, Laney brushed her hand over the tips of Addie's curly hair and got another smile from the little girl. Laney found herself smiling, too. Yes, this was definitely magic.

"I'll go into the other bedroom so you can be with her," Laney told him, but when she started to stand, Owen took hold of her hand and kept her in place. He didn't say anything. He just kept his grip on her while he continued to watch his daughter.

"I've been thinking about setting up a safe house and moving Addie there," Owen finally told her long moments later.

That didn't surprise her, not with the repeated attacks, but Laney thought she knew why that had put such an unsettled look on Owen's already troubled face. "You wouldn't be able to go with her."

"No. I'd need to be here, to see this investigation through to an arrest. Plus, it might be a good idea to put some distance between her and me."

"Distance between Addie and *me*," Laney corrected. She sighed, groaned. "I'm the target."

Owen quickly shook his head and caught her chin to force eye contact. "Maybe you were the sole target in the beginning, but those shots have been fired at me, too."

"They wouldn't be if you weren't with me," she pointed out just as fast.

Now he was the one to sigh, and he stared at her a long time before he said anything else. "So far, the attacks have happened when we were outside, and the hired thugs haven't managed to get close enough to this house to fire any shots inside."

That was true, but she was about to argue that it

could change, that this latest gunman might be the first in a string of others to come. But she could see the risk of taking the baby out on the road—even in a cruiser. Yes, a cruiser was bullet-resistant, but shots could get through. They'd just had proof of that.

"The ranch hands are willing to keep guarding the place?" she asked.

Owen nodded. "I suspect Jack will have to leave. Raylene, too. But Eli and I can stay here. And we have you for backup."

That was more than just a little vote of confidence. It actually caused some of the tightness in Laney's chest to go away. Owen trusted her to be part of this.

"Thanks," she managed to say, half expecting him to ask why she'd said that.

He didn't. Owen reached out, sliding his fingers over her jaw. To her cheek. And then to the back of her neck. He leaned in slowly. So slowly. Until his mouth brushed over hers. Almost immediately, he pulled back, their gazes connecting. A dozen things passed between them. Unspoken words but they still understood.

The need.

The ache.

The impossibility of it all.

Laney felt every one of those things, in every inch of her, and she was certain Owen did, too.

"Kissy," Addie said, clapping.

The moment between Laney and Owen was gone, replaced by another one that seemed even more important. And possible. Using the side of the tub, Addie got to her feet and dropped a kiss on Owen's cheek before doing the same to Laney.

"Kissy," Addie repeated, beaming with that incredible smile.

Yes, this was more important.

Owen scooped Addie out of the tub and into his lap and showered her with loud kisses that had the little girl giggling. Addie leaned over and spread some of those giggles and kisses to Laney, including her in a moment that she didn't deserve to share. But it was a moment that she'd never forget.

It didn't last, though. Owen's phone rang and even though Addie was only a toddler, she seemed to understand the importance of it because she moved into Laney's lap when Owen took out his phone. Laney saw Kellan's name on the screen, which was probably why Owen didn't put the call on speaker. Not with Addie right there. He wouldn't want to risk her hearing anything about the dead gunman.

To make sure Addie was spared that, Laney got up and shifted the little girl onto her hip so they could go out into the adjoining bedroom. Keeping hold of her hands, she let Addie jump on the bed, something that Francine had let her do. Of course, that seemed like a lifetime ago.

Everything did.

She'd come here, lying, looking for Hadley's killer. That had seemed the most important thing in the world. In some ways, it still was. But now it wasn't just about finding justice, it was about putting an end to the danger so that this precious little girl, Owen and his family would be safe.

Laney pulled Addie back into her arms when Owen entered the room, and she could tell from his expression that he'd just gotten more bad news.

"Rohan Gilley's lawyer just visited him at the sheriff's office, and after he left, Gilley told Kellan that he was finally ready to talk," Owen explained.

She shook her head, not understanding his somber tone, because it was good that the hired gun had broken his silence. "And?" Laney prompted when Owen didn't add anything.

Owen dragged in a breath through his mouth. "Gilley said that Emerson is the one who hired him."

Chapter 13

*E*merson.

Owen had already cursed his brother-in-law, but he kept cursing under his breath every time his calls to Emerson went to voice mail. Where the hell was he? Since Nettie wasn't answering her phone, either, Owen could only guess that Emerson had gotten wind of Gilley's "confession" and had gone on the run.

To avoid being arrested for murder.

That only caused Owen to silently swear even more, and the profanity wasn't just aimed at Emerson. He aimed plenty at himself. All the signs had been there, and Laney had said right from the get-go that Emerson had killed her sister. He hadn't listened and now they were in this mess.

"No one in Emerson's office has seen him," Eli relayed when he finished his latest round of calls.

Eli and Owen were only two of the people looking for Emerson. Gunnar and Raylene were back at the sheriff's office. Kellan was no doubt doing it, too, though he likely had his hands full with Gilley and getting the warrant not just for Emerson but for his financials. Because he'd been swamped and since there'd been no evidence to hold him, Kellan had cut Terrance loose. Temporarily anyway. Terrance would be making a return trip to the sheriff's office for further questioning. That might not even be necessary, though. If they could arrest Emerson and get him in the box for questioning, he might confess all.

Might.

And he might deny it, just as he'd denied the affair with Hadley. At least, he'd denied it until he'd had to face those pictures.

"I'm sure it's occurred to you that Gilley could be lying through his teeth," Eli pointed out.

Owen nodded. Yeah. In fact, that had been his first thought. After all, Gilley wasn't exactly a responsible, law-abiding citizen. He could have simply grown tired of being in a cell, waiting for a plea deal, and had decided to strike out.

"If there'd been no circumstantial evidence against Emerson, Kellan probably wouldn't have even told me what Gilley had said," Owen answered. "But there is evidence."

Eli made a sound of agreement. "And it doesn't help that he's gone AWOL. If that's what happened."

Owen looked at his brother, who was at the living room window. "You think something could have happened to him?"

"Depends on if he's really a killer or not. If it's Nettie or Terrance, then Emerson could be the next victim. They might try to make it look like a suicide."

Owen could definitely see that happening, but maybe before anyone else died, Emerson would come in and give a statement.

"You should get some rest," Eli added when Owen groaned and rubbed his eyes. "I'll be fine to keep first watch. Better yet, why don't you make sure Laney is okay?"

Eli took something from his pocket and tossed it to Owen. Only after Owen caught it did he realize what it was. A foil-wrapped condom.

Owen scowled at him.

"You think you'll need two of them?" Eli asked in his best smart-mouthed tone.

Owen scowled some more. But he slipped the condom into his pocket, causing Eli to smile. It made Owen want to punch him. Or thank him. Before he could decide which, he turned and made his way up the stairs.

He checked on Addie first and saw that she was sacked out in her crib. Francine and Gemma had taken the bed and were asleep, too. Only then did he remember he'd told them that he'd likely be getting up in the middle of the night for watch duty. Obviously the women had decided to make that easy for him by switching around the sleeping arrangements.

Owen checked on Laney next because he hadn't had a chance to talk to her since the Gilley bombshell about Emerson. And no, "checking on" her didn't have anything to do with the condom.

Probably not anyway.

Her door was open, but his heart dropped to his knees when he didn't see her inside. A few seconds later, she came out of the hall bathroom. She was wearing a robe several sizes too big for her and was toweling her wet hair.

"Emerson?" she immediately asked, and her whispered voice hardly had any sound.

He shook his head, saw the mixture of disappointment and frustration go over her face, but she didn't say anything else until they were in the bedroom. "Emerson might not be guilty."

Since that was the same conversation he'd just had with Eli and then with himself, Owen nodded and shut the door so they wouldn't wake Addie, Francine or Gemma.

"Gut feeling?" he asked.

"Just trying to give him the benefit of the doubt. I want the attacks to stop, but I want to make sure the right person pays for that." She paused. "Even if Emerson killed Hadley, it doesn't mean he hired those thugs."

Owen believed that, too. That, of course, put them right back to not having a clear suspect.

He stayed by the door while she continued to dry her hair and pace. Owen figured she wouldn't be getting a lot of sleep tonight, either. However, when the towel shifted a little, that was when he saw the cut on her right temple.

"You're hurt?" he asked, going to her.

"No. It's only a little cut."

He didn't have to ask how she'd gotten it. It'd been when the gunman had shot through the glass. He hadn't seen it earlier because her hair had covered her.

No, she wouldn't be getting any sleep tonight.

She looked at him, forced a smile. "You do know it's not a good idea for you to be in here, right?" she asked.

"I know." He didn't hesitate, either, and had no doubts about that. It was a *very bad* idea.

But he didn't budge.

There was a storm stirring inside him, and it spread until he thought there wasn't any part of him not affected by it. All fire, and it was edged with danger. He thought maybe if he'd been facing down gunmen, it wouldn't have felt as strong as this.

Laney must have sensed that storm because her breath kicked up a notch. It was heavy, causing her chest to rise and fall as if she'd just run a long distance. He saw the pulse on her throat. Took in her scent, something beneath the soap she'd used in the shower.

Her scent.

It roared through him even faster than the storm.

He had a dozen arguments with himself as to why he should turn around and leave. And, one by one, he lost every one of those debates. Because right now there was only one thing that mattered. One thing that he knew he had to have.

Laney.

Owen went to her, pulled her into arms and started what he was certain he would regret soon enough. He kissed her.

From the moment she'd stepped from her shower and had seen Owen, Laney had figured it would lead to this kiss. She hadn't seen any way around it. That didn't make it right.

No. Owen would almost certainly feel guilty about this. Once the heat had cooled down, he would consider it a lapse in judgment. But she wouldn't. She would see it as her one chance to be with him.

And she would take it

Even if Owen wasn't hers to take.

Laney melted into his arms, into the kiss. It wasn't hard to do. She wanted him more than she wanted her next breath, and with that clever kiss, he was giving her everything she needed. The taste of him. The fit of her body in his arms. The feel of his mouth on hers. And she got even more of that when he deepened the kiss.

Both his mouth and hands were rough. Rushed. Maybe from the same fiery need she was feeling or because he didn't want to pause long enough to change his mind. But Laney made him pause. She pulled back, met his gaze, looked straight into those storm-gray eyes. She didn't say a word. Didn't have to. She just gave him those seconds to reconsider.

Their gazes held. So deep. So long. And it wasn't necessary for them to have a conversation. He told her all she needed to know when his mouth came back to hers. Owen snapped her against him, his hand slipping into her robe and pushing open the sides.

She was naked beneath, something he soon discovered when his fingers brushed over her nipple. He still didn't stop. Didn't even hesitate when he lowered his head and took her nipple into his mouth.

The fire shot through her, flooding the heat to the center of her body. Oh, she wanted him.

Owen didn't stop with the breast kiss. He trailed his mouth, and tongue, lower to her stomach. He might have gone even lower if she hadn't stopped him and pulled him back up.

"You're wearing too many clothes," she protested and immediately tried to do something about that.

She fumbled with the buttons on his shirt and then

cursed his shoulder harness when she couldn't get it off him. Owen helped with that, kissing her and backing her across the room. At first, she couldn't figure out why he wasn't taking her to the bed, but then Laney realized he'd locked the door.

Good grief. Anyone could have walked in on them, and his daughter was just across the hall. That reminder gave her a moment's pause that might have lasted longer if Owen's next kiss hadn't sent her back into the melting mode. Mercy. The man could kiss.

And touch.

Yes, she soon learned he was very clever at that, too. With his hands skimming along her body, he moved her toward the bed, easing her back on the mattress while his fingers found their way between her legs.

The touch took her breath away and caused the pleasure to spear through her. But soon, very soon, it wasn't nearly enough. She wanted him, all of him, and that started with getting him naked.

"Still too many clothes," she complained. "Get them off now."

That finally spurred him to a different kind of action and, while still kissing her, he shucked off his shirt. Laney finally got her chance to touch him. His chest was toned and perfect like the rest of him. She ran her hand down to his jeans to get his belt undone.

And she unzipped him.

She gave in to the heat from the kisses and touched him, sliding her hand into his boxers. Touching him. A sound came deep from his throat. Part groan, part pleasure. She saw urgency come to his eyes. Felt it when he shoved his hand in his jeans pocket and took out a condom.

Laney pushed off his jeans and boots as he put on the condom. Both ate up seconds and caused the pressure to soar. *Now*, she kept repeating in her mind. *Now*.

Owen gave her now.

With the fire and need consuming them, he pushed into her and she closed around him. Owen stilled for a moment, his eyes coming back to hers. More long moments. But these seemed...necessary. As if they both had to know that this wasn't ordinary. That it wasn't just the heat. No. It was a lot more than that, whether they wanted it to be or not.

He was breathing through his mouth now. Heavy, sharp gusts. But still, his eyes—dark and heavy—moved over her, taking her into his mind just as she'd taken him into her body.

When he started to move, he did it slowly. Long, easy strokes. Stretching out the pleasure. That didn't last, either.

Couldn't.

The urgency returned with a vengeance. Something primal that was bone-deep. His need to finish this. The strokes came faster. Deepened. Kept pace with her quick, throbbing pulse. The need came faster, too. Demanding that now, now, now.

Owen gave her that, too.

He pushed into her until the climax slammed through her. Her vision pinpointed just him before it blurred. Before the only thing she could do was hold on. And take him with her.

Chapter 14

When Owen came back from the bathroom, he'd expected to find Laney already dressed and either pacing or working on the laptop. But she was still naked and apparently asleep. She was on her stomach, her hand tucked like a pillow beneath her face. She looked... well, peaceful.

And beautiful.

No way would he convince his body otherwise. Not a chance of convincing it—or rather, certain parts of him anyway—that he didn't want her all over again. That wouldn't have been such a bad thing if one of those parts hadn't been his heart.

Hell.

He hadn't just had sex with her. He'd made love to her. Big difference, and he was honest enough with himself to not try to downplay it. Sex was easy, often with no strings or ones that didn't matter. But there'd be important strings with Laney. Not from her. He was guessing she'd give him an out and say that it didn't matter. She wouldn't be doing that for herself but rather for him.

Owen wouldn't take an out. He'd never been the sort to dismiss his feelings, which meant he was going to have to somehow work out this guilt going through him about Naomi. In a way, it felt as if he'd cheated on her. Or worse, it felt as if he'd finally gotten past her death. And that was worse than the guilt.

Pulling in a long breath, he eased down next to Laney on the bed. She automatically moved closer to him, draping her arm over his chest, and he felt the muscles tense in her arm. She opened one eye, looked at him and frowned.

"You're dressed." She started to scramble away from him, probably to put on her clothes, but he dragged her against him, holding her.

She didn't move away, but she did look up at him. He recognized suspicion in a person's eyes when he saw it. Suspicion. Then lust. She glanced at the door, probably to see if he'd shut it. He had.

"I'm naked," she said. "You're not. I think this would probably work better if you were naked, too."

That made him smile, and Owen brushed a kiss on the top of her head. He just wanted a moment, with her like this in his arms. It didn't settle the guilt trip in his mind, but it sure as heck settled the rest of him.

She levered herself up, touched her fingers to the bunched-up part of his forehead. "What is it?" she asked.

Owen wasn't sure he would have told her, but he

didn't get the chance to decide because his phone buzzed. He'd turned off the ringer so that it wouldn't wake Addie, Francine or Gemma, but the buzz came through loud and clear.

Emerson's name was on the screen.

"Put it on speaker," Laney insisted as she got to her feet and began to dress.

Owen did, but he turned down the volume. "Where are you?" Owen immediately asked.

"I'm driving to the ranch. We need to talk."

Yeah, they definitely needed to talk, but Owen didn't want Emerson within a mile of the ranch. "Go to the sheriff's office. Kellan's there and he'll talk to you."

Emerson made a sound of outrage. "You're my brother-in-law, not Kellan. I want to talk to you."

"The hands have orders not to let anyone on the ranch." Owen spelled it out for him. "They won't let you on."

Emerson cursed. "Didn't you hear what I said? We need to talk. I can't find Nettie, and I think someone's trying to kill me."

Owen didn't say "Welcome to the club," but that was what he was thinking. Laney, too, because she rolled her eyes. "What makes you think someone's trying to kill you?" Owen prompted.

"Because a car's been following me. I've got a gun, but if these are hired killers, they'll be a lot better shot than I am."

"Funny you should mention that. Rohan Gilley, the gun we have in custody, said you were his boss."

That brought on a whole new round of cursing from

Emerson. "He's a lying SOB. I didn't hire him. I haven't done anything wrong."

"Nothing other than lying to keep your affair with Hadley a secret," Owen reminded him.

"I didn't kill her!" Emerson shouted. "I didn't kill anyone, and I sure as hell didn't hire Rohan Gilley."

Owen had no idea if that were true, but even if he believed him, he wouldn't let Emerson on the ranch. They were on lockdown, and it was going to stay that way until they were no longer in danger.

"Go to the sheriff's office," Owen repeated. "Give your statement to Kellan. If there's someone following you, someone who intends to do you harm, then Kellan can also put you in protective custody."

"Is that where Nettie went?" Emerson snapped.

Owen didn't have a clue, but since that might urge Emerson to go there, he settled for saying, "Could be. You should check and see. And do it soon, Emerson," Owen added just as the man ended the call.

He had no idea if his brother-in-law would actually do that, but maybe he would so they could begin to start putting together the pieces of this puzzle.

By the time Owen put his phone away, Laney was completely dressed. Something that didn't please the nonheart part of him. He considered getting her out of those clothes again and going for another round, but he didn't have a second condom and wouldn't ask Eli for one.

Well, maybe he wouldn't.

Owen was pretty sure the moment Eli saw his face, his brother would be able to figure out what had gone on. Heck, Eli might even volunteer another condom then—even though the timing sucked. Owen mentally repeated that part about the timing, got up and faced Laney.

"I'm going down to relieve Eli for a while," he said.

"I'll go with you and grab something to eat."

Until she'd added that last part, Owen had been about to tell her to get some rest, but since she hadn't eaten anything all day, he didn't want to nix a good idea. He might even be able to grab a bite, as well.

Apparently, good sex spurred the appetite.

Owen peeked in again on Addie before Laney and he made their way down the stairs. And yep, Eli did figure it out. The corner of Eli's mouth lifted in a smile, but he thankfully dropped the expression when Laney came in. She greeted Eli and went straight into the adjoining kitchen.

"Don't say a word," Owen warned Eli.

Eli didn't, but he did chuckle. If it was loud enough for Laney to hear, she didn't react. She started making sandwiches from some cold cuts that she took from the fridge.

"Why don't you get some sleep?" Owen suggested.

"Will do after I fix me one of those sandwiches." Eli traded places with him, and Owen moved to the window as his brother went into the kitchen with Laney.

It was dark outside. No moon. But there were security lights on the road leading to the house. Owen had debated as to whether or not to turn them off. Debated keeping off all the lights inside, too, so that no one would easily be able to see they were there. However, he'd nixed the idea since the security lights would make it easier for the hands to see if someone tried to get onto the ranch.

Owen was less than a minute into his watch duties when his phone buzzed again. He silently cursed, figuring it was Emerson. But no, it was Terrance. Owen answered, putting the call on speaker because both Laney and Eli had entered the room, no doubt to listen.

"Are you at the sheriff's office?" Terrance asked, continuing before he gave Owen a chance to answer. "Because I need to see you."

"I'm a popular man tonight," Owen grumbled. "What do you want?"

Considering Terrance had blurted the first part of his conversation, it surprised Owen when the man went silent. Owen was about to repeat his "what do you want" demand when Terrance finally spoke.

"Look, I need to explain some things, that's all." Terrance definitely didn't sound like his usual cocky self. "Your brother, the sheriff, made it clear that he's looking at me for Nancy's murder."

"Yeah, because she worked for you," Owen was quick to remind him.

"She did, but I swear I didn't have anything to do with her murder."

That was the second time tonight that someone had denied being a killer. Owen wasn't any more inclined to believe him than he was Emerson.

"I didn't kill Nancy," Terrance went on. And he paused again. "But she did get into that bank box to get the pictures."

Laney dropped the bag of chips she'd taken from the cabinet and hurried closer to Owen. Eli moved closer, too, eating his sandwich. While he wasn't hurrying, it was obvious his attention was nailed to the conversation.

"I'm listening," Owen told Terrance.

"Once I made the connection between Hadley and a safe-deposit box, I wanted to know what was inside," Terrance admitted.

Owen's jaw tightened. "Why? Because you thought there was some kind of evidence in there that would get your conviction overturned?" And yes, that question was loaded with sarcasm.

"No. I was guilty of assaulting Laney, and I served my time," he quickly added. "I just thought there might be something that would…punish Laney. Something to give her a dose of the same pain she gave me when she didn't do her job and vet the gold digger who drained me dry."

Owen was about to point out that Terrance had been the one stupid enough to fall for a con artist, but Laney spoke before Owen could.

"Punish me?" Laney repeated. "How?"

Terrance muttered some profanity. "I thought it would bring back bad memories for you. Something that would make you feel guilty for not finding your sister's killer." He paused. "When I told Nancy this, she took it upon herself to get into the bank. I never hired her to do that, never encouraged her."

Owen doubted that. There'd likely been plenty of *encouragement*. Payment, too.

"How'd Nancy get the key to the box?" Owen queried.

"I'm not sure. She didn't tell me."

Owen doubted that, as well. There was a slim chance that Nancy could have bribed someone at the bank to get her a duplicate key. Also a slim chance that Nancy had killed Joe and got the key from him. But all of this pointed straight back to Terrance.

"Nancy acted of her own accord," Terrance declared. "Because she thought it would be a favor to me."

"A favor?" Owen challenged. "She committed a felony. This is more than just a favor."

Terrance made a sound of agreement. "She had a thing for me and probably thought I'd be so grateful that it'd start up something personal between us. It didn't."

Owen would give that some more thought later, but for now he wanted to keep pressing for details. Then he could sort out what were lies and what were truths.

"What happened when Nancy went to the bank?" Owen asked.

"She called and said the only thing in the box was a bunch of pictures. Pictures of Hadley and the married DA. I wasn't sure how I could use those, but I told her to copy them, put them in online storage and then put the originals in a safe place."

"And then you killed Nancy?" Owen finished for him.

"No! Of course not." There was plenty of emotion in his voice now and some of it sounded like regret. "Nancy asked if she could make some money off the pictures, maybe by getting the DA to buy them. I told her no, that I didn't want her to do that." Another pause. "But I think she tried. I think that's what got her killed."

Yeah, maybe killed by Terrance himself because

the woman had disobeyed his order. "Who murdered Nancy?" Owen demanded.

"I don't know, but I refuse to be blamed for her death. I won't let your brother come after me and try to stick me behind bars." The anger was back with a vengeance, and his voice started to rise. "I won't go back to jail."

"You won't have a choice about that. If there's any proof whatsoever that you paid Nancy to go to the bank—"

"There isn't," Terrance interrupted. "Because I'm innocent, and as far as I'm concerned, this will be the last conversation I have with Laney, your brother or you." With that, Terrance ended the call.

Owen wasn't so sure about this being the last, but he hoped that Terrance would truly stay out of Laney's life. That would definitely happen if Terrance was arrested for murder.

"If Terrance was telling the truth about Nancy," Laney said, "maybe the woman used the courier so she'd be one step removed from the blackmail. In fact, she could have paid someone to contact the courier service."

As theories went, it wasn't a bad one, and if that was what happened, then Terrance could indeed be innocent. But that left them with the same question he'd just presented to Terrance. Who killed Nancy?

Eli was still chowing down on his sandwich when his phone buzzed. "It's Jeremy," he relayed to them. Jeremy Cranston, one of the ranch hands. Eli took the call on speaker.

"I just spotted someone in the back pasture," Jeremy said. "A man. And he's got a rifle."

* * *

Laney's stomach tightened into a cold, hard knot, and she realized this was something she had been expecting. Something she'd prayed wouldn't happen.

But here it was.

"The armed guy isn't close to the house," Jeremy added a moment later. "I saw him through the binoculars as he came over the fence. Should I leave Bennie here and head out to that part of the pasture?" Laney knew that Bennie Deavers was the other ranch hand helping them guard the immediate area around the house.

"No," Owen answered. "Just keep an eye on the intruder. He could be a lure to get us to go after him."

Oh, God. She hadn't even considered that. She should have, though. Laney should have anticipated that whoever was behind this would do anything to get to her.

But why?

She still didn't know, and that tore away at her as much as the fear for Owen, his family and the hands.

"Have you seen anyone else?" Owen asked Jeremy. "Maybe somebody on the road?"

"Nobody. Don't have to tell you, though, that there are a lot of acres. A lot of ways for someone to get here if they're hell-bent on it."

No, Jeremy didn't have to tell them. And yes, the person after her was definitely hell-bent.

She thought of all the old trails that coiled around the ranch and fed out into the roads. Once they'd been used to move cattle and equipment before the roads had been built. Now they could provide access to someone who wanted to get close without being seen.

"Keep an eye on all sides of the house," Owen instructed as he turned off the lights. Eli went into the living room and did the same. "Just keep an eye on the gunman and text Eli or me when he gets closer to the house."

Eli had already moved to the front window to keep watch when he ended the call. Owen moved to the kitchen window, but he looked at Laney.

"Have Francine and Gemma move Addie into the tub," he said. "You go in the bathroom with them."

"Yes to the first. No to the second," Laney argued. "You need backup, and I not only have a gun, I know how to use it."

Laney didn't give him a chance to answer. She ran up the stairs to get Addie to safety. Gemma must have heard her coming because the woman stepped out into the hall.

"There's an armed man in the pasture" was all Laney said, and Gemma hurried back into the room to scoop up Addie.

"Francine, get up," Gemma insisted, already heading to the adjoining bathroom. Thankfully, Addie didn't wake up, and Laney hoped it stayed that way.

The nanny sprang off the bed, her eyes wide with fear. Fear that Laney couldn't soothe because the danger had returned. "I'll come back up when the threat is over," Laney assured her. She prayed that wouldn't be too long.

Of course, after this threat was over, Owen would no doubt make the decision to move Addie. This was the second intruder in only a handful of hours, and he had to get his daughter out of harm's way. That meant taking the little girl to a safe house—away from Owen. And Owen would almost certainly insist that Laney go into a safe house, as well. Not with Addie, though. No. The best way to protect Addie was to get her away from Laney.

Once Francine and Gemma had Addie in the bathroom, Laney made sure all the upstairs lights were off and then hurried downstairs. Since Owen was still in the kitchen and Eli at the front of the living room, Laney went to the side window positioned between the two areas. They could cover three sides of the house in case this armed thug got past the ranch hands.

And the wait began.

It was impossible for Laney to tamp down all the fear that was rising inside her. Impossible to keep her breathing and heartbeat level. But she forced herself to remember her training. She didn't have nearly the level of expertise that Owen and Eli did, but she'd taken self-defense and firearms classes. Maybe, though, it wouldn't come down to any of them using those skills.

The room was so quiet that Laney nearly gasped when she heard the sound. Not an intruder. It was Eli's phone that dinged with a text message.

Volleying glances between the window and his phone, Eli read it. Then he cursed. "Jeremy said he lost sight of the armed idiot and thinks the guy went behind the trees."

Laney wanted to curse, too. That definitely hadn't been what she'd wanted to hear. Now the guy could be anywhere, including much too close to the house.

"Keep watch," Eli reminded them as he slipped his phone back into his pocket.

She did. Laney's gaze went from one side of her area to the other. Trees, yes. A white rail fence. And she could see the edge of the barn behind the house. What she couldn't see were any signs of a hired gun. Since Owen had a much better view of the barn, she glanced at him just as he glanced at her. And he shook his head.

"Nothing that I can see," he said.

"How's the security system rigged?" she asked. She was certain that Owen had already mentioned it, but she wanted to make sure.

"There are alarms on all windows and doors, including the windows on the top floor. If anyone tries to get in, we'll know about it."

Good. It was especially good about the alarms being on the second story of the house. Laney doubted the intruder could get a ladder past the ranch hands, but even if by some miracle that happened, he wouldn't be able to just break in without alerting them.

Her heart skipped a couple of beats when she saw something move by the barn, and Laney automatically pivoted in that direction. It got Eli and Owen's attention, and she heard them shift their positions, too. Then she saw the yellow tabby cat skirt out from the barn and dart across the yard.

"It was just the cat," Laney said. Even though she couldn't actually hear Eli and Owen take breaths of relief, she figured that was what they were doing. She certainly was.

Eli's phone dinged again, putting her heart in her throat as she waited for him to relay the text. "Jeremy caught sight of him by the left side of the barn."

The barn. Much too close. And possibly the reason the cat had run.

She couldn't see the left side of the barn from her position, so she shifted, moving to the other side of the window. She still didn't have a clear view, but she could see more of the barn.

As she'd done earlier, Laney took aim in that direction. Just as she heard another sound. One she didn't want to hear.

A gunshot.

Owen saw the rifle a split second before the bullet crashed through the kitchen window right next to where he was standing.

Almost immediately the security alarm went off, the shrill, clanging sounds pulsing through the house. The bullet had been loud, deafening even, but the alarms were drowning out sounds that he wanted to hear.

Like any kind of movement in the yard.

If this armed thug was coming closer to the house, Owen darn sure wanted to know about it. Plus, he needed to make sure Francine and Gemma weren't calling out for help.

"Kill the alarm," Owen shouted to Eli.

His brother was closer to the keypad by the door, and besides, the shooter was obviously at the back of the house, where Owen was.

Using the wall as cover, Owen glanced around the window frame at the barn. He didn't see anything, but he knew the guy was there, hiding in the shadows. Waiting to do some more damage. He got proof of that when he saw the rifle again.

Owen immediately fired, but the shooter must not have been hit because he managed to get off a shot. A second bullet came crashing through what was left of the window. The guy fired a third shot, then a fourth, but Owen couldn't tell where the last two had landed.

He prayed they hadn't gone upstairs.

Just the thought sent his heart and fear into overdrive. He knew that Francine would have Addie in the tub where she'd be relatively safe, but he didn't want *relatively* when it came to his daughter. He wanted this idiot gunman dead so he couldn't send any more lethal shots anywhere near the house.

The house went silent when Eli turned off the alarm, and Owen immediately listened for Francine. Nothing, thank God. And he added another thanks when he didn't hear Addie crying.

"I've reset the security system," his brother said. "But I had to turn off the sensors on the windows. *All* the windows," Eli emphasized. "It was the only way to shut off the alarms."

That wasn't ideal, but at least the doors would still be armed, and if the gunman came through a window, he'd have to break the glass since they were all locked. Owen knew that because he'd checked them all himself.

With his attention still on the barn, Owen heard the dinging sound of a text message from Eli's phone.

"Jeremy's been hit in the leg," Eli relayed, tacking on some raw curse words. "Bennie says it's not bad, and he's tying off the wound."

Good. Owen definitely didn't want the hand dying, but the injury basically took out both men who'd been guarding the house. It pinned them down so they might not be able to shoot the gunman even if they caught sight of him.

"Should I call for backup?" Laney asked.

Owen purposely hadn't looked at her—because he hadn't wanted to remember that she, too, was in danger, but he glanced at her now and shook his head. "I don't want anyone else coming into an ambush."

In fact, he wanted her away from the window, but the truth was, with the hands out of commission, Owen needed her eyes and gun right now. Laney seemed ready to give them both. She certainly didn't look as if she might fall apart. Just the opposite. She had a firm grip on her weapon and had it aimed in the direction of the barn.

"I'll call Kellan and an ambulance," Eli volunteered. "But I will tell them to hold off, to keep some distance from the house. I agree. I don't want anyone else gunned down tonight."

Owen listened while his brother made the quick call. That would put Kellan and the EMTs on standby at least, and he hoped like the devil that no one else got hurt. Well, no one other than the idiot who'd shot Jeremy.

He dragged in a hard breath and held it while he continued to take glances out at the barn. He couldn't wait long, though. Despite having Bennie there to help, Jeremy would soon need medical attention. Besides, Owen couldn't have any more shots being fired into the house.

"I see him," Laney blurted. Before Owen could even respond, she fired, her shot blasting through the window. The glass practically exploded from the impact.

Laney ducked back. Barely in the nick of time because the gunman returned fire, sending a shot right at her. This one didn't just take out more glass but also a chunk of wood from the window frame. A reminder that those bullets could go through the walls.

Owen saw the blood on Laney's face. No doubt a cut from the flying glass or wood. And it turned his stomach. She was hurt, and even though it was probably minor, he hated that this snake had been able to get to her. Hated even more that the injury could have been much worse.

Laney didn't even react to the cut. She adjusted her position again, still staying by the window, and Owen quit glancing at her so that he could keep his attention nailed to the barn.

The seconds crawled by as he waited, his finger on the trigger. He knew that Eli and Laney were doing the same thing, but Owen didn't hear or see anything.

When the seconds turned to minutes, Owen knew he had to do something. Jeremy needed help, and they couldn't just stand there. He was going to have to do something to draw out the gunman.

"Eli, keep low but come back here," Owen instructed. "I'm going to duck out from cover. When he takes aim at me, shoot him."

"No," Laney insisted. "You could be shot."

Yeah. But so could everybody else in the house. Owen didn't say that to her, though. He just waited until Eli was in position on the other side of the window. Owen gave him the nod and leaned out from cover.

Nothing.

No rifle barrel. No gunman.

Where the hell was he? Owen was about to ask Eli

to text Jeremy to see if he had eyes on the gunman, but before he could do that, Owen heard something that shot fresh adrenaline through him.

The alarm from the security system.

Someone had tripped it, and that someone was in the house.

Chapter 15

Laney tried to tamp down the jolt of fear she got from the alarm, but it was impossible not to react.

The gunman was almost certainly inside.

She forced her mind to clear so she could do a quick review of the house. Eli had said the windows were no longer armed so the intruder must have come in through a door.

Laney could see both the front door in the foyer and the back door in the kitchen. They were closed, so that left two other points of entry. The one at the side of the house off the family room. Or the one that led from carport area and into the house. Either one of those could give him access to the kitchen.

Or the back stairs that led to the second floor.

"Addie," Owen said over the clamor of the alarm.

Eli nodded. "I'll go up and guard the door." She

saw the same fear and concern in his eyes that was no doubt in hers.

Eli had likely volunteered because he was closer, right at the base of the front stairs. Without waiting for Owen's response, he disengaged the security system, silencing the alarms again, then barreled up the steps, taking them two at a time.

Owen hurried into the living room with her, positioning them so they were back to back. He didn't have to tell her to keep watch of the foyer in case the gunman came that way. He did the same to the back of the house.

Even with the silenced alarm, it was still hard for Laney to hear, but she picked her way through her throbbing pulse so she could listen. Nothing. Not at first. And then she heard what she was sure was someone moving around.

Owen must have heard it, too, because the muscles in his body stiffened even more than they already were. "It came from the family room," he whispered, automatically switching places with her so that he faced that direction.

Laney didn't like that he'd done that to take her out of the line of fire, but she knew that was an argument she wouldn't win. No way would Owen just stand there and let her face danger when he could do something about it.

Owen cursed softly when something or someone bumped against the wall. Not in the family room. Laney was almost positive this sound had come from the carport area. That caused the sickening dread to flood through her.

Because it meant there were likely two killers.

Her gun was already raised and ready, but she tried to steady her grip. A shaky hand wasn't going to help them now. Especially since it was possible the two thugs had coordinated an attack. They could come after them at the same time, trapping them in the crossfire.

That put a crushing feeling around her heart to go with the dread that was already there. Owen could be killed. And all because of her. Then these monsters could go upstairs and finish off everyone in the house. That meant she and Owen had to stop them before they got a chance to do that.

Owen's phone dinged, the sound she recognized as a text from Kellan. But Owen didn't take his phone from his pocket. She was thankful for that. Laney didn't want anything to be a distraction right now even though the message could be important.

Laney kept watching. Kept waiting. With her breath so thin, she felt starved for air, and her shoulders so tense, the muscles started to cramp.

She heard another sound. Not footsteps this time but rather a car engine. She didn't risk looking at Owen, but she saw the slash of headlights coming straight for the house.

Kellan.

Maybe.

Eli had told him to stay back to avoid being ambushed. Maybe Kellan had decided against that, which would explain the text to Owen's phone that he hadn't been able to check. If Kellan had indeed decided to come forward, she hoped he wouldn't be shot.

She glanced over her shoulder when the sound and lights got closer. In the distance, Laney could hear the sirens. Too far away to be the vehicle approaching the house.

And it was coming too fast.

There was a loud crash, and it felt as if it shook the entire house. The impact sent the front door flying open, and that was when she realized the car had collided with the front porch.

Maybe this was a third gunman. Or some kind of ruse to distract them from the two who were already in the house. If so, it worked, because the person who staggered through the front door got their attention.

Emerson.

"What the hell is going on?" he grumbled. "The ranch hands wouldn't let me in, and I had to bash through the gate."

The headlights on the car were out now, maybe damaged in the collision, making it was hard to see Emerson in the dark foyer. However, she could tell that he wasn't armed, or rather that he didn't have a gun in his hand, which was probably the only reason Owen hadn't shot him on sight.

Even in the darkness, she noticed that Emerson's eyes widened when he looked at them, and he shook his head as if dazed. Maybe drugged or drunk. Something was definitely wrong.

"What the hell is going on?" Emerson repeated, his words slurred.

"Why are you here?" Owen asked. He had his gun aimed at his brother-in-law while his gaze fired all around the area.

Emerson opened his mouth, closed it and scrubbed his hand over his face. "Something happened to me. I'm not sure what."

Laney had no idea if he was telling the truth, but even if he was, she had no intention of trusting the man. This could all be some trick to make them believe he was innocent when he could be the one pulling the strings on the hired guns. He could have already given them orders to attack.

"Get facedown on the floor," Owen told Emerson. "Put your hands behind your back."

Good. That way, they could maybe restrain him until they could take care of the intruders.

"You're arresting me?" Emerson howled. Now the anger tightened the muscles in his face. "Who the hell do you think you are?"

"I'm the lawman who's going to take you down if you don't get on the floor." There was plenty of anger in Owen's voice, too.

Emerson made a sound of outrage and moved as if he might charge right at them. He didn't get a chance to do that, though, before someone reached out from the side of the stairs and latched onto the man.

Then the person put a gun to Emerson's head.

From the moment Emerson staggered through the door, Owen had figured that things were about to go from bad to worse. He'd thought that maybe Emerson would just start shooting.

Or order his goons to shoot.

And maybe he would still do that, but for now it appeared that one of those hired guns had taken him hostage. *Appeared*, Owen mentally repeated. There was no way he was going to take this at face value.

Owen immediately grasped Laney's arm and pulled her to the side of arched opening that served as an entrance to the family room. As cover went, it wasn't much, so he made sure he was in front of Laney.

"Do anything stupid—*anything*—and the DA dies," the man behind Emerson growled.

Owen didn't recognize the husky voice and, even though it was hard to see the man in the dark shadows, he got a glimpse of part of his face. Owen didn't recognize him, either.

"Let go of me," Emerson yelled and tried to ram his elbow into the gunman's stomach.

The gunman dodged the blow, bashed the butt of his gun against Emerson's head and curved his arm around his neck. Emerson continued to struggle as the man tightened his choke-hold grip.

"What's going on down there?" Eli shouted. "I texted you to tell you that Emerson charged past the hands. Did he make it all the way to the house?"

"Yeah. I'm handling it," Owen answered. "Stay put," he added to his brother when he heard a sound he didn't want to hear.

Addie crying.

"She's okay," Eli quickly said. "The noise just woke her, that's all."

Owen released the breath that had caused the vise-like pressure in his chest. His baby was safe. For now. He needed to make sure she stayed that way.

"Are you working for Emerson?" Owen asked the gunman.

The guy snorted out a laugh. "Does it look like he's my boss?"

A desperate person out to kill them could make this look like anything he wanted. That included setting up a fake hostage situation. But it didn't look fake. Didn't *feel* that way, either. Emerson's head was bleeding, and he was gasping for air. Plus, there was that panicked look in his brother-in-law's eyes, which looked like the real deal.

"Things obviously didn't go as planned," the man said. "My partner's missing. Maybe your sheriff brother took him out, but he's not answering."

That was possibly Kellan's doing or one of the hands'. Either way, Owen was thankful there was only one of them. But that did make him wonder.

When had it happened?

He'd heard two sets of footsteps—Owen was certain of that—so did that mean Kellan was in the house?

"Because things got screwed up, I need to get out of here, and I'm going to use the DA here to do that," the gunman insisted. "Since it appears he's messed up his car by running it into your porch, I'll be taking that truck parked out front. If you don't have the keys, I'll start shooting, and that woman you're trying to protect just might be the one who takes the bullet."

That sent a shot of anger spearing through Owen. Laney had already been through too much to have this piece of slime threaten her.

"It's okay," Laney whispered to Owen. "Better me than Addie."

He hated that she would even have to consider that. But he was also thankful for it. She was putting his daughter first.

"Give him the keys," Emerson insisted when the man eased up on the choke hold. He sputtered out a cough. "If not, he'll just kill us and take the keys."

Owen stared at him. "You seem pretty cooperative for someone who's being used as a human shield."

Emerson looked Owen straight in the eyes. "I don't want to die. I don't know who's doing this, but we need to get this would-be killer out of the house. My niece is upstairs."

It twisted at Owen to hear Emerson say that. He didn't know if Emerson had genuine concern for Addie the way Laney did or if this was part of the act. Either way, if Emerson left, it would get the gunman away from Addie.

"The truck keys are on the foyer table," Owen told the gunman.

Owen saw the man's gaze immediately go in that direction. The keys were indeed there, and Owen was going to let him take them. Let him go outside, too. And then he would do what he could to stop him so that ambulance could get onto the grounds for Jeremy.

The thug got Emerson moving and he was careful to keep Emerson in front of him. "Take the keys," he growled at Emerson when they reached the foyer table.

Emerson did. His hand closed around the keys just as a shot rang out. For one heart-stopping moment, Owen thought the thug had shot Emerson, but the gunfire had come from the back of the house.

Hell.

The other gunman.

Maybe Kellan hadn't disabled him, after all.

The gunman jerked back, snapping Emerson even closer to him as he put the gun to Emerson's head. Obviously he didn't think the shot had come from his partner.

"I said I'll kill him, and I sure as hell mean it," the gunman yelled, but he wasn't speaking to Owen. "Stay back or the DA dies."

There was another blast of gunfire.

Then another.

Owen cursed and glanced around, trying to figure out who was doing this. Not Kellan. No. His brother would have called out to them to stop from being shot by friendly fire.

"I think the shooter's near the back stairs," Laney whispered.

That was Owen's guess, too, and it sent his heart to his knees. Because the gunman could be heading up to get to Addie.

"Eli, watch the back stairs," Owen called out to his brother. He knew Eli was already doing that, but he wanted him to have a heads-up.

"Eli won't let a gunman get into the bathroom," Laney reminded him.

Owen believed that. Eli would do whatever it took to protect the little girl, but that didn't mean a gunman couldn't get off a lucky shot.

"I swear I'll kill him," the gunman repeated. With his choke hold still in place, he maneuvered Emerson into the doorway.

Just as there was another shot. This one hadn't come from the back stairs, though. From the sound of it, the gunman had fired from the living room. That meant he was coming closer.

But something wasn't right.

If this was the second gunman, why did the one holding Emerson suddenly look so concerned? Maybe because he thought it was Kellan.

No. It was something else.

"Move," the gunman ordered Emerson. The thug got him onto the porch as another shot came their way. This one slammed into the door frame right next to the gunman's head.

"Stop or I'll kill you," someone said, the voice coming from the living room.

Owen immediately saw the gun the person was holding. Aimed not at Laney and him but rather at the gunman who had Emerson.

And that someone was Nettie.

Laney instantly recognized Nettie's voice. At first, she thought the woman was there only because she'd followed Emerson. But then she saw Nettie lean out from the arched entry of the living room. One look at her from over Owen's shoulder and Laney knew that Nettie was responsible for the attacks.

Nettie was the person who'd been trying to kill them.

And had maybe murdered Hadley, too.

Emerson shook his head, his expression registering a mix of shock and relief. Then fear. "Nettie, you need to run. This man will kill you."

Nettie definitely didn't run, but she did stay partly behind the cover of the wall. A wall she'd easily be able to duck behind if anyone started shooting.

"Boss," the gunman said, confirming what everyone had already figured out. Everyone but Emerson, that was.

"Boss?" Emerson snapped. "You idiot. That's my wife, and she didn't hire you." He fired some wild-eyed glances at Laney and Owen before his attention settled on Nettie.

Laney saw the realization register on Emerson's face. He groaned. "No. Nettie, not you."

Nettie didn't deny it. "Let go of him, Stan," she ordered the gunman.

Stan was making some wild-eyed glances of his own,

and there was fear all over his face. "I don't think that's a good idea. It wasn't my fault he came running in here. He crashed his car into to the porch and just bolted in."

"You should have taken care of the situation before that." Nettie's words were arctic cold and so was the look in her eyes. "Let him go."

So, Nettie was going to save her husband. Maybe. But certainly she didn't think that Emerson and she could just walk out and resume their lives.

"Nettie," Emerson said, his voice cracking. "What have you done? What are you doing?"

"I'm cleaning up your mess. You weren't supposed to be here. I told the housekeeper to sneak you a sedative, that you were going off half-cocked and would do something stupid to ruin your career. Your life."

So that was why Emerson had looked drugged. Because he had been.

"I'm trying to fix things," Emerson pled. The gunman tightened his choke hold when Emerson tried to go to Nettie.

"No, I'm fixing things," Nettie argued. "*Again*. First, with that bimbo you were seeing and now with the mess from those pictures."

"Hadley?" Emerson said. "You knew about Hadley?"

"Of course I did," Nettie snapped. "She called me crying, and said you'd broken off things with her, but she wanted me to know all about your relationship. That's what she called it. A *relationship*. Well, I showed her the price she had to pay for sleeping with my husband. I ended her miserable life."

Oh, mercy. Laney felt as if she'd just been punched in the stomach. Nettie had been the one to murder Hadley. It didn't make it easier, but at least now she knew.

"Damn it, I'm your wife," Nettie snapped, aiming a glare at Emerson, "and you cheated on me."

"I'm so sorry." Emerson's eyes shimmered with tears. "God, I'm so sorry."

Nettie dragged in a breath. "I know, and that's the reason you'll live through this." She looked at Owen now. "But not you. Not Laney. You were smart to tell Eli to stay put, because that means he'll live, too. Or rather, he will, if you cooperate."

"Cooperate how?" Owen's voice was just as cold as hers, and while Laney couldn't see his face, she suspected he matched Nettie glare for glare. "You came here, firing shots, ordering your hired goon to fire shots, and each one of those bullets put my daughter in danger. And why? Because you got your feelings hurt when your husband slept with another woman?"

No more coolness for Nettie. The rage tightened her face and, for the first time, Laney saw the hot emotion that had spurred Nettie to not only kill but to plot to kill again.

"Hadley didn't just sleep with my husband," Nettie growled. She didn't shout, but there was a low, dangerous edge to her voice now. "She tried to blackmail me. Blackmail! I wasn't going to let her get away with that."

"So, you murdered her," Owen said. "And then you killed Joe and Nancy."

Nettie didn't deny that, either. "Cleaning up messes— again." Her mouth went into a flat line. "I didn't know that Nancy had put the pictures on a server."

"How'd Nancy even get the key for the box?" Laney asked.

"From me. I took it that night from Hadley, but I didn't know which bank. It took me a while to find that.

But none of this matters. People will forgive Emerson when they learn of the affair."

Laney nearly laughed, and it wasn't from humor. "Do you honestly think that Emerson and you are just going to walk away from this?"

"Yes, because Terrance will get the blame. I've set all of that up." Nettie shifted her attention to Stan, her hired gun. "Let go of my husband."

Stan shook his head. "If I do that, what's to stop you from killing me? You might think of me as part of this mess you want to clean up."

Smart man, because that was no doubt exactly what Nettie was thinking. She could kill Stan, Owen and Laney, and walk out. In Nettie's delusional mind, she might actually believe that everything would be fine.

"Let go of my husband," Nettie repeated and took aim at Stan.

"Nettie," Emerson said, the plea in his voice. "Just please put down your gun. Everyone, put down your guns."

Laney knew that wasn't going to happen. Judging from their expression, so did Stan and Nettie.

"Owen?" Eli called out. "Everything okay down there?"

"Tell him yes," Nettie insisted, her eyes narrowing again. "If you want to save your daughter and him, tell him yes."

Laney could practically feel the debate going on inside Owen. No way did he want to do anything that would risk more gunfire, but even if he did as the woman asked, there were no guarantees that Nettie wouldn't just kill Owen, Stan and her and then go upstairs to do the same.

"Tell Eli yes," Nettie repeated, "or the next shot I fire will go into the ceiling. Maybe into the very room where you're hiding Addie."

Emerson frantically shook his head. "No. You can't do that. Nettie, you can't."

Her expression said otherwise, that she would indeed do the unthinkable.

There were at least fifteen feet of distance between Nettie, Owen and Laney with the foyer and the base of the stairs between them. Emerson and Stan were half that distance. Emerson must have realized he was the one who could get to her first because he rammed his elbow into Stan's stomach. This time, it connected, and the gunman staggered onto the porch before he took off running.

Emerson didn't run.

He launched himself at Nettie.

And the shot blasted through the foyer.

Chapter 16

Owen cursed when he saw what Emerson was about to do, but there had been no time to stop the man. No time, either, to stop the shot that Nettie fired when Emerson lunged toward her.

His brother-in-law made a sharp groan of pain and dropped down right in front of Nettie.

Owen immediately saw the blood spreading across Emerson's chest, and the heard the feral scream that Nettie made. A scream that would almost certainly send Eli running down the stairs if Owen didn't do something about that fast. No way did he want his brother rushing to help. Nettie was still armed and might shoot him.

"Stay put," Owen yelled up to Eli.

Nettie was still screaming, but the sound of Owen's voice must have snagged her attention. She looked at him, her eyes dazed. Maybe in shock. But it didn't last. She took aim at Owen and fired.

Owen shoved Laney back behind the arched opening. It wasn't good cover since the bullet went straight through a chunk of the drywall, but it was better than nothing.

"This wasn't supposed to happen," Nettie said, her voice a sob now. She was obviously crying. "Oh, God. Emerson wasn't supposed to get shot."

"He needs an ambulance," Owen insisted. "There's one waiting outside. All you have to do is put down your gun and I'll have Kellan send in the EMTs."

"Please," Emerson begged, "do as he says, Nettie. I need help. I'm bleeding out."

Owen glanced over and saw that Nettie, too, was still behind cover, volleying glances between Emerson and him. Emerson was clutching his stomach, moaning in pain, and yes, he was bleeding out.

Nettie shook her head, obviously trying to decide what to do. If she saved her husband, the man she supposedly loved enough to kill for, then she would be arrested for multiple murders and the attacks.

"I love you, Nettie," Emerson added. Maybe he did. Or maybe Emerson was just trying to do the right thing and calm Nettie enough to get her to put down that gun.

"I can't go to jail," Nettie said. Owen could hear the panic in her voice. "I can't live without you."

Emerson tried to speak but his eyelids fluttered down.

"No!" Nettie yelled and fired a shot at Owen. "He's dead. He can't be dead."

"He's not," Owen assured her while he glanced out

from behind cover. He kept his attention nailed to Nettie. "Look at his chest. You can see he's still breathing."

Owen had no idea if that was true. Emerson could indeed be dead, but if so, there was nothing Owen could do about it. However, he could do something about Nettie. He got that chance when the woman hurried to her husband. That was all Owen needed.

"Put down your gun, Nettie," Owen warned a split second before he stepped out and took aim at her.

Nettie shrieked, bringing up her own gun, and he saw the madness and rage in her eyes. She was going to kill him. Or rather, she would try. And that was why Owen made sure he pulled the trigger first.

He sent two shots slamming into Nettie's chest.

Laney stepped out to Owen's side and pointed her gun at Nettie. But the woman wasn't down. Despite the bullets Owen had put in her, Nettie might have gotten off another shot—at Owen—but Emerson caught Nettie's leg and dragged her down to the floor with him.

Owen rushed toward them, ripping Nettie's gun from her hand and passing it back to Laney. He didn't want to give Nettie another chance to kill them. But the woman had maybe given up on that. Sobbing, bleeding, she pulled Emerson into her arms.

Despite his heartbeat pounding in his ears, Owen still heard the footsteps and automatically pivoted in their direction at the top of the stairs. It was Eli, who cursed when he looked at the bloodbath in the foyer.

"The gunman ran," Owen relayed to his brother. "He could still be somewhere on the grounds."

"I'll go up and stand guard outside Addie's door," Laney offered.

Owen hated to put her in the position where she

might have to defend herself, and his child, but he preferred that to sending her out to look for a hired gun. He nodded, wishing he could say more to her, but he would save that for later. Later, when he was certain there was no chance of another attack.

Eli and Laney passed each other on the stairs as his brother came down. Eli took out his phone. To call Kellan, Owen quickly realized.

"I'll look for the gunman and check on Jeremy," Eli offered. "But I won't go far," his brother added as he hurried out the front door.

Owen didn't put his gun away in case Stan returned, but he went closer to Emerson and Nettie and tried to figure out what to do to save them. Not that he especially wanted to save Nettie, but he would try. There was no way, though, that he could tamp down the hatred he felt for her. She'd not only tried to kill him, Nettie had endangered plenty of people who he loved.

Including Laney.

That realization came out of the blue and hit him damn hard. But he shoved it away and used his left hand to apply some pressure to the wound on Emerson's chest. There wasn't much he could do for Nettie. The gravelly rale coming from her throat let him know that she was on her last breath.

"I'm sorry," Emerson said. "I swear I didn't know she was behind this. I didn't know she had planned all of this or I would have stopped her." He grimaced, groaning in pain. "I thought it was Terrance."

So had Owen. Or at least, Terrance had been one of their suspects but so had Emerson and Nettie. And Nettie had planned to use Terrance's suspect status to frame him for the murders and attacks.

Owen whirled around at the sound of yet more approaching footsteps—these coming from the front yard.

"It's me," Kellan called out to him.

Owen didn't allow himself to relax because there were still too many things that could go wrong. But he was glad when his brother came rushing in.

Kellan glanced around, as Eli had done, clearly assessing the situation before his attention settled on Emerson and Nettie.

"Nettie did this," Emerson said and started crying when he looked at Nettie, realizing that she was gone.

"Nettie did all of this," Owen added. "She confessed to killing Hadley, Joe and Nancy. She hired the gunmen. And she was going to set up Terrance."

Kellan nodded. "Eli just cuffed one of her guys. Said his name was Stan Martin. He's talking in case we need any more info."

Good. But Owen figured they wouldn't need more. Not with Nettie dead.

"How's Jeremy?" Owen asked.

"He's not hurt too bad. He'll need to go to the hospital, but it can wait for a little while."

Kellan motioned to someone outside and several moments later two EMTs came rushing in. Owen stepped back so they could start to work on Emerson. He was still bleeding, but he was very much alive, and that was more than Owen could say for Nettie.

"If you've got this, I need to check on Addie and the others. Laney," Owen said under his breath. "I need to check on her."

Kellan gave him the go-ahead while he stooped down to talk to Emerson. Owen heard Kellan read him his rights. A necessity because even though it didn't appear

Emerson had anything to do with the murders, he'd still obstructed justice and lied during an interview. It might not land him in jail, but it was almost certainly going to cost him his legal license and his job.

It seemed to take forever for Owen to make his way up the stairs. His legs, and heart, felt heavy, and there was still way too much adrenaline pumping through him. That lightened a little when he spotted Laney. She was exactly where he'd expected to find her, standing guard outside the bedroom door.

She looked at him, their gazes immediately connecting, and he saw the relief in her eyes when she ran to him. "Addie's okay," she said. "They're all okay. I just checked on them, and Addie's fallen back asleep."

Owen pulled her into his arms and another layer of that heaviness vanished. With all the shots that had been fired, it was somewhat of a miracle they hadn't been killed.

"Nettie?" she asked, easing back.

"Dead."

He paused to let her absorb that and everything else that went along with it. The woman who'd made their lives a living hell was gone. Now they had to deal with the aftermath and the nightmares.

Laney shook her head. "I'm sorry I didn't see sooner that Nettie was the one. I was looking too hard at Emerson to realize the truth."

Owen sighed. Leave it to Laney to apologize for not recognizing a jealous woman hell-bent on covering up her husband's affair. Because he didn't want her apology, or for Laney to feel regretful in any way for this, he brushed a kiss on her mouth.

She definitely didn't melt against him, didn't give

him one of those smoldering looks. Her reaction was that tears sprang to her eyes. So Owen kissed her again. This time he heard that slight hitch in her throat and thought maybe there was a little melting going on. This time when she pulled back, he definitely saw some.

Felt some, too.

Laney gave him a small smile, one he figured took a lot of effort on her part. "I'll be okay. I'll just wait out here while you see Addie."

A few days ago, he would have taken her up on that offer. But since this was now, tonight, he slipped his arm around her and opened the bedroom door.

"It's me," Owen called out. "You can unlock the bathroom door."

Seconds later, he heard someone do just that. He also heard mutterings of relief. Saw relief, too, on Gemma's and Francine's faces when Gemma opened the door. The face that he didn't see was Addie's. But he soon spotted his little girl asleep on a quilt inside the tub.

"Don't go downstairs. Not yet," Owen instructed the women. "Kellan's down there, and he's fine," he added to Gemma.

Clearly relieved, Gemma gave him a hard hug and went into the bedroom to look out the door and into the hall. He was betting she would wait right there until Kellan came up for her.

"The gunman is dead?" Francine whispered and then checked over her shoulder to make sure Addie hadn't heard. She hadn't.

"Arrested." Owen had to pause again. "Nettie's dead, though. She's the one who did this."

Owen figured in the next few hours, Francine would learn a lot more about what had gone on. Everyone in

Longview Ridge would. But, for now, that was enough information.

Francine went to the bed and sank onto the foot of it. She didn't come out and say it, but Owen figured she'd done that to give him some alone time with Addie. He wanted that, but he took Laney's hand to make sure that "alone time" included her, too.

Owen sat on the floor next to the tub, easing Laney down with him. He didn't want to wake Addie, but he had to brush his fingers over her cheek and hair. She stirred a little but settled right back down.

"I hope she won't remember any of this," Laney whispered.

That was his hope, too, but he would certainly remember it in crystal clear detail. Both the bad and the good. Because plenty of good had come out of this, too—including what had happened between him and Laney just a couple of hours earlier in the room across the hall.

Owen wanted to hang on to that, but when he looked at Laney, he saw yet another apology in her eyes. Tears, too. This time he didn't sigh. He huffed and hauled Laney onto his lap.

"This wasn't your fault. There's no reason for you to be sorry." With that, he kissed her again. This time it wasn't just to hush her but because he needed to feel her in his arms. Needed his mouth on hers.

And that was what he got.

He felt it. Not just the heat, though, but also the feelings that went deeper than just the lust. He felt everything for her that he hadn't been sure he could ever feel again. Yet, here it was. Here she was, right on his lap and kissing him back.

This time when he pulled back, he didn't see a trace of an apology. Thankfully, didn't see any tears, either, so that meant the kiss had done its job. Now he wanted to carry it one step further.

"I love you," Laney blurted before he could say anything. "I know, you'll probably think it's too soon, that you're not ready for it, but I can't change what I feel for you. For Addie," she added, glancing at the baby. "I love you both, and even if that sends you running, I wanted you to know."

Owen opened his mouth but still didn't get a chance to say anything.

"Please don't run," she whispered, pressing her forehead to his. "Just give it a chance and see where it goes."

"No," he said. This time he saw the flash of surprise and hurt in her eyes, and that was why he continued—quickly, "I don't need to give it a chance. Don't need to see where it's going, because it's going exactly where I want."

Laney blinked, shifted back enough so she could study his face. She smiled a little. "To bed?"

"Absolutely. The bed...and other places."

Her smile widened and she kissed him. It went on a lot longer and became a lot deeper than Owen had planned because he hadn't finished what he'd wanted to say. That was why he broke away.

"Other places like my house," he said. "That I hope you can think of as your house, too."

Laney's smile faded. "You're asking me to move in with you?"

"I'm asking for a whole lot more than that. I'm in love with you, Laney."

She froze, her eyes widening, and for one heart-stopping moment, he thought she was going to say that she didn't believe him. But then she threw herself back into his arms and gave him an amazing kiss. One that told him that this was exactly what she wanted, too.

Now it was Owen who smiled. For a few seconds anyway, but the movement in the tub had both of them looking at Addie. She was no longer asleep. She sat up, looked at them. And grinned.

"Da-da," she said, reaching for him.

Laney and he reached over and pulled her from the tub. Holding both Laney and his daughter, Owen knew that he had exactly what he wanted in his arms.

* * * * *